SILVER WOOD COVEN

THE COMPLETE SERIES

Books One through Five

By Hazel Hunter

RESCUED

SILVER WOOD COVEN BOOK ONE

By Hazel Hunter

CHAPTER ONE

"EXCUSE ME, MISS," a man with a rasping baritone said, "but can you tell us where the secret gardens are?"

Summer looked up from the dog-eared paperback she was reading to smile at a pair of elderly men sporting cameras and a Central Park guide book.

"They're not really a secret. This is the Italian garden, and the English and French gardens are on either side."

She pointed in the appropriate directions.

The shorter, heavyset man hooted with delight.

"I told you this was it, Jimmy."

"No, Arthur, you said if we went too far north we'd get mugged," his taller, rail-thin companion chided, and winked at Summer. "You come here often, young lady?"

Summer couldn't tell him she actually lived in Central Park.

"Yes, I do. It's quiet, and I like the flowers."

That they were blooming in late fall under a slate-gray sky that promised frost before midnight was something else she couldn't explain.

Arthur raised his camera to snap a shot of the vibrant pink peonies clustered around Summer's bench while his companion made a show of breathing in the crisp, flower-scented air.

"I can't believe how gorgeous it is here, Jimmy. Miss, how do they get all this stuff to bloom so late in the year? It's October, for crying out loud."

Summer felt an odd but familiar tug in her chest, and hoped ignoring it would make it go away for once.

"The people who look after the park do a wonderful job," she said.

Jimmy's face wrinkled with concern as he nodded at the battered backpack next to Summer. "You all right, sweetheart?"

No, it seemed it wasn't going away. It would never go away.

"I'm fine," she lied as she stood and slung the backpack, which contained every possession she had in the world, over her left shoulder. "I hope you gentlemen enjoy the gardens."

"Wait," Arthur said. Now he looked worried as well, and dug into his trouser pocket. "You look like you could use something to eat. Here." He took a ten-dollar bill from his wallet and offered it to her. "Have lunch on me and Jimmy, okay?"

Summer didn't want or need to take his money, but arguing with him would only make things worse.

"That's really kind of you, thanks."

She tucked the bill in her back pocket and smiled at them before making a hasty retreat, glancing back once to see both men no longer watching her.

The strange pull she felt in her heart had already faded away. She wished the weird things that happened when she felt it would, too. Something about her drew complete strangers over to talk to her, and when they did they always offered help. They seemed obsessed with giving her things, too. Inside her backpack she had two jackets, seven hats, and innumerable packets of gum, granola bars and breath mints. She also had almost three hundred dollars in fives and tens. Even hard-hearted native New Yorkers, who were skilled at ignoring the homeless and needy, came to her. They offered to help her find everything from a job to a safe place to sleep. At least she now had the latter, thanks to a puppeteer. He'd insisted on giving her the spare key to the little cottage where he put on shows with his troop during the day for kids.

"You know it's illegal to stay in the park at night, and now there's some pervert going around raping the women he finds here after sunset," he told her as he pressed the key into her hand. "In this cold weather you'll need the shelter, too."

It had been increasingly difficult for Summer to dodge the nightly police sweeps, and find spots to sleep where she wouldn't be noticed by them or the criminals who crept in after dark looking for victims. She was particularly concerned about the rapist, who had already assaulted four women over the last month and had nearly beaten two of his victims to death.

Despite the offer of safe shelter she couldn't help asking.

"Why are you doing this? How do you know I won't steal anything?"

"You wouldn't," he said, with the assurance of someone who had known her all his life. "Not a lovely girl like you. Now come on—I'll buy you a hot dog."

Summer didn't know what to do about her effect on people. She certainly wasn't doing it on purpose, and with the thousands of visitors and locals that came to Central Park every day she couldn't avoid people altogether. She also couldn't leave the park because she had nowhere else to go. Refusing to take what anyone offered her made them even more insistent—to the point they wouldn't leave her alone until she did. One boy from the Bronx had followed her around the park for hours, tearfully pleading with her until she finally accepted the brown bag lunch he'd been carrying. As soon as she had taken the bag from his hand, however, he went on his way, whistling cheerfully.

It's almost like a relief for them to help me, she thought, *and then they seem to forget about me the moment after they do. But why?*

Summer walked back through the Vanderbilt gate to Fifth Avenue and turned south to take the long walk to the 79th Street Transverse, which crossed the center of the park. After three months she felt as if she knew every inch of the eight-hundred-plus acres of New York City's biggest nature retreat. She also loved the Conservatory gardens with a passion, now that they seemed to be returning.

Why the gardens had come back to life was another mystery. Since Summer had begun spending most of her days in the northeast corner of the park, which was not as popular with visitors, it was as if fall was reversing itself. The lawns, shrubs and trees had grown greener and more lush, and flowers had begun blooming again. As with the generosity effect she had on strangers, Summer didn't want to believe she was responsible. Then she had sat down to read on a bench covered in red and brown leaves, and when she got up to take a walk an hour later she saw that all of leaves nearest to her on the bench had turned green.

Suddenly the hair on Summer's nape prickled, and she slowed her pace toward the Miner's Gate. For weeks she'd been convinced someone was watching her. But whenever she looked around she could never catch sight of who it was. Although she knew she should have felt frightened of being secretly watched, whenever she sensed the watcher she felt warm and safe, as if she were being guarded instead of stalked.

Summer had hoped she might cross paths with someone who knew her, but if that were the case why didn't the watcher come and speak to her?

A laughing toddler running after a bouncing ball scurried past Summer and appeared to be heading straight into the busy street after it. As she turned to chase after the little girl, a tall, broad-shouldered man climbed out of a sleek black sports car. Watching him scoop up the child and her runaway ball with one arm made Summer stop in her tracks. He moved as silently and effortlessly as a big cat. He wore his blond hair in a short, military-precise cut that emphasized the rugged masculinity of his striking features and gave him the look of a gladiator. His plain gray T-shirt and black trousers clung as if sewn onto his heavily-muscled frame. He was so tall Summer doubted the top of her head would reach his shoulder—and she was no shrimp.

Summer took a step toward him and then halted again as a semi-hysterical woman rushed past her toward the man. He handed the little girl and her ball over to her. As the young mother clutched her child and gushed her thanks, the man nodded and looked directly at Summer.

Whoa.

The impact of the man's gaze made her take a step back and hold her breath. She'd never seen a guy with such beautiful eyes. Long and narrow, they had a slight tilt to the corners that gave him an air of mystery. As he moved, the sun illuminated his irises, which were so green they looked like polished jade between the golden filigree of his thick lashes. But the intense way he looked at her was what made her heart skip a beat.

Are you the one who's been watching me? Do you know me?

As if he could read her thoughts, the big man inclined his head, before he climbed back into his car and drove off.

CHAPTER TWO

MICHAEL CHARBON GLANCED at the
rearview mirror to see Beauty, the woman he had
been watching for weeks, still standing by the
Miner's Gate. Stopping the child from running
into traffic had been imperative. He would never
allow an innocent to die simply to maintain cover.
Now that he had exposed his presence, however,
the target knew what he looked like. Monitoring
her activities in the park would now be more
difficult, although he couldn't keep his distance
much longer.

*Any Wiccan you can capture alive is to be brought in
for interrogation,* Nathaniel Harper, his mentor and
Temple Master of the North Abbey, had said. *If
that is not possible, or you find one using their evil to harm
mortals, you are to engage and terminate.*

Michael felt the familiar stab of guilt as he

drove to the west side of the park. He had not yet decided if he should bring in Beauty. While he was suspicious of her, he still had no proof that she was bespelling the humans around her. He'd watched the scenario play out dozens of times, and it always went the same way: the mortals initiated contact and after a moment offered the woman food, clothing or money. As for Beauty, she did nothing that made him believe she was casting lures or using charms, and she seemed genuinely startled whenever someone made an offering. On several occasions he had observed her trying to refuse the gifts, something she would hardly do if she were using magic to wheedle them out of the powerless.

Nor could Michael be certain that Beauty was Wiccan, for he had never witnessed her using any form of magic at all under any circumstances. Every time he came close enough to the woman to sense any power she might be concealing, she gave off the same simple warmth and ordinary life energy as any other mortal in the park.

Michael found a spot for his car and walked from it through the Hunter's Gate toward the cottage where the woman had been hiding from the police every night. He couldn't even condemn her for breaking in, for he'd seen her use a key to access the back door—doubtless another gift from one of her many protectors.

They all do *want to protect her,* he thought as he walked to the vantage point he'd been using to watch the cottage. Everyone seemed driven to help Beauty; this in the middle of a city where no one stopped for anything, not even a toddler chasing a ball.

Michael walked up to his makeshift observation post, a remote spot between two large stones concealed by a thicket of trees. As he situated himself he checked the angle of the sun. The night would be creeping up over the horizon in less than an hour, which would send Beauty hurrying to the cottage that lay a few hundred yards away. He had been tempted to break into the place one afternoon before she arrived so that he could observe her unseen from within, but he didn't entirely trust himself to be alone with her.

As he waited Michael once more silently mused on everything he found fetching about Beauty. She had the body of a dancer, with long, strong legs, an elegant torso and graceful arms. Watching her use her slim hands to caress a flower had made him wonder how they would feel on his skin. He didn't allow himself to dwell on the ripe curves of her breasts and bottom—looking at either too long made his cock hard as an iron pike —but then so did staring at her solemn, full-lipped mouth. His hands itched to sift through her mane of dark, sun-streaked, chestnut brown hair to discover if it was as silky as it was thick, and breathe in the scent of her flawless, translucent flesh to learn if she smelled like the flowers she was always admiring. Her looks had entranced him so much that he'd even nicknamed her Beauty.

Now he had looked into her eyes, and he had even more to brood on. Until today he had never been close enough to see their color. It was unsettling to find they were a jewel-like blue flecked with gold and green and violet, like dark opals.

A woman like that, with eyes so rare and magnificent that they made the heart clench, could enrapture a man with a glance. Perhaps her loveliness was the only magic Beauty possessed.

Michael felt an aching heat spread through his lower belly, and glanced down to see the heavy bulge of his erection distorting the front of his trousers. He'd been plagued by lust all his life, a particular embarrassment that even taking his vow of chastity had been unable to dispel. Over the centuries he had wrestled with his unruly needs, which no amount of prayer or self-denial could curb. He'd regularly fallen from grace by slipping away from the temple, secretly seeking out women to relieve his hunger for the delights of the flesh. For until he did, nothing else could give him ease.

Beauty could, Michael thought, leaning back against the rock as he allowed himself a moment to imagine it. The woman had been blessed with a ripe, strong body, as if the Almighty had fashioned her for his pleasure. Her breasts would fit sweetly into his big hands, and her strong thighs would cradle him easily when he mounted her. As thin and delicate as her skin was, Beauty would be quick to arouse, and once he played with her pretty body he could ease his thick cock inside her sweet pussy, and let her soft, wet heat envelope him as he stroked into her, over and over, until she writhed under him and begged for her release.

Michael closed his eyes as he silently repeated the avouchment Nathaniel had taught him. *In the fight chastity is security. My body belongs to the order. I am a Templar warrior, pure of heart, mind, flesh and spirit.*

Reminding himself of the reasons he was supposed to live a celibate life cleared the unchaste thoughts from his head, and shame over his inability to do so finally tamed his rebellious cock. When he opened his eyes the sun had begun its final descent behind the city's skyscrapers, and twilight crept across the park.

The sound of a woman's cry, cut off almost as soon as it rang out, made Michael straighten and peer down at the cottage. He saw two people struggling: one large hooded figure dragging a smaller form backward into the brush.

Using the darkness and the trees as cover, Michael ran down toward the cottage, taking care not to make any noise as he approached the now-thrashing shrubs. He heard fabric tearing, and then a man's grunt of pain. Michael pulled out his dagger as he plunged in after the pair.

"Let go of me," a frantic female voice cried out in the shadows just ahead of Michael. "No, stop it. I won't let you—"

"Stupid whore," a vicious male voice hissed. "Bite me again and I'll cut off your nose."

Michael saw the rapist drop down atop his victim, laughing as he ripped her clothes, and felt his blood boil. He threw his dagger, and it grazed the rapist's arm. With a high-pitched shriek the man stumbled to his feet and fled. Michael started to go after him and then stopped when he saw who lay cringing on the ground.

Beauty.

He knelt down beside her, reaching for her at the same time she clutched at him. In moments she was in his arms and gasping into his chest.

"Do not be afraid. He is gone now," he said. Awkwardly he stroked her hair, which felt as rich and heavy as a silk shawl. "Are you injured?"

Beauty shook her head, and then raised her wobbling chin to gaze at him.

"No. He didn't have time. Thank you. I couldn't–"

She burst into tears.

Michael cradled her close, tucking her head under his chin and making soothing sounds as she sobbed. Throughout the centuries he had seen women after they had been raped, too many times, and knew how it violated their gentle spirits as much as their bodies. She shuddered against his chest like a frightened and captive bird. Fury welled for her attacker, even as her sobs pierced his own heart. Finally, her weeping calmed.

"Do you want me to take you to the emergency room? Or should I call for the police?"

"No, please, don't do that. I'm all right," she said quickly. She moved away from him, a separation he felt keenly. "I didn't see his face, so I couldn't describe him."

That wasn't why she'd refused, but Michael

wasn't going to press her for the truth when she still seemed so shaken.

"You have been living in the park for some time now."

Beauty stared at him before she slowly nodded. "And you're the one who's been watching over me."

Michael stood up, bringing her with him. For a moment he could only stare. The young woman he'd seen from afar was as enchanting as he'd imagined. It took every ounce of will he possessed not to wrap his arms around her again. But when she swayed unsteadily, he took hold of her shoulders.

"The man who attacked you may return to try again," he said. She glanced over her shoulder. "I want you to come with me so I can keep you safe, until I can arrange a place for you to stay."

Her lower lip trembled, as she stared up into his face. He could only imagine how that must sound. But she'd already guessed that he'd been watching her. They'd nearly met earlier in the day.

"You would do that?" she whispered.

"I think you know I would."

"I do," she whispered. Like a trusting child she put her hand in his. "Somehow I do. Thank you."

"It is nothing." He took a moment to brush

away some of the dead leaves clinging to her jacket. "I am Michael Charbon."

"I call myself Summer," she said, "but I don't know what my real name is. I can't remember anything about my life, or what happened to me before I woke up here in the park three months ago. It's all just one big blank."

CHAPTER THREE

RIDING IN MICHAEL Charbon's sports car as
he deftly made his way through Manhattan made
Summer wonder just how wealthy her savior was.
She didn't know a great deal about cars, but the
sinfully comfortable leather upholstery and
polished chrome and mahogany dash had to be
custom-made. Michael didn't wear any jewelry, but
his clothes were made too well to be off the rack.
Then there was the dagger he'd slipped into the
glove box before they'd left the park. Aside from
the blade, which appeared to be razor-sharp, a
blue jewel as big as her thumbnail had sparkled
from the center of the artfully carved golden hilt.

*He can't be a cop. So why would a rich man even bother
watching a homeless woman?*

Summer wanted to ask him, but she had the
distinct feeling he wouldn't tell her the truth—a

certainty that also made her feel annoyed with herself.

So besides making people generous and bringing gardens back to life in the fall, I'm also psychic. But if I am, then why didn't I sense that maniac was going to jump me?

Michael gave her a sideways glance.

"Why did you choose the name Summer for yourself?"

"I took the name one day when a man saw me picking up some trash in the park. I guess he assumed that I worked for the Conservatory." The memory of that day made her smile. "He said he'd never seen the park look so good in summer. I thought it made a good name."

"Did you realize you had lost your memory right away, when you first woke up in the park?" When she nodded, Michael asked, "Why did you not get some help?"

"I was afraid," she said. Summer thought of the blood-stained clothes in the bottom of her backpack. "I didn't know what had happened to me, and when I tried to remember it gave me an awful headache. I wasn't sure who I could trust, either."

Michael drove into the entrance of the parking garage of a towering private building. He parked in a numbered slot by the elevator. Once he shut off the engine he turned to her.

"Why are you trusting me?"

"You saved my life," she said. Summer wanted to tell him about the strange wave of pleasure she'd felt sweep through her from the first moment she'd seen him, but then he would think she was crazy. "Why are you protecting me?"

He gave her a narrow look. "Perhaps I am like all the others who have been drawn to you."

"So you know about that." Of course he did. He'd been watching her for weeks. "You're not like them, you know. If you were, you would have walked away after saving me."

"Indeed." His mouth flattened. "Is that part of the enchantment?"

"Trust me, Mr. Charbon, this thing that makes people give me stuff is not enchanting. It's scary, and strange, and no matter what I do, I can't stop it," she said, and then immediately regretted her sharp tone. "I don't mean to sound ungrateful. I wouldn't have survived this long without the generosity I've been shown. It's just…"

She lifted her shoulders.

"Unnatural?" he suggested. But before she could reply he climbed out of the car and came around to open her door. "Come." He held out his hand. "You must be exhausted."

Summer had never felt more alert or energetic, and when she placed her hand in his, the warmth and strength of him seeped into her, racing up her arm and into her breasts. She watched his face, and saw the grim line of his mouth soften as he helped her out of the car. He released her hand almost immediately, making her wonder if she was reading too much into his reactions, and then she saw him surreptitiously open and close his hand by his side, as if he was trying to shake off something.

He feels it, too, she thought as he ushered her into the elevator, and pressed the button for the penthouse level. *But he doesn't want to.*

Once the elevator stopped, Michael escorted her down a strange hallway with white, unadorned walls and a flat, black carpet to the only door, where he entered a code on a keypad. She heard the door unlock itself and watched it swing inward.

"That's pretty neat," she said.

"It saves time, and discourages thieves."

He gestured for her to walk ahead of him, and then followed and closed the door, which locked itself. As he switched on the lights Summer took a moment to look around.

The apartment was enormous, with high

vaulted ceilings and a large, open living space. His furnishings were simple and minimalistic, and the art hanging on his walls was modern and graphic. What amazed her was that everything was either black, white or gray—not a single spot of color appeared anywhere—and there were no books or pictures or any form of entertainment.

"If you would like to wash up," Michael said as he crossed the room to open the white blinds, "the bath is down the hall, to the right."

"A shower would be great," Summer said. She had been sponge-bathing and washing her clothes in the cottage bathroom at night, using the sink and some hand soap. "Do you have a washer and dryer?"

He glanced back at her.

"In the utility room, next to the bath. Use the robe hanging on the door while you are laundering your clothes. I have to make some calls, and I will order some food for us as well. What do you like to eat?" He saw her expression and the corner of his mouth hitched. "Of course. You can not remember. Perhaps some Italian—I have never met anyone who dislikes it."

He took out his mobile and began scrolling through a contact list.

Summer resisted the urge to tiptoe as she went

back to the bathroom, which had been done in gray and white and was so clean she could have eaten off any surface. The oversize shower with its multiple spray heads made sense—Michael was a very large man—but his cake of white soap looked handmade, and the shampoo in the unmarked bottle on the shower shelf smelled of lemon because it had actual bits of lemon peel in it.

"Maybe he has sensitive skin," she murmured as she turned on the shower, adjusted the temperature, and began to strip out of her clothes. She paused only to glance at the door, which she hadn't locked, before she finished undressing. "Okay. If he comes in here, he can scrub my back."

Summer knew she was being reckless, and now that Michael had her alone he could do whatever he liked to her. She also knew that he wouldn't. He was big and strong, and a little scary. She knew he'd used that jeweled knife to stop the rapist. Yet from the moment he'd saved her Michael had been incredibly gentle with her. She had no illusions about herself. She was homeless and blank-brained and living like a wild thing in a public park. Her amnesia might even be a symptom of a serious mental illness.

With one phone call he could have handed her off to the police. Instead he was out there ordering Italian food for her, and making arrangements for her safe-keeping.

Summer slipped on the luxurious, black silk robe, found the utility room and started her clothes in the washer. Michael was still on the phone when she slipped back into the bathroom. She hung up the robe. As she stepped inside the shower, she moaned a little as the warm water cascaded over her from all sides. After three months of bathing from a sink, being able to shower felt like pure luxury. But she only allowed herself a minute to indulge in the bliss before she reached for the shampoo and went to work on her hair. With the cold weather moving in she'd only been washing her hair once a week, so now she took care to lather and rinse her head several times before using the bar soap on her body.

Her hands and jaw and legs felt sore, probably from her struggles with the rapist, and Summer was certain she'd have some bruises on her upper arms and back from him grabbing her and throwing her to the ground. The thought of how close she'd come to being badly beaten as well as violated made her hands shake, and then without warning a flash of something loud and bright red exploded in her mind.

You fucking bitch.

The soap slipped from her fingers as she tried desperately to hold onto the fragment of memory, but pain blossomed and consumed it as it hammered inside her temples.

As Summer bent over to retrieve the soap her knees wobbled and her throat tightened, and a fearful despair swamped her. Everything around her blurred. She knelt down and hunched over, covering her mouth with her hand to stifle the sobs she could no longer hold back.

• • • • •

Michael stood outside the bathroom door and listened to the shower, which did not entirely mask the sound of his Beauty weeping. He lifted his hand to open the door, and stopped. Instead he rested his palm against the center of it. If he had been another man he would have gone in and comforted her. But if she had been another woman, they never would have met.

His encrypted mobile buzzed in his pocket, and he retreated back to the front room to answer the call. "Charbon."

"It's me," Troy Atwater said. His mellow tenor

sounded guarded. "Safe to talk?"

"Yes." He walked over to the window to look out at the city's lights. "I found one of yours—a homeless woman. She has been living in Central Park since August. Tonight I had to intervene when she was attacked by a rapist. I prevented the assault, but the bastard escaped."

"Name?"

"She cannot remember it, or anything about her life before she woke up in the park. She calls herself Summer." He glanced back at the hall leading to the bath. "Nor does she know *what* she is."

Troy grunted. "Does she have any power?"

"She compels strangers to generosity. They give her food and clothing and a little money, but nothing that would be noticed." He thought of the gardens. "She also makes plants and flowers flourish. She claims she is not doing it deliberately, that it simply 'happens.'"

"She's probably untutored," Troy said, "and since she's lost her memory—"

"She is of no use to the Temple Master, " Michael finished for him. "If I take her in, he will have her tortured and then terminated. She is young and comely, so I have no doubt our inquisitor will take his time."

"In keeping with the Templar creed of never suffer a witch to live, but do have some fun with her first," Troy muttered, followed by an obscenity in a dead language. "They are not worthy of you, Paladin."

The old nickname made Michael's jaw tighten.

"We are not talking about me, Pagan. Can you provide the woman with refuge and instruction?"

"Of course," Troy said with a sigh. "When and where can we meet?"

"Midtown, in front of the Renaissance," Michael said. He hated going to Times Square, but no one from the North Abbey frequented it, and the heavy tourist foot traffic would provide cover. "Be there in two hours."

He switched off the mobile and considered hurling it across the room.

Only the chime from the entry intercom made him pocket the device and go to attend to the food delivery.

By the time he had set out the meal, he could hear the dryer in the utility room. Then Summer emerged from the hall. Her hair was wrapped in one of his white towels, and her body was swamped by his black robe. The combination of the two only served to highlight her delicate features. Her weeping had left her eyelids slightly pinkened and swollen, but her skin glowed and she smelled of lemon and castile soap.

"Thank you for letting me use your shower," she said politely as she approached the table. Her opal eyes widened when she saw the containers he'd set out. "Please tell me that you've invited over a small army to help eat this."

"I was not sure what you would enjoy." He pulled out a chair for her and tried not to look down at the way his robe clung to her body. "There is a little of everything."

She peered into one of the jumbo size containers.

"A little that could easily feed ten of me." She sighed and smiled up at him. "I'm sorry, Mr. Charbon. I haven't had a proper meal in a long time."

"Please, call me Michael." He retreated to his kitchen. "Do you drink wine?"

"I'd rather have ice water, if you don't mind," she said, and grimaced a little. "I don't want to drink on an empty stomach, plus I don't remember if I like wine."

She was nervous, Michael realized, probably because he kept looming over her. He forced himself to back away and brought her a glass of ice water. As he set it down, he took a seat on the opposite side of the table and helped himself to some ziti and fruit. He watched her select a simple salad and some plain bread.

"I do not often dine at home," he said, hoping to put her at ease. "It is always easier to pick up something while I am out. I am very fond of Japanese and Thai food."

She nodded and took a sip of her water. "How long have you lived in the city?"

Michael imagined telling her the truth and smiled a little.

"Longer than I care to admit. I hated it when I first came here—so many people living so close together seemed unnatural—but in time I came to appreciate the modern conveniences."

Her brows rose. "Where did you grow up? In the country?"

"Near Paris, actually, but I spent much of my youth traveling in the Far East."

It was close enough to the truth.

"You don't have an accent." Summer studied his face. "I would never have guessed you were French. You speak perfect English."

"You do not have an accent either. That might be a clue."

Her eyebrows arched at his observation. Looking into her opal eyes, he felt as though he were falling. They made other hungers swell inside him, and he pushed aside his plate.

"Why were you crying in the shower?"

"I was thinking about what might have happened, if you hadn't saved me." Her gaze took on an over-bright shimmer, and she got up abruptly. "I should go and check on my clothes."

Michael was halfway out of his chair to follow her before he cursed himself. Whatever pagan powers she possessed, they were now affecting him, too.

For a moment he considered surrendering to them. He wanted nothing more than to go her, and take her in his arms, and assure her that he would never let any harm come to her. He could see himself leaving the order for her, and taking her away to a place where they'd never be found by the Templars or the Wiccans. There she would be his, the woman of his dreams, and he could live as other men. He could know love with Summer, and perhaps even have children. He could be husband and father and neighbor, and never again have to bloody his hands for the sake of a mission he no longer believed in.

Temptations so often test the faith of the very purest of heart, my son, Nathaniel Harper's pleasant voice intoned from Michael's memory. *You are burdened by so many because the Almighty intends you for greatness. Someday you will lead us all, I know, but first you must prove yourself worthy.*

Michael did want to lead the order, for only as Grand Master could he change the path of Templars. Instead of hunting the Wiccans, he could guide his brothers to co-existence with them. A new era of peace and tolerance might even allow them to work together toward protecting humanity and steering the world away from global destruction. If he had a destiny, he wanted it to be that.

With his resolve returned, Michael cleared away the food and tidied the table before he went down the hall to the utility room. Summer stood folding her laundered clothes into a neat pile.

"We must soon leave," he said.

"Oh!" she gasped. Startled, she turned toward him, and one side of his robe slipped down. "I didn't hear you." She followed his gaze to her bare shoulder and made a face as she pulled it up. "It's too big for me."

Michael saw something on her shoulder, but before he could make it out, the pull of her power twined around him, tugging at him as his mind filled with a sensual fog. As he moved closer to her he forgot his resolutions and destinies, and focused on the soft, sweet promise of his Beauty's mouth. A small dent in her lower lip fascinated him. It hinted that she had been worrying it with the edge of her teeth. He wanted to soothe it with a kiss, and taste it with his tongue.

The clothing in Summer's hands inexplicably fell to the floor as she came to meet him, her eyes filled with some nameless promise of pleasure.

"What's happening?" she whispered.

"You have held me enchanted for weeks," he murmured as he pulled her against him. "I can not resist it any longer." He bent his head until his mouth hovered a breath away from hers. "This once, Beauty. Only this once."

Her mouth felt made for his, soft and welcoming, and when a low sound parted her lips he tasted her sweetness, giving her his tongue to stroke hers as he urged her closer. The press of her firm breasts burned into the vault of his chest as he lost himself in the kiss, his hand moving to cradle the back of her head and tangling in her damp, heavy mane.

Summer clutched at his arms, her nails pricking his flesh and sending a jolt of heavy need into his groin. He tucked his arm under her bottom and lifted her off her feet. The rub of her sweet curves against his coiled muscles made him gasp.

Then the edges of the robe fell open.

Summer wrenched her lips from his.

"Michael, please," she breathed. "We can't do this. It's not…us."

She sounded confused, as if her own words puzzled her. But somewhere through the haze of desire, her words rang true. Slowly, he lowered her back onto her feet. But as he did, he allowed himself to take a long look at her ripe curves and tight pink nipples. Willing his hands not to touch her, he dragged the robe closed and belted it. As he did she covered his hands with hers, and he closed his eyes and fought against the beast of need roaring inside him.

"I'm sorry," she whispered. Now she touched her hands to his cheeks, her slim fingers cool against his overheated skin. "I don't want to do this to you."

Her words must have broken the spell, for his head instantly cleared, and he took a step back to break the physical contact between them. The last surge of carnal madness quieted, and he was able to look at her again without wanting to lunge at her.

"You should get dressed, and then we will go." He saw her expression. "You cannot stay here."

Summer began to reach out to him and then let

her hand fall to her side.

"But why not? We have some kind of connection, you and I. I could feel it."

"You felt your power overtaking me, and it dragged you along with it," he told her bluntly. "I believe you were born a witch."

She blinked at him, pulling the robe up tighter. "A witch? I don't think I deserve–"

"A Wiccan with powers of magic. A real witch." She gaped at him.

"Are you serious? Like Halloween, that kind of witch?" She shook her head. "That's crazy. Witches are just fairytale villains."

"They exist in the real world," he said. "They look like ordinary humans, but they have powers like yours. They are called Wiccans, and you may be one of them." He held her gaze. "Search inside yourself. You know you have power."

Though she looked as though she'd argue, she only bit her lower lip. He stared mesmerized for a moment before coming back to himself.

"I am sending you to them so they can determine if you truly are a Wiccan. If you are, they can train you to control your power."

She gave him a sharp look. "How could you tell I'm one of them? Are you a witch, too?"

"No. I am not Wiccan." He turned away. "I

know what you are because I am a witch hunter."

CHAPTER FOUR

AS MICHAEL DROVE toward Times Square, Summer tried to work out everything he'd told her. Since she had never considered witches could be real, it was just as difficult to believe Michael hunted them. She wanted to dismiss everything he'd said as delusional, and would have, except for how she'd survived in the park. Then there had been that moment in his apartment, as if they'd been drawn together by unseen forces for a kiss. One minute she'd been folding her clothes, the next she'd plastered herself all over him. If she was a witch, then why would she be throwing herself at a witch hunter?

"Wait a minute." She turned to stare at him. "You weren't watching over me at the park, were you? You were *hunting* me."

"I was observing you," he said flatly, "to

determine if you were using your power to harm humans. Had you done so, I would have hunted you down and…stopped you."

"Why would I hurt humans? I'm human," she pointed out, and then frowned. "I am human, aren't I?"

"You are mortal, for now." He glanced at her and sighed. "Summer, I do not have all the answers you want. Atwater will have to explain it to you."

"You mean the guy who is taking me away to meet my witchy people?" She saw him nod once. "So then he's one, too, right?"

"He is a warlock. Witches are female," Michael said. "Before you ask, yes, I also hunt warlocks."

"But not him," she guessed. "Your friend Atwater, you have him on speed dial to come rescue homeless women who have forgotten that they're witches, or don't know that they are, or whatever my deal is."

"The warlock is not my friend," he said, his expression darkening. "We have some history together that forged a truce between us, but he has no more love for me than I for him."

"Oh, well, that makes me feel so much better." She sat back and stared at the traffic ahead of them. "Tell you what, why don't you just drop me off at the park? I was doing fine there."

He made a turn into a dark alley and shut off the engine before he turned to glower at her.

"In the park you were living like a beggar, bathing from a sink, eating handouts, and hiding from the police. How is any of that fine?"

"There are plenty of people in the city who have it a lot worse than I do." She clenched her fingers to keep her hands from shaking. "Besides, whatever made me lose my memory probably happened in the park. Maybe someone is there right now, looking for me."

"Such as the man who tried to rape you tonight, perhaps?" He got out of the car and came around to open her door. "Come. We must walk the rest of the way, and Atwater will not wait forever."

Summer ignored the hand he offered her and climbed out, shouldering her backpack as she stalked out of the alley. Everything Michael had told her was beyond unbelievable. Any ordinary person hearing him go on about witches and warlocks and powers would have called the police and had him carted off to Bellevue.

The only thing keeping Summer from running as fast and as far away from him as she could was the unshakeable sense that he wasn't crazy, and that everything he had told her was true. Michael did behave like a hunter. The effect she had on people and gardens could only be called magical. And what she'd felt just before they'd been shoved together to share that weird, mind-boggling kiss back at his apartment had been decidedly supernatural.

She glanced at Michael, who looked as bleak as she felt.

"If you're not Wiccan, what are you?"

"I belong to the Poor Fellow-Soldiers of Christ and the Temple of Solomon," he said, and steered her around a corner.

The name sounded terribly familiar to Summer, but not in a good way.

"Is that a veteran's association?"

"No." His mouth twisted. "We are more commonly known as the Knights Templar."

Summer almost tripped over her own feet. "Excuse me. You're what?"

"You heard me." He gave her a sour look. "Stop gaping at me like that."

"Michael, even I remember that the Templars were wiped out in the Dark Ages." When he shook his head, she frowned. "Okay. So what does that make you? A priest, or a monk?"

"We regard ourselves as warrior-priests." He

stopped at an intersection and waited for the light to change. "My parents gave me to the order when I was an infant. I honor them with my service to the Almighty."

"By hunting witches," she said. Of all the professions she imagined Michael to have, being a priest was not one of them. "So why aren't you wearing a robe or a collar or something to warn unsuspecting women to avoid throwing themselves at you?"

"We Templars rarely have much contact with women." He took hold of her arm and peered across the street. "He is here." He turned to her and slipped a small card into the front pocket of her backpack. "That is the number for my mobile. Call me only if you are in danger and you can not find Atwater."

The prospect of leaving Michael finally hit home. Summer wavered, caught between panic and nausea. She swallowed past a constriction in her throat.

"Won't you let me stay with you? You've got enough room at your place, and I won't be any trouble, I promise."

His expression softened. "You belong with Atwater and your people. They can protect you, and help you become what you were meant to be."

Summer tried hard to keep her tears from welling, blinking them away.

"It's because you're a priest, right?"

"It is what I was meant to be."

He took hold of her hand and led her across the street to the front of the hotel.

Summer saw a dozen men in front of the hotel, but when a tall, dark-haired man stepped out of the shadows she somehow knew instantly that he was Atwater. He moved with the same silent, lethal efficiency Michael possessed. His eyes scanned the faces around him before he approached them. His build was less bulky than Michael's but no less intimidating, for he had a purposeful fluidity in his movements that reminded Summer of something silent and deadly slicing through the water, like an orca.

"You took your time, Paladin," the man said. His voice had a pleasant, melodic quality that sounded as silky as Michael's voice was rough. He didn't hesitate to extend his hand toward the other man. "What did you do, stop for souvenirs?"

"You complain too much, Pagan," Michael said, and clasped Atwater's strong forearm as he did the same, something Summer had only seen done by actors playing ancient warriors in a movie. "You must take her from the city at once. I am not the only hunter in this sector."

"Watch for my flame trails," Atwater said and turned to Summer. "I'm Major Troy Atwater from the Magus Corps, Miss Summer. I'll be transporting you to Silver Wood coven in New Hampshire."

"It's just Summer."

She had never seen a man with such heavenly blue eyes, which perfectly matched the glints in his silky mane of shoulder-length black hair. His features were equally striking, and just looking at the sensual fullness of his mouth made her own lips tingle. The fact that she was so strongly attracted to him should have made her feel ashamed, or even angry with herself. But instead her head was swimming. She was torn at leaving Michael, had nearly begged him to keep her. Yet the man to whom he gave her exuded a calm power that summoned something deep within her. The nearness of Michael behind her and this new man in front of her stoked a new desire. Somehow standing between them was exactly the place she should be.

"Why do I have to go so far away?" she blurted out.

Troy exchanged a silent look with Michael.

"The Templars and our people are enemies," Troy said. "If his comrades discover he's been harboring you, he will be regarded as a traitor— and Templars hate traitors even more than us."

Summer's throat tightened as she turned to Michael. "You didn't tell me that."

"It is of no consequence now. Go with Troy, and be happy, my Beauty."

He touched her cheek briefly before he nodded to the major and walked away.

Summer stared after him, while her stomach knotted so tightly she pressed her hand to it.

"This isn't right," she said. "He can't just go like this." She stared up at Troy, who was studying her face. "He wanted me to stay with him. I could feel it."

"Lady, you're radiating so much power right now soon everyone within a three-block radius is going to want you to move in with them." Troy took her arm and guided her away from the front of the hotel at a brisk pace. "Michael has been alone for…a very long time. He's used to it, and it's what he wants. Now I need you to put a lid on your ability before you start a riot."

Summer saw some of the interested looks she was getting from everyone they passed.

"I could do that?"

"I'm one of the most powerful warlocks on the east coast, with body wards that can deflect even the most lethal spell, and even I want to take you home and chain you to my bed." When she gave him an irate glare his beautiful mouth stretched into an unrepentant grin. "There, that's better than looking like you just lost your best friend."

"I think I just did," she said and glanced back over her shoulder, but Michael was gone. "How do I put a lid on my whatever-it-is?"

"Your power is linked to your emotions, so calming down would be a good start." He stopped by a brand new, dark green Jeep and unlocked the passenger door, holding it open for her. She hesitated. "We really do need to get out of here before another hunter picks up your trail, or that cop over there decides to shoot me for stealing the love of his life."

Summer saw a patrolman across the street giving Troy an ugly look, and how he had his hand resting on his sidearm.

"Right," she muttered. Reluctantly she climbed in and buckled her seatbelt.

Troy went around and got in behind the wheel to start the engine.

"Michael told me you were swaying humans in

the park to show you compassion. When did the desire compulsion drop into the mix?"

As he pulled away from the curb she had two abrupt, warring urges: to throw herself at Troy, and to jump out of the Jeep and run all the way back to Michael's apartment.

"I don't know what you mean."

He reached over and took hold of her hand, and drew it to the side of his strong neck. He pressed her fingertips against his skin so she could feel the frantic thud of his racing pulse.

"This is what I mean."

Summer felt a shivery thrill, and an aching need to move her fingers down so she could pull the edge of his shirt free from his jeans and slip her hand inside it.

"*I'm* doing that to you?"

He nodded, letting go of her hand. "Me, Michael, and anything male that comes near you, I imagine."

"That's never happened before now." She stared at her hand. "Back at the apartment there was a moment…we kissed. But if Michael's a priest, that had to be me compelling him to do it?"

"Probably," Troy said, as he steered the Jeep around a corner, up a ramp, and onto the freeway.

"When Michael became a Templar, he took a vow of celibacy."

She heard the odd shift in his tone. "You don't approve."

"I think it's unnatural," Troy admitted. "But sex is as sacred to all Wiccans as it is profane to the Templars. Probably another reason we don't get along."

"Well, I'm sorry I did that to you," Summer said. "I'll try not to in the future."

"Don't worry about it. It'll take about five hours to drive up to Silver Wood, so why don't you lower your seat and take a nap?" Troy suggested. "I'll wake you up when we get close."

"We need to stop at one of those big box stores on the way," she said. "I need to pick up some necessities."

"Silver Wood will provide whatever you need," he assured her.

"Does Silver Wood have a nice selection of lingerie?" Summer asked sweetly. "Because I've been wearing and washing out the same bra and panties every day for the last three months, and at this point, new underwear is not only necessary, it's a deal-breaker."

Troy chuckled. "Yeah, I guess it would be."

CHAPTER FIVE

STOPPING AT A store for Summer to make her necessary purchases took only fifteen minutes, and by the time they reached New Haven, she had fallen asleep. Once Troy cloaked her with a sound-damper spell, he took out his mobile and called in to Magus Corps headquarters in Boston.

"Major, according to the roster you're supposed to be on leave," the duty officer told him.

"I am, but there's been a complication." He quickly related the situation and what he knew about Summer without mentioning Michael Charbon. "I'm transporting her to Silver Wood for evaluation. I'll stay there with her until we can determine the cause of the memory loss and where she is in her development, but I'd like to consult with Artephius on some details."

"I'll transfer you." The officer put him on hold,

and after a short interval the line clicked and a stern, querulous voice answered it. "You know what they say about warlocks who can't relax or take time off. They turn into me."

Troy grinned. The old warlock had helped found the Magus Corps, so he wasn't exaggerating —and due to his great age, there was no one among their ranks more familiar with oddities and aberrations among their kind. "I'm sorry to disturb you, Arte, but I need your expertise on how to best deal with a foundling. She's an untutored witch whose ability appears to be in flux."

"Are you annoying her, too?" the older man asked. "That generally ramps up power levels among females."

"The flux is not in intensity. It's in effect," Troy said. "She seems to be a green witch who generates a proximity field with a strong compassion compulsion. When I met her, however, I felt physical and emotional desire for her."

Artephius grunted. "That's certainly refreshing. Witches are usually the ones groveling at your feet. To what degree did it affect you?"

"I'm still fighting a fairly vicious urge to carry her off, mate with her and spend the rest of eternity guarding her and getting her pregnant." He sighed. "This shouldn't be happening. Aside from the fact that I have no desire to take a mate, I'm carrying full body combat wards."

"It's not her ability that is arousing your inconvenient yearning," the old warlock said. "Our particular gifts are bestowed at birth. They can be diminished or strengthened, but they cannot be altered or supplemented. It's more likely that you're dealing with a spell she's cast, or a curse that was placed on her."

"She can't cast spells yet, and even if she could I'd sense it." He glanced over at Summer's peaceful face. "Why would someone curse her to be desired by any man who comes near her?"

"Think about it," Artephius told him. "With such a lure she'd be constantly pursued and fought over no matter where she went. She'd have to live in an abandoned monastery just to get any sleep. Rather a nasty curse to use against a female."

Although what the old warlock said made sense, Troy still wasn't convinced.

"This wasn't happening with her before tonight. What would trigger that kind of curse?"

"There's the usual assortment, but I'd wager he fixed on her own desire as the catalyst," Artephius said. "The moment she felt an attraction to someone, it would activate. Did she show any particular regard for you when you met?"

Troy frowned. From her behavior he knew Summer had definitely been attracted to Michael, but from the moment he'd looked into her gorgeous eyes he'd sensed her interest in him as well.

"She may have. What would be the motive behind such a curse?"

"Revenge. This sort of malicious magic is quite common among vindictive cast-off mates, and obsessed, spurned lovers." He uttered a sigh before he added, "It's an unconscious, pathetic cry for attention as well. Along the lines of, 'If I can't have you, then every other man in the world should know my suffering.'"

Troy wanted to find whoever had cursed Summer and introduce the bastard to a whole new world of pain.

"How do I dispel it?"

"Find the Wiccan responsible and persuade him to give you the curative," the old warlock said. "If he refuses, you could try killing him, but that doesn't always work. He may have crafted the curse to become permanent upon his death."

"It may be a while before I can identify him,"

Troy admitted. "She's lost all of her memories."

"I imagine the nasty little bugger who cursed her also wiped her mind to protect his own identity," Artephius said. "Until you can restore her memories, you'll have to compel the curse to go dormant again."

That made him think oddly of Michael. "How do I do that?"

"If her desire activated it, then her satisfaction should render it inactive." The old warlock chuckled. "Give her pleasure, Major. I'm sure you're up to the task."

That he was. Troy felt his cock swell at the prospect of burying it between Summer's legs.

"I'll consider that option when I've known her for a little longer than sixty minutes. Is there another way?"

Artephius made a tsking sound. "Always the gentleman. You might cast a body ward over her, and see if it acts as a barrier. Or isolate her away from all males. Good luck, Major."

Troy thanked the old warlock before he switched off his mobile and took a side ramp into a deserted rest area. Once he parked he looked down on his beautiful, slumbering passenger before he climbed out and walked away from the Jeep.

Putting nearly one hundred yards of distance between him and Summer didn't entirely dispel the yearning inside him, but it tempered it to a more manageable level that would allow him to focus on the ward. He glanced at a water fountain outside the restrooms, and checked the parking lot once more before he dropped his own body shielding and summoned his elemental power.

Water began to burble out of the drinking fountain, and swirled around the basin drain before it danced back up and cascaded over the side. Troy guided it to him with a wave of his hand, lifting and shaping it into a large rectangle before he flicked his fingers. The water divided itself into a net of shimmering drops which dwindled smaller and smaller until they dissolved into a mist.

Ward of water, protect unseen the woman Summer from all that harm outside and within. So may it be.

As Troy cast the spell, his power infused the misty net with a brilliant blue glow. It drifted across the parking lot to the car, where it funneled into the vehicle through the radiator grill. The interior of the Jeep took on the same shimmering glow for a moment before it enveloped Summer, and then shrank as if it were being absorbed by her clothing. Once the light vanished Troy felt the desire still throbbing inside him ease, although it didn't disappear completely.

Of course it won't, he thought. *You actually do want her.*

It had been months since Troy had taken the time to indulge his needs with a female. Now and then he would seek out a witch he knew to be uninterested in mating or monogamy for a night. He always enjoyed spending a night sharing the pleasure and power of sex with a woman, but despite being invited to return to her bed he never did. Serving in the Corps made relationships difficult, as he often had to travel and spend weeks or even months away on assignment.

That isn't the only reason, Troy thought, once more recalling how furious his father had been when he'd told him that he had volunteered for the Corps and was leaving Silver Wood. For years Abel Atwater had expected Troy to succeed him as High Priest. To say he did not take kindly to being thwarted was like saying the sun was a little warm. Abel had refused to say another word to him.

Erica Buchanan, the new High Priestess and his mother's best friend, had been the only one to say good-bye. *For all his stony looks and cold silences he loves you, Troy*, she'd said when she'd hugged him good-bye. *Remember that.*

Troy's current conscription would end on the new year, and part of the reason he had taken this leave was to decide if he wanted to continue to serve. As a warlock with elemental power he knew how valuable he was to the Corps, and he believed in their mission. He just wasn't certain how much more of his life he wanted to devote to battling Templars.

He hadn't seen or spoken to his father since the day he'd left the mountain, but over the years Erica had kept in touch, sending a letter every few months with news of his family and the coven. That was how Troy knew his brother Wilson had mated with Aileen Smith, the green witch Troy had initiated just before he left Silver Wood. She and Wilson were expecting their first child by the Winter Solstice. Wilson would not be happy to see Troy, either. His younger brother had always resented Abel's preference for Troy, and now that he had mated with Aileen he would probably not welcome the return of his mate's former lover.

When Troy climbed into the Jeep he removed the sound-dampening spell from Summer, and passed his hand over her to check the body ward. Wherever the shadow of his hand fell her body briefly glowed bright blue, indicating the presence of the shielding spell.

Summer turned on her side to face him and opened her eyes.

"Are we there?" she asked, her voice low and drowsy.

"Not yet," he said and touched her cheek, remembering how Michael had made the same gesture. Her skin felt like warm satin against his fingertips. "We're at a rest stop. Do you need to use the facilities?"

"No." Her brow furrowed, and she caught his hand before he took it away. "Why are my clothes damp?"

Troy grimaced. The ward had passed through her garments to adhere to her form, and because she was clothed had left behind some residual traces of the water he'd bound it to.

"I cast a protective spell over you," he told her carefully. "It will help you with controlling your ability."

"It might not be working," she whispered as she reached a hand to him. "You still look like you want to, you know, find some bed chains."

"I do, but that's not magic," he said, and rubbed his thumb across her palm. "It's you."

· · · · ·

Summer felt the same tug pulling at her that had flung her into Michael's arms, but this time she found the strength and will to shove it back and stop it from taking her over.

"This is a bad idea," she said. She took her hand away and unclipped her belt before groping for the adjustment handle. "Maybe I should get in the back seat."

"Good idea. There's more room." Troy's seductive expression changed like lightning into a teasing grin. "I'm kidding. The ward is working just fine, and you're safe from me."

Troy leaned over to help with the seat at the same time it tried to pop back into an upright position. It pushed her forward and straight into the hard plains of his chest.

"Sorry," she said, awkwardly twisting in place, only to find their faces close.

His warm breath caressed her lips, and the startling blue of his eyes pierced hers.

"Is that what happened with Michael?" he asked, his voice husky.

"No," she whispered. She gave into the desire welling up inside her and grabbed the front of his shirt. "This did."

Jerking him forward so she could kiss him

properly was a huge mistake. So was slipping her hand over the back of his neck. By the time his tongue glided against hers she didn't care. Troy's cool scent flooded over her, stroking her skin like a night breeze. The hot passion of his mouth sent streaks of an answering need burning through her. She could feel his big body tensing over her, his muscles coiling and his hands tightening on her upper arms. Her heart pounded knowing that he wanted her just as badly.

Troy dragged his mouth from hers. "Gods, Summer, no. Stop. We have to stop."

He pushed himself back from her, rubbing a hand over his face and taking in several deep breaths.

She gasped and sat back in her seat. Her hand flew to her chest, as though she could still her thrumming heart.

"Are you all right?" he said.

"Yes. I mean no. I…" She pressed the heels of her hands against her eyes. "What *is* this?"

"Search me. I've never felt anything like it. I think we'd better… Give me a minute."

He climbed out of the Jeep.

Summer lowered her hands and watched him pace back and forth outside. His fists clenched and his chest heaved as he struggled for control.

Without him beside her she was able to calm down and reassert her own will, and once the ache infusing her body ebbed she opened the door and got out.

Troy turned to her, his expression guarded. "Stay over there."

"I'm not going to seduce you in a rest area," she said, and hugged herself. "I wanted to apologize. I can't remember, of course, but I'm pretty sure I never behave like that."

"You did with Michael," he reminded her, his jaw set.

"Yes, because it's my goal in life to seduce all celibate witch hunters," she countered. "Along with complete strangers who act like jerks after they kiss a woman."

"Okay, it wasn't all you." He made a frustrated gesture. "Look, we need to set some rules or we're never going to make it to Silver Wood. We'll end up trying out the Kama Sutra in the Nympho Newlyweds Suite at some gaudy Atlantic City hotel."

A giggle escaped her, and Summer pressed a hand to her mouth, but it was too late. She gave into the helpless laughter, and heard Troy join in. Soon they were sitting together on the curb, clutching their sides and gasping as they tried to control their mirth.

"Okay," Summer said and wiped away the tears streaming down her cheeks. "No offense, but I really don't want to elope with you. So is no kissing rule number one? It should be."

"No touching of any body parts," Troy advised her, his voice lower and rougher now. "I don't suppose you could quit being so damn gorgeous."

"Not unless you have a spell that can make you hideous, Handsome." She sighed. "I really am sorry, Major. I'm not doing it deliberately, I swear."

"At least we're aware of how powerful our chemistry is," he said. He gave her a sideways glance. "Call me Troy, okay? I'm on leave, and I think we've just zoomed past the point of polite formalities."

Summer nodded. "It's getting late. You want to try getting in the car again?"

"Yeah, we'd better." He stood and started to reach down to help her up before he pulled his hand back. "Sorry."

Once they were back on the road Summer shifted away from Troy so there would be no accidental contact between them.

"Can you tell me something about this place where you're taking me?"

"Silver Wood is in the White Mountains," Troy said. "It's a bit isolated up there, and we have our mountain warded to provide defense and to prevent strangers from intruding. Most of the coven lives at the pavilion, which my parents built when they left their home covens to form their own. It's a big, rustic place set far back in the woods, but it's quite comfortable. The coven is committed to living in harmony with nature."

"This coven, it isn't like a cult, is it?" Summer asked. "I mean, I'm not going to have to shave my head, and wear skirts all the time, and have babies with six different men, right?"

"You can wear what you want, and have as many kids and lovers as you like," Troy said blandly. "You should probably keep the hair, though. It gets chilly up there in winter."

"Good point," Summer said. She noticed his tone had grown a little cold as he spoke of the coven. "Do you live there when you're not working?"

"No, I left some years back. My father is the High Priest of the coven, but we haven't spoken since I joined the Magus Corps." He rubbed his thumb over the Celtic band he wore on his right hand. "There might be a bit of family drama while I'm there. I'm his great disappointment."

"At least you know you have a dad to disappoint." She rubbed at her shoulder, which ached a bit. "I'd like to find out if I have family somewhere. If I ever remember where I'm from," she added. "Michael said I have no accent."

"You don't," Troy said, and frowned. "You also speak a little slowly, though, and your pronunciation of words is textbook perfect. I don't think English is your birth language. *¿Habla Español? Sprechen Sie Deutch? Parlez-vous Français?*"

"Je parle Français," Summer replied without thinking, and then gaped at him. "Oh, my God."

"So do I, lovely lady," Troy said in flawless French. "Do you remember who taught you to speak English?"

"I think it was…ah." Pain stabbed into her temple, and she pressed her fingers against the spot. "It hurts to think about it."

"Then don't," he said, switching back to English. "Tell me about the first thing you can remember. Michael said you woke in the park."

"Yes, back in August. I was in a ditch, buried under a mound of dead leaves." Recalling how confused and terrified she'd been on that awful day still made her shudder. "When I crawled out it was almost dawn. I found a better hiding place up in a tree and stayed there for the rest of the day."

"So you felt the need to hide?" Troy asked. "Were you afraid for your life?"

"Not exactly." She bit her lip. She couldn't tell him about the blood spatter staining her clothes, or how none of it had been hers because she'd had no wounds. "I couldn't remember anything, not even my name, and I thought someone might find me and ask questions and think I was a crazy person."

"Did you have that backpack with you?" When she nodded, he eyed it. "Once we're at Silver Wood I'll ask Erica to scry it. She's better at scrying location, but sometimes she can divine from other objects."

"Scry?"

"It's a form of foretelling, although Erica's particular scrying ability is more like a psychic GPS. If you ask her where something or someone is, and give her a mirror and a map, she can usually find it." He smiled fondly. "She's the High Priestess of the coven, and unmated, but she tends to mother everyone."

Summer wondered what Erica would be able to read off the clothes she'd washed.

"What about your mom?"

Troy's expression darkened. "My mother died during a Templar attack. She was protecting me, actually."

"I'm so sorry," Summer said, and almost touched his arm before she remembered their new rule. "That must have been terrible for you." She wondered under the circumstances how he could be friends with Michael, but recalled how the Templar had insisted that they weren't friends. "This war with the Templars, will it ever be over?"

"Not as long as we keep killing each other," he said, sounding tired now. "I had hoped one day we could change things for the better. But there are too many extremists on both sides who would rather we all die than agree to live in peace."

"Not Michael," Summer said firmly. "It wasn't my ability that made him save me from that rapist. He did that all on his own. He may be on the wrong side, but he's a decent man."

Troy nodded. "Maybe someday we can convince him of both."

CHAPTER SIX

SOME TIME LATER Summer was awakened by the first rays of sunrise, and sat up to see they were traveling up a narrow, winding road. When she looked out the passenger window she saw the steep side of the mountain stretching down to a V-shaped pass filled with ice-silvered trees.

"Wow," she said, then yawned to pop her ears. "This is beautiful."

When she turned her head toward the windshield she saw Troy was driving straight into a enormous pile of boulders blocking the road.

"Look out!" she shrieked, bracing herself for the impact.

"Wait," Troy said and accelerated. Just as they were about to smash into the rocks they vanished. "That is one of my father's better illusion spells. He can adjust it to the weather and make it look like a mud slide, snow avalanche, even some fallen tree trunks."

"Really," Summer said, and fell back against her seat. She pressed a shaking hand to the base of her throat where her pulse hammered frantically. "How clever. Are there any more, or can I have my heart attack now?"

"Well, don't worry if you see a three hundred pound tiger jump on the hood," Troy said. "I think my father got rid of the real one." He chuckled at her incredulous stare. "I'm kidding. That's the only one, and it's just there to keep the hikers and campers off our mountain."

"Sure, laugh it up now," she grumbled. "When we get up there I'll just give you a nice big kiss in front of your family."

"Don't tempt me," he muttered as he took a right turn at a fork in the road and drove up a much narrower trail into a dense thicket.

Once they cleared the trees Summer sat up to gaze at an enormous two-level structure made of rough-hewn cedar that had been built into a grove of towering evergreens. Too large to be a house, the building had been designed to look like a natural part of the forest, as if the trees had woven their branches together over untold centuries until they formed the roofs and walls.

"Welcome to Silver Wood," Troy said.

Walkways made from multi-colored, irregular-shaped slate wove around the outside of the pavilion, while artfully-placed pots and baskets of ferns and flowers added an unseasonable note of nature to the eaves, window sills and front decking. White smoke drifted from several large chimneys fashioned from rounded river stone. From a nearby barn a half-dozen dogs bounded out to surround and bark at the car as Troy parked near some pickup trucks and ATVs.

Summer watched Troy as he regarded the front entry. "You don't want to go in, do you? Is it going to be that bad?"

He shrugged. "I have my own spread a couple miles from here," he said. "If my father doesn't want to offer us his hospitality, then we'll stay at my place." He climbed out.

As Summer joined him she saw a petite, red-haired woman in a long green dress come out onto the front deck and clap her small hands twice. All of the dogs stopped barking and sat down to grin and pant.

"Haven't I taught you scallywags better manners?" she scolded as she stepped down from the deck. She stopped in her tracks when she saw Troy's face. "Troy, oh, my dear." She hurried across the space between them to hug Troy tightly. "Why didn't you tell us you were coming for a visit?"

Now that she was closer Summer saw that the older woman had luminous green eyes and some silver strands weaving through her shoulder-length red curls. What made her heart twist was also seeing the long, jagged scar that ran diagonally across her face from her temple over her nose to end at the lobe of her ear. Summer didn't look away from the scarred woman but wondered how she could have survived such a horrible injury. From the depth and breadth of the scar the poor woman's face must have been almost cut in half.

"It was a last minute decision," Troy was telling her. "Erica, I'd like you to meet Summer. Summer, this is Erica Buchanan, High Priestess of the Silver Wood coven."

"Hello," Summer said and smiled, and then found herself being hugged and kissed on both cheeks.

"You are very welcome here, my dear girl." Erica drew back and beamed at her for three seconds before she blinked and her smile slipped. "Troy, why have you shielded her with one of your water wards?"

"That and Summer are a long story, Erica," Troy said and looked over the older woman's head at several other people who had emerged from the pavilion. "We'll get to it a little later."

The first who followed Erica out was a stout, smiling man with the same curly red hair tied back in a ponytail. He was wearing a battered leather apron and well-stocked tool belt over his denim overalls. At his side was a younger, heavily-built man who seemed almost as wide as he was tall. He had slicked-back hair the color of old brass and wore a white dress shirt and pressed trousers that looked almost incongruous next to the older man's work clothes. Another pair flanked them, and Summer saw one of them bore a faint resemblance to Troy, although he was shorter and darker, and had a trim beard. His companion, a waifish-looking young woman with black hair and large, luminous gray eyes, rested her frail hands on her protruding belly. She looked almost too thin to be so heavily pregnant.

The final person to emerge from the pavilion stood apart from the rest with his arms folded and his jaw set in an only too familiar hard line. Since physically he was an older, slightly heavier version of Troy, and had the same heavenly blue eyes glaring out beneath the same peak in his silver-streaked black hair, Summer knew he had to be Troy's father.

"Look who has come home for a visit," Erica said. She turned toward her people and spread her arms wide, as if she wanted to hug them all, too. "Our dear Troy has brought a friend with him as well. This is Summer."

Nearly everyone gave Summer looks of varying suspicion. Only the stout man trundled over, and before she could stop him he seized her hand to bestow a smacking kiss on the back of it.

"Ewan Buchanan, blessed be."

Summer exchanged an uneasy look with Troy before she smiled at him. "I'm definitely, ah, blessed."

"Pay no mind to my brother," Erica said and rolled her eyes. "Ewan always has to be the first in line to charm the ladies. Now let me attend to the formalities." The older woman drew Summer to her side and guided her up to where Troy's father stood on the deck. "Summer, may I present the High Priest of Silver Wood coven, Abel Atwater. Abel, help me welcome Troy's friend Summer."

The older man gave her a long, silent look before he loomed over her and offered his hand.

"Well, girl? Have you no manners?" he boomed when she didn't take it.

Troy was by her side a heartbeat later.

"Summer has been cursed and cannot be touched. Hello, Father."

"Troy," his father said flatly. "Do you bring this cursed woman with you everywhere, or have you presented her merely for my benefit?"

Cursed? Is that what he'd decided had happened?

Erica took Summer's arm and led her back to the others to introduce them.

The well-dressed body-builder was named Lachlan Darrow, whom Erica said served as Abel's assistant and helped run the various business concerns of the coven.

"A pleasure to meet you," Lachlan said to Summer, although he didn't try to touch her.

The young couple turned out to be Troy's younger brother, Wilson, and Wilson's wife Aileen.

"Welcome to Silver Wood," Wilson said. His tone hovered one degree above icy, and he kept glancing back at Troy and Abel. "Are you from Boston?"

"New York City," Summer said and turned to smile at his wife. "You look ready to be a mom."

"By the New Year at the very latest, I hope," Aileen said, her small face glowing as she gave Summer a sweet, dimpled smile. "How did you meet Troy? Do you work together?"

"A mutual friend introduced us, actually."

Summer glanced at Ewan, who was talking to Lachlan and seemed to have no particular interest in her now. She also felt no tug inside as she had with Michael and Troy. Her gaze shifted to where Troy and Abel stood. The two men appeared to be having a very terse conversation. From the way Abel was now glaring in their direction she guessed Troy was telling him about her.

"Would you excuse me for a moment?" she said.

Once she joined the men they stopped talking and turned toward her.

"Mr. Atwater, I don't want to impose on you and your family. If you would rather I not stay here—"

"So she does have manners," Abel said, eying her. "Until we ferret out the truth about you, and what is to be done about this curse you carry, you are to remain with Erica, Aileen or one of the other women of the coven. You will also avoid having any physical contact with the men."

She gulped. "I couldn't stop Ewan in time—"

"So I saw," Abel said and turned to Troy. "You may use the northwest rooms. Your brother and Aileen are living in the cabin Wilson built for them over the summer."

"It's better if we have separate rooms," Troy said. "We're not sleeping together."

"You brought her here, so you'll guard her every night. How you do it is your business," Abel said and turned away. "We breakfast together in an hour in the dining hall."

"Thank–" Summer started, only to watch the older man stomp back inside. "You."

"He's angry with me, not you," Troy said and took her backpack before they followed Abel.

Inside the pavilion was even more impressive, with blazing stone fireplaces, cozy hand-made furnishings and walls hung with intricate tapestries. As Troy guided her through a labyrinth of corridors back to their rooms she saw open doorways leading to a library, a weaving room, a glass-walled hothouse, an enormous kitchen and a long dining room with a table large enough to feed forty or more. She also saw some rooms she couldn't identify: one with a raised platform around which huge floor pillows were scattered, another half-filled with racks of plants hanging upside down, and a third with some sort of shrine.

"How big is this place?" Summer asked as Troy stopped at a pair of double doors and opened them.

"I don't know anymore. It looks like my father has been adding on since I left." Once she walked in he followed and closed the doors behind them. "I apologize for the way he spoke to you. It's difficult for him to be empathetic when all he wants to do is thrash me senseless."

Summer grimaced. "If he's that hostile then maybe we should go to your place."

"I think now that he's vented his spleen he will come around," Troy said. He scanned the room, which had other doors on either side, and was comfortably furnished in soft green colors. "You can have the bedroom. I'll sleep on the couch." He went over and crouched in front of the hearth to start building a fire.

"Troy," she said andwaited until he looked up at her. "I didn't feel anything when Ewan kissed my hand, and he hasn't shown any interest in me. Why didn't the 'curse' affect him?"

"I don't know," he admitted. "Maybe my body ward is better than I thought it was."

Or maybe, Summer thought, *the curse isn't what you think it is.*

CHAPTER SEVEN

BY THE TIME the sun rose Michael finished his last sweep of the park. He drove to the east side, to one of the oldest churches in the city. He felt frustrated that he had not been able to find the rapist who had attacked Summer, convinced the man was a rogue warlock. Michael knew rape could be a powerful element in dark magic, and that if the Wiccan was deliberately assaulting females in order to augment some spell, he would have no qualms about terminating the vicious brute.

He will pay for terrifying her, with his worthless life.

Inside the church, four humans pretending to work nodded to Michael as he made his way around the scaffolding and piles of construction materials toward the unfinished altar. There he slipped into an elevator hidden behind a curtain and pressed the only, unmarked button on the panel, which lowered the cab through the basement into the sublevel of the North Abbey.

It had been Temple Master Nathaniel's idea to base their east coast headquarters beneath the decaying church, and use the excuse of renovating it to hide their real activities.

"No one goes to church anymore," he had said. "No one will set foot in one that's falling down around their ears. Once our humans finish repairing the old beauty—at a snail's pace, naturally—we'll simply have the church declared a private monastic retreat. Perhaps for lepers. That should keep the tourists away."

Down at the sublevel Michael stepped out and removed his dagger and gun, which he left with the Templar on guard duty. Cold air poured in from ducts that snaked up to outside air vents, bringing along with it the hard, sour smells of the city. As Michael walked down the long corridor to the command center, where Nathaniel oversaw all the Templar operations within their assigned quadrant, he smelled the mossy incense the humans burned to try to mask the dankness. For some reason the cloying smoke and claustrophobic lack of windows always made him feel as if he were walking into a tomb where the dead were being feted and worshipped.

The command center itself resembled a massive strategic data site, with longs rows of narrow desks and computers manned by the humans who monitored various media feeds for any sign of Wiccan activity. On one wall hung an enormous map of New York and other surrounding states that was regularly marked with flags and pins indicating pagan-related incidents or suspected gathering places. A massively complex radio array constantly swept the police bands and fed the calls into another computer, which flagged any activity suspected of being perpetrated by their enemy.

In the midst of all this technological bustle, the Temple Master worked from a school teacher's desk, where he reviewed reports, took phone calls from his men and the faithful, and directed a staff of more than a hundred mortals and twice as many Templars.

Nathaniel was always busy, and yet when he saw Michael approaching he closed the file he was reading and rose to his feet. Short and rather stout, the silver-haired Temple Master still had a commanding presence that made larger men feel like awkward, overgrown boys.

"Michael, you should have reported in hours

ago." His steel-blue eyes softened with visible affection. "I was growing concerned, my son."

Michael went down on one knee before his master and mentor, bowing his head as he pressed his fist over his heart in the proper salutation.

"Forgive me, Master Harper. I was hunting a rogue warlock whom I discovered has been assaulting and raping human females in Central Park."

"This is news to me," Nathaniel said and gestured for him to rise. He waved over his shift supervisor. "Bring me all the data you have on women who have recently been raped or assaulted in Central Park." Once the supervisor hurried off he smiled briefly at Michael. "Sit down, my boy."

Michael lowered himself onto the small chair beside Nathaniel's desk and shook his head when one of the humans stopped and offered to fetch him coffee.

"It seems rather busy for a morning shift," he said to his master. "Has something come up?"

"Something will, in due time," Nathaniel said and checked his watch. "I have summoned all our brethren in the field to attend me this noon, and I will want you at my side."

"All of them?" Michael said and frowned. "May I ask for what purpose, Master?"

"That can wait. You and I have a far more troubling problem to discuss." Nathaniel removed a file from his desk and handed it to Michael. "This conniving witch presents a very grave threat to our mission."

"Indeed," Michael said, barely able to control his shock when he opened the file and saw a picture of a blood-soaked, terrified Summer staring back at him. "Who is she?"

"We do not know her name, although she was brought into the country from Canada. We managed to turn the human transporting her to our cause, but before we could secure the exchange she attacked. Before she escaped she murdered our sympathizer and five of our best mortal guards." Nathaniel sighed heavily. "I have just received a report from Gideon that she was spotted last night in Central Park. It is now your sole priority to locate and capture this woman, and deliver her to me."

Michael quickly skimmed through the report, which stated only that a woman matching Summer's description had been spotted bespelling humans in the Conservatory gardens.

"Why was she brought into this country? Was she running from our brothers to the north?"

Nathaniel abruptly rose. "Walk with me, my

son."

The Temple Master led Michael through the data center and out into the sparring chamber where off-duty warriors often came to work off their various frustrations by practicing their fighting skills. Today the room was empty, except for the weapons waiting to be wielded. Nathaniel took down an ancient shield that long ago had nearly been cut in two.

"This was carried by Grand Master de Sonnac into his final battle." Nathaniel's diamond ring glittered as he traced the battered surface with his thick fingers. "I remember how fiercely he fought that day. Exhausted, half-blinded, and yet he refused to let another take his place at the head of the charge."

Michael hung his head. "He was an inspiration to us all, Master."

"I think he would still be with us, had his men not failed to protect him." Nathaniel hung the shield gently back in its place. "Michael, this witch we seek is no ordinary Wiccan. She knows how to find The Emerald Tablet. Do you know what that is?"

Michael frowned. "From what I recall, it was an ancient grimoire destroyed by the pagans after the Crusades."

"Not destroyed—hidden by the heretics. The Emerald Tablet isn't simply an old spell book, my son. It is the oldest and most powerful grimoire ever written. Within its pages are the secrets to controlling all forms of magic, nature and the elements, and perhaps even time itself." The Temple Master gazed up at him. "Whoever possesses the Tablet will wield unimaginable power. There would be no stopping them, you see."

Michael felt sick. "You believe we should have such power? When it comes from a source so ungodly as this?"

"We are at war, my boy. A war that spans so many centuries, and that has taken far too many of our brothers from us. It has gone on too long now." Nathaniel touched his shoulder in a comforting gesture. "I know how repugnant it seems, when we have already devoted so much of our lives to eradicating the plague of the magic-users. But once we have the Tablet, we will finally have the means to end it. We will turn the tables on them, and use the pagans' own devilish powers to scour all of them forever from the face of the earth."

The door to the sparring chamber opened, and a short, bald human bowed respectfully toward

Nathaniel. When the Temple Master nodded in return, the clergy aide hurried over to them.

"Master Harper, Steward Edmunds wishes to speak with you prior to the assembly." The clergy aide, Augustin Colbert, didn't spare Michael a glance. "He indicated that it is a matter of some urgency."

"So it always is with Gideon," Nathaniel said. He gave Michael a rueful look. "I will see you at the noon assembly, my son."

Michael bowed his head, but kept an eye on Augustin as the two men retreated. He knew the clergy aide despised him, and had been spying on him for some time now. While he was certain that the little man was interested only in what he could use to somehow disgrace Michael in Nathaniel's eyes, he would not be above enlisting the help of Gideon Edmunds, Nathaniel's steward, who had no love for anyone but himself.

Knowing Nathaniel would meet with Gideon in his private chambers, Michael left the sparring room through the maintenance access door, and descended down a dimly-lit stairwell into the equipment room that provided heating and air conditioning for the North Abbey sublevel. During his incarceration after the seventh Crusade, Michael had learned how to use his hands to pick up the vibrations of voices through solid walls and floors, something he was peculiarly sensitive to. He now employed the trick by placing the palms of his hands on the wall that stood between the equipment room and Nathaniel's chamber.

Only to see if Gideon or Augustin knows more about Summer, he promised himself.

$$\bullet\ \bullet\ \bullet\ \bullet\ \bullet$$

Gideon Edmunds stood before the plain mirror on the wall in the Temple Master's chambers and inspected his reflection. He had not aged since attaining immortality, but he was changing in a strange fashion. He no longer bothered with sleeping, as that contributed to his unfortunate ailment. A year spent entirely awake had added a permanent pinkish color to the whites around his black eyes. He also had a mild tic at the corner of his mouth that came and went. Thus far he had managed to disguise it by chewing on the end of a cigar.

In the beginning he had not understood what was happening to him, and suspected he had been cursed. With great effort he had captured and secretly imprisoned an ancient pagan. He had tortured him while demanding to know what he was suffering from, and why. The old warlock had given him a ghastly grin, his teeth gleaming scarlet with his own blood.

"Not all souls were meant to live forever," the fool had said. "The path of eternity is littered with madmen caged by their own shattered minds."

Gideon had enjoyed making the warlock suffer for weeks after that, until finally the old man's higher brain functions had shut down. He became little better than a lump of twisted, burned, tattered flesh. Gideon had finally tossed the living corpse into a furnace and let him burn to ash, but the pagan's words clung to his thoughts like leeches, and had sucked at his vitality for the next five decades as he grew progressively worse.

Despite the pagan's claims, immortality sickness was quite rare. It had struck only two Templars known to him over the centuries. Gideon could well remember one who had begged their temple master to decapitate him before the brain-eating spiders crawling inside his skull could escape and attack the rest of the order. The other brother who had fallen ill had simply walked into the sea one night. His bones washed ashore some months later. While he felt no such inclination to end his own life, Gideon concealed his symptoms and began his personal, sacred quest to find a cure.

A century had passed, but Gideon was no closer to a cure than he had been in the beginning. He had found various ways to manage his mental aberrations. Thirty years ago a spell provided by a rogue witch in exchange for safe passage through the city had effectively tempered his then-growing paranoia. It was what he had done to the witch before she managed to escape that had led to the most effective means of dragging himself back from the brink of insanity.

He had not intended to rape her. Females held no allure for him, and he had successfully kept to his vow of celibacy since becoming a Templar. Before torturing her, however, he had stripped out of his clothes to prevent them from becoming soiled with her blood. She had misinterpreted his actions and begged him not to violate her with such fear in her eyes that he gladly did just that.

Although he took no pleasure in the rape itself —it disgusted him to merge his sacred flesh with her profane body—her agony and terror pleased him immensely. It had also oddly restored his own clarity of thought, so he repeated the violation over and over. That she had escaped in the end always vexed him, but it had also led him to another truth. After finding the pagan gone, in his anger he attacked a mortal female, dragging her into a dark alley and raping her behind a pile of crates. The relief he experienced proved to be just as pervasive. It made it clear he did not need to sully himself by fucking a pagan woman to preserve his mind—until last night.

He had spotted the witch Nathaniel had been searching months for, and stalked her back to her lair. Gideon was not supposed to know anything about her, since Nathaniel preferred to keep him as ignorant of his plans as the rest of the Templars assigned to the North Abbey. But as the Temple Master's steward, Gideon had unlimited access to Nathaniel's rooms. He had installed listening devices so he could know if the old man suspected anything about his ailment. In the process of monitoring every conversation, Gideon had discovered that the young witch for whom Nathaniel searched knew the location of the Emerald Tablet, an ancient grimoire rumored to be so powerful it could make whoever possessed it unbeatable. What interested Gideon was the fact that the Tablet also contained the incredibly old healing spells that could cure any illness.

Gideon's failure to capture her still needled him. Trying to rape and beat her into submission had been foolish, but Gideon could no longer be anywhere near a female without becoming savagely furious and aroused. If he hadn't cloaked himself with a body shield he might have been disabled or even killed by the man who had come to the witch's rescue.

I should have cut off her nose, Gideon thought, absently rubbing the hand she'd bitten during their struggles. *The hole in her face would make it easier to find the bitch.*

"Gideon," Nathaniel Harper said as he waddled into the chamber and smiled broadly. "Augustin tells me you have an urgent matter." Augustin trailed in his wake.

"Unhappily I do, my lord." As he bowed before the Temple Master, Gideon imagined drawing his sword and using it to slice through Nathaniel's pudgy neck and part his fat head from his shoulders. "Baldwin has sent word that the pagans are preparing for a mass gathering for their winter celebration. He claims twelve covens will be traveling into the area, and another five groups who wish to organize their own heathen circles."

Nathaniel stroked his weak chin. "He did not indicate before that it would be so many. With so many in one place at the same time, we cannot fail to carry out our sacred duty."

The only duty Nathaniel had, Gideon suspected, was to his own advancement and self-glorification.

"You will be quite busy arranging the strike, my lord. Perhaps I should take over handling Baldwin now, to relieve you of that worry."

The Temple Master gave him a chiding look.

"You never could abide not being in the know, could you, Steward?" Gideon began to protest. "It matters not," Nathaniel said, cutting him off. "I cannot afford any mistakes with this informant, so I will continue to personally attend to Baldwin. Thank you, brother."

Gideon bowed again, primarily to hide his anger. "As you command, my lord."

"Why is your arm bleeding?" The Temple Master nodded at Gideon's sleeve.

He glanced at it and saw it was wet with blood.

"A human attacked me from behind in the park last night when I was searching for the escaped witch. I will have it attended to by the healer, my lord."

Augustin smirked. "You, wounded by a mere human? I cannot imagine such a thing, Steward Edmunds."

"He stabbed me from behind," Gideon said as he imagined pressing his thumbs into Augustin's face until his scum-colored eyes popped out of their sockets. "Like so many cowardly mortals do when faced with a superior adversary."

"See the healer before you attend the assembly," Nathaniel ordered. "Augustin, take a team and sweep the park again. Show the sketch we had made of the witch's face to the humans who work there. Someone must know more about her. Gideon, stay a moment, if you would."

Augustin bowed low before the Temple Master before he retreated. Once he had gone, Nathaniel's expression turned grim.

"No mortal could have come within ten yards of you without your knowledge. It was either a pagan, or one of our own. Why did you lie?"

Gideon swallowed against the urge to hurl the foulest obscenities he knew in the Temple Master's face.

"I cannot say who it was. I could not see how badly I was hurt, so the wound forced me to flee to safer ground. Do you wish me to be entirely candid about such matters in the presence of your human clergy aide?"

"No, of course not," Nathaniel said. He paused for a moment then continued. "Do you think it could have been Michael Charbon who attacked you?"

"Michael?" Gideon said and made a contemptuous sound. "That muling mortal-lover only draws a blade with a pencil on paper."

"He was tracking a rapist last night in the park," the Temple Master said and gave him an unpleasant smile. "Perhaps he mistook you as one. It would not be the first time he interfered with you toying with a helpless mortal."

Gideon hated Nathaniel's seneschal almost as much as the Temple Master.

"Charbon confessed to attacking me?"

"No, he believes the rapist was a warlock," Nathaniel said. His thin silver brows arched. "You have not gone over to the side of the enemy, have you, Steward?"

"My lord, if you believe that to be true…" Gideon went down on his knees in front of the Temple Master, and tilted his head back. "Then end me now, for I could not live knowing you suspected me of being a traitor."

"Have a care, Gideon. Someday you will make a foolish offer like that to a more suspicious man, and it will be accepted. Now get up." The Temple Master folded his hands into the wide ends of his robe's sleeves and glanced past him, his thin lips stretched to a satisfied smile. "Alvis. It has been too long."

"My lord," a high-pitched male voice said.

Gideon turned to see the largest Templar who still walked the earth bend himself into a low, fervent bow. When he straightened the light leapt from his white-blond hair into his eerie blue eyes, which were so faded by centuries in the sun they sometimes looked solidly white with only tiny dots for pupils.

"Welcome back, Snowman," Gideon said.

Nathaniel's deadliest assassin ignored him as he gazed down at the Temple Master with the usual fawning sycophancy. Alvis worshipped Nathaniel Harper almost as much as he did the Almighty.

"I have heard that we assemble to slaughter a great many pagans, my lord." Delight made his girlish voice a little shriller than usual. "Is this so?"

"We come together to discuss it today," Nathaniel told him. "Can I count on you to help us prevail, Brother?"

Alvis pulled the battle axe he kept strapped to his back over his shoulder and presented it in salute. "Show me where they are, and I will chop them into pig food."

CHAPTER EIGHT

TROY PULLED OFF his shirt and used it to wipe the sweat from his chest before he buried the tip of his axe in the chopping stump. He hung the shirt around his neck before he threw another half-dozen split logs to the pile in the barrow. Even with the temperature dropping it felt good to be working outdoors. A faint, frosty mist diffused the afternoon sunlight, and he suspected from the rapidly-chilling air they could expect a freeze before morning. He could smell the hearty Irish stew Erica had bubbling in the kitchen, and the yeasty-sweet scent of the herb bread Aileen was baking to go with it. The coven's dogs lay in a loose ring around him, content to watch him work.

Home. It wasn't his anymore, but that didn't change the way it felt to be here.

It had been seven days since he'd brought Summer to Silver Wood, and while they weren't any closer to discovering who she was or how to dispel the curse she was carrying, the last week had gone better than he'd expected. The women of the coven had treated Summer with their usual warmth and kindness, with Erica taking her under her wing and helping her adjust to life among the Wiccans. Aileen was now working with Summer in the mornings to develop her touch with plants, and even his father spent an hour each night trying to restore her memory with his power of persuasion.

Troy had been given a noticeably cooler reception, but after abandoning the coven to join the Magus Corps he hadn't expected to be welcomed back into the fold. His father remained coldly civil, and the other men tolerated his presence, but Wilson was still actively avoided him. Only Erica, Aileen and Ewan had been openly friendly, although Wilson kept descending at regular intervals to whisk his frail wife back to their cabin to rest.

"It's because you initiated me, you know," Aileen told him one morning when they had a moment alone together in the kitchen. "I've tried to convince Wilson that you and I were never meant to be, but he can't seem to get over it."

Troy didn't regret the brief romance they'd shared, which had ended even before he'd left the coven.

"I had no idea he was jealous. He's an idiot, my brother." He smiled down at her belly. "Have you divined what you'll be having?"

"No, and if you can tell, you're not to tell me," she warned. "This baby is my first, and I know it's going to hurt, a lot. If I'm going to get through the labor I need something to look forward to."

Erica did her best to bring Troy and his father together at every opportunity, but Abel seemed uninterested in anything but the preparations for the Winter Solstice gathering and following the traditions of the season. He spoke to Troy only when necessary, and usually just to give him another list of chores that needed attending. Troy didn't mind. When he'd lived at Silver Wood he'd spent more time in the yards and the barns than he had in the big house. A door shut sharply and light footsteps came approaching him from behind.

"I'm sorry to interrupt, Major, but we need to have a discussion about something."

He grinned a little without looking at Summer. She only called him "Major" when she was unhappy or annoyed.

"What's the matter now?"

She came around to stand in front of him and planted her hands on her hips.

"Erica just told me about this sacred moon drawing thing."

"Drawing down the moon," he corrected. "We'll hold the ritual the next time it's full. What's the problem?"

"Oh, you know, the part about how we do it. Sky clad, which she tells me means we all get naked and go outside, at night, in the woods. This would be the same woods where the bears and snakes and tigers live."

Troy chuckled. "There are no bears or tigers on the mountain, and the snakes are hibernating."

"So then I'm safe courting hypothermia by stripping down in front of a dozen guys," she said, nodding. "Assuming my curse doesn't decide to kick in. If it does, then we're going to have a problem. Or an orgy."

"Summer, the body ward I cast over you is working fine. No one is going to be affected by the curse—and it's clothing optional. You can opt to go naked, or opt not to." He saw where she was staring and quickly pulled his shirt back on. "Joining the ritual circle now will be a lot easier than when the covens gather for Winter Solstice. Then you're talking about three hundred guys, most of whom will be celebrating in the nude for at least three or four nights that week."

She rubbed her forehead and looked up at the sky.

"Why can't Wiccans celebrate another way? What's wrong with sitting around the fireplace and drinking hot cocoa and swapping ghost stories?"

"Nothing, but that's what humans do. We're not human, and our rituals date back centuries before secular religion got everyone uptight about nudity." He gave her a sympathetic look. "If you feel that uncomfortable, I'm sure Abel will excuse you from the circle."

"Oh, no," she said and held up her slim hands. "Your father has already informed me that I'm not excused from anything, ever. To be a proper witch I have to grow my own herbs, mix my own potions, cast my own runes, and take part in all the rituals. Even that one with the disgusting green stuff Erica smeared all over my face."

He thought for a minute. "That wasn't a ritual. That was a cleansing."

"What did it clean? Do you know how long it took me to get that gunk off my face? I was about to borrow some sandpaper from Wilson." She sighed and hunkered down to scratch one of the retrievers behind his ears, which instantly drew all the dogs over to her. "Okay, okay, be patient, you guys. I only have two hands."

Troy watched the dogs rubbing and nuzzling themselves against her in their collective bid for attention, and silently wished he was covered with fur and walked on all fours. Sleeping on the couch in their rooms was uncomfortable enough, but knowing one door was all that stood between him and Summer in a bed, kept him tossing and turning most nights.

Once all the dogs were piled around her, Summer sighed happily.

"I love dogs. They never give you the evil eye for screwing up witch stuff. Are you going to be chopping wood for the rest of the afternoon?"

"No, I'm finished," he said and crouched down beside her. "Do you want to do some gardening?"

"Been there, weeded that. Also, Erica kind of kicked me off garden duty today." Her shoulders slumped. "How was I supposed to know dandelions aren't weeds? They are to humans. And how come Wiccans use them to make salads and wine, anyway? Can't you people just grow lettuce and grapes, like everyone else?"

Troy bit back a laugh. "I think you need a Wicca break."

"Oh, boy, you would not believe how much." Summer perked right up. "Can we go for a hike, or a supply run into town, or let me emigrate to Australia?"

"We'll take a drive over to my place. I've been meaning to get over there and make sure it's ready for winter so my father doesn't have to." He stood, and waited for her to do the same before he nodded at the pavilion. "Get a jacket and some good walking shoes. I'll let Erica know we're going."

Summer grinned like a girl and hurried back inside, while Troy headed for the kitchen where Erica was washing dishes.

"Your green witch has a black thumb," the High Priestess grumbled as soon as she saw him. "I thought she was supposed to be gifted with plants."

"Sorry about the dandelions," Troy said, and took down one of the wicker hampers and began filling it with fruit, bread and cheese. "We're going to head over to my property so I can have a look around and see if there are any issues that need tending before the snow comes. We won't be here for dinner."

"So I see," Erica said. She dried her hands and retrieved two unlabeled bottles from a rack on the wall. "Spring water with citrus and a bit of honey," she said as she offered him the pair. "She doesn't drink wine, and you need to keep your wits about you."

"Nothing is going to happen," he assured her as he placed the bottles in the basket. "If it was, it would have already in our rooms."

"Not really," the older woman said blandly. "I put a charm under her bed to keep you out of it."

Troy cleared his throat. "A charm?"

"Just a small one," she said and pinched the air with her fingers. "Oh, don't look at me like that. She's very lovely, and you're quite virile, and then there's this desire curse. I considered it being proactive."

"Thank you, I think," Troy said and kissed her brow. He tucked the hamper under his arm. "How hopeless is she in the garden, really?"

Erica's expression grew pained. "She's never been taught anything, or if she has she can't remember, so she may improve in time."

"That bad, huh?"

Her red curls bobbed as she nodded. "A swarm of starving gophers might be less destructive, but not by much."

"I don't agree," Aileen said as she came into the kitchen with a basket of freshly-picked herbs. She looked completely unashamed about her obvious eaves-dropping. "Summer is hopeless in the garden because she's not an herbalist. She has no empathy with growing things, nor any real interest in the green arts. I think her gift with plants is a side effect of some other power."

Since Aileen was one of the most gifted young herbalists among Wiccans, Troy knew she spoke from experience.

"Do you know what her power could be?"

The young witch gestured for both of them to follow her out into the kitchen garden, and pointed to some rather uneven rows of thriving dandelions.

"She came back at midday when you were working at the loom, Erica. I watched from the window as she replanted them. She didn't know what she was doing, but look at all the new shoots."

"When I saw them in the weed basket they were already wilting. They should be dead now," Erica said. The High Priestess knelt down beside the bed and ran her fingers wonderingly over the plant's yellow-flowering heads. "They are bigger and greener than they were before she pulled them out." She stared up at Troy. "This is what she was doing in the park?"

He shrugged, and helped the older woman to her feet.

"She doesn't just make things grow like I do," Aileen said. "I think Summer can bring dead plants back to life. Perhaps she can do the same with people."

"Like a necromancer," Erica murmured. "But without those horrid spells and sacrifices."

"Have you ever known a witch to have a natural resurrection ability?" Troy asked. Erica shook her head, and Aileen did the same. "All right. I'll get in touch with Boston tonight and ask them to search the archives again. There has to be some record of this somewhere."

"Troy, she's not evil," Aileen said suddenly, and touched his arm. "I have felt the goodness in her."

"We all have," Erica said. "But to reanimate life is a black magic. If that is her true gift, my dears, then I'm afraid she was born cursed."

CHAPTER NINE

AFTER TEN MINUTES on the still-scary winding mountain road, Summer saw no sign of any cabins or houses.

"Why did you build this place of yours so far away from the rest of the coven?"

"I didn't. It's part of the Atwater family's original settlement." He detoured onto a dirt road and skillfully avoided a large pothole. "Hang on, this is where it gets bumpy."

Summer gripped the sides of her seat as they made their way up a steep portion of the road and then went down again, with thick brush crowding in on both sides.

"Maybe we should have brought a machete," she said.

"No one comes out here," Troy said. He drove around a pile of rocks that had spilled onto the road and then made one last turn into a clearing where most of the grass and brush had turned brown. "There it is."

About half the size of the pavilion, Troy's house sat like an enormous horseshoe left on the edge of the clearing. A glass-fronted A-frame loft dominated the center of the structure, and more curved, glass panels flowed out in two stacked-level wings. A blend of the modern and primitive, its weathered pine posts and gleaming steel roof supports had a pleasing symmetry that brought a smile to her lips.

"It's amazing," she murmured. She turned to see him staring at it with a brooding frown. "You did a wonderful job with it."

"My mother actually built most of it. Her ability allowed her control over anything made of wood."

He climbed out of the Jeep and waited for her to join him before he walked with her up to the center of the house and unlocked the door.

Inside white dust cloths draped the furnishings, and aside from a few spider webs in the corners the walls stood bare. Still, Summer could see how much care had gone into finishing the golden oak floors and walnut roof beams, and how vibrant the amber paint covering the walls still was.

"Did you grow up here?"

"No," he said and went over to check the large fireplace. He picked up some logs from the rack off to the side, and stacked them on the iron grate. "Would you see if there's some kindling in the back room there?"

Summer walked in the direction he pointed and found herself in another, larger room. Here the tables and chairs had not been covered, and for a moment she was stunned by the intricately carved woods that had been painstakingly fashioned into the dining set. When she ran her fingertips over the highly-polished surface of the table, the wood grain felt as smooth as glass. Intricate Celtic knot work had been chiseled into the backs of all of the chairs.

Troy appeared on the other side of the table, and frowned at it before he regarded her.

"More of my mother's work. She was very gifted with wood."

"Are you kidding? It looks like she was the Michelangelo of wood," Summer murmured. "So what's your ability? Dog herding? Super wood chopping? Homeless witch saving?"

His expression grew remote. "We'll talk about it later."

"Okay. Kindling, right, sorry."

She went over to the hearth at the other end of the room. But when she reached down to the open-topped metal box containing bits of fluff and curly wood shavings, a faint heat touched her fingers.

"Troy, someone built a fire here recently."

She bent down and blew a breath over the ash in the grate, making the banked coals flare to life.

"Probably Wilson," Tory said from behind her. "He used to come here whenever he missed our mother." He came over and retrieved the kindling box. "If you want to have our picnic in here, we can. The meadow's pretty much dead."

"Whatever you'd like," Summer said. She could feel how tense he was, and smiled brightly. "Why don't I go get the hamper?"

"Sure," was all he said, as he bent down again to place more kindling and wood over the embers.

Sensing Troy needed some time alone, Summer slowly walked out to the Jeep. She took a few moments to gaze at his property. Across the edge of the meadow facing the house she saw a frost-edged creek that hadn't completely iced over. In the trees she spotted a small barn and storage sheds. Several old paths still ran every which way through the meadow. She grabbed the hamper and followed one down to the creek. The water appeared crystal clear, and on impulse she bent down to plunge her cupped hand into it for a drink. For a moment the setting sun reflected off the rippling surface, turning it red–

A harsh male voice began jabbering behind her eyes, and his words were a solid stream of ugliness and fear.

Tell them. Tell them now. You have to tell them where it is, you fucking bitch, or we're both–

A gunshot blasted in her ears and a wave of thick, warm wetness splashed all over her. Summer threw herself to the ground and covered her head with her arms.

"No, please, stop. I don't know. I don't know–"

Her ears filled with a wet, choking sound, and when she lifted her head, she was standing in a dark parking lot between two cars. Their headlights blinded her. Her clothes were covered in blood, and something heavy slumped against her legs. Slowly she glanced down. There was a ragged hole where his eyes and nose should have been. His thick, wet scarlet lips twitched.

Tell them, he mouthed.

Summer screamed, scrambling to her feet. She ran blindly for the trees, staggered and almost fell before she righted herself. But she immediately took another tumble as her feet slid down the icy bank of the creek. She wheeled her arms wildly as she tried to regain her balance. But the water suddenly rose out of the creek and formed into a giant hand that scooped her up and carried her through the air until a pair of hard hands snatched her and dragged her back down to the ground.

A huge curtain of water fell over her, soaking her clothes and plastering her hair over her face, and she screamed again.

"No!"

"Summer," someone said. The man holding her was also wet. She struggled against him, but he ducked his head when she tried to claw his face. "Summer, it's me." He brushed the wet hair back from her face. "It's all right. I've got you."

She recognized him. "Troy?"

She froze, horrified to see her nails so close to his eyes. She jerked her hand away.

"What was that?" she gasped. "The water just grabbed me."

"Stand still."

His eyes took on a blazing blue glow, and suddenly drops of water began rising like rain in reverse.

When Summer looked down she saw the drops forming on her clothes and beading on her hair before they lifted into the air. Above their heads the drops stopped and hung in a shimmering cloud, each tiny drop catching the sunlight and splitting it into hundreds of thousands of tiny rainbows.

Troy spread his fingers and pushed them toward the creek. Summer watched the cloud of water fly to the creek and fall into it. He glanced down at her.

"Dry now?"

She touched her clothes and hair, which weren't even damp.

"*That's* your ability?"

"I'm a water elemental. I can control water in any form," he said and plucked a small twig from her hair. "Why were you screaming?"

Summer felt her temples beginning to throb and grimaced.

"A big hand made of water scooping me up in the air wasn't enough reason?"

He shook his head. "Before that, when you were kneeling by the creek."

"I saw something in the water. Something red." She squinted up at him. "It brought back a memory. It was dark, and there were two cars. A man was yelling at me to do something. Then there were shots all around us, and blood." She ducked her head. "Too much blood. All over me."

Troy's grip on her arms tightened.

"Summer, what happened to the man? Did he harm you?"

"He was afraid of me. Then his face exploded." The pain in her head began hammering as if it were trying to break out, but she grew distant from it, as if her mind was moving away from her body. Blindly she smiled at Troy. "You're not afraid of anything. I like that about you. You will make a fine mate."

"Summer, listen to me carefully," Troy said, his voice low and soothing now. "What did you do to the man? Were you afraid? Did you defend yourself?"

What he was saying horrified her, but she was drifting away from her feelings, too.

"I couldn't save him. I wanted to, but it was too late. I had to run away."

Troy was asking her something else, but she was so far away now she could barely hear him.

"What?" she said.

"How did you kill him?" Troy repeated, louder this time.

"Kill him? No, I couldn't… I would never."

She heard a train roaring through her head, and then the world up-ended into blackness.

• • • • •

Warmth and the scent of wood smoke surrounded Summer as she opened her eyes and saw a crackling fire. Beneath her was a sinfully soft down comforter spread over a mattress, although she wasn't in a bed. She was curled on her side, her back pressed against a broad, hard chest, and a heavy arm circled her waist.

"This is nice," she murmured, watching the flames through half-closed eyes. "How did I get here?"

"I carried you," Troy said softly in her ear. "You fainted in my arms, and I couldn't let you go." He paused. "You look beautiful in the firelight."

Summer shifted onto her back so she could see his face. The fire loved him, too, and streaked his thick black hair with glowing gold.

"Is this the curse talking, or you?"

"Me," he said, his gaze moving all over her face. "Do you remember anything?"

"Floating. Pain. More pain." She watched him prop himself up on one elbow. "And weirdly-behaving water. That's all. Did I say anything this time?"

"Nothing that made any sense." He rested his

hand on her belly and rubbed his thumb across the dent of her navel. "Except that I would make a fine mate."

She'd said that? She felt her cheeks flush. But his hand on her belly was moving insistently, and it made her bold.

"You'd make a fine anything," she said lowly. Warmth flickered to life beneath his broad palm, as she covered his hand with hers. "I know it's only been a week, but it's time to find out now, isn't it? About us, and how it could be."

"I already know," he said, and lifted her hand to his mouth. He pressed his lips to her palm. "Let me show you."

Troy rolled on top of her, bracing himself with his hands to keep the bulk of his weight off her as he settled his lower body between her thighs. As soon as he dipped his head she met his mouth halfway, her lips parting as she accepted his hungry kiss. He used his wicked tongue to stroke hers, and worked an arm under her to lift her up in a sitting position. His hands got busy unbuttoning her blouse and slid it down her arms.

"Oh," she gasped, breaking their kiss as he unclipped her bra and covered her bare breasts with his hands. "You're fast."

"I've been thinking about this every night since

we got here. Believe me, this is slow." As he stroked his fingers over her nipples he watched her eyes. "It's a good thing that couch can't talk, either."

"Really," she murmured. She smiled as he pulled his shirt over his head and dropped it. Her hands slid over his tightly-muscled chest. "If it could, what would it say?"

He leaned forward to whisper against her ear.

"Stop rubbing your cock, and go give it to that beautiful lady in the next room." He drew her hand down to the thick bulge in his crotch. "She'll know how to play with it."

"I can't really remember," Summer said, but cupped the heavy length of his erection, squeezing it a little before she reached for the button of his jeans. "Maybe I should do a little hands-on research."

"Now who's fast?" Troy teased as he took her hand away and lifted her up to stand with him so he could strip off her jeans and panties.

He hissed in a breath when she leaned closer to rub her curves across his ripped abs. He lowered his head to touch his brow to hers as he cradled her breasts and massaged them. She pressed herself against his erection and slowly gyrated. He hissed again.

"You have a hundred years to stop doing that."

"Wimp," she said breathlessly as he tugged on her tightly-puckered nipples.

"So beautiful."

He clamped his hands around her waist and lifted her off the makeshift mattress until he could suck at her breast.

Summer twined her fingers through the heavy, straight mass of his black hair. She let her head fall back as the sweet rasp of his mouth sent a burning flush from her breasts to her pelvis, where it tightened into a knot of hot need. His hungry licking and suckling made her curl her legs around him, and she felt his hand tighten on her bottom as the soft curls of her sex whispered over his corrugated abs.

Troy's strong arms lowered her back to the comforter, and after nuzzling each breast again he moved away from her. Dazed, it took her a moment to search for him. She watched as he took a condom from his pants and proceeded to strip. His body was magnificent—chiseled slabs of muscle rippling under taut skin. But as he pulled his pants down, his erection sprang free. He sheathed the curving length of it with a condom, as wet warmth flooded the apex of her thighs. That he had enough sense to protect them both in this crazy passion made her feel oddly cherished.

"I should have thought of that," she breathed, as he towered over her. "Thank you."

He knelt between her legs and ducked his face under her jaw.

"My pleasure," he whispered against her throat.

He kissed his way down the center of her torso, pushing her thighs apart to bare her sex to his heated gaze. He placed a delicate kiss to the right of her mound. He looked up at her, his blue eyes blazing now, and then buried his mouth against her.

A cry spilled from Summer's lips as Troy's tongue pushed between her folds and laved over her clit, lashing it again and again before he shifted and penetrated her with his tongue. He worked it in and out of her clenching opening, stimulating all her most sensitive nerves before returning to torment her nub with another wet, passionate stroking. She felt the pleasure gathering inside her and arched her back, shamelessly rolling her hips so that she was working her sex against his tongue as much as he was licking her with it.

"Inside you," Troy growled. He loomed up over her, his big body coiled as he wrapped his fist around his heavy shaft and pressed the slick, straining bulb of his cockhead against her. "Take me inside you, Summer. I need to fuck your sweet pussy before I explode."

She reached down to guide him, and then moaned as he pushed the broad head inside. She whimpered a little at the stretch, and he stared down at her, his eyebrows knit together.

"Gods, you're as tight as a virgin," he muttered, his big hand stroking her hair. "Maybe you are. I don't want to hurt you." He began to draw back.

She wrapped her arms around him. "Please, don't leave me like this. I don't care. I need you."

His brilliant blue eyes stared into hers. "Tell me if you want to stop."

Troy braced himself over her, looking down at her face as he began to move in short, gentle strokes, giving her more and more of his pulsing thickness.

"*Oh gods*," she gasped.

She shivered uncontrollably as her body stretched to accept him. They were a tight fit, but he felt so hard and good inside her.

"Yes, my lady, that's it," he said, grunting between the words as his strokes grew longer and slower. "You can take all of me. We were made for this, you and I."

Once he had penetrated her to his root he went still, closing his eyes briefly as he relished the full merging. Summer felt their body hair tangle and clutched at his arms. His erection had filled her so completely she didn't know where she ended and he began. What she did feel for the first time was the protective body shield he had given her, which now felt like a heavy, hot blanket about to smother her.

"Troy," she whispered, staring up into his hot eyes. "Take away the body ward."

He dragged in a deep breath. "You're sure?"

When she nodded frantically he muttered a few words and a glowing mist drifted away from Summer, and the stifling sensation vanished.

Now she could feel him as she never had before, the delicious heat and glide of his skin against hers, the salty tang of his sweat mingling with her own. She ran her hand over his shoulder and down his arm, circling his wrist with her fingers. She curled a long leg around his, her eyes intent on his face, as she contracted her soft wetness around his shaft to massage every inch he gave her.

This man is thine now, an old woman's voice inside her whispered in a tongue only her heart understood. *Do with him what thou will.*

As if Troy had heard, his big body tensed for a moment over hers, and then relaxed as he began to move inside her, his shaft swelling even thicker as he slid out and forged back in. He bent his head to touch his lips to hers, using his tongue with the same gliding thrust of his cock to taste her. When he looked into her eyes she saw an endless sea of wanting in his.

He looks at me the way Michael did, Summer thought, but couldn't hate herself for thinking of the big Templar.

"Michael," Troy muttered, his mouth tight, and then shook his head as if to clear it.

"It's all right," she murmured, and pressed her palm to his cheek. "I know. I feel it, too." Desire was burning her up now, the suddenly insane need for him. "This is our night. Show me how it can be with you, Troy."

He hesitated another moment before he groaned and gathered her against him, his hips working hard between her thighs as he shafted her over and over with deep, forceful thrusts.

"Is this what you wanted?" he breathed. "Can you feel that? I've wanted to do this since the first moment I laid eyes on you, my sweet witch."

Summer's breasts heaved as she writhed under him, her sex growing slick as he impaled her over and over with his steely girth, until the desire inside her blossomed into a ferocious need.

Troy seemed to sense how the new hunger gripped her, for he pulled back onto his knees, cradling her hips as he fucked her harder and deeper, his thumb burrowing between her folds to stroke steadily back and forth over her clit.

"There it is," he muttered, his eyes narrowing as he watched her breasts bounce. "I want it, Summer. I want to feel it squeezing my cock. Give all your wanting to me, my lady."

Her spine bowed as she took another thrust, feeling it from her toes to her lips, and then cried out as the hot delight sizzled through her to burst into fiery pleasure. Dimly she felt Troy stiffen and jerk, his groan of satisfaction pleasing to her ears, the pulse of his shaft inside her softness almost as sweet as if he had filled her with his seed.

Not yet, the old cronish voice inside her murmured. *Thee must wait.*

Troy rolled to his side, his eyes closed and his face suffused with pleasure. He held her and stroked her back as their heartbeats slowed. But he was the first to drift into sleep, murmuring under his breath as he did.

Summer caught the words and frowned.

Something about his brother?

• • • • •

Michael Charbon arrived back at his apartment after another long day on patrol. Since announcing the plan to raid a mid-winter mass gathering of covens Nathaniel Harper had been as demanding of his men as he was secretive about the exact location. He had also been disappointed by Michael's repeated failure to produce Summer.

You must find her, my son, the Temple Master told him. *The Emerald Tablet is too important to our cause now. If we can recover it before we move against the pagans, we can assure our victory.*

After showering and picking at a meal he didn't want, Michael sat before the fireplace and brooded over his increasingly vexing dilemma. With Nathaniel so convinced that Summer was the key to prevailing over the pagans, Michael knew he could never allow her to fall into the hands of the Temple Master or any of his brothers—particularly Gideon, whom Michael now knew was the rapist who had attacked her. Something was very wrong with Gideon as well, but Nathaniel's steward was the least of his problems. He was almost convinced that the attack his master was planning would be carried out to the north—and Silver Wood might be one of the covens at the gathering.

If Nathaniel captured Summer during the raid, he would have her tortured to try to discover the location of the Tablet. Since she had no memory of her life before she came to Central Park, she couldn't tell him what he wanted to know. She would likely die on the rack after weeks of agony.

No. Everything in Michael rebelled at the thought of Summer falling into Templar hands. *I would kill her myself first.*

Michael closed his eyes and let his head fall back against the cushions. Attending to his duty and doing what he thought was right could no longer be aligned or fit together. He had tried to follow the true path, and serve the order with honor, but he knew the mass extermination of pagans was wrong. No victory in war could be honorably decided by genocide.

Won't you let me stay with you?

The memory of the last time he had spoken with Summer swept over him, and his mouth curved a little as he remembered her lovely eyes, and how they beseeched him. He had wanted to keep her for himself, and there would always been a part of him that regretted sending her away. He could recall perfectly every second of the few hours they had spent together. On several nights since she had left, he had thought of the wild, abandoned kiss they had shared while he stroked his cock. When he spilled his seed over his fist, he had not felt a single twinge of shame.

That is because you belong to me now, Michael, Summer's voice whispered in the darkness. *When you come to me, I will show you how it will be.*

He could not go to her, but he could imagine it. His fantasy of her took him away to a soft bed of white before a blazing fire, where Summer lay naked and slumbering, her lovely face peaceful. Michael knelt beside her to brush a strand of silky hair back from her cheek, and traced with his fingertip the high curve of her cheekbone.

Dark opal eyes opened to gaze up at him. "Michael."

"I am here," he murmured, trailing his hand down her throat and over her collarbone.

Touching her naked breast made his cock lengthen and stiffen. He brought her hand to it, wrapping her cool fingers around his girth.

"You've been thinking about us," she whispered.

He stretched out beside her, using his palm to massage her hard nipple. He pressed his cockhead into the soft notch between her thighs. The sweet, wet warmth of her honey spread over his aching bulb.

"You are wet for me."

Summer nodded solemnly. "I want you. You knew that when I kissed you."

Michael reached down to stroke her sweetness, and felt other fingers caressing her folds. His eyes narrowed as he saw Troy rise up behind Summer, his blue eyes reflecting his own shock.

"Paladin," Troy said and tilted his head as he studied him. Then his mouth hitched. "So we share dreams outside prison cells, Brother."

"We are not brothers," Michael said. He glanced down at Summer, who rolled over and began kissing the pagan's long, hard shaft. "I will leave you to it."

"Don't go," Troy said as he cradled the back of Summer's head with his hand. Her mouth enveloped the reddened dome of his cockhead. "Her hunger is for us both."

Michael saw Summer lift her hips and spread her legs, presenting him with the slick, sweet, jewel box of her sex.

"You must give her all of it, Brother," Troy murmured as he guided Summer's bobbing head. "Your hard cock, deep inside, where she needs it."

Michael should have felt repelled by the pagan's suggestion, but he crawled over to kneel behind Summer, and stroked her heart-shaped buttocks with his rough hands. He looked at Troy again, who nodded and watched as Michael fisted his throbbing cock and brought it to her opening.

Summer moaned and let Troy's penis pop from her lips. "Yes, please, Michael."

The pagan brought her head back to his crotch. "Greedy little witch," he said. As her head bobbed, he looked across her back at Michael. "I want to spill inside her mouth while you pump into her pussy."

Michael pressed in, and groaned as her hot wetness clasped his cock. The feel of her squeezing his shaft made his hips recoil and thrust heavily against her as he gave her his full length.

"That's it," Troy crooned. "That's what she needs. Suck my cock while Michael fucks you, sweet lady. Show us how much you need us to pleasure you."

Michael couldn't stop himself from plowing into Summer's tightness any more than he could avert his gaze from her mouth as it rode the pagan's stiff penis. His hips bucked against her, and when he crouched over to cup her bobbing breasts he felt her trembling.

"Help me play with these lovely tits," Michael said.

Troy nodded, and his hands joined Michaels as they caressed her. "Later we can suck them together and play with her little nub until she comes."

Summer groaned, her whole body shaking now.

Michael felt his balls drawing tight and shifted his hands to her hips. "I cannot hold back."

"Not anymore," Troy said as he and Summer began to fade away. "Come to us, Brother."

Summer lifted her head and gave him a pleading look. "Soon, Michael. You have to come soon."

"Summer," Michael whispered.

He sat upright, and looked down to see his own hand pumping his stiff penis. He wanted her so much he had been masturbating in his sleep, something he had never before done. He felt a stab of loneliness so acute it bit into his chest like a blade.

At least she and the pagan had each other. All he had were dreams that could not come true. So he would sin alone.

Slowly Michael sat back, and watched his cockhead grow darker as he continued to stroke his shaft. The remorse he should have felt for yet

again violating his vow of celibacy never rose
inside him, nor did he feel particularly disgusted
by his fantasy of sharing Summer with Troy.
Everything about it had felt immensely arousing
—and completely right.

Michael imagined Summer's luscious mouth
suckling the pagan's cock while his own pushed
deep inside her pussy. He came like a fountain, his
shaft jerking over and over as the thick jets
spurted over his fist.

He fell back and closed his eyes, enjoying for
once deep satisfaction from an act that usually felt
hollow and shameful.

"Thank you, Brother."

CHAPTER TEN

ERICA BUCHANAN FINISHED reading through an ancient book of the dead and carried it back into the warded vault where the coven kept books considered too dangerous to leave out in the open. The passages about necromancy had been very detailed. Although reading through them left her feeling as if her mind were coated with a thin layer of foul slime, at least she knew that what Summer had done with her dandelions was probably not the product of an evil nature.

As I know only too well.

Erica's single brush with the most evil-natured being she had ever encountered had nearly killed her before altering her life forever.

As she closed the vault and resealed the spells guarding it, the door to the library opened. Abel came in to scowl at her.

"You should be abed, madam."

She sniffed. "You should mind your own business, sir." She went back to the desk to collect the notes she had made for Troy. "Am I needed?"

"You are always needed," Abel said. He came around the desk and pulled her into his arms. "That is why you should be abed, with me."

Erica smiled as he bent his head to kiss her, and when he tried to heft her up in his arms she broke off the kiss with a laugh.

"Abel Atwater, we are too old to be doing this in the library, of all places."

"Well, then, should we do this?" He plunged his hand in the front of her blouse to gently squeeze her plump breast. "Or perhaps this?" His other hand splayed over her bottom and brought her hips to his.

Erica glanced at the door. "You neglected to lock that again." She untangled herself from his embrace and patted his chest. "I will come to your bed in an hour."

"Or sooner, if you want to be pleasured." He arched one dark brow. "I may fall asleep."

She eyed the broad bulge of his erection. "Somehow I doubt that. An hour." She stood on tiptoe to kiss his cheek before she took her notes and went out into the hall, only to nearly walk into Lachlan. "Did you need something, my dear?"

The younger man's sly blue eyes met hers in a guileless stare. "I was looking for Wilson."

More likely he had been eaves-dropping, Erica thought. Of all the men in the coven, Abel's assistant was the one she trusted the least. He always seemed to pop up where he wasn't supposed to be. She also suspected his frequent trips into town were not always, as he claimed, to deal with coven business matters.

"I saw him go out to the barn after dinner," she said. "Perhaps he's still there."

Lachlan inclined his head and strode off.

Annoyed now, Erica headed to the kitchen, where she found a tired-eyed Aileen standing over a pan of milk on the stove. As she always did when she saw the young witch, Erica forced her mind to blank and her mouth to smile.

"Are you still having trouble sleeping?"

"Yes, and it's Wilson's fault. With all his tossing and turning lately I can barely close my eyes for three seconds straight. So tonight I'm drugging him." She turned off the burner and poured the warm milk into a tumbler before adding some powdered chamomile. "Are Troy and Summer over at his place?"

"Yes. They'll probably be back in the morning." Erica had tried to check on them with a quick scry, but something had blocked her vision. "You two should stay here tonight. Wilson has no business dragging you in and out of here on cold nights."

Aileen yawned and nodded. "He says we should help with the preparations for the gathering, but I think he wants to keep an eye on other developments and, of course, me. Just in case I decide to seduce his brother with my awesome body." She patted the curve of her bulging belly.

"The more they love, the stupider men become," Erica said firmly. "What do you think of inviting Summer to join our circle?"

"After knowing her only a week?" Aileen frowned. "I really can't say. She seems very nice, and she's a hard worker, but I'm not sure she's ready. She's a bit resistant to our ways."

"A bit, yes," Erica said with a sigh. "You were so different when you came to us—so eager and willing to learn. You spoiled us for all other newcomers."

"I was so desperate to be part of a family that I think I would have done anything to fit in," the younger woman admitted.

Erica felt the void in her chest expand. "Was it

so terrible with the people who adopted you?"

"No, they were very kind to me. I never wanted for anything." A wistful flicker passed over Aileen's thin face. "But they were human, and I was Wiccan, and as I grew older I realized how different we were. Sometimes I caught them watching me, too, as if they were afraid of me."

"Anyone would be proud to have you as a daughter, my dear girl." Erica kissed her brow before she handed her the tumbler of warm milk. "Now go to bed, and if that mate of yours continues to wake you, kick him out of it."

The younger woman gave her a sleepy smile and patted her belly.

"Maybe I'll have the baby do that. Lately I think the little one has been playing soccer with my bladder."

Once she was gone Erica went out into the garden to sit on her meditation bench, where no one would hear her crying, but instead found her brother occupying it.

"Ewan, what are you doing out here so late?"

"Couldn't sleep. I ran out of sheep to count, so I thought I'd admire the Lady and tally her starry courtiers." He moved over and patted the empty space on the bench. "Sit, sit."

Erica perched beside him, smiling as her

brother wrapped an arm around her shoulders. All around them tiny fireflies winked on and off like blinking eyes, thanks to the warming spell that kept the garden protected from the harsh temperatures of November.

"Aileen can't sleep because her mate is restless. What's your complaint?"

"I have more than one," Ewan said. "Troy and Abel, Troy and Wilson, Troy and Aileen, and of course Troy and this untutored witch with no memory." He winked at her. "Troy always seems to be involved in my worries. Perhaps we should send him back to the Magus Corps."

"You worry too much about everyone." Erica knew her brother was very sensitive to the moods of other Wiccans, and often became distressed when there were conflicts within the coven. "What do you think of Summer?"

"She's kind and lovely, and the dogs adore her. That's good enough for me," he said with a chuckle. "But then, so does Troy. I would not deny the boy his chance to take a mate, but if they choose to stay…"

Erica made a face. "Abel will begin pressuring Troy to take his place as coven leader, which Wilson will hate, and Summer will not understand, and ultimately will drive away Troy and put us back to where we were, on either side of this rift."

"I'm not on anyone's side. Those two are so alike they will be butting heads for eternity," Ewan said, and gave her a shrewd look. "Best you stay out of it, Sister. I know you love Troy like a son, but you need to attend to our lineage."

Not this again, Erica thought. "We can talk about it another time."

"Wait, wait. I've printed out profiles for some new prospects for you to consider." He reached into the front pocket of his overalls and removed a stack of folded printer paper, which he pushed into her hands. "All are Wiccans, in good standing with their covens, and all in need of a fertile mate. All will be attending our gathering, and some are actually quite handsome, too."

Erica kept her expression bland. She and Abel had been casual lovers for years, but she had insisted on them keeping it concealed from her brother and the rest of the coven. After having a prophetic nightmare about seeing the High Priest butchered during a bonding ceremony with her, Erica also refused Abel's many requests to formally mate.

"Brother, as I've told you, I'm quite happy being single and childless," she lied.

"Doesn't hurt to look, does it?" Ewan patted her hands. "You might find a man with whom you can finally be happy."

"I am too old and set in my ways now, my dear." Before he could begin another argument over the matter she kissed his cheek. "When you run out of stars to count you should try the lightning bugs. Good night."

Erica retreated to her rooms to bathe and prepare for bed, but when she emerged from the bath she found Abel stretched out naked on her bed. He was looking through the profiles Ewan had given her.

She put her hands on her hips. "I thought you were going to wait in your rooms for me."

"I grew tired of waiting. Ewan is still matchmaking, I see." He tossed aside the paper and reached for her, drawing her down beside him. "I locked the door this time."

"We must be quiet," she said and switched off the lights. She unbelted her robe and pulled it off, draping it over the foot board. "Aileen and Wilson are just down the hall."

"Mate with me," Abel said as he rolled on top of her, "and we won't have to sneak around anymore."

Erica's temper suddenly flared up. "I don't want

to be a mate, or a mother, or anything but myself." She wrapped her legs around him. "Now, either pleasure me, or go back to your own room."

Even in the darkness she could see the slow smile that stretched across Abel's face as he pressed into her. He rubbed her soft nipples, teasing them to hardness before using his tongue on them while he inched into her.

Erica focused on relaxing and welcoming him, keeping her eyes closed as she reminded herself that this was her friend and lover, and not the monster that had destroyed her life and ruined her for all men.

Years of love-making had taught Abel what she liked, and he gave it to her with a deep, slow pumping of his shaft, his hands stroking her breasts, his mouth mapping her face with teasing kisses. She felt a moan rise up in her throat, but Abel clamped a hand over her lips.

"Shhh," he whispered. He nodded at the door. "Someone is out there."

His hand and the prospect of being discovered sent Erica into a panic, which Abel misinterpreted as passion. He pressed her face against his shoulder as he murmured lusty, sexy words against her ear, his cock hammering into her now.

Erica held on and closed her eyes, trying not to shake herself to pieces as he finished. Once he had he rolled away from her, he quickly fell asleep. Silently she retreated to the bath to take another shower. The hateful memories that haunted every inch of her scarred body had to be scrubbed away.

CHAPTER ELEVEN

TROY WOKE TO the sound of birdsong, and saw a sprig of green in front of his nose. He sat up to see that he and Summer lay in the center of the meadow in front of his house, which was no longer frost-covered or dead. Thick, soft green grass dotted with wildflowers extended in a broad circle around them, and also streaked over to the house and back to his Jeep. Down at the creek more grass and blooming flowers clustered at the spot where Summer had fallen.

Memories of the night he'd shared with her came flooding back to him. He smiled as he recalled how beautifully she'd responded to him. Although she obviously had little experience, Summer had been an eager and exciting partner who took as much pleasure in his satisfaction as her own. Her frank sensuality and willingness to be as playful as she was passionate had aroused him so much he'd spent most of the night buried inside her.

The fact that they had ended up sleeping in the meadow didn't worry him as much as what effect it would have on her.

"Summer," he said, stroking her cheek.

"I know. It's everywhere I walked." Without opening her eyes she snuggled closer. "The question is, how did we get out here? I don't remember getting up and leaving the house, do you?"

Troy recalled falling asleep with her in his arms in front of the fireplace.

"More of your mysterious magic?"

"Sure, blame me for everything," Summer said and stretched before she propped herself up and looked around. "Even more interesting, we're both still naked, but I'm not cold at all. You?" When he shook his head she concentrated for a moment. "Something brought us out here, but it wasn't me." She turned her head to scan the meadow and yawned. "I would kill for some coffee. This isn't a Wiccan version of a practical joke, isn't it?"

"Not in my coven," Troy said and pulled her over on top of him. He stroked his hands down the long, lovely lines of her back. "Kiss me."

Summer obliged by lowering her head and daintily touching her lips to his.

"Good morning," she said. As she felt him rub his erection between her thighs she smiled. "That would be lovely, but you don't have a condom on you, Major."

He nipped her chin. "How do you know?"

"We used all three that you had last night." She braced her hands against his chest and rested her chin on top of them. "So unless you made good on your threat to go back to the pavilion for more, you're out of luck."

Troy rolled her onto her side and reached down to slide his hand between her legs.

"There are other ways, my lovely lady."

"We shouldn't. They're going to be worried about us," she predicted. "Plus if we go back, you can restock and then we can…" She waggled her eyebrows at him.

"Oh, we will, have no doubt," he grumbled, and scooped her up in his arms as he stood and walked down to the creek with her. "Hold on to me."

Summer shrieked as a small tornado of droplets rose from the creek and pummeled their naked bodies with icy water before spinning away and dropping back into its source, leaving them both chilled but clean.

"Why did you do that?"

"We needed a cold shower, and I doubt there's any coffee here." He set her down on her feet and lowered his head to kiss her thoroughly. "I don't feel the curse anymore, do you?"

Summer looked as if she was going to say something, closed her mouth quickly, and then grimaced.

"I don't really know. You'd better re-ward me, just in case."

Troy used water from the creek to invoke another shielding spell, but when the misty water net tried to wrap itself around her it slid to the ground and formed a puddle around her feet.

Summer stared down at it. "So that's not good."

"Be still," Troy said and passed his hand over her body. There was a new barrier of energy in place. "It's you. You've warded yourself."

"I don't know how to do that," she countered. "I'm still on the basic curative herbs and flower poultices lesson."

"Come on, I need to get you back to the pavilion," he said and reached for her hand without thinking. His fingers passed through her ward without hindrance, which shouldn't have been possible. When he took her hand, he felt the field of energy around her stretching to envelope him. "You don't have to protect me, Summer."

"I'm not," she insisted. "It's just doing it on its own." She turned her head to look at the other side of her body. "Something's wrong with it, though. Like something's missing."

"Don't worry, we'll figure it out."

He walked with her back into the house, where they went into the dining room to retrieve their clothes. Troy came to an abrupt halt when he saw his mother's carved furnishings, which over night had sprouted tiny branches with new leaves.

"Whoa," Summer said. Her eyes widened before she gave him a panicky look. "This is not me. I couldn't have done this, I swear."

Troy released her hand and walked over to one of the chairs. He carefully inspected it before he stroked a bright green leaf that had sprouted from the end of the armrest. It was so odd and yet so lovely a thing that it immediately invoked the image of his mother's smiling face.

"If I did this, I am so sorry," Summer was saying. "I never meant to ruin it."

"You didn't. My mother was so kind-hearted that she never cut down a single tree. She carved only from wood that had already fallen and died.

She would have loved to see this." He glanced over at her. "Thank you."

Again she looked as if she wanted to say something, only to turn away. "No problem."

As they dressed Troy saw how she kept frowning at the down comforter where they had made love.

"What's wrong?"

"Do you see those?" She pointed at some long depressions in the surface of the covering. "The little one in the middle there is where I fell asleep, and you were on that side, right?"

He eyed the spot. "I think so, why?"

Her hand shifted to indicate the depression on the other side of the spot she'd made.

"Who was there?"

"No one," Troy said. Yet as soon as he said that he remembered a pair of jade green eyes staring at him from the shadows. "I must have rolled over during the night."

Summer gave him a long, silent look.

"Right. That's the only logical explanation."

Once they dressed Troy used his power to douse the fireplace. Outside the rejuvenation of the meadow had expanded several more feet and was moving into the trees, where several oaks were beginning to put out new leaves.

"If it wasn't so pretty, it would be creepy," Summer said, and hugged herself. "How could I be doing this? I haven't even cast my first spell yet."

Troy had considerable power as an elemental, and knew other warlocks with similar abilities who could command fire, air, light and even huge herds of animals to do their bidding. In all the centuries he had walked the earth, however, he had never seen anything like what Summer could do simply by walking across a meadow. Yet just as he was about to tell her that, he realized he had not yet revealed that he and the other Wiccans were immortal. That and the doubt and fear in her eyes made him draw her into his arms.

"We'll find the answers," he promised her. "Together." He kissed her brow and then reached into his jacket for his phone. "Let me call Erica and let her know…" he stopped and stared at the distorted screen.

"What is it?" Summer glanced down at the phone, and then went still.

Troy turned the phone over in his hand to check the back before he met her gaze.

"I got the case at an art shop." He touched the little olive branch growing out of his shattered display. "The guy makes them out of olive wood."

CHAPTER TWELVE

IN THE NORTH Abbey sparring chamber Alvis Berenson came at Michael with his practice staff aloft in a full frontal attack. But at the last moment the giant warrior whirled around in an attempt to strike from the side. Michael parried the hard blow and rolled his wrist, circling the wooden staff with his own before knocking it from Alvis's ham-size fist.

"You are like the fucking bee," the Norseman grumbled as he retrieved the weapon. "Always darting in to sting instead of battling face to face like a man."

"You are not a man, Brother," Michael told him flatly. "You are a mountain, and to fight you from the front is like trying to push one aside. With a finger."

He gave him a properly respectful bow.

Alvis uttered his high-pitched laugh as he bowed in return.

"You have a quick tongue, Charbon. May your sword arm be as strong in the coming weeks."

They hung up their practice weapons before leaving the sparring chamber and stripped out of their clothes before stepping into the adjoining sauna. It was a rare indulgence Nathaniel had installed for the use of his warriors after their bouts. The other Templars sitting inside the steamy chamber rose and left as soon as they spotted Alvis, who watched them go with a contemptuous smirk.

"Why are you the only one who does not shun me, Charbon?" Alvis asked as he tossed a dipper of water onto the heated rocks that generated the steam.

"I expect they have heard the stories about your berserker days among the Vikings," Michael said and leaned back against the wet wooden wall behind him. "They fear what they do not understand."

"So they shun what they fear." Alvis spat on the floor. "Like mortals, they are."

"Any man who beholds you knows his heart to quail, Brother," Michael told him. "You are eight feet tall, and three times wider than any of us."

"I cannot help my size," Alvis grumbled. The Norsemen sounded sullen. "In my village, when we were not off a-Viking, I was worked like a beast because of it. I bore the yoke on my shoulders, and dragged the plowshare across the fields. If not for our lord, Master Harper, I expect my bones would be buried there now."

Michael nodded. "So would we all be dead and dust."

"As we are alone I would speak to you about a concern," Alvis said and rubbed a huge hand over the bristling hairs that covered his skull. "You have been watching Gideon of late. I see the wariness in your eyes. Do you think him a traitor?"

"No," Michael said honestly. "But there is something amiss with him. Have you seen his mouth working?"

Alvis nodded. "He chews on that cigar to hide the twitch. Sometimes when he comes in of late, he stinks of women and fornication."

Michael felt startled. "You think he is violating them?"

The roof beam shoulders shifted. "It does not matter. Women are the daughters of Eve. They condemned us all to sin and suffering. If he returns the same to them, they likely deserve it—

and he cannot be held accountable for his sins anymore."

Hearing that from the most fervently devout Templar Michael had ever met confused him. "Why not?"

"Eternity is what plagues Gideon now," Alvis informed him. "He suffers from immortality sickness, and can no longer be trusted to serve and protect our lord, or carry on the work. When we strike at the pagan gathering in the White Mountains, I will stay behind to perform the kindness of dispatching him. Then I will join you there."

Hearing the location of the attack made acid bile surge up in Michael's throat. Silver Wood coven was located in the White Mountains of New Hampshire. To keep from puking in front of the Norseman, Michael asked a question.

"Does the Temple Master know about your plans for Gideon, Brother?"

"He ordered it," Alvis said. "You will be leading the men into the fray, so I wished you to know how it would be at the rear." He studied his face. "You are pale now. Surely you have heard this is what is always done, to release our ailing brothers from their torment."

Michael nodded. "I did not imagine Gideon to

be so stricken. It is a terrible way to lose a brother." He stood. "I must report for patrol duty. Thank you for the match, Alvis."

Michael showered and dressed as fast as he could, so he could get to his car and call Atwater from his encrypted phone. On his way out of the old church, however, he was intercepted by Nathaniel.

"My son, I need to speak with you," the Temple Master said. "I am deeply troubled by your lack of progress in tracking the witch who escaped us."

"Are you equally concerned about your steward going mad?" Michael countered without thinking, and then felt the burn of regret. "Forgive me. Alvis just informed me about Gideon's condition, and what is to be done about it."

A flicker of anger passed over Nathaniel's features before he sighed.

"It was a very difficult decision. As much as I wish we could save Gideon, we cannot allow our brother to descend into lunacy and run amok. You will say nothing to the other men about this, Michael. It is a private business."

He ducked his head. "As you wish, Master."

"Soon we may never again have to end the suffering of an ailing brother," Nathaniel continued smoothly. "With all the wisdom and power it contains, I feel certain that the Emerald Tablet can be used to cure immortality sickness." He reached up to pat Michael's cheek. "Find the witch, my son, and bring her to me, and we may yet still save Gideon."

Michael bowed and then watched the Temple Master walk away before he went to his car and pulled out his encrypted phone from where he kept it taped under the driver's seat. He dialed Atwater's number only to hear it go directly to voice mail. He opened his mouth to leave a message before he abruptly ended the call.

This was no longer about Templars and Wiccan, it was about life and death. Summer was the key to finding the most powerful grimoire in existence. If the pagans used her to find the Tablet, they would have the means with which to wipe out their old enemies. If it fell into the hands of the Templars, they would do the same. Anyone wielding such a weapon would rule the world, and since both sides were immortal, that would be for all eternity.

I know what my duty is, Michael thought. *That is why she was brought to me.*

He programmed the GPS before he called the North Abbey. Augustin Colbert answered.

"Let Master Harper know that I have received a

new lead on the whereabouts of the witch, and I will be traveling out of state to follow up."

"Where are you going?" the clergy aide asked.

Michael glanced at the GPS display, which showed he would arrive in the White Mountains of New Hampshire in four hours.

"Philadelphia."

CHAPTER THIRTEEN

THE SHOUTING MATCH between Troy and Abel started shortly after they arrived back at the Silver Wood pavilion, and was loud enough to carry from the library to the kitchen.

"That sounds like Troy refusing to follow his father's orders," Erica said as she stopped chopping carrots and cocked her head toward the bellowing.

"How can you tell?" Summer asked as she tried to make out what sounded like gibberish to her.

"She speaks Welsh," Aileen said as she stirred the large stock pot of soup bubbling on the stove. "I'm still learning." She paused to listen. "I can't be sure, but that sounds like Abel throwing some shade at you, Summer. I don't think he likes you sleeping with his son very much."

"Aileen," Erica said and gave her a look of

reproach before she said to Summer, "We didn't know the two of you were romantically involved."

"We're not. We just had sex." Summer felt an odd fuzziness in her head and sat down on one of the stools by the counter. "It was terrific, but we're not getting married or anything."

Aileen giggled. "Wiccans don't marry like humans. We mate, generally for life."

"Well, then we're definitely just having sex," Summer said.

As the shouting grew louder Erica wiped her hands on a towel and took off her apron.

"I think I'd better step in as referee," she said and hurried out.

"Would you go and clip a few chives from the garden, Summer?" Aileen asked as she peered into the soup pot. "They're the long green shoots next to the dandelions."

"Gotcha."

Summer stood and shook her head to try and clear it as she walked toward the door to the hothouse. Then went still as the world went away.

In the darkness, flashes appeared behind Summer's eyes: Aileen, limp and dripping, being carried into Erica's bedroom by Troy; Troy tearing open the sodden dress to reveal a huge, blistering burn over Aileen's small breasts; Troy's fingers touching the white handle of a knife that was sticking out of the side of her belly; bright red blood welling from around the knife, which bobbed as Aileen convulsed; a white-faced Erica rushing to the end of the bed where she stopped and stared at the younger woman; Troy turning his head to shout at the High Priestess. *Erica, help me. The baby—*

Summer turned around to see Aileen struggling to move the stock pot from the stove to the counter, a knife still in her hand. The knife had the same white handle as the one in her vision. The bottom edge of the heavy pot wedged against the side of the burner. Aileen frowned as she gave it a hard tug.

No.

Summer lunged forward as the pot tipped, and everything around her and Aileen froze, as if time itself came to a complete stop. The bizarre moment allowed her to knock the knife from the pregnant woman's hand and drag her back out of the way. As she jerked Aileen around and shielded her with her body, time snapped back into play, and the pot tipped over. Boiling soup splashed against the back of Summer's jeans as the pot and the knife fell to the floor with a crash.

Aileen stared at her in horror. "Summer. *Oh,*

Gods."

Aileen's wide eyes shifted over her shoulder to the huge steaming lake of soup on the floor.

"It would have scalded half your body," Summer said, her voice hollow and cold. "You would have slipped in the soup, and fallen onto the knife, and miscarried the baby. Then you would have bled to death. Take me outside, please. Now."

Aileen helped her into the garden, and closed the door behind them.

"You saw it before it happened, just now. You stopped it," Aileen said and swallowed hard. "Summer, you stopped everything. I felt it as you pulled me out of the way."

"I don't know what I did in there," Summer said and felt herself beginning to tremble. "Aileen, please don't tell anyone about this."

"You saved my life, and the life of my child." Aileen took hold of her hands. "I would do anything for you, Summer."

The other woman was shaking even harder than she was.

"Sit down," Summer said. She guided her to one of the garden benches. "Stay here. I'll clean up."

Summer returned inside, where she found Erica

standing in the doorway staring at the mess on the floor.

"We had a little accident. It was my fault."

"So I see," the older woman said and frowned at her. "Where is Aileen?"

"She's taking a rest break in the garden. I didn't want her to slip and fall." At least that much was true. Summer went to the utility closet and took out the mop and bucket Erica kept there. "I'm really sorry about screwing up the soup."

"We can have a salad and sandwich for dinner tonight," Erica said and gave her a sharp look. "I told Troy and his father to take it out to the barn, but they went in opposite directions." She paused. "Are you all right, my dear? You look very pale."

"I'm fine," Summer said and produced what she hoped was a rueful grin. "A little shaken up, is all. No, please," she added as Erica started to reach for a kitchen towel. "Let me do this. It's my mess."

"All right. I do need to speak to Abel about his temper anyway."

Erica gave her a sympathetic smile before she retreated.

By the time Summer mopped up the soup from the stovetop and the floor she felt steadier, and quickly washed the offending pot and knife before she rejoined Aileen, who was sitting and cradling her belly with her thin hands.

"All clear in there. You okay?"

"Thanks to you, yes." Aileen walked back inside with her and surveyed the mopped floor. "I wish I could still drink. I think I could polish off an entire bottle of wine by myself right now."

Summer poured her a cup of tea from the pot Erica kept under a cozy and sat down with her at the work table.

"I might drink it for you."

"Summer, what you did to save me…" Aileen shook her head. "I understand why you want me to keep it secret. No Wiccan has such power."

"I don't know how I did it," she admitted, "but I think I better figure that out first before we let everyone know I can stop time."

"You should talk to Troy about it," Aileen said and took a sip of the tea and sighed. "He is a water elemental, and in all the centuries he's lived he may have seen something like this."

Summer frowned at her. "Centuries?"

"I thought you knew." She made a face. "Wiccans are immortal, like the Templars. Well, we're not born that way, but once we are initiated we never again have to fear age or death."

Summer couldn't quite wrap her head around

the idea that Troy had lived for centuries, so she tackled Aileen's claim.

"But I saw you die in my vision."

"It is difficult, but we can be killed. When we are in our first century of life we can also choose to die." She touched her belly. "If I knew my child had passed on, I think I would want to go with the little one."

Something occurred to Summer. "You said the Wiccans are immortal, like the Templars. Are all of them immortal, too?"

Aileen nodded. "That is why I think we became enemies. We are the only immortal races in the world, so only we can really oppose each other." As more angry voices came from the front room she frowned. "That's Wilson."

Summer accompanied her out to where Troy and his brother were standing toe-to-toe and arguing in Welsh. Judging by how furious their expressions were neither one of them appeared interested in backing down.

At the sight of them Troy took a step toward Summer and then staggered away as Wilson's fist connected with his jaw. A moment later the two men were pummeling each other. They went down together to wrestle back and forth on the floor.

"Really, Troy?" When he took no notice Summer propped her hands on her hips and simply watched them. "The two of you. I hope I'm an only child."

"I was, and it kind of sucks," Aileen said, before she called out, "Wilson, come on. That's enough now."

The men ignored them until Abel Atwater came into the room carrying a bucket of water, which he tossed over them. The water drenched Wilson, but at the very last second Troy stopped the wave over him and sent it flying through an open window into the yard. It dropped as a pile of ice cubes. The dogs came running to happily attack the cubes, but then stopped short and filed silently into the house behind Lachlan, who glared down at Troy.

"Haven't you done enough to him?" Lachlan demanded.

He reached down to help Wilson up, but the younger man shook him off. After giving Aileen a sullen look he stalked out of the house.

The dogs surrounded Troy and began to wag their tails even as they bared their teeth in unwilling snarls. He looked over at Lachlan as he wiped some blood from his chin.

"Call them off, now."

The dogs returned to their normal happy selves as soon as Abel's assistant waved a hand. He hurried out after Wilson.

"Lachlan can control any warm-blooded animal," Aileen said, her mouth flattening. "Except himself."

Without another word she retreated back to the kitchen. With a final look of disgust and still holding the bucket, Abel followed her.

That left Summer alone with Troy, who now looked a little sheepish.

"I'm sorry about all this. My father isn't too happy about us, and every time I glance at Aileen my brother thinks I'm trying to steal his wife and first born from him. What have you been doing?"

"Oh, you know. Hanging with the witches, cleaning up the kitchen, finding out you're immortal." She tucked her arm through his. "Let's take a walk."

• • • • •

Troy took Summer through the woods to the source of his creek, which spilled down over a cliff side into a deep spring-fed pool. Over the years he and his father had hauled the rocks they cleared from the pavilion's yards and gardens to pile them at the water's edge. Summer climbed up to one flat rock they often used for diving. She sat down and gazed out at the view.

"This place is so beautiful," she said as Troy joined her, taking a seat. "I'd never want to leave it if it were mine. So why were you fighting with your dad over me?"

"I wasn't, until he called you a Templar spy." Troy picked up a pebble and tossed it into the pool. He hated that his father was so suspicious of outsiders, but it seemed even more ludicrous now that he had to explain it to Summer. "He believes it's the only rational explanation for your amnesia. He thinks they deliberately mind-wiped you so you wouldn't remember that you are spying for them."

"That's an interesting alternative theory," she said and handed him another pebble. "And your brother thinks you're going to steal his wife because…"

"Aileen and I were involved, a long time ago. We ended it, and we're just friends, but Wilson is convinced that I still have feelings for her." He uttered a bitter chuckle. "He accused me of bringing you here to confuse and distract him so I could seduce his wife. Who, if you haven't noticed, is eight-and-a-half months pregnant."

"Yeah, but she's still pretty hot," Summer said and gave his shoulder a friendly bump with hers. "Don't look so depressed. I like you. Ewan likes you. Erica likes you. Lachlan…hey, did I mention Ewan likes you?"

"Ewan likes everyone." Soothed by her good humor, he pulled her onto his lap. "I'm sorry I didn't tell you about the immortality factor. I was waiting for the right time."

She rested her head against his shoulder. "Like when? Your birthday? How old are you going to be this year? Twenty-nine, for the five hundredth time?"

"We stop counting after five hundred." He rubbed his thumb across her full lower lip, and smiled a little when she kissed it. "Why don't we go back to my place? I've restocked my condom supply, and it's much quieter and nicer there."

"I would like that very much," she said and pressed his hand to her cheek. "But you can't keep using me to avoid dealing with your family problems." He gave her a narrow look. "Your dad has every right to be suspicious of me. *I'm* suspicious of me. Plus you got me from a Templar, remember?"

He shook his head. "Michael is different."

"For which I am very grateful, but it doesn't

change the facts. I don't know who I am or how I got to Central Park. I could be anything." Her expression tightened. "And we don't know all of what I'm capable of doing yet."

"You are not a Templar spy, because if you were, they would have already overrun the place," Troy told her, and helped her up before he circled her waist with his arms. "As for your abilities as a witch, we just have to test you. There's a very old test, in fact, that should prove what you are."

She gave him a wry look. "Oh, yeah? What is it?"

"The dunking test." He pulled her against him and jumped off the rock, laughing as she shrieked on the way down. They plunged into the ice-cold water.

Summer surfaced with him, gasping and squealing before she took her hand and shoved a handful of water at his face. He stopped it so that it hung between them, and she gave him a dirty look.

"Don't you dare."

Troy laughed and used the water to lift her up onto one of the long, sun-warmed rocks, where he climbed out and sat down beside her to dispel the water from her hair and clothes.

"Never mess with a water elemental in winter,"

he advised her as she sat up.

"Come here," she said and grabbed the front of his shirt.

She pulled him down on top of her, her lips meeting his in a ferocious kiss.

Troy's residual anger over fighting with his father and brother shifted into something far more urgent. He tore open her blouse to get at her breasts, sucking one and then the other as he unfastened her jeans and shoved them and her panties down to her knees. As she worked them off he pushed down his own trousers, pausing only long enough to sheath himself with one of the condoms. He hoisted her legs up around his hips and guided his iron-hard shaft to her damp sex.

"You're the one who really makes me crazy," he told her as he rubbed his cockhead against her before pushing it between her slick folds. "Look in my eyes. I want to see yours as I take you."

Sinking into her softness made him swell even bigger, for she was as wet and hot as a hungry mouth. The way her lashes fluttered as she caught her breath and tightened around him made him feel a fierce satisfaction. She could kid and pretend nothing mattered to her, until he got his cock inside her. Then things got very, very serious.

He laid her down on their clothes.

"That's it. Feel me filling that soft, sweet, little pussy," he crooned as he stroked into her. He needed her too much to do anything but fuck her, deep and hard, his cock pumping like a piston for the engine of his lust. "Does that feel good? Are you going to come for me?"

"Troy, oh, yes." She clung to him as she made a whimpering sound, her slim hips rolling under the power of his thrusts. "Please, please."

He took hold of her legs and pushed her knees back almost to her shoulders so he could forge deeper into her fluttering softness. He pounded her pussy as his rigid shaft prodded the edge of her cervix. Summer writhed, her pretty breasts heaving as she took everything he gave her, and then she released a wild wail as her body shook uncontrollably.

Troy jerked his cock out of her, stripping off the condom. He worked his fist up and down his shaft. But when she reached up to help him, the touch of her cool fingers made him instantly come. The pleasure exploded from him in long, silky white ribbons of cream. He watched them lace across her belly and breasts and felt the satisfaction of having marked her with his seed, for she was his woman now.

He fell beside her, his chest heaving as he closed his eyes and let the sunlight bathe his sweat-shined hide.

"Gods, that was amazing," he breathed. "You are the sexiest woman I've ever touched."

"I'll let Wilson know that," she said primly, and turned her head to press her lips to his shoulder. "Maybe he'll stop imagining things. By the way, if you dunk me in that icy pool again, I'm going to be the last woman you ever touch."

CHAPTER FOURTEEN

WHEN THEY RETURNED to the pavilion
Summer learned everyone except Ewan had gone
into town on an impromptu shopping trip that
she suspected had more to do with cooling off
and putting some distance between Troy and his
family than any actually necessary errands.

"You'll know when things will go back to what
passes for normalcy around here," Erica's brother
told her as they watched Troy head off to the
chopping stump. "We'll have too much fire wood,
more game than we can eat, and very shiny cars
and floors."

She frowned. "Why?"

"Everyone deals with stress in different ways.
Troy chops wood. Wilson goes hunting. And
Abel?" He lifted his shoulders. "He waxes.
Everything."

Summer nodded slowly. "I wonder what I do."

"Maybe you're one of the lucky ones, like me." He gave her a wink. "I'm never stressed. It's because I never take sides. I just go hang out with the dogs in the barn until the yelling is over."

"Great idea." She reached down to scratch behind the ears of a grinning Irish setter. "Next time I think I'll join you."

Summer went back to their rooms to shower and change, and while she dressed she thought about what Aileen had said. She did need to talk to someone about what had happened in the kitchen, and Troy was the logical choice. If she could stop time without even thinking about it, then she might do it someday and be unable to restart it.

She also wanted to tell him about the condition she'd been in when she'd woken up in the park. If her blood-soaked clothes were proof that she had hurt someone, she needed to know now before she got any stronger.

After Summer dried and braided her hair, she felt her shoulder itch, and pulled back her blouse to see if she'd gotten an insect bite. Her skin twitched, but there was nothing there. She rubbed some skin cream over the spot before she buttoned up and left the room.

Outside she found the axe and a huge mound of chopped wood by the stump, but no Troy. She walked across to the barn before she noticed the Jeep was missing from the yard.

"So he took off without me," she told the dogs, who herded around her briefly before they bounded off to follow Ewan into the house. "Yes, abandon me, too. It's the story of my life."

Summer started to head back to the pavilion when she heard what sounded like someone whispering her name. She turned around until she heard it again, and then moved in that direction.

"Hello? Is someone there?"

She stepped over a fallen tree trunk and moved through a small sea of fern toward a thicket of firs. The soft-needled trees perfumed the air with the smell of Christmas.

"Hello? It's Summer."

A pair of hard hands seized her from behind, and hauled her up against a broad chest. A damp, smelly cloth came over her nose and mouth. She looked up to see Michael's green eyes fill with regret.

"I am sorry, my Beauty," he told her as her vision began to gray. "But you must come back to me now."

STOLEN

SILVER WOOD COVEN BOOK TWO

By Hazel Hunter

CHAPTER ONE

SUMMER WOKE UP alone in the dark. Feeling dazed and sluggish, she grimaced over the faint burning sensation in her nose and the awful taste in her dry mouth. When she tried to touch her face she discovered her wrists had been bound together. Shifting her legs revealed the same thing had been done to her ankles, and that she'd been left on top of a bed with cool, clean, silk sheets.

She rolled onto her side to push herself upright with one elbow, squinting as she turned her head. She couldn't make out any details of her surroundings. Her first impulse was to shout for help, but that might bring whoever had taken her and left her tied up. The last thing she remembered was walking in the woods outside the pavilion. Whoever had done this obviously had grabbed her there, but who? And why?

Sensory memories began scrolling through her mind: her name being whispered softly, the firm grip of hard hands, a cloth with a terrible chemical smell clamped over her mouth and nose. The remorse in his cool green eyes and his voice as he'd said to her: *I am sorry, my Beauty, but you must come back to me now.*

"Michael?"

Summer was shocked as much by the memories as the croaking sound of her own voice, and the stabbing pain that bounced inside her head and just as quickly vanished.

Struggling against the knots binding her proved useless, so she wriggled toward the edge of the mattress, hoping to ease herself off. When she reached it the silk sheet under her slipped, and she fell to the floor with a loud thud.

She heard heavy footsteps outside the room and rolled, hoping to wedge herself under the bed, but a door opened and the sudden brightness made her freeze like a doe caught in headlights.

"Summer," Michael Charbon said and lifted her with his strong arms. He placed her back on the bed and ran his hands over her, checking her arms and legs before peering at her face. "You should not have woken so soon."

"I guess you didn't use enough drugs."

Her voice still sounded horrible, but what upset her more was the sense of relief she felt as soon as he touched her, and the pleasure she took in looking at him.

Tall and powerfully built, Michael strongly resembled a warrior ready to fight for his life in some dangerous arena, but she wasn't afraid of him. She wanted to wrap her arms around him and run her fingers through his short-cropped golden hair and listen to his deep voice rumbling in his broad chest. He had made her feel safe and protected from the moment they'd met, when she'd been a homeless amnesiac in Central Park. He had saved her from a dangerous rapist.

The problem was that Michael wasn't her friend. He was a Templar witch hunter, and she was a witch. He had abducted her from the safety of Silver Wood, the coven that had taken her in and had been training her to control her power. What was even more confusing was that Michael himself had arranged to send her to Silver Wood to keep her safe from the Templars.

He obviously changed his mind, or he wouldn't have brought me back to New York City. So why do I still want to throw myself in his arms and kiss him until neither of us can think straight? To cover her confusion Summer asked, "May I have some water, please?"

He nodded and left her, returning a minute later with a chilled glass bottle. He uncapped it and held to her lips.

Summer drank half the contents before she gasped and turned her face away. "No more, or I'll be sick." She ignored the wonderful heat and smell of him as she glanced around her. "This is your bedroom, isn't it?"

"Yes," he said, capping the bottle and placing it on the night stand. "You should try to sleep a few more hours now. The effects of the drug should wear off by morning."

The light came from behind him, shadowing his features, but Summer could hear the concern in his tone. She'd felt the same thing in his touch. Maybe he hadn't brought her here to hurt her.

"Michael, why did you bring me back? I was happy with Troy and his people—and I was safe with them, too. You knew I would be. You sent me to them."

"It was a mistake," was all he said. He switched on the bedside lamp before he rose and walked over to look out the bedroom window. "Have you remembered anything more?"

"No, but I've discovered a few things." Summer checked the distance from the bed to the door, and wiggled backward until she could prop herself up against the pillows. "I've been cursed, but the curse stopped working a couple weeks ago. It turns out I'm also not a green witch, and I suck at actual gardening, but I can bring dead plants back to life." She leaned over and began to unpick the knot in the cords around her ankles.

"That we knew from the effect you had on the Conservatory gardens," he said softly.

"This would be more like I killed the plants first, then replanted them because I felt badly, and whoosh, they grew like wildfire." Once her ankles were free, she shifted over toward the edge of the mattress as silently as she could. Slowly, she swung her legs over. "Everyone was pretty nice about it, but then, they're nice people." She stood and took a step. Her legs felt a little numb but supported her weight. "How have you been?"

Summer didn't wait to hear his answer, but tiptoed across the room and stepped out into the hall. She fled down the hall toward the front room and freedom. She was a few inches from the entry door when a big arm encircled her waist and dragged her back against a big, hard body.

"I would have made it if you hadn't drugged me," she muttered as he swept her up in his arms and carried her back to the bedroom. He placed her back on the bed and retied her ankles together. Tired now, she watched him knot the cords. "So what have you been up to? Is winter your busy season for hunting and torturing witches, or do they give you some time off for the holidays?"

A muscle in his jaw tightened. "I am not a torturer."

"Then why am I tied up, Michael?" She watched his eyes, which looked haunted, and felt a surge of anger. "Did you want me to be helpless, and entirely at your mercy? I am. I have been since the night you saved me."

"You are the least helpless female I know," he said. He got up from the bed and pulled the coverlet over her. "I would never harm you, Beauty. You know this."

"I know you knocked me out, tied me up, and took me away from people who were helping me. From Troy, who trusted you." She wanted to sound angry, but it came out exhausted. "What are you going to do now? Turn me in to the Templars? Since they do like to torture witches, that's going to inflict a lot of harm, me-wise."

"I will help you regain your memories, and then I will move you to a safer place." He bent over and switched off the lamp, and then briefly

185

touched her cheek. "Go back to sleep, Beauty. I will be watching over you."

Just to spite him she wanted to stay awake for the rest of the night, but her eyelids went on strike and the rest of her body wouldn't cross the picket line. Until the drugs wore off she wouldn't be able to escape Michael, if that was even the right thing to do. As she drifted off she thought of Troy, and how frantic he must be by now. In the morning she would have to persuade Michael to call him, and at least let him and the coven know she was safe.

CHAPTER TWO

SUMMER KNEW SHE was dreaming when she opened her eyes again. She stood in the center of a beautiful formal French garden that she had never seen—and yet somehow still knew.

"Of course you know it, *bébé*," said a pleasant female voice. And older woman with flowing brown hair and jewel-bright eyes took her arm. They strolled along a path made of polished flat circles of violet-green jasper. "You played here when you were a little girl. When we were hidden from the greed of the world."

Although she spoke in French, Summer understood every word. She also saw that with every step they took the beautiful flowers and plants around them began to wilt and grow brown.

"Why does the garden die?" Summer asked.

"They found me. I always knew they would, but I didn't think it would be so soon." The woman stopped and clasped Summer's hands in hers. "Forgive me, *bébé*. When you bring your mates together, and come into your power, you will understand."

"My mates?" Summer's eyes widened as the woman's body grew transparent and then faded away. "No, don't leave me again. *Maman*."

"Summer," said a man's voice.

Troy's smooth tenor sounded as if it came from a great distance. Summer hurried through the dying garden toward it, reaching out for her lover.

"Troy, please, I'm here."

Darkness enveloped her, whirling her away to the meadow in front of his home. The sunlight poured over her with all the bright heat of mid-summer. Troy stood just a short distance away, his tall body shrouded in a green mist. His heavenly blue eyes glinted as he stared at her. When she took a step toward him he held up his hand.

"Don't come any closer. If you do I'll lose you again."

She wanted to run to him, and throw herself in his arms, but when she tried to take another step something held her rooted to the ground. She glanced down and saw her feet tangled in a thick mat of wildflowers that were growing incredibly fast and twining their stalks around her legs.

"Troy, help me."

"I'm trying," he said. "Erica is looking for you. I can see you in the mirror, but you're sleeping. Do you know where you are?"

"I'm in New York," she said. "Michael took me back. Troy, he doesn't want to hurt me. I'm safe for now, I think, but something's wrong. He has me tied up."

"You hold on," Troy said, his voice filled with fury now. But like the older woman his body turned transparent and began to fade. "I'm coming. I'll find you, I promise."

Tears stung her eyes as she reached out to him. "Don't hurt Michael, Troy... *Troy.*"

The wildflowers abruptly dragged her down into the earth, the soil swallowing her up as she plunged deeper and deeper–

"You have nothing to fear from me."

Summer opened her eyes to see Michael sitting alone in an armchair before a fire. He held out his hand to her, and without thinking she hurried to him, flinging herself into his arms.

"Do not cry, Beauty." He pulled her onto his lap and held her like a child, tucking her head under his chin and stroking her back with a soothing caress. "I am here. Nothing can hurt you now."

She lifted her head. "*You* hurt me, Michael. Why did you take me?"

"He is falling in love with you. I saw it in my dreams." He studied her face. "And you care for him. You gave yourself to him."

"I care for you," she whispered. "I would have stayed with you."

"It could never be, my Beauty." He brought her hand to his mouth and kissed her palm. "I am a priest, and you are a pagan. I belong to the order."

"None of that matters." Power bloomed inside as Summer pulled her hand away and pressed it over his heart. "You are mine, Michael Charbon."

Wildflowers shot up around the armchair weaving around them and enveloping them in a soft, fragrant cocoon. Michael's eyes filled with awe and wonder, but no fear, and as Summer touched her lips to his she heard once more the old crone's voice.

This man is thine now. The triad is now complete. Do with him what thou will, Guardian.

• • • • •

Michael woke with a muffled groan, and

immediately knew three things: he had not been cocooned by wildflowers, he had fallen asleep in his armchair, and had been dreaming. The weight on him was not made by his guilt but by Summer, who lay sleeping in his arms.

Michael knew he should carry her back to the bed, but he would not have another chance to look at her or hold her like this again. So he filled his eyes with her, from the top of her thick, sun-streaked brown mane to the high, elegant arches of her pretty feet.

The changes in her were subtle but he could see them: the healthy bloom to her skin, the silkiness of her hair, the serene smoothness of her brow. She had begun to lose the gauntness inflicted by living homeless in the park. It was obvious she had been well cared for during her time at Silver Wood.

Summer shifted, snuggling closer to him and slipping one hand to rest against his chest. Michael went still as he saw the shredded, burnt cords hanging from her wrist. He looked down at her feet and saw the bonds around her ankles had suffered the same fate. Had she used some Wiccan magic to free herself? If she had, why had she come to him instead of escaping?

Troubled now, he gathered her up carefully and

carried her back to his bed, where he removed the ruined cords before tucking her in. She frowned slightly before she sighed and settled onto her side, resting her cheek against her hand.

Michael clenched his fists as he stood over her, his cock swelling and his heart hammering in his chest. He wanted to wake her with kisses on her luscious mouth and long neck as he unbuttoned her blouse to bare her beautiful breasts to his eyes. His hands ached to cradle them and squeeze them as he suckled her and tongued her until she cried out for his cock. She would feel like hot honey on him as he sank into her–

Summer murmured something in her sleep, and a tear slid down her cheek as she repeated it: "Troy."

This is the fool I am, Michael thought bitterly. *Standing here wanting her while she dreams of him.*

His phone buzzed in his pocket like an angry wasp, and he retreated, closing the door to the bedroom before he answered it. "Charbon."

"Michael, my son. I was told you were traveling to Philadelphia." Nathaniel Harper's tone was sharp with annoyance. "Did you find the witch there?"

"No, master." It was not a lie. He had found Summer in New Hampshire. "She is not there."

"I am sorry to hear that," Nathaniel said as his tone grew chilly. "With Gideon's illness we are in need of the Emerald Tablet more than ever, and only she can lead us to it. Still, you are making more effort with this task, so I will not complain."

Complaining was all Nathaniel had done since assigning him to find Summer. The traitorous thought shamed Michael, and he closed his eyes briefly.

"Thank you, Master."

"You should know that my steward left the Abbey yesterday without permission and has not yet returned," Nathaniel said, his voice tight now. "It seems he has taken Augustin with him as well. If you see either of them, do not attempt to confront Gideon alone. Contact me and I will send Alvis to help you contain him."

Michael felt sick. Gideon Edmunds was a ruthlessly trained fighter with centuries of experience in battle, and the immortality sickness he suffered was known to inflict extreme, delusional paranoia on those it afflicted. He could easily wage a one-man war on humans and cut a path of death and destruction through the city.

"Has he shown any signs that he has become unstable?"

"None that I have observed, but he has been

concealing much from all of us. This, too, he may have hidden." The Temple Master sighed. "Whatever the state in which you find him, my son, remember that he is still our brother, and worthy of our respect and care for his loyal service to the order."

Unlike me, Michael thought, hating himself even more now. "Yes, Master."

After he switched off the mobile he took down one of his paintings and opened his wall safe, removing one of the spell scrolls he kept there. In this Michael had also secretly defied Nathaniel, who had expressly forbid every Templar from employing any form of magic while carrying out their duties. Since Nathaniel planned to use the Emerald Tablet, the oldest grimoire in the world, to wipe out the Wiccans, Michael no longer felt any guilt over his own modest collection.

The scroll he removed detailed an alteration spell, which he had used more than once on himself during his patrols in order to evade notice. Like the others he had written it himself, as he had long ago learned he had a natural inclination for spell casting. He'd also learned a great deal about magic in the past by observing Troy Atwater, who had used it more than once to save both their lives during their escape from the

Saracens.

He took in the words and let them linger in his mind as he replaced the scroll, and then walked back to his bedroom. Summer lay sleeping so peacefully he almost changed his mind, but he knew it had to be done before someone came to the apartment and saw her.

Because it felt right Michael rested his hand on the top of her head, unconsciously willing the power in her to help him as he cast the spell.

Cloak this woman with a lad's guise, of light hair and dark eyes. All who behold her will see nothing but that which is he. So may it be.

An amber light shimmered over Summer, cloaking her in the illusion that altered her feminine form to that of a tall, lean young man. Her long tresses lightened to a white-blonde and shrank to a short cap of hair around a solemn, lean face. Even her clothes shifted to more masculine versions in plaid and denim. By the time the light vanished Michael could see no trace of Summer's true form in the lad who lay sleeping.

Forgive me, Beauty. He touched a cheek that appeared flat to feel the sweet curve beneath the illusion. *I wish I could be anyone else for you.*

CHAPTER THREE

"SUMMER."

THROUGH THE green mist Troy lunged for her hand, and felt his own smash into something hard. Glass shards pelted his face and chest as he bellowed her name again, only to find himself in a candlelit room, his hand bleeding. Erica Buchanan's hands shook him hard enough to rattle his teeth.

"Troy Atwater, look at me." The High Priestess of the Silver Wood coven turned his bewildered face away from what was left of the shattered mirror on the table so that he looked into her tear-filled green eyes. "Yes, you're here, with us. You're home." She gave him a tight, fervent hug.

Troy dragged in a deep, steadying breath as he shed the last traces of the spell that had, at least for a few moments, allowed him to communicate with Summer.

"Why did you bring me back? She was in the meadow with me. Right there, not more than a hundred feet away. Damn it, I could smell her."

"Dream-speaking can seem very real," Erica said, her red curls falling around her scarred face as she bent over to wrap a soft cloth around his bloody fist. "But you were not in the meadow. You never left this room."

Troy rested his brow against his uninjured hand, recalling every detail he could remember. "She was afraid, and begged for my help. She's back in New York." An ugly anger welled up inside him. "He took her. That son of a bitch."

"Troy, we will sort this out, I promise," Erica said. "For now you must rest."

"I don't have time for that." He began to rise, and found himself being shoved back in the chair by his father's hard hand. "What are you doing? I have to get on the road before morning."

"It's almost noon," Abel Atwater told him, dragging his hand through his silver-streaked black hair. "The spell took you so far into that witch's mind it took all night and this morning for Erica to bring you back."

"What?" He glanced at the windows, and saw the slant of the sunlight confirmed the time.

"How could a simple dream-speaking have kept me enthralled for twelve hours?"

Erica exchanged a look with Abel before she said, "I don't think it was the spell, my dear. While you were in communication with Summer your eyes filled with green light. I've never seen anything like it in all my years."

"Neither have I, but I can tell you what it means," Abel said flatly. "She's more powerful than you—than any of us. So before you even think about going after her, consider what she might do to this coven if you bring her back."

Facing his father was like gazing into a mirror at his future self. They shared the same striking features, bright blue eyes and long-limbed, strong physiques. Their manes of dark hair even sprang from the same widow's peak. What Troy could never understand was how they could look so much alike and be so completely different in mind and heart.

As High Priest of Silver Wood, Abel had every right to protect his people, but Troy knew this wasn't about Summer or any threat she might pose. His father had always had an unyielding, suspicious nature. He still thought he had the right to control every aspect of Troy's life. Years ago he had driven Troy to leave Silver Wood to join the Magus Corps, and now he was trying to stop him from saving a woman who had become not only his friend but his lover.

You can't keep using me to avoid dealing with your family problems, Summer whispered from his memory. *Your dad has every right to be suspicious of me.* I'm *suspicious of me.*

Troy stood and turned his back on his father as he said to Erica, "Thank you for helping me locate her. I'll call when I can."

He went to the room he had shared with Summer and took his overnight bag out to pack. Another time his father's obstinacy might not have provoked him so strongly, but learning that Michael had taken Summer had sent his temper soaring into the red ranges. He knew Summer cared for the Templar, and Michael must have felt something for her, or he would never have risked bringing her to Troy.

Why would he take her back to New York, when he knows what the order will do to her if she's captured? Troy knew Michael's struggles with loyalty and honor better than anyone. *Has he finally given up, or gone over the edge?*

The sound of a throat being cleared made Troy turn around to see Erica's brother, Ewan Buchanan, standing on the threshold.

"I'm sorry, Ewan, but whatever it is will have to wait. I'm leaving."

"Over which I heard my sister and your father shouting." Ewan's merry brown eyes took on a sorrowful tinge. "Troy, I know this is none of my concern—and you know I try very hard to stay out of these familial tussles—but perhaps you should wait a day before you travel. Only to rest," he added when he saw how Troy's jaw set. "So that you are fully ready to rescue young Summer."

"Every moment I delay places her in greater danger," Troy said. He stuffed some clothes in the bag and went to the cabinet where he kept his weapons. "I can rest when we return."

Ewan laid his hands on the upper curve of his heavy belly.

"As long as you're sure. Where have they taken her? Is there anyone at the Magus Corps I can call to send assistance?"

"She's somewhere in New York City, and no, the Magus Corps doesn't handle this sort of thing."

That was a lie. He could make one call and have the city under siege by his comrades by nightfall. Troy was almost tempted to, for Michael was a formidable fighter. But for centuries he had kept hidden from everyone the outrageous pact he'd made with the Templar. This, too, had to stay between them.

"I can find her myself, Ewan. Don't worry."

"May the Lord and Lady watch over you," the older man said, making a benevolent gesture of blessing before he retreated.

Troy made it to his Jeep before his younger brother, Wilson, Abel's apprentice, Lachlan, and every dog in the coven intercepted him.

"I'm going after Summer," he told them.

But when he pulled the driver's door open Lachlan's heavy hand slammed it shut. The dogs began to collectively growl. Troy spun on Lachlan.

"You really don't want to fuck with me now, Dr. Doolittle."

Lachlan's face turned red. He'd always been sensitive about his ability to control animals.

"Abel said you're not to leave the mountain."

"Abel doesn't have a say in it," Troy said and shifted his gaze to his brother's dark face. Although Wilson looked nothing like him, he could see their father's intransigence seething in his bitter, dark eyes. "You've wanted me gone since the day I brought Summer here, and now you're going to stop me?"

"Give us a minute, Lachlan," Wilson said and waited until the apprentice warlock reluctantly stalked off. "I don't give a damn what you do. Go, come back, it doesn't matter to me. But Aileen is about to have our baby, and we don't know anything about this woman except that she can't control her power. That makes her dangerous, and a threat to my mate and my child."

"You're wrong, Husband," a soft voice said from behind them. "Summer would never harm us. As it happens, she saved my life and our baby."

Troy turned to look at Aileen, whose luminous gray eyes were dark with worry and fear.

"What do you mean?" Troy demanded.

"I promised Summer I wouldn't tell anyone," the pregnant witch admitted. "But she can control some of her power now, and she used it to prevent a bad accident from happening to me." She regarded her husband. "The baby and I would be dead now, if not for her."

Wilson paled. "Why didn't you tell me?"

"I might have, if you weren't running around acting like a jealous idiot." She turned to Troy and handed him a small leather bundle. "Some healing potions you may need on the journey. The vials are marked."

"Thanks, little sister."

To annoy his brother he kissed Aileen's cheek before tossing his bag in the back and climbing in behind the wheel.

Wilson drew his wife back from the Jeep, a possessive arm around her thin shoulders as he glared at his brother.

"Try not to get yourself hacked to pieces."

"I'd never make you that happy, Brother."

Troy started the Jeep and drove off.

CHAPTER FOUR

DAWN ROUSED SUMMER from a green darkness, and when she opened her eyes she saw gray silk sheets, black carpeting, and white walls. Michael's apartment. Her captor now sat dozing in a chair beside the bed, the thin morning light revealing two day's worth of whiskers shadowing his face.

She sat up, glancing down at her unbound hands, and went still as she saw long, masculine fingers and square palms.

Her hands were not her own.

Slowly she climbed out of the bed, standing on sturdy, long-toed feet that looked nothing like her own. She raised her head to see the reflection in the mirror above Michael's dresser, and saw a frightened, young man staring back at her with big brown eyes. When she raised her hand to touch her cheek, he did the same.

Am I dreaming again?

Summer walked toward the mirror until she stood six inches from it, and extended her hand. The young man did the same, and touched his fingertips to hers. Which looked exactly like his fingertips.

That's me. I'm a man.

Summer backed away from the mirror, running her hands down her body to feel her breasts where she saw a flat male chest, and the curves of her hips where she saw only flat, lean flanks. Now she could also feel the energy humming over her skin. She was carrying some sort of new body ward. Unlike Troy's, this clung to her like invisible paint, and was many times stronger than the spell he'd cast.

Michael did this.

She heard a low rumble and turned to see her captor stirring. She took a step toward him, intending to slap him awake, and then backed away. She was so angry she was afraid to touch him—afraid of what the unknown power seething inside her might make her do.

Get away from him. Now.

Carefully she moved back through the open doorway and out into the hall. She walked silently through the apartment to the front entry, which she found locked.

She reached out to the keypad beside the door and closed her eyes, recalling what she had seen Michael do the first time he had brought her here. She slowly punched in the same numbers, and the door unlatched and opened.

She darted out and ran for the elevator, changing direction at the last moment for the emergency exit. As she shoved the door open and fled down the narrow stairwell she heard the heavy thud of footsteps running over her head. She climbed onto the handrail to slide down to the next landing, and the next, until she reached a padlocked iron gate that closed off access to the remainder of the stairs. A small sign bolted to the gate read *Under Construction, In Case of Emergency Use Fire Escape* with an arrow that pointed to the small window beside her.

Summer thumbed the window lock, but when she tried to open it she discovered it had been painted shut. At the same time she heard Michael on the stairs two flights above her. She pulled off the plaid shirt she wore, wrapping it around her hand to protect it before she punched her fist through the center of the glass. The window shattered, and she knocked the big, jagged pieces away before she climbed out onto the icy metal slats of the fire escape platform.

A big hand reached out and clamped around her ankle.

"Summer, stop."

She tried to kick herself free from Michael's grip, but he used her struggles to unbalance her, and she fell on her bottom hard before he dragged her back inside. She struck at his face and chest with her fists, opening her mouth to scream, only to be turned around and clamped against his chest, one of his hands pressed firmly over her lips.

"I will not hurt you, you know that," he murmured as he lifted her off her feet and carried her easily up the stairs. "Stop struggling. There is nowhere you can go that they will not find you. You must stay here with me."

Once they were back inside the apartment he set her down, murmured some words and took his hands away. Light shimmered as the body ward vanished, and Summer's body returned to its natural appearance.

"So you did that to me, too," she said and realized she was standing there in her bra. She shook the broken glass from the blouse around her fist before she simply dropped it. "Why?"

He looked away from her. "Changing how you look is the only way I can keep you safe."

"Is that what you're going to tell your Templar pals?" She eyed the door, and wished she'd taken the elevator down instead of the stairs. "That I'm, what, your boyfriend?" She frowned. "Is that why we can't be together? You'd rather have a man in your bed?"

"What? No." His green eyes turned frosty as he glared at her. "I cannot have a female here. I told you that Templars avoid women."

"That's right, you're a warrior-priest. You're not allowed to have fun at all." Suddenly furious, she went to him. "Or have you decided to break your vow of celibacy, Michael? Is that really why you brought me back?"

He went rigid as he looked over her head. "I can never be with you. I belong to the order."

Summer slapped him, and as the pain of it blazed over her palm and up her arm, she watched the red mark of her hand appear and then fade almost instantly from his cheek. She couldn't hurt him, and knew he wouldn't strike back. But thinking straight took a back seat to her temper, which went from seething to nuclear so quickly she thought she might explode.

"I don't care about your order, or your vows, or

your prissy rules." She shoved his chest, which was like trying to push over a brick wall. "And you're lying. You're not afraid of them. You're afraid of *me*."

Now his gaze dropped to her face, and his mouth tightened. "Go back to bed."

"Sure, no problem. I like your bed. The silk sheets feel amazing." She traced a rough heart shape over his sternum with a shaking finger. "Why don't you join me? Isn't that what you really want?"

"Summer." He sounded like he was grinding his molars together now. "Enough."

"You could have had me before you sent me away. But that's all right. I was with your friend, Major Atwater, at Silver Wood. *Several* times." Her hand flew up to his neck as she pressed closer. "Would you like to hear what Troy did to me? Maybe it will give you something new to think about the next time you take matters into your own hands."

His big hands clamped on her shoulders as if to thrust her away, but his fingers moved against her skin with caressing gentleness. The practiced indifference faded from his features as he tugged down the straps of her bra.

His touch sent an explosion of sensations

through her.

"I dreamt of you with him," he said, his voice growing deeper and rougher. "I watched you pleasuring him with your mouth." He cupped her chin to lift her face, and stroked his thumb across her lips, parting them to test the edge of her teeth. "I watched while I buried myself in your wet, hot softness." He slipped his other hand between her legs, pressing his fingers against her. "Here."

Summer felt the anger inside her shifting into a different heat, one that flooded into her breasts and burned down into her lower belly.

"Don't fool with me, Paladin." She used Troy's nickname for him deliberately, to remind him of the other man in her life. "I'm not going to walk away again."

"You asked what I wanted." He began mapping her face with his mouth, his fingers sliding into her hair, his palm stroking over her thigh and hip to settle at her waist. "It is you, Beauty. I want you. Only you. Always you."

· · · · ·

Summer linked her hands behind Michael's strong neck as he lifted her off her feet, and met his lips with a sigh of relief. His mouth began the kiss as a reverent caress, but when she opened for him and he tasted her with his tongue, his grip tightened and he ravished her mouth.

An image of Troy doing the same thing came over Summer, and the emptiness she felt since being taken from him returned like the throb of a wound. But it wasn't guilt over offering herself to Michael—it was frustration, as if she still wasn't complete.

Why do I want them both? What woman needs two men?

Michael broke off the kiss and nuzzled her neck. "Do not think of him," he muttered, as if he could read her mind. "This night belongs to us."

Summer closed her eyes. She had given Troy his night alone with her, and now it was time to do the same for Michael. But soon she needed them together with her, her pagan and her paladin. Something in her sensed that it was the only way they would survive the coming horrors. She opened her eyes to see Michael watching her face.

"Michael, if we do this, it can't be undone." It meant more than becoming lovers, but she didn't know how to put it into words. "Be sure this is what you want."

"You are the only certainty in my world anymore, Beauty."

He brought his mouth to hers, and kissed her so gently their lips barely brushed.

He is yours, the old crone inside her head murmured. *Take him now.*

Summer cradled his face, fastening her open mouth over his to taste him. The moment her tongue touched his, Michael groaned, and his arms tightened around her. He held her so that her sex pressed against the thick ridge of his erection, and the heavy hardness made her go soft and wet. Summer vaguely realized the shifting movement under her came from Michael's legs as he carried her back to his bedroom. They were going to do this, and knowing that ignited such a desperate desire inside her that she heard herself moan. Michael didn't put her down but rolled onto the bed with her, his big body pressing hers against the cool silk, his hands dragging hers up over her head.

It took him another minute to stop kissing her long enough to breathe, and then he simply gazed down at her with the expression of a starving man presented with an endless banquet.

"What you said to me is the same for you. I know you were with Troy—that you care for him.

If you wish me to stop, it must be now, or not at all."

Summer loved the faint tremor in his voice as much as the insistent nudge of his erection between her legs.

"Troy is important to me, but so are you." She grabbed handfuls of his shirt and pulled him down so that their noses bumped. "And you're not going anywhere, pal." She covered his mouth with hers.

Michael kissed her as ruthlessly as he stripped her, his tongue gliding in and out as his hands tugged and pulled and tore. He had her gasping when he sat up to yank off his shirt.

Summer stared at his chest, which was broad and heavily paved with muscle under his golden skin. As brutally gorgeous as he was, she could also see dozens of old scars marring his skin. All of them appeared to be from blades, which made her throat tight as she touched one jagged mark with her fingertips.

"So many battles," she whispered. Until now she had never considered how violent Michael's life as a Templar had been. "Will you ever stop fighting?"

"I have tonight."

He tugged her panties down her legs and sat

back on his haunches to look at her nude body, his hands curling into fists on his thighs.

Summer grabbed his arms and used them to haul herself upright. Touching his skin made her palms tingle and her mouth water. She pressed her lips to his shoulder. When he didn't move she wondered if he'd changed his mind.

"If you want to slow down, it's fine. I know the first time can seem a little scary."

Bitterness darkened his expression. "I wish you were my first, but I have broken my vows many times." He stared at her breasts before he met her gaze. "I have never been with a woman like you, Summer. None of the other females I have lain with ever cared for me. I paid them to take me."

She felt an immense tenderness flood her. "Then I think that makes me the first in your heart."

He shook his head. "I tell you I have been with whores, and you console me."

That the Templars had forced him to live a celibate life angered her, but the shame he felt over trying to secretly escape it broke her heart.

"I'm not here because you hired me," she said softly. "I'm in your bed because I want to be with you. What do you want to do with me, Michael?"

"Give you everything you need. Make love to

you in the way you want." His chest heaved as he dragged in a deep breath. "And fuck you until neither of us can walk."

His poetic, graphic honesty pleased her, and Summer smiled and lay back, thrusting out her breasts and parting her thighs. "Take off your pants first. I need you naked."

Michael climbed off the bed to unfasten his trousers and step out of them. Like Troy he was not circumcised. But his shaft was so erect that his cockhead had emerged from his ruddy foreskin. The thick bulb was engorged and glistening with a drop of his cream. Summer's thighs quivered as she realized she was going to have all that inside her in only a few moments.

He smiled a little at her. "You look worried."

"I have no idea why. You're only built like a stallion." Summer watched him take a condom from his nightstand and sheath himself. "Just how recently have you been hiring those ladies to help you break your vows, anyway?"

"Not for a long time. I bought these after you left me." He sounded disgusted with himself. "I do not know why."

"I do." She smiled. "Come here and I'll show you."

Something seemed to snap inside Michael, for

he took hold of her ankles and dragged her to the edge of the mattress with one tug. He loomed over her, the heavy shaft of his penis in his fist, and crouched as he moved it between her thighs.

"I have you now, my Beauty," he said softly as he pressed in. His broad cockhead parted her and pushed inside to penetrate her. As she arched her back he held her waist and moved his hips in short, powerful thrusts as he gave her more and more. "This is what you wanted. Take it. Take it all."

Summer shuddered as his girth stretched her softness, filling her so completely she wasn't sure if she could take all of him. Then she lifted her hips and felt the thick bulb of him prod her cervix as his balls pressed against her, warm and velvety.

"There, yes," he crooned. "You are so sweet on me."

The smell of him rolled over her, hot and dark like a midnight in July, and made tiny beads of sweat frame her upper lip. She couldn't help tightening around him, caressing him and holding him with her slick muscles. She watched as his whole body tensed.

"Now it's your turn," she said, drawing his big hands up to her breasts. "Take me, Michael."

He gripped her mounds as he slid out of her, and then thrust back in with two hard, deep jabs that sent a shockwave of aching delight through her belly. He squeezed her breasts, watching her nipples as they flushed and puckered. He gave her his full length again and again, pumping his cock in and out of her.

Summer curled her legs around him, pulling him in hard with every penetration, moaning softly as he went deeper. The way his cockhead collided with the inner curve of her cervix made a shocking jolt. It sizzled with the heat and friction of his fucking.

"Beauty, my Beauty," he chanted as he plowed into her, his calloused fingers tugging at her nipples relentlessly. "You like my cock in your little pussy? I think you do. You feel like an oiled fist on me."

As he glided over a particularly sensitive spot inside her, she pressed her heels against the backs of his flexing thighs and pulled his head down to her breasts.

"So pretty," he murmured. He licked one hard nipple, toying with it before he covered it with his mouth and sucked. He worked his tongue on the underside to press it against the edge of his teeth.

Seeing his lips sealed over her and feeling the

delicious suction made Summer's clit pulse frantically. She grabbed handfuls of the silk under her as she writhed against him.

"Please, Michael. That's so good."

He pulled her up so that her body was supported only by his hands and skewered on his penis.

"Put your arms around my neck. I am going to fuck you hard now."

Summer cried out as she did as she was told, and he splayed his hands over her ass and worked her on his cock. His hot green eyes narrowed as he watched her breasts bounce with every thrust, and smiled as she shivered and clutched at him.

"There, yes, that is what you need." He grunted as he pounded her pussy over and over. "Take what you need, my Beauty. I have it in endless measure. I can fill you like this as much as you need. Your pleasure is right here, right now. Take it and come for me, lovely one. Let me see it in your eyes."

The orgasm swept over her with bone-melting power, sending her into a dark palace of sensation. She hurtled through room after room of sweet, hot pleasure until she thought the passion of it would make her melt into nothingness.

Michael placed her on the bed and covered her with his body, still thrusting inside her but with slow, soul-stirring strokes.

"I knew when you came to me it could be like this." He brushed the damp hair back from her brow, and kissed it before he gazed into her eyes. "I wish you were mine."

She touched his cheek. "I am."

"I mean like humans—married to me, my wife." He thrust deeper and faster. "I would keep you in this bed and fuck you until your pussy overflowed with my seed." He cupped her nape, studying her drowsy face. "I would fill your belly with my babies." He forged into her so deep his cockhead lodged in her cervix, with only the thin shield of the condom between them. "You would never go to sleep without me inside you."

"I'd never want to." She kissed him.

Summer held him as he groaned and shook, and when he pressed his hot face against her neck and came, she stroked his shoulders. She closed her eyes with the silent wish that Troy was there with them, holding them both, loving her as much as her paladin.

CHAPTER FIVE

MICHAEL WOKE TO the sound of his door chime and Summer sprawled naked atop him, her limbs entwined with his. Gently he moved her to one side, smiling as he heard the faint grumbling sound she made before her breathing slowed again. They had spent all of the day and most of the night wrapped around each other, leaving his bed only to shower and raid his pantry. His Beauty had fed him and teased him and pleasured him, and had in turn writhed and cried out under him as he brought her to climax again and again.

Once he pulled on his trousers Michael paused only to cover her before he went to see who had disturbed them. As he peered through the peep hole he saw the lower vault of a powerful chest and felt his blood turn to ice. Only one Templar assigned to the North Abbey stood that tall, and he was the most unforgiving, fanatical and deadliest immortal Michael knew.

"Charbon," Alvis Berenson bellowed in his oddly high-pitched voice as he pounded on the door with one massive fist. "Attend me now."

There was no time to hide Summer. Michael could only compose himself before he jerked open the door and scowled up at the huge Norseman.

"Do you mean to wake the entire building along with me?"

"Twill do them good to rise at a proper hour." Alvis had to duck his head to step inside, and when he straightened he glanced around, his pale eyes narrowing as he took in Michael's furnishings. "I have heard tales of how you live like a mortal." He made a circuit of the room, touching various things before he turned on Michael. "What need you with all this frippery of theirs?"

"I sometimes bring humans here to question them, or enlist their aid for our mission. If I kept it empty, they would have nowhere to sit." Michael went to draw the blinds. "It also offers an excellent prospect of much of my patrol sector."

"Aye, so it does. Had you a mortal slut to warm your bed and cook for you, you'd be just like the rest of these black-hearted sinners." Alvis joined him and peered down at the streets below. The sunlight glittered in the white-blonde stubble that covered his scalp, and the honed edge of the battle axe he wore strapped to one massive shoulder. "Master Harper has told you about Gideon and Augustin?"

"I spoke with him yesterday," Michael said and had a terrible feeling that Summer was not only awake but eavesdropping on them. "Has there been any news of them?"

"No. Gideon well-lined his pockets from the master's safe, and filled three bags with weapons from the armory." Alvis eyed him. "Automatic rifles and large-caliber hand guns, and enough ammunition to mount a month-long siege. What I cannot fathom is why he took that sniveling idiot clergy aide."

"Augustin's family shares their blood line with our Grand Master," Michael said. "Gideon knows the value of a political hostage."

The Norseman sniffed. "Gideon's brains are melting to mush. I doubt he knows the value of a ha'penny." He frowned and drew in another, longer sniff before his eyes widened. "I know that female stink. Have you been dallying with a woman, Charbon?"

"No," a low, husky voice said from behind them. "That was me."

Michael turned with Alvis to see Summer in her male guise, and stopped himself from reaching for the Norseman's axe.

Alvis's astonishment turned quickly to fury as his cheeks mottled with purplish patches. "Did you lay with this boy, Brother Charbon?"

"Hey, I don't do guys," Summer said and scowled as she spoke in a thick Brooklyn accent. "Mr. Charbon hired me to look after his place when he's outta town. Only this time I brought my girl over so we could, ya know. He walked in on us and made me kick her out of here."

As Alvis's suspicious gaze bounced between him and Summer, Michael struggled to keep his expression bland. "The boy took advantage. You know how they are."

"Go and bathe," Alvis finally told Summer. "You yet stink of your whore."

"Whatever," Summer said and sauntered off to the bathroom, and as soon as the door closed Alvis shook his head.

"Once these mortal boys begin pestering females they are useless for anything else," he told Michael. "I say get rid of him."

"I was planning to," he countered. "Now why

have you come? Am I needed at the Abbey?"

"No." Deep lines bracketed the Norseman's mouth as he looked out once more at the view. "Charbon, I am troubled, and I come to seek your counsel." He saw Michael's expression and added, "I cannot speak of this matter to Master Harper."

Since Alvis worshipped Nathaniel Harper almost as much as he revered the Almighty, Michael knew it had to be something that might cause a rift between them.

"You can always confide in me, Brother."

"I have prayed mightily on it," Alvis said, "but to no avail." His pale eyes burned into Michael's. "It is this business with the Wiccan wench you seek, this witch who can lead us to the Emerald Tablet. Master Harper has told you how he wishes to acquire the relic so that we may turn the pagans' filthy magics against them?"

"If I can ever find the witch," Michael said.

According to the Temple Master, the location of the Emerald Tablet lay locked in Summer's memories, which was one-half of the reason he had taken her from Silver Wood.

"The master regards this as a strategy, but to me, to trifle with their spells and enchantments is to do the devil's work for him." Alvis thumped a ham-size fist against his enormous chest. "My heart knows this. If you believe in our cause, then you know it, too."

That the enormous assassin despised pagans and considered them evil was well-known among the Templars. What surprised Michael was the Norseman's condemnation of Nathaniel's plan. He'd never known the big man to question anything the Temple Master ordered.

"What say you, then?" Alvis demanded

"Master Harper has tasked me with finding the witch," Michael said carefully. "I am sworn to carry out his orders, so that is what I must do. Once I bring her in, she will be interrogated until she reveals the location of the tablet. I cannot prevent that either, Brother."

"Aye, you must do as you are told. But when you find her"—one massive paw landed on Michael's shoulder like a blow from a fifty-pound sledge—"I beg you first summon me, that I may do the work as the Almighty directs."

A torrent of icy fear spilled inside Michael's gut. Alvis's intentions were only too clear. He intended to kill Summer before she could be questioned, so that the location of the Emerald Tablet would remain a mystery. Michael had no intention of turning her over to the Norseman, but if her identity were ever revealed…

"I can do as you ask, Brother," he lied, "but you know that Nathaniel will never forgive you for thwarting his plans."

The roof beam shoulders lifted and fell. "In this I must hold myself accountable to a higher authority." He gave Michael's shoulder a rough cuff, which nearly knocked him onto his ass. "I knew I could trust you to walk the same path as I. You are a true servant of the temple, Charbon."

CHAPTER SIX

NEW YORK CITY in November was a gray, choked rat's maze, Troy decided as he inched his way through rush hour Manhattan traffic. He'd have done better to park across the river and continue his quest on foot, but he didn't want to give Michael or any of his Templar comrades the chance to catch him out in the open. Once he rescued Summer, he needed to get her out of the city as fast as possible.

Finding one witch in a metropolis of eight and a half million people might have been an impossible task, but Troy felt sure Michael Charbon would lead him to her. Thanks to the blood-brother bond they had formed long ago in the depths of a Saracen hell hole, locating the Templar required only a simple tracking spell.

By doing so Troy was aware that he was

breaking the truce that had stood inviolate between him and Michael for centuries, but he didn't care. *The bastard dishonored it first by taking Summer. He snatched her right from under my nose.* Troy wouldn't rest until he had her back, and Michael Charbon's blood on his blades.

He emerged from gridlock to follow the tracking spell to an exclusive residential area, where the tether turned around a corner and disappeared into an alley. Troy parked the Jeep at the corner and glanced down the alley to see Michael talking to a giant Viking carrying a battle axe.

So you do have friends, you son of a bitch.

His eyes narrowed as the two men clasped hands. The bigger man had to be another Templar. The giant shrugged into a heavy parka that covered the weapon on his back before he and Michael walked out of the alley.

Troy quickly ducked down and watched the two men pass before he climbed out of the Jeep. He waited until Michael and the giant parted ways before he began following his former ally. As he did a faint scent teased his nose, like that of a distant garden. Troy's head pounded as new rage poured through him.

Summer's scent was all over Michael, as if he

were carrying her in his arms, which was only possible if they had been close.

Troy curled his hand around the hilt of his long dagger, but he forced himself to release it. Stabbing Michael would not kill him. Very little would. He also still did not know where the Templar was keeping Summer. Now was not the time to attack. When it came time, however, he would not hesitate. If he had forced himself on Summer, he would die. Badly.

He followed Michael for several blocks until the Templar disappeared into a high-rise residential building. As the door closed behind him, Troy walked up to the white-gloved doorman.

"Do you know that man who just went inside? Does he live here?"

"We don't give out information about the tenants," the doorman told him, and made a rude gesture. "Move along, pal."

Troy walked a short distance away and waited for a passing car, and flicked his fingers. A wave of watery slush from the gutter crashed over the doorman, who sputtered and swore.

"You all right?" Troy said as he walked up to the man and seized his wrist. He used the dirty water and ice saturating his uniform to channel a compulsion spell. "Tell me what I want to know."

The doorman's eyes emptied of all emotion as he spoke in a monotone. "I know Mr. Charbon. He lives in the penthouse."

Of course he did. Michael and his scum Templar brotherhood had more wealth squirreled away than every drug cartel in the world combined.

"Is there a woman with him now?"

"His sister," the doorman said. His mouth curved. "Beautiful girl. She was asleep when he brought her home, so he carried her up."

Troy eyed the top of the building, and then glanced across the street. "Forget me and what I have asked you."

He drew the slushy water out of the man's uniform and sent it back into the gutter before he lifted the spell.

The doorman gave him a surly look. "You again? I told you, Mister, beat it."

Troy trotted across the street and eyed the row of buildings until he spotted one with a rooftop view that offered the right vantage point. Entering that required him to bespell a bearded man carrying in two bags of groceries.

"You can get on the roof through the maintenance door on the seventh floor, and then walk up the back stairs," the man said as he led

Troy inside. "It's a long walk up, but the service elevator's been out of order since August." He gave him an odd look. "You're not planning to jump, are you? We had a jumper last year, and Mrs. O'Reilly nearly had a stroke when she saw the mess on the sidewalk."

"I'm merely going to have a look at something."

Troy released him from the spell before taking the elevator to seven, where he climbed ten more flights of stairs to reach the roof access door. The cold, exhaust-scented air greeted him as he stepped outside and disturbed a pair of pigeons perching on a satellite dish. Troy walked to the edge and stepped between two huge fan units to look at Michael's floor, and saw the Templar had left the windows open, and a young man stood looking down at the street.

Troy didn't recognize the lad, but he felt rocked to his core when he saw Michael come up behind the boy and wrap his arms around his narrow waist in what was clearly an intimate embrace.

What is this? The Paladin has a boyfriend?

Michael reached down to rub his hand over the boy's crotch. Just as Troy began to turn away light shimmered between the lovers, and the boy transformed into Summer. He expected her to struggle or even fight off the Templar, but instead she leaned back against him, her lips curving and her thighs shifting apart.

Behind Troy a water tank made an ominous bubbling sound as steam began to seep from its top vents.

Troy controlled his rage-driven ability, but he couldn't stop watching them. Summer touched Michael's hands, and then turned and embraced him, her slim hands curling over his shoulders as he kissed her. Troy watched Michael tug away Summer's blouse and bra before he bent his head to nuzzle her breasts. His big hands first cupped and then squeezed the tight curves of her buttocks.

A tight throbbing in his crotch made Troy glanced down, and he was dumbfounded again to see the evidence of his own erection bulging in his pants.

The hell…?

He had to brace a hand against the side of one cooling unit as need poured through him, as hot and fierce as if he were the one touching Summer. That he felt no shame or disgust stunned him as much as his arousal.

It's Summer's curse. It must be.

When Troy glanced again at the windows across the street, he saw that Michael and Summer had disappeared.

Troy swore as he moved along the roof ledge, peering in each window until he saw them again. The room they had gone to was darker, but he could still make them out. What he saw made his cock throb and his balls tighten.

The Templar had stripped to the waist, and Summer stood completely naked now. She was caressing Michael's arms and shoulders as he fondled her breasts, kneading the soft mounds and rubbing his thumbs over her nipples. He bent his head to kiss her, and Troy could see he was giving her his tongue, filling her mouth over and over with it.

His own mouth dried as he tasted her on his own lips. He felt her touch warming his skin. He felt her hips shimmy against him, her lower belly rubbing his cock, and the faint scrape of her fingernails as she dragged them over his skin.

Even the most powerful transference spell couldn't make him feel another man's pleasure, not when he stood cloaked in two layers of combat body wards. Yet with each passing moment that he watched them he felt the phantom sensations growing stronger, until it was as if he held Summer in his own arms.

It took all of Troy's strength and self-discipline

to turn away, but that made no difference. The enchantment seized him fully, taking over and flooding him with hunger and desire as it stroked his body and tugged at his cock. He staggered toward the building access door, wrenching it open as he stumbled inside and fell to his knees, his heart hammering in his chest and his hips surging forward as he groaned.

Troy knew Michael was fucking her now, his big body pinning hers to his bed as he drove his penis into her softness over and over and over. The same thing was happening to him, and caught in the trap of the enchantment, Troy had no choice but to go along for the ride. He rolled over and felt her under him as he worked his hips, feeling the sweet wetness of her caressing his rigid shaft with each thrust. In his ears he could hear her low moans, and felt Michael's voice rumbling in his own chest.

Beauty, you are trembling. Do you need me to suck your pretty tits again while I plow your pussy? Will that make you come hard for me? I know you want to, I can feel it on my cock. Give those sweet nipples to me…"

Troy clenched his teeth, but then he felt the pebble of her nipple graze his lips and he latched on, sucking her as he fucked her deeper and harder, his cock pounding into her. He felt her arch under him as she writhed on his shaft, her pussy clamping around him as she came with a low, wild cry.

Troy tore open his trousers and held his jerking cock as semen jetted from the thick shaft. It pulsed beneath his fingers as he felt Michael come, both of them grunting and thrusting into Summer's wet tightness. When he finally emptied himself he rolled over onto his back and stared up at the dome light overhead. His body shuddered with the aftershocks of his climax.

Not my climax, Troy thought as he closed his eyes. *Michael's and Summer's.*

Sex was sacred to all Wiccans, and as an immortal Troy had been actively enjoying women for centuries. He considered the pleasures of the flesh to be natural and necessary to the enjoyment of life. He had even lain with two women on more than one occasion, and each time felt no shame, even when they had turned to pleasure each other. He recalled two witches from Sweden who had spent a long weekend showing him just how skillfully one woman could make love to another.

He had also had chances to indulge himself with other warlocks. While he liked the company of men, he never found himself aroused by the thought of having sex with a member of his own gender. Yet feeling Michael's cock as if it were his own had been the second most exciting experience of his life.

Just as being with Summer had been the first.

What had just happened to him went so far beyond anything in his experience that he didn't know how to feel about it, or the emptiness he felt now.

I should have been there with them. Part of it. Part of them.

He dragged himself to his feet, and cursed his ridiculous thoughts as he shoved his still-hard cock inside his pants and headed for the stairs.

· · · · ·

Once she had come back down to earth, Summer rested her chin on Michael's damp chest and studied his face.

"You look very thoughtful for a man who just promised to take me to Tahiti."

"I am thinking." His green eyes closed as he looped an arm around her shoulders. "But I made no such vow."

She kissed his right nipple, which was small and brown and puckered against her lips. "Yes, you did. Right after you said my breasts were as beautiful as roses blooming in moonlight." Her brow furrowed. "Or was it sunlight?"

"Sunlight," Michael said and stroked his big hand over her rumpled hair. "You were never meant for darkness, Beauty. Although I should take you to task for calling out the name of another man while you were in my arms."

"I know. That was terrible of me." She laid her cheek against his heart. "Only one problem."

"I know." He sighed. "I said his name, too."

It had been the strangest thing. One moment Summer had been gripping Michael as he stroked in and out of her, and the next she had felt Troy on top of her, as if he had somehow gotten between the two of them. But even that wasn't quite right. When Michael kissed her breasts she felt Troy's mouth, and when he sucked her nipples, it was Troy's tongue that caressed her. Then she heard herself call his name at the exact moment Michael had muttered "Troy" against her breast. Summer rolled over onto her back and stared at the ceiling.

"Michael, while we were making love…I could feel him. I swear, I could *taste* him. What's happening to us?"

"I cannot say." He got out of bed and walked

naked over to the window. "He is close. I think he has come after you…and me."

"Oh, yes. He will definitely come after you," Summer said and pressed her hands over her eyes. "Damn. Why did you take me from Silver Wood? Why didn't you just tell us about this Emerald Tablet?"

"You were supposed to be in the shower, not listening to me and Alvis," he said and glanced back at her. "How did you manage to reinstate the body alteration spell?"

"I don't know. I just did it. Excuse me for being a little concerned about leaving you alone with the pagan-hating giant guy." She sat up. "Let me call Troy, and I'll explain that you had only good intentions, and that I'm okay, and that he shouldn't try to encase you in ice the minute he sees you."

"You do not know anything about my intentions," he reminded her as he walked back to the bed, and sat beside her. "I have explained nothing to you."

She felt like slapping him again. "Michael, do you think I would have jumped in bed with you—twice—if I thought you were going to hurt me?" She slid off the side of the mattress and picked up her clothes. "First we defuse Troy, then you can tell us why you dragged me back here and what exactly this Emerald Tablet is."

The sound of a fire alarm blasted through the apartment, and Summer shrieked as icy water sprayed over her from a sprinkler above the bed.

"It is too late," Michael shouted as he pulled on his trousers. "He is here." He ran out of the bedroom.

Summer dragged on her soggy clothes as fast as she could, and when she hurried out to the front room she found Michael standing in a cage of ice, and Troy freezing the spray from the sprinklers into thousands of sharp-looking icicles that floated around Michael on all sides as if waiting to strike.

"Troy, no!" Summer yelled. She stopped in her tracks, afraid of taking another step and setting him off. "It's okay. Michael didn't hurt me."

"I know," he said through clenched teeth. Frost glittered in his black hair as well as his furious blue eyes.

"He protected me from the Templars," she reminded him. "He still is. He's not the enemy."

"He took you." Troy's fists bulged, and icy spikes shot out of his knuckles. "He took you from me."

"Summer, you should go out in the hall,"

Michael said quietly, never taking his eyes off Troy. "Now, please."

She knew what would happen if she did, and stepped between her two men. "You are not fighting over me," she told Troy. As she heard the ice shattering behind her, she turned around to face Michael. "We're all friends here, remember?"

"Bullshit," Troy snarled, at the same time Michael said, "He is not my friend."

"Please." Summer held up her hands. "Stop. Now. For me, okay? I care about both of you."

"You mean you fucked both of us," Troy said.

"I think it is too late for reason, Beauty." Michael stepped out of the remains of the cage. To Troy he said, "Perhaps we should step outside to discuss our situation."

Troy gave him an ugly smile. "Oh, yeah. Let's chat in the hall."

As the two men advanced on each other, Summer grabbed Troy's arm. "There will be no discussing or chatting or dismembering." She turned to Michael and planted her other hand in the center of his chest. "I said—"

All three of them went still as a ring of power expanded through the room. Everything froze in time, just as it had when Summer had saved Aileen from falling onto the knife.

This is why we were brought together, Summer thought, her mind filled with a serene clarity. *Why I must bind them to me now. We cannot survive apart.*

Time snapped back into motion. The icicles hovering around them melted instantly and rained down onto the carpet with a tremendous splash. Troy uttered a low, confused sound and Michael murmured something in French.

Summer paid no attention to them. For the first time since she had woken up in the park she felt whole and safe and powerful.

"Yes," she whispered, and her voice rang out around them as if she had shouted the word through a mansion filled with crystal bells. "My sentinels."

Power poured through her and into the two men, who stared at her, their eyes filled with green light. She slid her hand up to Troy's cool cheek, and pressed her fingers over Michael's hammering heart, drawing the strength and feeling she needed from both of them. She could feel every nuance of their desire for her, and returned it with her hunger for them. She felt herself go utterly, completely wet and knew they were swelling and hardening for her.

"Thou art mine, Troy, Michele," she heard herself say in a language only she understood before the room began to dim. "My lovers. My defenders. My mates."

CHAPTER SEVEN

"IF YOU'RE HAPPY and you know it, clap your hands."

Gideon sang the cheerful tune with great gusto, as it suited his mood to perfection. He paused only to roll down the van window and spit the shredded remains of his last cigar out the window at a young mother pushing a stroller along Fifth Avenue. As she flinched away he chuckled.

"Or stick that in your poxy quim, you filthy whore."

"Master Edmunds, please," Augustin begged from the back of the stolen florist van. Gideon had shackled him beside the driver whose skull he had bashed in and several dozen of the sweetest bouquets of flowers this side of a cemetery. "If you would return to the Abbey, I know Master Harper will do everything in his power–"

"To slay me," Gideon finished for him, roaring the words along with a hearty laugh. "Of course he will, Colbert. It is after all, the proper thing to do when a noble Templar knight goes mad. I am mad, you do realize that? If you're happy and you know it, I mean."

"You are ill," Augustin said softly, insistently. "It is not your fault."

"Aye, that's the truth of it," Gideon said and checked the street signs before he made a turn and cut off a taxi. When the driver rolled down his window to shout obscenities, Gideon aimed for his face and fired the Beretta. "What was that?" He called out before he fired a second time. "I'm the son of a what, my good fellow?"

Gideon kept firing, and the taxi's windshield sprouted several crackled holes as it veered away and struck a parked car.

"When you covet eternity, you also court madness, Colbert. They will not tell you that when you are made immortal. If you're happy and you know it…" He paused in his singing to check the rearview mirror, and scowled when he saw the driver emerge from the taxi, his face gleaming with broken glass and bloody scratches. "Fuck me, how could I miss such a fat head?"

Augustin crawled toward the front of the van

until he huddled against the back of the center console. "I wish only to live to serve the order."

"Wrong, wrong, wrong," Gideon said and slapped him in the back of the head. "You wish only to serve yourself and live forever. It's what I wanted, and look at me now. Crazed from a hundred years of holding off immortality sickness. That's also known as fucked five ways to Hades, in the event you were wondering. And if you're happy and you know it, clap your hands."

Aside from the constant mouth tic and a few itchy sensations on the inside of his skull, Gideon actually felt very good. His prospects were looking up now that he had money and weapons and a mortal hostage and a van filled with pretty flowers. All he needed was Charbon to tell him where to find the witch who had hidden the Emerald Tablet. Once he caught the grubby slut he would rape her until she told him where it was, and use it to cure himself. Then he would go back and rape her a few more times. He might even put her on a leash and make a pet of her, like every bitch should be kept.

He had told all of this to Augustin several times, but it pleased him to tell him again, and to sing to him a few more choruses of his happy tune. The clergy aide sniveled again about going back to Nathaniel, but several cheerful blows of Gideon's fist put a stop to that.

"So here we are," he said and stopped across the street from the building where Charbon resided. He peered around until he saw the way to the back. "I am going to need your help with Michael now, Augustin. You will be the bait, and your face will surely show it, if you're happy and you know it."

"Yes, Master Edmunds."

The clergy aide sounded annoyingly nasal, and when Gideon glanced down at him he saw the human's nose was now crooked and streaming blood. The boy had a decidedly sullen expression.

"Did I do that? I beg your pardon." He took out his handkerchief to offer it to the mortal. "Here. Mop yourself up now, lad. There's work to be done." Which reminded him of another song. "Just whistle while you work." He tried to whistle the notes that followed, but his mouth tic made it impossible. "Well, then, I guess I'll never work again. Suits me."

Gideon parked in the alley behind Charbon's building and opened the side door to yank Augustin out of the back.

"Please, Master Edmunds." Swaying on his feet, he extended his manacled wrists. "I will help you capture Brother Charbon, but you must first release me."

"Bollocks." He straightened Augustin's collar. "You'll run off the moment I free you, and then I'll have to chase you down and cut your throat and hide your body. I simply don't have the time for that now, dear boy. Oh, Danny boy. Do you know that song?"

Augustin shook his head helplessly.

"You're entirely fucking useless." He slapped the cringing human on the arm and thrust a bouquet of roses between his shackled hands. "Chin up. I forgive you for it. And you needn't cower until Charbon comes out of his lair. Then you should weep and carry on about how I've abused you and you're terrified of me and all the other nonsense banging about in your idiot human head."

"I want to help you, Master," Augustin moaned.

"So you shall," Gideon said and jerked him close enough to lick the blood from his nostrils. It tasted sweet, or perhaps it was the smell of the roses. His senses had gone topsy-turvy on him of late. "And if you do this very well, I'll leave you here, Colbert. You can crawl back to Nathaniel and weep all over him about how poorly I treated you. He might even reward you for your loyal resistance. If you whistle while you work."

Gideon reloaded the Beretta and hung two machine guns over his shoulders before tucking a shotgun under his arm and adding a few more handguns to his jacket and trouser pockets. He was tempted to buckle on his sword, but he had no inclination to be sporting with Michael Charbon. He would shoot out his kneecaps first to disable him, and as soon as his brother knight gave him the location of the witch he would shoot him in the neck and head until he was effectively decapitated.

Gideon plucked a daisy from another bouquet and tucked it into his breast pocket. "That's better."

Augustin hobbled into the building, dragging the leg with the ankle he'd foolishly shattered trying to escape from Gideon. His face turned white beneath the new and old blood, and his mouth crimped to a hard line.

"If you're happy and you know it, Augustin, you really should clap your hands," Gideon advised him as they took the elevator to the penthouse level. It came to an abrupt halt a few floors below as a red light flickered on and an alarm sounded. "What is this?"

"There must be a fire, Master," Augustin said

and peered at the panel with the buttons and pointed to one. "If you press that, the doors will open and we can crawl out."

Gideon rammed his fist into the panel, and frowned as it crumpled and sparks flew out.

"Now your face will surely show it," he said.

He grabbed Augustin's skull and bounced it off the panel, beaming as the elevator's doors opened a scant inch. He wedged his fingers in the gap and shoved them aside before hoisting Augustin through the narrow space and climbing out after him.

The door to the emergency stairwell was locked, which greatly annoyed Gideon. He kicked it open and dragged the semi-conscious Augustin with him up to the penthouse landing. He stopped there, peering through the window before he huddled down with his mortal helper for one last pep talk. He slapped him a couple times.

"Go to his door, bang on it, and plead for him to give you sanctuary," Gideon explained. "When he opens it, collapse and stay down until I finish him. You must stay down or I will shoot your head off, too. And your face will surely show it, Augustin. In little tiny pieces all over the corridor. Are you ready, my boy?"

The mortal closed his eyes and nodded.

Gideon gave his brow a tender kiss. "Excellent."

• • • • •

Michael caught Summer's arm as she fell, and Troy grabbed the other.

"Take her outside," Troy said.

He lifted her into Michael's arms before he turned his back on them. Michael watched for a moment as the warlock stretched out his arms, pulled the water out of the carpets and furnishings, and funneled it back into the ceiling sprinkler heads.

Michael kept one eye on the pagan as he carried Summer onto the balcony and held her against his chest.

"Beauty," he murmured.

He kissedher forehead and cheeks. At first her skin felt fever-hot against his lips, but it rapidly cooled to a more normal warmth as the color returned to her cheeks. She stirred, frowning as her eyelids fluttered and opened.

"Michael, what…?"

"You fainted." He sat down on the concrete and held her in his lap. "You also melted Troy's ice daggers into water, held both of us powerless, and very possibly stopped time."

"Really? Okay." She glanced back into the apartment, where Troy was standing in the now-dry room and watching them. "Did I do something about his temper, too?"

"I cannot say yet." Michael nodded to Troy, who walked out onto the balcony with them. "She is confused."

"So am I," Troy said. He rubbed the place on his arm where she had touched him during the incident. "Summer, what the hell was that?"

"I wanted you to stop fighting, so I guess…I stopped you." She winced and pressed her fingers against one temple. "Ow. Why does remembering always hurt?"

"I think you were made to forget," Michael said and stood. He held Summer until she was steady on her feet. "Come inside, both of you. Come and sit with me. It is time I told you everything."

He brought out a bottle of wine for him and Troy, and a glass of water for Summer as they sat down together at his table. He began with what little he knew about Summer, and Nathaniel's plan to capture and torture her until she revealed the location of the Emerald Tablet.

The moment Michael mentioned the relic

Troy's expression darkened. "The tablet is the most powerful, well-hidden grimoire on the planet," he said darkly. "Not even the Magus Corps knows where it's concealed."

"Neither do I," Summer said immediately, and then sat back. "You think that's why I have amnesia? Because I did know where it was, and someone made me forget to protect it?"

"I cannot say," Michael admitted. "Whether or not Nathaniel locates the tablet, he still intends to attack a gathering of covens. I think Silver Wood may be one of them."

Troy scowled. "How could he possibly know about us?"

"Someone among the Wiccans has been passing information about the covens to the Temple Master," he told him. "The identity of the informant is known only to Nathaniel, who calls this traitor 'Baldwin.'" He turned to Summer. "All of this is why I came for you, Beauty."

Troy's fist tightened around the stem of his wine glass. "Were you going to bother to tell me about the attack on the gathering, Paladin? Or were you only interested in saving your new girlfriend?"

"Hey," Summer said sharply before Michael could reply. "I'm not his girlfriend. I'm his lover.

I'm also your lover. Somehow we're all going to have to deal with this." She rested her forehead against her hand and peered sideways at Michael. "Right now I want to know about me. Nathaniel arranged to have me delivered to him, right? So where did I come from, and who betrayed me?"

"You were brought here from Canada," Michael said. "Nathaniel bribed the mortal who transported you here to bring you to his men. Something went wrong at the exchange, and they were all shot to death."

"So I'm probably French-Canadian." Summer swallowed hard. "Did I kill those men?"

He thought of what Nathaniel had told him, and what he personally knew about his Beauty. "No. I do not believe it was you."

"Neither do I," Troy said, covering her hand with his. "It's not in you to kill."

"There's something in me," she countered, nodding toward the center of the room. "It's big, and it's bad, and it stopped both of you. I'd say given the right circumstances it could be pretty lethal."

"Then why did you not use it to kill the rapist?" Michael asked. "Or me when I took you from Silver Wood?"

Troy nodded. "He's got a point, Summer.

You're not a killer."

She didn't look entirely convinced, but some of the tension left her shoulders. "Okay."

"Once I had moved Beauty to a safe location I also had every intention of warning you about the attack, Troy." Michael felt the old bitterness rising like bile in his throat. "I am still a good traitor."

"Saving the lives of hundreds of innocent men, women and children is not a betrayal of your faith, Paladin," Troy said. "It's exactly what it should be."

"I wish the rest of the order agreed with you." Michael heard someone hammering on his door, and frowned. "Now what?"

Troy got up and went to look through the peephole. "Are you expecting a bleeding bald man who looks like someone repeatedly kicked the crap out of him?" he asked as he drew his dagger.

"No," Michael said and joined him to have a look, but barely recognized Augustin. "He is the Temple Master's clergy aide. He was abducted by an insane Templar yesterday."

"An *insane* Templar?" Troy echoed.

"It is too much to explain now," Michael said. "Troy, take her into the bedroom. Whatever you hear, do not come out."

"No," Summer said and put her hand on his

chest where it still burned. "If you open that door you'll die, Paladin. I can feel it."

Troy put his nose to the side of the door and drew in a deep breath before he looked at Michael and nodded. "I can smell sweat from two men. One isn't human."

"Gideon. Of course." Michael's mouth twisted. "Troy, can you block off the hall on either side of the door with ice?" He looked at Summer. "Out of sight, down the hall."

As Summer retreated the pagan nodded, and stretched a hand toward Michael's kitchen. Water flew out of the sink tap and formed a curtain in the air. With a wave of his hand Troy sent it through the tiny gaps around the edges of the door and into the hall. A moment later frost grew on the surface of the door like icy fur.

Troy jerked the frozen door open, and caught the shivering, bloody human standing outside, his hands clutching a bouquet of frozen roses.

"Easy, pal," Troy said.

As gunfire blasted the wall of ice outside, Augustin Colbert stared up at Michael. "Gideon wants the witch. Give her to him."

"I think not," Michael said and tapped his temple, knocking him out.

Troy muttered something under his breath and

splayed his hand over the clergy aide's slack face. He then hauled the wounded human over to Michael's sofa and dumped him there.

"We have to get out of here, now," Troy said.

The gunfire abruptly stopped, and Michael heard the door to the emergency stairs down the hall slamming shut.

"Gideon," Michael muttered.

He and Troy went out into the hall, where Troy melted the ice barrier, but by the time they got to the stairwell they found it empty. Michael looked down through a shattered window at the alley, where he saw Gideon climb down off the slightly caved-in top of a florist's van and hoist himself inside before driving off.

"How did he get down there so fast?" Troy muttered.

Michael saw fresh blood edging the broken window glass. "He jumped."

"Okay, so he's definitely batshit crazy." He gave Michael a sideways glance. "Did you hear what she said right before she fainted?"

Michael nodded. "It sounded a little like French, but it was beyond me."

"Same here," Troy said and rubbed the back of his neck. "So how does a still-mortal girl with no memory speak a language too old for you and me to understand?"

Michael shrugged. "I am still trying to fathom how she stopped time." He hesitated before he added, "What happened between us has nothing to do with her feelings for you."

Troy's expression turned wry. "Same here."

They returned to the apartment, where Summer was sponging the blood from Augustin's slack face. "His nose is broken, and so is his ankle, but I think he'll be okay." She stood. "What are we going to do now?"

"I cannot leave until I find out more about this attack Nathaniel has planned," Michael said, "including anything about Summer he may still be keeping from me." He looked over at Augustin. "I can take him back to the Abbey. Nathaniel will have him taken from there to a private clinic he uses for our humans. Since he is his assistant he will go with him. That will give me a chance to search the Temple Master's chambers."

"You mean us," Summer said. When both men looked at her, Summer smiled brightly and shifted back into the form of the young man. "We're going with you."

CHAPTER EIGHT

AT THE SIDE entrance to the old church Troy
eased Augustin Colbert from his shoulder to the
makeshift litter they had fashioned out of two
sparring staffs and a blanket. He stepped up to
take the end Michael was holding. He looked at
Summer in her boy's guise on the other end.

"Not another word out of you. Let Michael do
all the talking."

She nodded.

The Templar unlocked the door and led them
through a labyrinth of unfinished renovations to
the elevator concealed behind the altar. They took
it down to the sublevel of the North Abbey. Troy
kept his own expression bland as they followed
Michael out and waited as he was questioned by
an armed guard. Augustin's battered appearance
supported Michael's highly edited tale of Gideon's

attack at his apartment, and after a quick call the guard let them pass.

Troy inspected the design of the Abbey as they carried Augustin down the corridor. Built like a bunker, the structure sported thick concrete walls reinforced with sheet metal and steel support beams every dozen feet. He glanced up at the quarried stone that formed the ceiling, which reminded him of how the Egyptians built their ancient tombs. A bomb could go off in the church overhead and Troy doubted it would disturb a mote of dust at this level.

Nathaniel met them halfway down the hall. "Is he alive?"

As Michael repeated the story, Troy continued leading the way into the Templar command center. Until this moment no Wiccan knew the location of the North Abbey, and now that he did Troy felt conflicted. It was his duty to report everything he discovered about the Templar stronghold to the Magus Corps, but as soon as he did, it would be targeted by their forces for infiltration and possibly destruction. It would make him no better than the Temple Master planning to wipe out the covens at the winter solstice gathering.

Everything about this situation with Summer

was wrong on so many levels. The Templars had made her a pawn in their quest to wipe out the Wiccans. If Troy reported the truth about her potential power to the Magus Corps she would be taken and isolated and studied until they could decide how to best use her against the Templars.

This war has to end. Enough have died.

Nathaniel had them carry Augustin to the Abbey's infirmary, where one of his human servants checked him over before confirming that his nose and ankle were broken.

"He will need the leg to be x-rayed and immobilized, Temple Master."

"Get him cleaned up," Nathaniel told him. "I'll take him myself." To Michael he said, "How could you permit Gideon to escape?"

"I did not," Michael said. "He jumped through a window and fell ten stories onto a van he had parked in the alley. Before he collapsed Augustin told me that Gideon is hunting the witch. Perhaps you can use that to lure him out into the open. I will go back on patrol and see if I can locate the van he is using."

For the first time Nathaniel noticed Summer and Troy. "Who are these men?"

"Humans I employ when discretion is required." Michael sounded unconcerned. "Alvis will vouch for them."

This was the moment when they would be exposed, Troy thought, or ignored. The Temple Master may have looked like a retired school teacher, but his mild eyes took in every detail of their guises.

Nathaniel approached him, and gave him a long measuring look. "The order is grateful to you for your service, mortal."

Centuries ago Troy had unwillingly served among the Templars who had carried out the Seventh Crusade. While he had despised every moment of that enslavement, he had learned every nuance of their protocols. He went down on one knee, bowing his head, and pressed his fisted arm across his chest.

"It is my honor, my lord."

"This one is promising, Michael." Nathaniel patted Troy on the head like an obedient dog before he returned to the exam table and said to the infirmary attendant, "Have my car brought around to the back for him."

Michael snapped his fingers, and Troy rose and followed him and Summer out into the corridor. From there the Templar took them through a series of passages into a mechanical room where he looked around before he went to stand beneath a large stone.

When Summer went to join him, Troy tugged her back. "You'll want to stick by me now."

"Why?" She frowned up at him. "What is he going to do?"

Troy put his arm around her. "Watch."

Michael reached up to press his hands against the stone, and closed his eyes. A shower of powdery dust rained down on his head as the block of stone shifted and then began to slowly slip out of place until Michael's arms bulged under the weight.

"Oh, my," Summer whispered.

Troy had seen the Templar move much larger rocks with only a touch, and once again wondered how Michael had been gifted with an ability so powerful it could almost be called elemental. Aside from the fact that Templars collectively avoided practicing magic, none of them had any powers beyond their superhuman speed, strength and stamina, and their ability to recover quickly from almost any injury.

Michael knelt down to place the massive stone on the floor before beckoning to them. "Come. Troy, you go first."

Troy put his boot in Michael's laced hands and when the Templar boosted him through the opening he caught the edge and pulled himself up into a dark chamber. He turned to help Summer through, and then watched as Michael jumped up and hoisted himself through the gap in the floor.

"How did you do that?" Summer asked.

"It does not matter," Michael told her, and went to lock the door before he switched on the lights. "Nathaniel keeps his files in the desk in the corner there, Troy. Summer, search the armoire. I will check the rest of the room."

The Temple Master's room contained a variety of priceless European art and antiques, including the high-topped scriptorium illuminator's desk. Troy easily picked the lock on the lower drawer, which revealed a tightly-packed row of unmarked folders. He took out one and skimmed through it, astonished to find it profiled the identities of the members of Sea Cliff, a coven on the coast of Maine. He found similar reports compiled on half a dozen northeastern covens, and while none of their locations were named, it was enough information to take down every major coven from Portland to Newark.

What made Troy's blood run cold was finding a copy of the original invitation that Abel Atwater had sent out for the Winter Solstice.

"You were right. He's coming after us," he said

and showed Michael the document before he replaced it in the file. "My father contacts other coven leaders only by courier spell, so there are no paper copies. The only way the Temple Master could have gotten this was from someone at Silver Wood who watched him cast the spell to send the message."

Summer brought over a wooden box inlaid with ivory and set it atop the desk. "Who has that kind of access to your father?"

"Lachlan and Erica," he said and thought for a moment. "Maybe my brother." He nodded toward the box. "What's this?"

"I don't know," she admitted. "I can't get it open. It doesn't seem to have a lid."

"It is a safekeeper," Michael said. "We use them for mementos."

He picked it up and turned it over, running his thumb along the seams until he felt something and pressed it in. The top of the box slowly slid to one side, and he reached in to remove an old bundle of stained, rough-woven cloth.

Summer peered at the rusty blotches. "That looks like blood."

Troy unfolded it to reveal a small cuff of intricately-worked bronze. "This is very old. Something made for a child. Do you know what it is, Paladin?"

Michael stared at it for a long moment before he shook his head.

"Wait," Summer said and reached out to stop him from folding it back in the cloth. "Give it to me."

When Troy handed it to her she tucked it in her hip pocket without explanation. "All right, what's next?"

While Troy inspected the remaining files Summer and Michael searched the rest of the room, but found nothing. Finally Troy located the file Nathaniel had compiled on Summer. But aside from the shocking photo and the account of the lone survivor from the exchange massacre, there were no new revelations.

"According to the guy who hid in the bushes, Nathaniel's men shot and killed one traitor, and tried to execute another, but their bullets bounced back on them." He closed the file. "As if by magic."

"I could have done that," Summer said, her voice trembling.

"If 'Baldwin' is Wiccan, so could he," Troy said and tucked the file back into the drawer. "I think we're done here, Michael."

They took a moment to set the room to rights

before descending back into the mechanical room, where Troy helped Michael heft the stone back in place. As he stepped back the Templar ran his hand around the edges to reseal the mortar.

"I thought they didn't use magic," Summer said to Troy.

"They don't, but Michael has picked up a few tricks since we were in prison." He grinned sourly at her reaction. "He didn't tell you we were cell mates?"

"We were not criminals," Michael insisted. "We were prisoners of war."

"We were invaders," Troy corrected. "Captured in battle and thrown in a Saracen dungeon and left there to rot."

Summer looked bemused now. "When was this?"

"The middle of the thirteenth century." He caught Michael scowling at him. "Hey, it wasn't my idea to go on the Seventh Crusade. I had no problem with the Turks conquering the Middle East. It was never my Holy Land."

"Save the history lesson for later," Michael advised him. "We have to get out of here before Nathaniel returns."

He led them through the passages to the elevator, which took them back up to the old church. On the way Troy mentally catalogued everything he had seen in Nathaniel's files to report to the Magus Corps. He'd also have to contact his father and have him warn the other covens about the profiles that had been compiled on them, as well as the Templar's plans to attack the winter gathering.

Abel would be furious, and the covens would demand someone be held accountable. Whoever the traitor was his days of informing on the Wiccans were now numbered.

CHAPTER NINE

LACHLAN DARROW FINISHED tidying the High Priest's study and went to the window to look out at the barn. Wilson had been working since dawn on the cradle he was building for the baby. But from the sound of the hammering coming from that direction Lachlan wondered if he was nailing it together or smashing it apart.

Awkward movement drew his eyes across the yard to Aileen's distorted, slender, corpulent figure. Her belly had yet to drop, so it would probably be several more weeks before she gave birth. He had tried to force himself to feel happy for Wilson, but every time he looked at his wife he wanted to puke. Especially now that her milk had come in prematurely, and every time she took a breath her breasts leaked. She smelled perpetually of the milk, which constantly left damp patches on her top.

Breeder, he thought, scowling. *Disgusting, fecund, lactating cow.*

If only Aileen hadn't gotten pregnant the moment she'd mated with Wilson it might have been so different. Forcing Wilson into fatherhood now when he was still grappling with immortality and his place in the coven had been utterly thoughtless. Lachlan couldn't understand why everyone in the coven didn't see that, but then he had never fathomed why everyone loved the herbalist so much. She always used that sweet, helpless facade of hers to manipulate everyone into doing her bidding.

Lachlan turned to find three of the coven's dogs sitting outside the door watching him. It was nothing new. His ability naturally attracted every warm-blooded animal within a hundred yards to follow him around like adoring groupies. He could also read their primitive thoughts, which were inevitably centered on food, sex or romping with the other members of their pack—which he often envied.

"Eating, fucking and playing," he muttered as he dispersed the dogs with a wave and stalked out of the chamber. "Wouldn't that be the life?"

"Oh, I don't know," Erica said as she walked up

beside him. "I think I'd have to have gardening in there somewhere." She gave him a gentle smile. "Rough morning?"

Lachlan was surprised by her sympathy. He knew Erica disliked him. But he could play along.

"After Abel lit into me again for not stopping Troy, and Aileen's latest false labor episode at breakfast, and Ewan still dithering on whether or not to put on the Clash of the Kings at solstice, which is going to require horses and viewing stands and body armor, all of which we don't have, and rehearsals, which we're running out of time for?" He shrugged. "Typical day at Silver Wood, really."

Erica grimaced. "Then perhaps I'll wait to tell you that one of the warlocks from Lily Garden coven is bringing his deaf human girlfriend to the gathering, and would like an interpreter to help him with signing everything for her." As Lachlan sighed she nudged him with her elbow. "Come and have a cup of tea with me."

He accompanied the High Priestess to the kitchen, where she prepared one of her flavorful herbal brews. They carried their mugs out into the garden.

"I know with the gathering only a few weeks away you have been very busy attending to all the details," Erica said. "Abel may not say so, but I know he does appreciate your efforts, Lachlan."

"He barely notices me," he said and cupped his mug between his palms. "I'm only useful to Abel when something goes wrong, and then it's to hold me responsible." He eyed her. "So he doesn't take it out on you, and mess up his next chance to share your bed."

A light blush pinkened her scarred face. "And I thought we were being so crafty and discreet."

Now Lachlan laughed. "The only person who doesn't know you're sleeping with Abel is Ewan, but he's always been oblivious. If you weren't immortal he'd probably assume you were still a virgin." He drained his tea. "I do have about ten thousand things to do today, so why don't you drop the friendly act and tell me what you really want?"

Erica's expression turned shrewd. "You're unhappy here, Lachlan. You have been for some time, but I think Troy's return has made things even more difficult. You might want to consider applying to another coven to join their circle." She paused before she added, "Once Aileen has the baby, you know that will be settled."

His stomach knotted. "I never thought otherwise."

"I think you once hoped he would tire of her, and now that you know he will not, you are waiting on some calamity to happen." She set aside her tea. "It serves no purpose, my dear. Even if he were to abandon Aileen and the child, Wilson would never turn to you."

Suddenly he couldn't bear another moment of her well-intentioned, patronizing kindness. "Thank you for your counsel, High Priestess."

He got up and walked back into the kitchen, dropped his mug in the sink, and headed out to his truck. He drove down the mountain at a furious speed, and stopped at the crossroads that led in one direction to town and the other to Portland. He pulled off the road and rested his brow against the steering wheel.

They'd been boys when they'd met at a summer gathering, drawn together by their mutual sullenness. Lachlan's parents had sent him to Silver Wood to be fostered by Abel after Lachlan had been involved in several vicious fights at school. Wilson had still had his mother in those days to buffer some of Abel's indifference toward him, but that summer she had also been preoccupied with teaching Troy how to control his elemental power, leaving Wilson to fend for himself.

Lachlan's fledgling power over animals had paired well with Wilson's ability to track anything that moved. They had spent long hours hunting together. Then they'd gotten lost in the woods one night, and had been forced to sleep together to stay warm.

Now Lachlan's penis grew long and hard as he massaged it and thought of those heavenly hours he had spent in Wilson's arms. Nothing sexual had happened between them, but it had been a revelation for him. Finally he understood why he had felt nothing for the pretty girls who had chased after him at school. He had been meant for Wilson.

Waiting for Wilson to notice him, recognize his love, and come to him had occupied every moment of Lachlan's existence. He'd been so faithful, too, those first years after he'd lost his heart.

He took the road to the city, taking out his mobile to hit the second number on his speed dial menu. Making the call always repelled him, and made him feel like a traitor, but he had to have something for himself. No matter how much he hoped, he'd always known it would never be Wilson.

Maybe Erica is right. Maybe it's time for me to get out,

while I still can.

"It's me," he told the man who answered. "I need to meet. I've got something for you."

CHAPTER TEN

"ICE, ICE, BABY," Gideon chanted under his breath as he limped into the florist's shop.

The dead body in the van was beginning to stink it up, so he carried the corpse into the back storage room and dropped it on top of the others he'd hidden there.

Now that he had also rid himself of Augustin he felt quite the unencumbered gentleman. He washed the congealing blood from his hands in the work sink. What amazed him was how clever Michael Charbon had been, to force a pagan warlock to do his bidding. Gideon knew from personal experience how difficult it was to compel the heretics to wield their magic for Templar purposes.

"Clever, clever boy," he said and picked up the blood-stained purse belonging to the shop owner and took from it a set of keys. "You'll have to teach me your tricks. I like ice. Ice is nice. Twice as nice."

He collected his things and walked out of the shop, and pressed the unlock button on the key fob until he saw the lights of a gold Mercedes flash at him.

"Ah, very nice, nice, ice nice, twice nice."

He strode over to the vehicle to peer inside. The white leather interior pleased him, so he popped the trunk and stowed his bags inside before getting in. He settled in and put the key in the ignition.

A uniformed police officer tapped the end of his baton against the driver's side window. Gideon rolled it down. The cop jerked his chin at his shirt.

"Cut yourself shaving this morning?"

"I haven't shaved in a few days. Shave and a haircut, two bits," Gideon said and glanced down. Blood spattered the front of his shirt. "Oh, this. I had to kill some people yesterday, and beat a man today. It's truly disgusting, how much you mortals bleed. Only women bleed. I like it when women bleed, don't you?"

The officer drew his weapon and backed up a step. "Step out of the car. Hands where I can see them."

Gideon sighed. "I can't open the door if I put my hands where you can see them. Or do this." He fired the Magnum in his hand through the door and watched the patrolman totter backward into the brick wall behind him. "You made me put a hole in my new car, too. That's not very nice."

He waited until the cop died before he rolled up the window and started the engine. By then more humans were running toward his car, or toward the dead patrolman. It was difficult to tell. He drove through them, knocking their bodies this way and that. He gritted his teeth as the Mercedes jolted over one who had the bad luck to fall under the wheels.

Once he was clear of the humans, Gideon sped across town toward Michael's building. Confronting the lad head-on had not turned out well. He needed to formulate a new plan. Perhaps he would stake out Michael, the way police officers on television did, and follow him until he led him to the witch. Or that warlock who made water into ice. A nice bucket of ice would feel very good on his itchy head right about now.

"That's the ticket," Gideon shouted to his reflection in the rearview mirror. "Ice, ice, baby."

CHAPTER ELEVEN

ALVIS MADE COFFEE for the old woman, sharing a cup with her although the stuff tasted to him like ass. Her fierce little dog lay on her lap, and whenever Alvis came too near, he bared his tiny pointed teeth. Even as he knew he could snap the pup's neck with a twitch of his fingers, he respected the diminutive animal for his courage.

"Your pet comes from very respectable blood lines," he told the old woman. "In my youth such dogs were used to pull sleds and carts, and to guard the halls of kings." He frowned. "I remember them being much bigger, however."

The old woman nodded, and sipped her brew from a cup that shook as much as her hand. "Are you going to kill me, sir?"

"I have not decided," Alvis said, but only to keep her from weeping. She had been doing that ever since he had set up his post in her apartment to monitor Michael Charbon. "I do not care for your sex, but you have not crossed me. I think you have behaved well for a female."

"Thank you," she said faintly before she nodded at the window facing the street. "What about this man you've been watching?"

"That is another dilemma. My master bid me bring him proof of his sins, and then we should decide what is to be done with him, but I think I must settle this now." Alvis frowned. "I had thought Michael Charbon a God-fearing, honorable knight. It is a great disappointment to me to discover he is a liar and a fornicator and a magic-wielding traitor."

The old woman cleared her throat. "Must he die for those things?"

"As I saw it with my own eyes, yes," he said and nodded at his laptop. It showed four views of the interior of Michael's front room. "Do you know, I questioned myself for placing those tiny cameras in Michael's lair? I told myself I was wrong in my suspicions. It shames me now, to think I confided in him about the witch and my desire to kill her before she could lead my master astray. He has been hiding her from all of us."

"I don't understand," the old lady said, slurring

her words now.

He hefted his axe. "It means I will take great pleasure cleaving him in two, and chopping to pieces that fornicating witch who despoiled him, and the pagan who controls those water demons."

Her rheumy eyes closed as she murmured a prayer under her breath.

"Now, now, old mother, there is no need for that," he said kindly. "If you have lived a decent life and avoided sin, you will surely end in the arms of the Almighty."

Her head nodded as if to agree with him, and then she sighed and slumped over, her last breath leaving her with a whisper. The air became slightly tainted as her bowels and bladder evacuated.

Alvis went to open the window to let out the stink of death. The powder from his poison ring worked so quickly but gently, and now the old woman could never speak of his presence to anyone but their Father in Heaven. He watched from there until Michael Charbon returned with the two men who had helped him move Augustin Colbert, and watched as they changed into the witch and the warlock.

He went to the old lady's wall phone and called the command center again. At last one of the humans connected him directly with the Temple

Master. "I have much of import to tell you, Master Harper."

"It will have to wait," Nathaniel said. "I am seeing to Augustin now. Where are you?"

Alvis knew that the Temple Master had great affection for Michael Charbon, and that he might be tempted to put that above his duty. It was that fear that made him lie. "On patrol in Manhattan."

"Good. Gideon was seen leaving Michael Charbon's building in a florist's van." The Temple Master described it for him. "Find Gideon, Alvis. If you must, end his suffering now. We cannot allow him to harm any other mortals."

"Yes, Master," Alvis said and hung up the phone. He picked up his battle axe. "As soon as I put an end to your other problem."

The small dog whined and nestled closer to his dead mistress, and closed his black eyes.

• • • • •

Michael watched Summer with Troy as they drove back to his apartment. They were easier with each other than with him, but they were Wiccan, and he was not. For all his centuries of life, devoted to a cause that demanded he relinquish every pleasure a man could know, he had never felt lonelier. He had been wrong to take her away from Silver Wood. He could see that now, but at least he could return her into Troy's care.

She will be happy with him, Michael thought, somewhat bemused at the pleasure it gave him to think of them together. *That will be enough for me.*

He walked with them to where Troy had left his Jeep, and listened as his pagan brother detailed their next move.

"We'll go back to the mountains, and talk to my father about moving the gathering. We'll also have to find out who has been passing information to Harper about the covens, and warn them that their identities have been compromised. We may be able to reach out to some Canadian covens and see if they know anything more about Summer." His fierce blue eyes met Michael's. "Gideon."

Michael nodded. "I will track him. As addled as he is, he will not be difficult to find."

"No," Summer said suddenly, and curled her hand around his. "You're not going after that maniac. You're coming with us. You belong with me and Troy now."

"There is no us," Michael told her, touching her cheek. "There is you and Troy. I must continue on alone here."

"Paladin…" Troy sighed. "It won't be easy, but

I think I can convince my father to offer you sanctuary. If he won't, then you can stay at my place."

The last thing Michael thought Troy would do is offer to harbor him.

"I must attend to Gideon, and you must warn the covens about the coming attack." When Summer began to protest, he bent his head and kissed her into silence. "You have given me so much, Beauty. Do this last thing for me now."

Her dark opal eyes widened, and she pushed him away as an enormous battle axe swung between them. It hacked into the side door of Troy's Jeep, causing an explosion of metal and glass fragments to pelt them.

"Michael," Troy said, and flipped him a dagger.

Then he grabbed Summer and dragged her to the other side of the vehicle. He shoved her behind him to shield her with his body.

Michael spun to face the white-eyed, grinning face of Death and backed away quickly.

"Alvis."

"Traitor," Alvis declared and yanked the axe out of the Jeep's door. He advanced on him, swinging the weapon from side to side. "Fornicating with witches and plotting with warlocks. Had I not seen it with my own eyes, I would not believe you could betray us so."

The eerie whistling of the blade slicing through the air was meant to terrify him. Michael knew with one blow that Alvis could end his long life. He never took his eyes off the Norseman as he backed toward his building.

He said to Troy in French, "When I draw him inside, get her out of here."

Alvis laughed and said in the same language, "I am not so ignorant as you think, traitor."

He turned on his heel and stalked toward Troy and Summer. With the dexterity of a much smaller man, he jumped on top of the Jeep. With a bellowing cry and hefting the axe above his head, he dropped on them.

Michael flung himself between the giant and Summer, driving the dagger into the side of Alvis's neck as the axe struck Michael's side. Pain billowed through him as he fell with the Norseman onto the sidewalk. He wrapped his fingers around the hilt of the axe, groaning as he pulled the blade from the deep wound in his side. He used the weapon as a crutch to push himself to his feet.

Alvis sat up and plucked the blade from his neck, sending a wide gush of blood spraying over his face and shoulder and chest. He grinned at

Michael through the ghastly red mask.

"Now you d–"

Using the last dregs of his strength Michael swung the axe at Alvis's neck and cut through it. He watched as the Norseman's head toppled off his neck and his enormous body slumped over.

Summer's voice rang in Michael's ears as he turned toward her, and reached out as he staggered and fell to his knees. Troy grabbed him and eased him down onto his back, his mouth flattening as he clamped a hand over the gushing wound in Michael's side.

"Paladin," Troy muttered. "You damn fool."

"Pagan," Michael gasped. He managed half a smile as he felt the life running out of his veins and the darkness encroaching. "You must protect her. No matter what happens, or what it costs." His gaze moved to Summer, who was kneeling beside him now and weeping. "She is… everything."

UNITED

SILVER WOOD COVEN BOOK THREE

By Hazel Hunter

CHAPTER ONE

SUMMER COULDN'T REMEMBER enough of her life to know how good or bad it was, but she could still measure her situation against her most recent experiences.

Waking up covered in blood in Central Park with no memory of who she was or how she'd gotten there? *Horrible.*

Having mysterious powers that revived dead plants and caused people to be generous to her? *Amazing.*

Nearly being raped by a deranged immortal maniac? *Terrifying.*

Finding out she was a witch, falling for both an immortal warlock and an immortal witch hunter, and bouncing between a secret coven in the New Hampshire mountains and a secret order of Templars in New York City? That went all over the scale: *Incredible. Confusing. Wonderful. Troubling.*

Yet even with the wide range of all those experiences, none of them had prepared her for what had just happened.

Summer stared at the dead body of the Templar assassin who had just tried to kill her with a battle-axe. The gory weapon lay a few feet away next to the assassin's decapitated head. If not for Michael Charbon diving in front of her and Troy Atwater, they would both be dead now. Michael, who had nearly been cut in two by the same axe, had pulled the weapon out of his body and used it and the last of his strength to kill the assassin. Now he lay with his head in her lap, unconscious and dying from the terrible wound in his side. The smell of blood tainted the cold, damp air, and she shook her head as something wailed in her ears.

Sirens. The police were coming. Of course they were. One man was dead, another soon would be, and while violence on the streets of New York City was common, a beheading was not.

"Summer, we have to go," Troy said and opened the Jeep door that had been axed by the assassin. He hauled Michael Charbon's limp, heavy body up from the blood-stained sidewalk. "In the car. *Now.*"

His commanding tone helped blast away Summer's shock-induced numbness. Troy served as a field investigator for the Magus Corps, and now he sounded as if he'd shifted entirely into his soldier persona. She quickly climbed into the back seat, helping Troy as he lifted the injured Templar into the Jeep. She cradled Michael's head with one arm and pressed her trembling hand over his wound. Blood was still streaming from it, but in that instant she knew what they had to do.

"Freeze the wound," she said.

"What?" Troy's shock turned to anger. "I can't."

"Your ability to control water can freeze his blood and tissues, Major, and it will buy us some time." Time to do what, she wasn't sure, but her instincts told her this was the right course. "Please, Troy. Do it now or he'll die."

The warlock's jaw tightened, but when she lifted her hand away he placed his over the wound. As he closed his eyes to focus, Summer glanced over her shoulder at the dead assassin's remains and the axe. She felt something move in her chest, a surge of power. She watched as a brilliant green light spread over the dead man and the weapon. When the light vanished, so had the body, the axe, and all of the blood.

I did that.

Summer didn't understand the Wiccan abilities she possessed, or why in a crisis they seemed to work independently of her. But her magic had never hurt anyone. Seeing that happen again also reassured her.

If I can make a dead body and a crime scene disappear, I can save Michael. I have to.

Troy's magic turned the air inside the Jeep frigid. Summer shivered as she watched the wounded Templar's pale face, and saw the frost creeping across the bloody fabric of his shirt. When Troy lifted his hand, ice encased the wound, and the bleeding had stopped.

"Don't ask," she said when the warlock glanced out the back window and saw what she had done. "Just get us out of here."

Troy muttered something in Welsh as he clambered in behind the wheel. He started the engine and headed down the street, just as blue and red flashing lights appeared behind them. Summer wanted to shout at him to go faster, until she realized he was driving at a normal speed to avoid drawing attention from the arriving cops. Once he turned a corner and was out of sight, he floored it. He deftly dodged through traffic and made quick turns until they were miles away and merging onto the interstate.

"We can't take him to a hospital, not with an axe wound," Troy told her. "He won't live long enough to make it to Silver Wood."

"I know," she said and looked ahead.

The highway stretched endlessly ahead of them as she felt Michael's skin growing cold and clammy under her palm. He was barely breathing now, and his face was so white it looked carved from alabaster.

"Troy, take the next exit, and find a place to park where we won't be seen from the road."

His hands tightened on the wheel. "I can't fix this, Summer."

She heard the pain in his voice and wished she could touch him, too.

"I know, but if you help me, I think I can repair some of the damage."

Troy drove off an exit for Pelham Bay Park and after a few minutes pulled off onto a dirt road that led into a thickly wooded area. Once they were safely out of sight, he parked the Jeep and turned around. His gaze moved from Michael's ice-encased wound to her face.

"So you think you can heal the dying now?"

"No. But I know I can bring dead things back to life, and when the three of us touch my power goes through the roof." She reached out to him with her free hand, but when he didn't take it she added, "We're the only chance Michael has. Please, trust me."

Troy got out of the driver's seat and came into the back with her. He lifted Michael's heavy, long legs and draped them across his strong thighs.

"You can't control this power of yours yet," he reminded her. "We could end up killing him."

Summer saw her own pain reflected in his brilliant blue eyes.

"If we don't try, he'll die anyway."

She reached down and clasped Michael's hand. Then she reached out to Troy.

"Gods help us," he muttered and laced his fingers through hers.

His touch kindled the power lurking inside her. It billowed and raced through her blood to every part of her body. This time she was expecting it. She wrapped her mind around it, riding it as it poured into Michael and Troy.

We cannot survive apart.

Summer stared down at the ice melting away from the terrible wound. She sent her love for Michael through her rejuvenating ability, willing his torn flesh to mend itself and restore his life. As she did, the other side of her power rose into her consciousness, cool and deliberate as it took control of her mind. She regarded the injured Templar with a fierce determination.

This warrior belongs to me. He shall not die this day.

The interior of the Jeep turned a glowing bright green as Summer's power funneled into Michael through his wound. It burned away his bloodied shirt to expose the full horror of the wound. But a lacy web of green energy quickly formed over it. Bright red beads began to drip steadily from her fingernails as well as Troy's. They slid across Michael's skin to the wound, where they sank inside him.

Summer looked up to see Troy staring at her, his eyes filled with the same green light. Although he was completely under her control physically, she could sense fear for her and Michael building in his heart. Although she wished she could reassure him, it was the other who spoke to him in his mind, offering a quiet promise.

Do not be afraid, Sentinel. Your brother shall live.

Beneath the glowing web the ruined muscles and torn blood vessels slowly knit themselves whole again. Once his internal tissues were restored the sliced edges of his skin stretched over them. The web contracted to a single line of green light that fused them together and faded away to reveal a new, raw-looking pink scar. His flesh was still horribly bruised, and his side swollen. But as the power retreated back inside her she knew that the promise would be kept. Michael would survive.

Gently she drew her hand away from Troy's. As soon as the contact ended his eyes returned to their usual radiant blue.

"Apparently you *can* heal people," he said, sounding rather dazed.

When she looked down, Michael's face had regained some color, and his broad chest rose and fell with easier, deeper breaths. His eyebrows furrowed just a little, and then his lips parted.

"Beauty," he breathed.

One side of his mouth curved up, but then fell, as he slipped away again.

• • • • •

Troy had four hours to think on the drive from Pelham Bay Park to the White Mountains of New Hampshire. Summer elected to stay in the back with Michael, wedging herself in one corner with the Templar's head still in her lap. He could see her reflection in the rearview mirror and regularly checked on her, expecting her to fall asleep during the long ride. Instead she sat very still and watched the passing scenery, her fingers gently stroking Michael's forehead.

She was watching over him, the same way Troy watched over her.

He knew of many skillful healers among the Wiccan, and even a few among the ranks of the Magus Corps who were exceptionally powerful. It would have been difficult for any of them to save a man as seriously wounded as Michael. None of them could have done it as quickly as Summer had.

Then there was the question of what to do about Michael Charbon. After nearly being cut in two by that giant assassin, it was obvious that he couldn't go back to the Templars. He had no family outside his brotherhood in the order. As far as Troy knew he was the only friend Michael had.

If we can even be called friends.

Over the centuries the truce they had struck up had kept them first from killing each other, and then had evolved into a reluctant alliance. They had exchanged information and even a few prisoners, but always in some effort to avoid more violence. It could not always be avoided, however. Troy knew Michael had killed at least as many Wiccans as he had Templars. But there had always been good reasons for those deaths. Michael had stopped dozens of rogue witches from preying on humans, while Troy had prevented at least as many lone Templars from attacking vulnerable covens or untaught Wiccans. They had done what was necessary, but only when given no other choice.

My father won't care. The moment Abel lays eyes on Michael, all he'll see is the enemy.

Troy thought of the year he had spent chained to Michael, and what they had done to survive and escape that Saracen hellhole. It had taken Troy another year to make it back to his home coven in Wales. The moment his father had laid eyes on him, as thin and exhausted as Troy had been, he'd not welcomed him. He'd sneered at him for being foolish enough to roam the world in pursuit of idle pleasures. That day had been the last time he'd ever felt any amount of love for his father.

"Troy," Summer said. When he glanced in the rearview mirror, Summer smiled wistfully at him. "Would you please stop at that rest area up there?"

He looked ahead and saw it was the same place where he'd pulled off the first time he'd brought Summer to Silver Wood.

"Of course."

Thinking she needed to use the facilities he parked near the rest rooms, but when Summer eased out of the back seat, she walked up to the driver's door.

"Come out here, please."

Troy quickly climbed out frowning. "Is something wrong?" His gaze shifted to the back seat. "Is Michael–"

Summer put her hands on his shoulders and stood on tiptoe to put her mouth on his. She pulled his head down to kiss him passionately, her lips as sweet as her tongue was bold. Troy clamped his hands on her waist to pull her into him, his muscles coiling as his need for her exploded into an almost violent hunger. He turned and shoved her against the Jeep, pinning her there with his body weight. He kissed her mouth and neck and covered her breasts with his hands, relishing the sound of her soft moan. The scent of her changed as her arousal blended with his.

A low groan from the back seat made them both freeze, and Troy forced himself to release her and step back. "Sorry, I…I'm sorry."

"I'm not," she said and frowned up at him. "I'm your lover, Troy. You can put your hands on me any time you like."

"So can Michael, apparently." There, he'd said it, and Troy hated himself the moment the words left his mouth. "Forget that. It's none of my business."

"No, you're right. He's also my lover. I told you that back in the city." She said it frankly, and with none of the shame he'd expected. "Now that I have you both, I'm not going to give up either of you. I want you to understand that before we return to Silver Wood."

He knew Summer was relatively inexperienced when it came to sex. While she had been an eager and generous lover with him, it had been obvious that everything they did had been new to her.

"Do you expect me to help you explain this *ménage* à *trois* to Erica and the others?" he asked.

He wasn't even sure he understood it all that well himself.

Summer shook her head. "We're not going to discuss it with them. This is our business." Her expression softened. "Sex is definitely playing a part in this. When I was with you at your house, somehow Michael was with us, too. I know you felt him as much as I did. The same thing happened when I was with him in his apartment. You were there with us, Troy. I could even smell you."

He thought of the strange spell that had come over him while he'd secretly spied on Summer and Michael making love.

"I was across the street watching you and Michael. Something took over—your curse, maybe—and I felt as if I were having sex with you. I didn't touch myself, and I still came."

"It's not a curse," she protested. "It's us. You, me and him. We're connected now." She glanced back at the Jeep. "I just don't know how or why."

On some level Troy agreed with her, but he knew sharing her with Michael would be difficult if not impossible. The Templar loved her so much he'd nearly died to protect her. He knew if he'd been in Michael's place he'd have done the same.

"If you had to choose between the two of us, who would you pick?"

She pressed her lips into a thin line, and shook her head. "I've already made my choice." She blew out an exasperated breath. "Let's go."

She stalked around the Jeep, and climbed in the front passenger seat.

Troy got in beside her. He could almost hear the anger simmering inside her, and found that as puzzling as her answer to his question.

"Look, I had a hard time at first, when I saw

you with Michael," he found himself confessing. "Then I remembered that I have no claim on you. You're not my mate. I also knew you had feelings for Michael before you met me." When she didn't say anything he sighed. "Summer, I've told you before that sex is sacred to all Wiccans. Therefore what you did with Michael is sacred to me. I do believe that."

She sniffed. "You're still jealous."

"Oh, yeah," he agreed. "Because I'm still a guy. I thought of you as mine when we were together at Silver Wood. I made that assumption again when you got out of the car just now and kissed me. I've had you, Summer, and I want you again. That's not going to change." He hesitated before he added, "Michael is going to feel the same, probably more so. He's not like us. He's been expected to live a celibate life for centuries."

She turned to face him. "You know something? I told Michael that you and I were together. In fact, I taunted him with it. He wasn't jealous. He understood. If I'd wanted only you, he would never have touched me. But that's the thing—I want you both. I need you both."

"Right," Troy said and felt a surge of frustration. "Let's be practical for a fucking second. Assuming Michael survives, and my father doesn't turn us away, do you really think you can handle juggling two lovers at the same time? Do we take turns with you? How are you going to make it work? Write up a fucking schedule?"

Summer curled over, covering her face with her hands as she made a strange sound. Troy thought she was crying until he heard the sound again and saw the way her shoulders were shaking.

"It's not funny," he told her.

She sat up and wiped her eyes with the heels of her hands before she answered him.

"You think I'd need a schedule for…" she trailed off into another spate of laughter.

Troy's lips curved a little as he realized what he'd said. "Sorry. But if you are going to make a schedule, can I have Saturday nights? Sundays are more Michael's territory anyway."

"Stop," Summer gasped. "I'm going to wet my pants."

"Okay," he said, laughing a little himself. "Okay."

Although she hadn't answered any of his questions, Troy felt a little better now. If they could laugh about it, they could work it out.

"I guess what I really want to know is why. Under all that scary power I know you're not a

wild thing. You're sweet, and I doubt you've had
more than one or two lovers in your life. So what
made you decide to take on both of us, lady?"

Some of the hilarity left her expression as she
sighed. "I don't know. I just feel it, here." She
pressed a hand over her heart. "Like it's the way it
has to be for me, and not because of the curse,
either. When I'm with you and Michael I feel as if
I'm exactly where I'm supposed to be. That the
three of us are connected by something more
powerful than we are. And when it comes to the
sex, I think…" She stopped and shook her head.
"Um, no. You don't want to hear this."

"It's okay," Troy told her. "Whatever it is, you
can tell me. After everything that's happened,
you're not going to shock me."

"This might," Summer said and took a deep
breath. Then faced him again. "I think I know
why I felt both of you when I had sex with you
individually. I think we're meant to be together in
that, too. We're supposed to have sex together.
You, me and Michael."

CHAPTER TWO

DESPITE HIS WORDS, Summer knew she had shocked Troy. Though he didn't explode into a jealous rage, he barely spoke to her for the remainder of the trip to Silver Wood. She knew nothing she could say would make it easier for him to accept, so she alternated between keeping an eye on Michael, who was still unconscious, and watching the passing scenery as the sun set. The sky turned a star-studded, black velvet.

A few miles from the mountain road that would take them to the pavilion Troy said, "When we get there stay in the Jeep with him, and let me talk to my father. If he isn't willing to give sanctuary to a Templar, we'll have to leave immediately."

Summer glanced back at Michael. "Can't we simply say that he's a friend who saved our lives?

It wouldn't be a lie."

"They'll sense that he's an immortal, and they'll know he's not Wiccan. The coven has despised the Templars since the attack that killed my mother." He slowed as he made the turn off for the mountain. "Under ordinary circumstances I wouldn't even try to bring him here, but Michael nearly died protecting us from Alvis. That kind of sacrifice is deeply respected by all Wiccans, and it should give us some leverage."

Summer felt her stomach knotting. "What if it doesn't, and Abel tells us to leave? Where do we go?"

"I can't take either of you to Boston. Magus Corps headquarters would know the minute we entered the city. They'd demand we turn Michael over to them for questioning. We'd have to head west, maybe to one of the bigger covens, but eventually the Magus Corps will send someone after us." He drove through the illusion of a snowy rockslide that Abel kept on the road to prevent humans from intruding on the coven's home territory. "This could end very badly, Summer."

"No," she said flatly. "I won't allow anything to happen to you or Michael. You belong to me now."

"We're supposed to be protecting you," he said and smiled a little. "And the way you say we belong to you… is that you talking, or your power?"

"Does it matter?" Thinking about it made her head hurt, and the fact that he was still questioning the fact that they belonged together annoyed her. "English isn't my first language anyway."

He gave her a sideways glance. "Hey, settle down. I can feel your power spiking, and the last thing we need is to set it off now."

Summer focused on controlling her emotions as Troy drove up to the pavilion and parked. Lights from inside the main house made the windows glow golden. The coven's pack of dogs scampered out of the barn and bounded toward the Jeep. Before they reached them, however, the entire pack came to a skidding halt and sat down to form a wall like furry bodyguards.

Lachlan, Summer guessed. The surly, blond warlock had the ability to control all animals. As Abel's apprentice he helped with running the coven, but he disliked Troy and often instigated conflicts between the Atwaters. He'd also used the dogs more than once to threaten Troy.

The only person who came out of the pavilion,

however, was Abel Atwater. The Coven Master of Silver Wood looked like an older, slightly heavier copy of Troy. From the harsh set of his expression Summer knew he wasn't happy to see his eldest son returned. Troy got out of the Jeep and closed the door.

"So despite my wishes, you've brought back that woman." Abel folded his arms. "That I could overlook, but you lead the enemy to us as well?"

That made Summer frown. From where he stood Abel couldn't see the backseat of the Jeep. He might have sensed him, but how could he have guessed Michael was a Templar?

"His name is Michael," Troy said and nodded toward the Jeep. "He nearly died to save me and Summer from a Templar assassin. That makes him our ally, and my friend." He paused. "He needs shelter, care, and time to heal. Because he saved us, he cannot ever return to the order. Out of respect for his sacrifice, I ask that the coven provide him with sanctuary."

"Respect?" Abel spat on the ground. "There is my respect for your turncoat Templar, boy."

"That's enough of that," said a woman's voice. The petite figure of Erica Buchanan appeared at the Coven Master's side, although her scarred face looked drawn and tired. "Troy, is Summer all right?"

"Yes, High Priestess. Our friend Michael was actually wounded protecting her and me with his own body." Troy took a step forward. "He will not hurt anyone, I promise."

"No, he won't," she said, as her voice grew chilly. "If your father gives his permission, you may keep the Templar here until he heals. But if he comes near me, or lays one finger on any female in this coven, I'll kill him myself." She turned on her heel and retreated inside.

Summer stared after the redheaded woman, completely confused. Erica was one of the gentlest souls she'd met among the Wiccans. But just now she sounded as harsh and unforgiving as Abel. Erica's threat bothered her, too. Why would she assume Michael would hurt one of the women of the coven?

Abel stared after Erica as well, jaw muscles working, before glowering at his son for another long, silent moment.

"Go on, then. Get him and bring him inside."

Troy came back to the car, but when Summer got out to help him move Michael he shook his head and hauled the unconscious Templar out by himself. He pulled him upright and then gently rolled him over onto his shoulder. He hoisted him

out of the Jeep and halfway over his back in a
fireman's hold before he turned and carried him
across the property.

Summer saw the dogs were still maintaining
their perimeter, and glanced down one side of the
line and then the other. With a collective low
whine the animals dispersed, scurrying back to the
barn with their tails between their legs.

Lachlan glared at Summer as she followed Troy
inside, but she ignored him to smile at Aileen,
who stood beside her husband, Wilson Atwater.
Abel's younger son had one arm around his wife's
slim shoulders and his free hand resting on her
hugely rounded belly. He looked about as happy
as his father had been to see them. Aileen offered
Summer a welcoming smile, but her solemn gray
eyes grew worried as she took in Michael's big,
limp form.

"Wilson," Abel bellowed from another room,
and Troy's brother reluctantly turned and
departed, at which point Aileen hurried to catch
up with Summer and Troy.

"I heard some of what was said," the young
witch confided to Summer. "Does your friend
need healing?"

"We'll check his wound, but I think all he needs
is rest and some TLC," Summer said. She heard

the sound of Abel's and Wilson's muffled shouting from the other side of the house and grimaced. "And maybe a bodyguard until he's back on his feet."

Troy carried Michael into the rooms he had shared with Summer, and carefully lowered him onto the bed.

"Aileen," Troy said, "could you make some of your orange-apricot tea for him? And add some molasses."

"Is this really the time for tea?" Summer asked.

"It's actually a Wiccan herbal tea treatment," Aileen told her. "Your friend needs fluids, and the apricot replaces the iron lost, which the orange helps the body absorb. The molasses will stave off shock and boost red blood cell production. I'll have it ready in a few minutes, Troy."

Once the pregnant witch hurried off, Summer closed the door and leaned back against it.

"I can understand why your father is upset, but what is going on with Erica? I've never seen her act like that."

"A long time ago she was captured and tortured by someone," Troy said as he used his dagger to cut off the remains of Michael's ruined shirt. "She refuses to talk about it, but I'm pretty sure it was a Templar."

"Is that how she got that scar on her face?" Summer asked, and when he nodded she felt sick. "Why didn't you tell me?"

"I'm not supposed to know. I found out about the incident from another Magus Corps officer." Troy gently felt around the fresh scar on Michael's side. "This looks better than I expected. You do good work, Dr. Summer."

"It would be nice to know how I do it," she said. She laid her hand over the scar, and felt the pulse of Michael's blood coursing through the repaired tissues and vessels. "He's very strong."

"Confused, too," Michael murmured, and opened his eyes to slits. "Where am I?"

"We brought you to Silver Wood. My father agreed to give you sanctuary. No, don't," Troy said as Michael tried to sit up. "You'll just pass out again, and I've already lugged your giant ass around too many times today."

"Wiccan weakling," Michael said, but subsided against the pillows. His cool green eyes shifted from Troy's face to Summer's. "Alvis?"

"He's dead," she said gently. "And you almost died saving us." A knock on the door made her glance over her shoulder to see Erica's brother cautiously peering in at them. "Come in, Ewan."

The heavyset man smiled as he stepped inside,

a work apron over his big belly and his red curls standing on end.

"I heard all the yelling and assumed you were back, Troy. Summer, blessed be, I'm so happy you've returned to us unharmed." He raised his eyebrows at Michael. "And you must be the Templar everyone is squabbling about. Welcome to Silver Wood, sir."

Summer performed quick introductions, and Michael nodded, his eyes tired but watchful. As Ewan drew Troy aside and spoke quietly to him in Welsh, Aileen returned with a tray containing a pot of tea, a mug and a small vial filled with a sparkling potion.

"A few drops of the potion will help ease his pain and allow him to sleep if he grows restless," she murmured to Summer as she handed over the tray. "I would stay, but Wilson has decided to move us back to the cabin tonight, so I have to pack my things."

Troy's younger brother was very jealous of his wife, especially around Troy, who had once been Aileen's lover. With a Templar in the main house as well, Wilson was obviously taking no chances.

"I'm sorry about this," Summer told her.

Aileen's gray eyes shifted briefly to Michael before she lowered her voice.

"Be careful, Summer. Ever since you were taken I've had the feeling that something dreadful is coming for you."

"Coming for me here at the coven?" Summer asked, thinking of the attack the Templars had planned.

The younger woman's mouth tightened.

"I wasn't sure, and I thought when you came back the feeling would go, but when I saw you tonight it only grew worse. Now I think it's already here. I think it's been waiting for you."

• • • • •

Once Michael had fallen asleep again, Troy left Summer with him and went with Ewan to talk to Abel and Erica.

"If you will allow me to help, I think I can bring them around, Troy," the older man said. "Neither your father or my sister are unreasonable." He grimaced as Troy gave him a pointed look. "Very well, they are at times, but I think they can persuaded to be less resistant."

They found the pair with Lachlan in the library, but as soon as Troy and Ewan stepped inside Abel's apprentice gave him a filthy look, stalked out and slammed the door behind him.

Erica also didn't seem happy to see him. "This is not the best time, Troy. Brother, perhaps you should retire for the night."

"The only thing I am tired of, Sister," Ewan told her, "is this endless bickering. Troy has brought important news that needs to be heard, and I want you to listen to him. And you, Abel. You may not be inclined to behave as a father to welcome your son home, but as Coven Master it is your duty to attend to the welfare of this coven."

Abel peered at the shorter warlock. "Have you been at my whiskey, old man?"

Ewan lifted his hands in a gesture of surrender. "I will go and talk to the rest of the coven about Troy's friend. You three need to work this out." After giving Troy an encouraging look he left.

Troy noticed that the warded vault where the dangerous books were kept was standing open. An ancient volume lay open on the reading desk by Abel. He recognized the grimoire as one of the shadow books the Magus Corps kept on a cautionary list of destructive magic resources.

"Has the coven decided to take up practicing black magic now, Father, or are you just that happy to see me?"

The older Atwater scowled. "What is this news

that cannot wait, boy?"

Troy debated on asking Erica to leave them, but decided instead to watch her as he related what details he knew of the attack the Templars had planned on the winter solstice gathering.

"You need to alert the other covens and cancel the gathering. Don't use your normal methods of communication, either. I'd also suggest we determine who among the coven members has been betraying us, and why. It has to be someone at Silver Wood who can access the spells you've cast, Father. The Templars had an exact copy of your invitation to the covens."

"You're sure about this?" Erica asked, sounding and looking genuinely shocked. When Troy nodded, she said, "Of course we'll cancel it–"

"No," Abel said, glaring at them. "We'll move the gathering to a safer location. No one will know the place except me and the coven leaders. Unless you believe I'm the traitor, and I'm passing information to the scum responsible for murdering your mother?"

Troy dragged a hand through his hair. "No, of course I don't. But is it worth risking hundreds of lives simply to have a Yule party?"

"If you had ever bothered to be part of this coven, you ignorant stripling, you'd know how important this gathering is," Abel said, his fists bunching at his sides. "We are a small coven. We have alliances to build, and resources to pool. There are a dozen groups who want to form new covens, which will add to our strength and numbers."

Troy could feel his own temper rising. "So do it another time."

"There are things that can't wait," Abel insisted. "Combat training for our younger members. Sanctuaries for the persecuted. We have to protect our people."

"Sounds very ambitious," Troy said and knew how determined his father was to expand his power base and bring outside covens under his sway. "But you won't do any of that if you're all dead."

"Now you even sound like a fucking Templar," Abel said. He strode up to him, shoving his face close. "Is that what you are now, son? Has that scum you brought under my roof turned you against your own kind?"

Of course he would think that. Abel saw things only in black and white.

"A long time ago Michael saved my life."

His father's expression darkened. "So he could use you—"

"Michael saved my life during the Seventh Crusade," Troy said and nodded as his father's eyes widened. "Those years I was gone, when you thought I was off wandering the world? I was, but not by choice. The Templars captured me outside Paris when they raided that coven you had foster me. I didn't run away. They put me in chains and dragged me along on their glorious quest."

Abel's jaw hardened. "Why would they take a Wiccan with them on crusade?"

"They saw me use my ability when we tried to fight them off. Soldiers need water, especially in the desert. So the Grand Master told me I was going to serve as his army's water bearer. When I refused, he put me in a cage and starved and tortured me until I cooperated." Even after all these centuries it still made Troy sick to remember those endless months of being dragged along with the crusaders. "They took me into battle with them, so I could steal the water from their enemies. When the Templars were finally overwhelmed and I tried to escape, I was captured and imprisoned by the Sultan Turanshah's men. They threw me in his dungeon along with Michael, the only Templar to survive."

Erica made a low, mournful sound. "Oh, Troy."

"Turanshah's dungeon made Hell look like a

garden party. Like the others they'd captured we were beaten daily, and given no food or water. The mortal prisoners all died, one by one. But I didn't, and neither did Michael. All we did was fight." He walked over to brace his arm on the mantle and stare down at the flames crackling in the fireplace. "When they discovered we weren't human, they began feeding us and treating our wounds. They brought us both back to health. Then they gave us knives and stood back to watch us fight. At first we did, gladly, but the blades were too short and dull to inflict lethal wounds. Once we were weak from blood loss and beating on each other they chained us together and threw us back in our cell."

Erica looked appalled. "Why would they do such a thing?"

"Our hatred for each other entertained them. They built a little arena on the sand, and brought Michael and I out of the dungeons every day to fight each other. They entertained themselves by making us use different weapons. Clubs. Whips." He closed his eyes for a moment as he remembered those endless, bloody battles. "Torches."

Abel walked away from him and stood at the window, his shoulders stiff. "How long did they make you fight the bastard?"

"It was difficult to keep track of time. Perhaps a year. If we were injured they would give us a day or two to heal, and then it was back to the arena." Troy saw how pale Erica looked and sighed. "It seems no hatred can endure when both enemies are made victims. Michael and I began helping each other. We planned our fights so our injuries looked worse than they actually were. We learned how often the guards patrolled, where they watched and where they didn't. We stole things we could make into weapons."

"You were planning to escape?" Erica asked.

Troy nodded. "I used my ability to help us tunnel out of our cell, but halfway through it collapsed on top of me. I would still be buried there if Michael hadn't crawled back to dig me out and drag me with him the rest of the way."

No one said anything for a long moment, but Troy saw Erica's expression turn to shame. Abel turned around to face him.

"Why did you never tell me any of this?" his father asked, his voice gruff. "When you came back to Wales, you let me think you'd been off gallivanting and wenching."

"As I remember it, you accused me of that the moment I stepped over the threshold," Troy said.

"And how could I tell you I'd befriended a Templar after I'd been made their prisoner and forced to go on crusade with them? I think you would have killed me yourself."

"I remember how thin you were," Erica said quietly. "I should have guessed. I am sorry, Troy."

"As I said, it was a long time ago." He turned to Abel. "When Michael and I were free, we forged a truce between us. We vowed never to fight each other again, and we have kept that promise. Michael brought Summer to me instead of turning her over to the Templar inquisitors. When one of their assassins attacked us, Michael took an axe in the side to protect us. You may hate him for what he is, Father, but you will damn well accept what he is not: our enemy."

CHAPTER THREE

THE STINK OF sweat and fear pervaded the private hospital room, blending with the lingering, sharp odors of commercial disinfectant, alcohol-based hand sanitizer, and latex gloves. A disposable, compartmented tray on the table beside the bed held the remains of an institutional meal: a half-cup of pudding, a blackening section of banana, and a small pile of overcooked, scrambled eggs. Monitors on wheeled poles flanked either side of the bed, displaying digital numbers. A PCA unit counted down another fifteen minutes before the press of a button would deliver another dose of morphine into the patient's intravenous tube.

"He kept singing children's songs," Augustin Colbert said, his broken nose making his voice thick and nasal. "He would be talking to me and then utter one of the lines from the lyrics. I think your steward has finally lost his mind, my lord."

Temple Master Nathaniel Harper nodded his agreement as he looked down at the battered face and body of his clergy aide. It aggravated him to have to put one of his people in a hospital, but Augustin's injuries had been too severe for him to recover at the Abbey infirmary. Since Colbert was a mortal he had the usual weaknesses, and in reality he had been beyond fortunate to escape from Gideon Edmunds with his life. An immortal Templar suffering from immortality sickness was probably the most dangerous, lethal force on the planet.

"I know he took you to Charbon's apartment, but why?"

Augustin frowned, and then winced as the furrowing of his brow caused the aluminum strip protecting his newly-set nose to shift.

"Charbon had something Gideon wanted. He sent me to his door to draw him out into the hall. Once I did, he planned to shoot him in the legs to disable him. That is all I can remember, my lord."

Gideon had sent them all on a merry chase as he had slaughtered his way across the city, dragging Augustin along as a hostage as he searched for the green witch who had the only cure for his condition. Every hour Nathaniel heard of yet another mortal found butchered, thanks to his former steward's descent into madness.

But why would Gideon go after Michael? He knew the two men had never cared for each other, but all Michael knew about the green witch was what Nathaniel had told him.

"You must try to recall what Gideon wanted from Michael," Nathaniel told Augustin. "It is of the utmost importance."

The clergy aide closed his blackened, swollen eyelids for a moment and then shook his head. "I am sorry, my lord. I was at Charbon's door, and then I woke up here. That is all I know." A tear slid down his cheek. "Please don't ask me to try to remember again. It makes my head hurt to think about it."

"Very well," Nathaniel said and suppressed an urge to slap the sniveling man across the face. Instead he forced himself to make the sign of the cross over him. "Rest now, my son."

When he stepped out of the hospital room Nathaniel beckoned to the mortal physician waiting in the hall.

"He is suffering from some sort of memory loss. What caused it?"

"It's not uncommon, considering the amount of physical and emotional trauma he suffered," the doctor said. "In addition to the broken bones he sustained several blows to the head and neck, and he was forced to walk on a shattered ankle. If the frostbite damage is severe enough to render his tissues necrotic, we will have to amputate his leg from the knee down."

"He has frostbite?"

Nathaniel cocked his head at the words, before he glanced at the window. New York City in November was chilly, but they had yet to experience even a soft freeze.

"Surely not in this weather."

"I doubt it was from typical exposure. Judging by the type of tissue damage to his arm, leg and torso, your man was subjected to sudden, extreme cold on only one side of his body." The doctor reached for Augustin's chart, flipping it open to show Nathaniel the photographs taken in the E.R. "His clothing was saturated on that side, and we found bits of ice still clinging to his shoe laces. It's almost as if he fell partway into a frozen lake and just laid there until the first layers of his flesh froze."

An ancient image prodded at the edge of Nathaniel's memory. But as he drew it into focus, it was coupled with a more recent one. He had to cock his head again. He remembered a thin and battered Wiccan huddled in a cart cage rolling through the desert. De Sonnac's water warlock, Atwater, who had been reportedly killed along with the blinded Grand Master during the Battle of Fariskur. He'd been able to find water in any place, and could even freeze it. The Wiccan scum had had the eyes of a demon, intensely blue and filled with hatred for his captors.

Nathaniel went still.

He remembered the mortal male who had carried Augustin on a litter into the Abbey. His hands balled into fists. Nathaniel had even praised him for helping Michael.

The order is grateful to you for your service, mortal.

The human had bowed his head and gone down on one knee, pressing his fisted arm across his chest.

It is my honor, my lord.

He'd also glanced up just as Nathaniel had turned away.

The same bright blue eyes.

Michael had been the only survivor of that particular battle. When he had escaped and returned to Paris, he had told Nathaniel that Atwater had been killed along with the Templars by the Saracens.

Michael had lied.

"Do what you can for him," Nathaniel told the doctor before he hurried to the elevator. Once outside the hospital he used his mobile to contact the captain of the guards at the Abbey. "Recall Michael Charbon at once, and when he arrives, secure him for questioning."

"We have intercepted a police report that described two men fighting in the streets, Master," his captain said. "From the witness descriptions it appears to have been Charbon and Berenson fighting over the green witch and another man."

"Alvis fighting Michael?" Nathaniel stopped in his tracks. "No, that's impossible. I personally gave Alvis the order to track Gideon."

"The descriptions of the men are very detailed, Master." The captain hesitated. "Four of the witnesses describe the smaller man beheading the larger. If this is true, Berenson is dead, but we cannot confirm it. The police found no remains, and the scene was scoured clean, as if by some magic."

Alvis, his finest assassin, dead. His body and the proof that he was murdered, gone. *By some magic indeed.* Nathaniel felt as if his blood might begin to boil.

"Was the third man at the scene described as having blue eyes and long dark hair?"

The sound of paper shuffling came over the line. "Yes, Master."

With his thumb Nathaniel switched off the mobile and stared blindly at the glittering lights of the Manhattan skyline. He would have his people check and recheck the reports, but the conclusion was obvious: Michael was in league with Atwater and the green witch. He had lied about them, shielded them, and had even killed Alvis to protect them. That Michael would one day betray the order had always been a risk, but Nathaniel had been convinced he would see the signs long before it happened. Now it seemed Michael had turned traitor right under his nose. Not even when he'd brought his Wiccan accomplices along with him, pretending they were mortals.

They were still inside when I left with Augustin.

Nathaniel trotted across the parking lot to where his driver had parked, and climbed into the back before the man could open the door for him.

"Take me back to the Abbey. Now." His mobile rang, and he answered it, impatient. "What is it now?"

"I don't mean to trouble you, Temple Master,"

a cold voice said. "I can stop calling, if you like."

"Forgive me, I thought you were someone else," Nathaniel said quickly. "What do you have for me, Baldwin?"

CHAPTER FOUR

MICHAEL FELT THE warmth of his Beauty beside him on the bed, and turned his head to look into her dark opal eyes. Summer smiled and touched his face, tracing the lines of his brow and nose and mouth before she leaned forward to brush her soft lips over his.

He breathed in the delicious scent of her, grateful and rather amazed to still be with her. He remembered every moment of his brief but epic battle with the Norseman.

"Alvis Berenson buried his axe in my side."

Pain flickered across her pretty face. "Yes, he did."

Recalling how he had pulled the battle axe from his own body, and used the gory blade to decapitate the most feared assassin among the Templars, gave him pause. The wound had been so deep he'd known it would end him. That knowledge had given him the superhuman strength to make that final blow.

"I should be dead."

"You should be," she said and rested her hand against the place where the heavy blade had struck him, the place that was now miraculously whole and only sore and swollen. "But you're not. You're with me and Troy, and you're safe. Go back to sleep."

Exhaustion tugged at him in agreement, but Michael didn't want to slip back into the darkness, not until Troy returned and could watch over her while he slept.

"Tell me about this place."

"This room is where Troy and I slept while we were here at Silver Wood." She wriggled against the mattress. "It's a nice bed. A little small for the three of us, but maybe we can ask for an upgrade."

He raised his brows. "You are planning to sleep with both of us?"

Her smile faded. "I'm not letting you out of my sight again, Michael Charbon. You'll be lucky if I let you go to the bathroom without me."

He would have chuckled, but she sounded so ferocious he didn't dare.

"Then we will have to make plans to go, and soon. By now Nathaniel knows I betrayed the order. He will send his best to hunt me down and bring me back. The only thing Templars despise more than the Wiccan are–"

She kissed him to stop him from speaking, and then pressed her fingertips against his mouth.

"You're not a traitor."

Michael kissed each of her fingers before fixing his gaze on her lips.

"Come here and do that again."

Summer's eyes darkened as she shifted closer, touching his cheek with her hand before she met his mouth with hers. Kissing her was like being caressed inside and out by very soft, warm feathers. He relished the sweet taste of her. As weak as he was, a moment later all he could think was how much he wanted to roll atop her and spread her legs. He would slide his aching cock into her softness, and feel her trembling beneath him as he worked it in and out of her tight, luscious pussy.

"Whoa," she said and drew back, breathless."Not a good idea right now, big guy. I don't want to tear something open."

"Such as your clothes? I will do it." He reached for her blouse.

"Behave yourself," she said and batted his hand away. Then her gaze shifted, as the door to the room opened, and her mouth curved. "Did your father change his mind and decide to kick us out?"

"No," Troy said and came over to sit beside her on the bed. But as he took her hand he looked over at Michael. "I told him about our time in Turanshah's dungeon, and what they made us do, and how you saved my life. He knows about our truce, too."

He and Troy had both sworn to keep their history secret, and had kept that vow for hundreds of years. For Troy to break that promise must have involved something more important than protecting each other. He also knew how heavy the burden of secrecy had been on his warlock comrade. Still, Michael pretended to scowl.

"So now what am I to do, Pagan? Find a priest and confess my own sins?"

Troy grinned. "You *are* a priest, Paladin. Absolve yourself." He stretched out beside Summer, folding one arm behind his head and reaching down with the other to clasp Summer's hand. "Seriously, I don't think Abel or Erica will give us any grief for now. They're going to be busy relocating the winter solstice. But as soon as Michael's feeling more mobile I think we should relocate to the old house."

"Agreed," Michael said. He stretched carefully and grimaced as the ache in his side grew more intense. "A day or two of rest should see me fully mended. How did you manage to heal my wound, Pagan?"

"I froze it to stop the bleeding," Troy admitted. "Summer did the rest."

"Don't ask me to explain," she said, before he could reply. "It was this thing inside me, and you two, and I don't know. Lots of scary green light."

"Then I thank you both."

Michael took her hand to bring it to his lips. But at that moment the light darkened, and the room vanished entirely.

Michael found himself standing with Troy and Summer in a strange, beautiful chamber lit by the golden glow of candles and flickering firelight. A tall, dark-haired, young woman in a diaphanous robe stood between two large, muscular young men wearing only trousers. One of the men was dark, and the other was very fair, and both were quite handsome.

Michael immediately stepped in front of Summer, and bumped shoulders with Troy as he did the same.

"Is this real?"

"I don't know," Troy murmured, "but it damn sure feels like it."

"Excuse me," Summer said and squeezed between the two of them. Her expression changed as soon as she saw the dark-haired woman. "*Maman.*"

The trio paid no attention to them as the men moved closer to the woman. The dark man slipped her robe from her shoulders from behind as the fair man untied the robe's belt. When the sheer fabric fell to the floor the woman stood naked, her head falling back onto the dark man's shoulder as the fair man clasped her by the waist.

"This is your mother?" Michael asked her.

Summer nodded slowly. "But I've never seen those men." Her hand tightened on Michael's as the fair man began kissing her mother's breasts. "Oh, boy, I don't think we should be watching this."

You are not watching, cherie. Summer's mother turned her head, and green light filled her eyes. *You are remembering.*

As both men caressed Summer's mother, Michael felt his own cock stiffen, but he could not look away from the lovers. What they did was not obscene but beautiful, like a dance. It also awakened his own memories of loving Summer, and sent a surge of longing through him so powerful he felt his hands shake. At the same time he felt a different desire flooding through him, and on some level knew it was coming from Troy.

"Summer, does your head hurt?" Michael heard Troy ask.

"Not at all." She tore her gaze away from the lovers to stare at him. "Do you know what this is?"

"Maybe." He looked over her head at Michael. "I've got everything you're feeling in my head right now. Do you feel the same connection to me?"

Michael nodded. "She is the conduit. We have to release her, I think."

"Together, on three." Troy counted, and when he reached three Michael released Summer's hand.

The vision disappeared, and Michael stared up at the ceiling from the bed, returned to the room and his own reality. Beside him Summer went limp, and when he turned his head he saw she was unconscious. Troy checked her pulse.

"She fainted again." His mouth tightened as he rested his hand on her brow. "I assumed these things were dreams, or visions, but they're not."

"They are memories," Michael said. Worried he might trigger another episode, Michael resisted the urge to touch her himself. "Evidently her mother had two lovers."

Troy gave him a pointed look. "Yeah, what a coincidence. Maybe this is why she's been so adamant about staying with both of us. She may be trying to follow in Mom's footsteps."

Michael didn't want to believe that what Summer felt for either of them was influenced by anything but her own emotions, but the similarities between the memory and their situation could not be ignored.

"Why would she try to relive her mother's life with us?"

"I have no idea, but there's something else you need to know," Troy said. "On the way here we argued about this little triangle she has going with the two of us. She told me that the strange things that have happened when she was with each of us meant that the three of us are supposed to be lovers. As in the three of us having sex together."

Michael recalled the dream he'd had of making love to Summer with Troy.

"So it is possible she is trying to recreate her mother's *ménage* à *trois*. Perhaps even unconsciously."

"Her *maman's* lovers certainly looked a lot like us," Troy' said. His attention was drawn back to Summer's face as her eyelids fluttered. "Hey, pretty lady. How's the head?"

"I'm fine," she said curtly. She sat up and climbed over Troy to get off the bed, and then turned and faced them with her hands planted on her hips. "I also heard everything you just said. Do you always talk about me like I'm a deluded nutcase while I'm unconscious?"

"Sometimes," Michael said before Troy could answer. "But mostly we wait until we are out of the room, or you are."

She made an exasperated sound and threw up her arms.

"I'm not crazy. I'm also not trying to be my mother. I can't remember my mother."

"You were doing an excellent job of it a few minutes ago," Troy said. "And any time you want to remember her again like that I'd be happy to go along for the ride."

"Stop kidding around," Summer said and began to pace. "There is no way I watched my mother have sex with two guys. In case you didn't notice, there was no one else in the room but them. I wasn't there."

"She is right," Michael said. "And I sensed that

her mother was mortal, didn't you?"

When Troy nodded and heaved a sigh, Summer glared at them.

"What does that have to do with it?"

"Your mother was Wiccan, Summer," he told her. "If she was still human, then she couldn't have conceived you yet. To do that, she would first have to be initiated by her lover, or lovers, as the case may be."

Her anger faded as she digested this.

"So how could I possibly remember something that happened before I was even born?"

"I don't think you did," Troy said slowly. "I think what we saw are your mother's memories."

CHAPTER FIVE

"BLOODY USELESS THING."

Gideon Edmunds climbed out of the battered florist's van and stalked around to the front where a white, oily smoke gently wafted out of the grill. The van that he had appropriated for himself back in New York City had turned into a dragon on him at some point during his journey. It had slowed from a steady speed to a slow crawl before it had belched, shuddered, and coasted to a stop.

It seemed to Gideon that it was also a female dragon, for it had died on him, as nearly all females were wont to do. One would expect more from an immortal reptile, but there was nothing to be done about it now. He should skin it and wear the hide as a trophy, but there didn't seem to be flesh to the damned thing. Before dying it must have enchanted itself to appear as nothing more than an empty vehicle.

He kicked one of the front tires with his boot. This new problem annoyed him almost as much as forgetting the words to all the cheerful ditties he had been singing on his latest crusade. He was also weary of driving himself.

"Am I not an immortal knight?" he shouted at the heavens. "Do I not deserve a chauffeur at the very least? How am I to focus on my quest if I am trudging about like a fucking serf?"

Snowflakes drifted down to land on his face, but curiously the frigid heavens themselves did not reply. The Almighty must be mightily preoccupied with how to smite Gideon's countless enemies, or properly reward him for his suffering.

What Gideon really needed was a mortal to serve him again. They were all very good at driving, and could be quite handy for other middling chores. He considered walking back to New York City to find Augustin Colbert, who had been tolerably acceptable as a servant, except that he couldn't remember whether or not he had killed Augustin. Also, it was too far away now.

He was in New Hampshire, according to the sign he had passed some miles back. *Welcome - Bienvenue to New Hampshire "Live Free or Die"* it had read. At the time he'd thought that a particularly touching sentiment. But now it seemed like a false promise, or perhaps even a threat. Did these New Hampshiremen truly intend to kill anyone who did not live according to their directive? He did not fear mortals, but they could prove quite bothersome. Perhaps as a cautionary measure he should just kill every human who crossed his path. After sitting and driving for hours he could certainly stand the exercise.

A moment came over him, breaking through the endless dance of his thoughts like a pail of cold water, and Gideon leaned against the van. The madness receded and rational thought returned to him. He had to find the green witch. He would force her to take him to the Emerald Tablet, or he would be trapped in the prison of his own insanity for the rest of eternity, or until one of his Templar brothers caught up with him.

Headlights appeared, and grew larger as a big car approached and then slowed to a stop beside the florist's van. Gideon squinted in the glare at the thick-bodied man behind the wheel of the old Cadillac. He had the usual idiot expression every mortal seemed to wear as he studied the van and then peered back at Gideon, but at least he had a functioning vehicle. Gideon walked over to the driver's window and tapped politely on it.

"Good of you to stop," he said when the window rolled down.

"Gotta watch out for each other on the road." The human grinned, showing very white teeth. "Need a jump?"

He would have to be crafty now, so that he didn't end up driving again, and this time with mortal brains splattered all about him.

"Actually a ride to the next town would be most helpful, sir."

The human nodded. "Sure, hop in."

As he went around to the passenger door Gideon wondered why the man was so obsessed with jumping and hopping. Was he a rabbit, disguised as a man, or a warlock, hinting at some sort of evil enchantment he intended to inflict? Since rabbits could not speak it was likely the latter. Warlocks were too damn much trouble to train as proper servants, too.

Stop thinking of such things. Focus on your purpose. You must find the witch.

"Good thing I stopped," the human said. "Not a lot of traffic this time of night. I'm Nick, by the way. What's your name?"

Gideon thought of the Templar who had led the conspiracy against him. "Michael."

Nick grunted his approval. "I gotta a cousin in Newark named Mike. You try calling anyone to come and get you, Mike?"

"I don't have a phone with me," Gideon said. He could smell something foul coming from the back of the vehicle, which at first he attributed to his madness. Unfortunately focusing didn't make it go away, so he began breathing through his mouth. "Is anyone expecting you in town?"

"Nah. I'm from Jersey. Had to drive up here to take care of some business." Nick eyed him. "You got people up here?"

"All my people died a long time ago," Gideon said and rubbed his nose. Why should he tolerate such a stench? Was he not the Almighty's most beloved warrior? "What is that smell?"

"Oh, I hit a raccoon coming out of Boston. Huge fucker." Nick flashed his too-white teeth again. "Got all mashed up in the wheel well. Guess there's still some shreds hanging on. I'll have to scrub her down good before I head home."

The smell *was* coming from something dead, but it had to be much larger than a raccoon. Still, to be polite Gideon nodded, and to distract himself from thoughts of using the gun in his pocket to blow Nick's brains all over the windshield, he began humming the tune of one of his happy songs under his breath. The happy songs kept him calm, and humans alive.

Nick began to hum right along, and toward the end even sang some of the words.

"All I can remember from that one is 'Head, shoulders, knees and toes,'" he told him. "Sang the shit out of that one back when I was a kid. So you're a florist, right?"

"Yes," Gideon lied. "I love flowers, don't you?"

The mortal stopped smiling. "Do I look like a pussy to you, Mike?"

Gideon studied him. "No, but you could be wearing a disguise. What's wrong with flowers?"

"Nothing, if you're a chick, or a fruitcake." Nick slowed and pulled off the road, putting the car in park and turning off the engine before he turned to face him. "You a pansy, Mike? You get in my car thinking we got a possible love connection going here?" He grabbed his crotch and fondled it. "You thinking about sucking on this, you fruitcake?"

Gideon frowned at him. "You're really very confused, aren't you? Even more so than I am. That's rather incredible, under the circumstances."

"Yeah?" Nick produced a small, snub-nosed gun and pointed it at Gideon. "Let's see if you understand me now. You're going to grab the shovel out of the back seat, you pansy, and walk out in the woods over there, and dig me a grave. A nice, deep, unmarked grave. If you do a good job, I might not even put you in it. Now get out of the car."

The mortal was a killer, Gideon thought with the last of his reasoning. When it faded away behind his madness, joy flooded him.

Oh, we're going to have so much fun now.

Gideon beamed as he opened the door and climbed out, and would have burst into song if only he could have remembered one. He had to settle instead for humming something bright and happy under his breath as he came around to the driver's side, and took a bullet in his chest when Nick got out and fired at him, and then another before he could wrest the weapon out of his pudgy little hand.

As Nick scrambled backward, Gideon glanced down at the holes in his shirt.

"That wasn't very nice."

He shot Nick in one kneecap and watched him drop, swearing and rolling and clutching his wounded leg, before Gideon reached inside and removed the keys from the ignition. He used the lock fob to pop open the trunk, and then went back to survey the source of the smell.

"Oh, dear." He lifted the edge of a very bloody sheet to have a better look at the pile of body parts. "Blind me, how did you get it into so many little pieces? Not with an axe, surely. These cuts are too neat."

Nick answered him with a sobbing screech of rage.

Gideon searched around until he found the little gas-powered chain saw, and grinned as he pulled it out of the trunk.

"Well, Nick, I'm quite impressed. What a shame you're not a Templar. I think we might have been the very best of friends."

He shook off some of the blood and gore still sticking to the chains before he went to stand over the writhing mortal and pulled the chainsaw's starter cord.

"So where did you begin with *your* victim, exactly?" Gideon had to shout for the mortal to hear him over the whining buzz of the tool. "Head, shoulders, knees or toes?"

* * *

Just before dawn Erica Buchanan finished brewing her calming valerian tea, and brought it with her out into the divination garden. Since she had planted the lavender borders the rest of the coven recognized it as her private spot and stayed out of it. It was the only place on the mountain where she could be sure to be left alone with her thoughts.

The mugwort and yarrow were growing well. The rising sun cast its first rays over the neat circular beds, and gilded the spiky leaves and clusters of tiny golden flowers. She would soon need to prune the star anise trees, which were growing overly woody. Then she would trim the basil sprigs growing in the pots she had placed against the back wall. Basil was a snobbish herb that refused to grow indoors or next to any other plant. Her coriander and dill, on the other hand, seemed drawn to each other, twining in delicate green embraces wherever their broad and feathery leaves grew close. A ghostly patch of white sage had begun creeping over the stone borders of its bed toward the rue, but it would not choke the life out of rue's bluish leaves. Even in the garden there were lovers.

Sometimes her coven reminded her of herbs. Abel was definitely coriander, strong and peppery, an herb of Mars, either loved or hated, and never simply liked. Aileen was the embodiment of lavender, sweet and pure, a flower of Mercury, comforting and soothing. Both were filled with love and yet struggled with it, thanks to her.

Because I am basil, Erica thought, sat back and closed her eyes. *I am just as stubborn and lofty, refusing to share myself with Abel or Aileen or anyone.*

Like the basil in the garden she might forever be alone, but she would serve the same purpose as the strong, fierce herb. She would protect her people, and exorcize the evil dwelling within the coven—just as soon as she could calm herself. She had to accept that one of those evil bastards now slept under the same roof, and would be sharing their table, and looking upon her with his damned eyes. And she would not scream and throw things at him, for he could not have the same eyes as that monster. Those dark, flat, lifeless eyes had avidly watched hers as he inflicted his brutalities on her, over and over and over, until she had begged him to kill her.

"May I join you?"

Erica opened her eyes and sat up to see Summer standing on the other side of the lavender border.

"Is anything wrong?" Erica asked. She began to rise. "I should start making the morning meal–"

"There's no need yet, High Priestess." The younger woman's voice was as soft and serene as her gaze. "Everyone is still asleep."

Erica wanted to resent the intrusion. She wanted to hate Summer, and shout at her to leave the mountain, and take that brute with her. All Summer had done since she'd first come to Silver Wood was cause trouble and turmoil. Erica wanted her peaceful, uneventful life back, so she could go on pretending it was just as real as every other Wiccan's. But Erica knew it wasn't the young witch's fault. She'd done nothing but try to help.

"Please," Erica said, nodding to the bench next to her. "Come and sit."

"This is a lovely spot," Summer said as she took a seat, and looked around at the lush, thriving beds. "It looks a bit like a compass."

"It's how one plants a divination garden," Erica said and noted the shadows under the other woman's eyes. "You look tired. You should go back to sleep for a few more hours."

"I couldn't. I had another vision last night, of my mother with two men." She grimaced, and her voice was strained. "It was something that happened before I was born, so Troy thinks I may have my mother's memories." She spread her hands out in a helpless gesture. "How is that even possible?"

"There are spells that can transfer thoughts

from one person to another," Erica said. "Coven leaders sometimes use them to teach their apprentices practices which cannot be spoken or written down."

Summer nodded, seemed as though she would say something, but paused. Finally she plunged on.

"Would her memories influence me in any way?" Her opal eyes searched Erica's. "For instance, would I do the same thing I remember her doing?"

Erica thought for a moment, and then shook her head.

"Memories have power only over the emotions. They might influence your mood, make you sad or happy, but they can't control you or force you to do things, if that's what you mean."

"Thank you," Summer breathed, closing her eyes for a moment. "That's a relief to know." She was a moment before she opened her eyes again. "Did Troy talk to you and Abel about what we learned in New York?"

Erica nodded. "Abel intends to relocate the gathering so the Templars cannot find us. I imagine Troy will handle determining who among the coven is passing information to them." She paused. "For some time now I have felt the presence of evil within the coven. Yet no matter how often I scry, I cannot see who it is that betrays us."

"I'm beginning to learn there aren't any easy answers," Summer said. "You can't blame yourself. Whoever has been passing information has obviously been doing it for years. They've learned how to conceal their treachery from everyone. When it involves something terrible, I think people become very good at hiding what they've done. You have to see the evidence of it in other things."

Erica frowned. "What do you mean?"

"You don't just dislike Templars, you hate them," Summer said calmly. "You despise them. When you looked at Michael last night, I saw that in your eyes, and heard it in your voice. Even now, when I say his name, you're digging your fingernails into your skin."

Erica glanced down and saw the oval ends of her nails about to cut into her palms. She immediately relaxed her hands.

"The Templars have been our enemies for centuries, my dear. My reaction is the same as any Wiccan would have."

"You mean any Wiccan woman who had been raped and tortured by a Templar," Summer said gently.

Erica didn't realize she had slapped the younger woman until she felt the sting of it on her palm, the sound still ringing in her ears. Horrified, she shoved herself to her feet and stumbled away. Without warning, hot tears began to fall. She wiped furiously at them, unable to make them stop. A sob welled up from somewhere deep inside, and escaped before her hands could clamp over her mouth.

Before Erica knew what was happening, Summer's arms gently wound around her. Without thinking Erica slumped against her, weeping uncontrollably on her shoulder.

"It's all right," the younger woman murmured, holding her.

They stayed like that for minutes as Erica struggled for control. A part of her life she thought she'd put behind her hovered closer than she'd thought. As her crying stilled, Summer led her back to the bench. They sat in silence, Summer not demanding to know anything, not doing anything but being there with her.

"Ewan warned me never to travel alone," Erica finally said, her voice still trembling a little. "In the old times it was dangerous for a woman to go anywhere by herself, but when we came to this country I saw how different it could be. American women were so independent, and I wanted that. I wanted to be free to do whatever I pleased. So I did, and when nothing bad ever happened to me I became less cautious. I stopped looking over my shoulder. I was so sure that no one noticed me, or suspected me."

"You were caught by a Templar," Summer said.

Erica nodded quickly. "Even when he took me I thought I could reason with him. I wasn't doing anything wrong. I'd just been visiting an old friend. I noticed the Templar was sick, and even offered to help him. I assured him I would do no harm to him, even as he was tying me up." She swallowed against a surge of bile in her throat. "And then he undressed, and ripped my clothes from my body. He beat me until I stopped screaming, and then made me scream again when he forced himself inside me."

From there she told Summer everything. How she had been tortured, and raped, and beaten so many times that she became like a mindless, battered doll. How the Templar had become bored with her indifference, and begun using a knife on her. The terrible wounds he had inflicted. The night he had forgotten to take his blade with him, and how she had nearly cut her wrists to the bone while freeing herself from his bonds.

"It was the middle of the night when I escaped, so no one saw me. I bespelled a homeless woman so I could steal her filthy clothes to cover myself," Erica said. She could almost smell the stink of those pitiful rags. "I called Ewan to come and get me, and hid in a subway tunnel until he did. He wept when he saw what the Templar had done to my face. I didn't tell him about the rest. A few weeks later I discovered I was pregnant with the Templar's child, and I left again. I couldn't kill my unborn child, but I couldn't keep it, either. I arranged an adoption, had the child in secret, and came home alone."

Summer went still. "Aileen is your daughter."

Aghast now, Erica stared at her. "How could you know that? I've never told anyone, not even Ewan. And she doesn't look like me at all."

"She does, when she smiles," Summer assured her. "But it's actually your hands. I noticed it almost right away. The shape and length of your fingers, the square palms, the graceful way they move. Aileen's are identical."

"I knew it was foolish bringing her here once she was ready to join the Wiccans, but I couldn't resist," Erica said, and sighed. "The first time I saw her I realized she was nothing like her father, and all I felt for her was love, and regret." A rush of panic filled her. "Please don't tell her any of this, Summer. For her to know the truth about how she was conceived would only hurt her terribly, and it's hard enough for me to live with the fact that I abandoned her."

"You did no such thing," Summer said, taking her hands and looking intently into her eyes. "You protected her life, and insured that she would have a good home." Her expression softened. "But I won't say anything to her, I promise." She paused and glanced at the house. "In return I'd ask something of you." Her opal eyes gazed deeply into Erica's, her face solemn. "I want your word that you won't do anything to harm Michael."

Erica was stunned. "Of course I won't hurt him. Do you honestly believe that I would try?" Before Summer could answer, Erica held up a hand. Given what she'd just revealed and the way she'd acted, it wasn't unreasonable. "I promise that I won't harm your Templar."

"Troy and I will take Michael over to the old pavilion tomorrow, and we'll stay there," Summer said. "That way Wilson and Aileen can move back to the main house."

Now she felt like a selfish old woman.

"Summer, I never meant to drive you away."

"You haven't," she said quietly, still holding Erica's hands. "It's just that the guys and I need some time alone. Could you tell everyone to keep their distance?"

"Of course. Yes, I can do that. If you're sure."

"Oh, yes." The younger woman's eyes took on a strange glitter. "The three of us need to settle a few things."

CHAPTER SIX

IT ONLY TOOK one day for Michael to get back on his feet. After showering and changing into clean clothes borrowed from Troy, he accompanied him and Summer to the old pavilion.

"I've stocked the pantry and woodpile, and cleaned out the fireplaces," Troy told them as he unloaded their bags from the back of the Jeep. "I'll air out the bedrooms today. Erica gave me a bunch of clean linens we can use."

Michael took a moment to look around at the silver-frosted trees and the icy ground of the meadow.

"You left all this to join the Corps, Pagan? I think you must be addled."

"You being an authority on the subject," Troy said and handed him a box of linens, which

Summer promptly took back out of Michael's hands. "He's not a cripple, lady."

"No, but he's on light duty, Major," she told him firmly, and instead handed Michael her purse. "You're not to pick up anything heavier than this, do you understand me?"

She strode off toward the house.

Troy stood beside Michael and watched the tight curves of her bottom as she crossed the meadow.

"I think we're in a little trouble here, Paladin."

"You do not have to tell me." Michael sighed. "I am holding the purse."

Once they were all inside, Summer took charge of making the rooms more habitable, and in between dusting, opening windows and storing their things, she issued orders like a drill sergeant.

"Troy, would you please turn on the main power to the house so I can turn on lights and get this food in the refrigerator? Michael, sit down over there and sort that box of linens for me. I need a set of king-size sheets, and see if there are any towels for the kitchen as well as the bathroom." She hurried out of the room, and then returned to frown at both of them. "I'm sorry, what are you waiting for? The *spring* solstice?"

Working together it still took most of the day before Summer declared the place barely livable and retreated to the kitchen to prepare an evening meal. Troy silently gestured for Michael to follow him outside to the old barn, where he raided a cooler and took out two bottles of beer.

"It would be whiskey, but she caught me trying to sneak it out of the main house," Troy told him as he twisted off the cap and raised his bottle. "To our lady. Do you think she was a platoon leader in her previous life?"

"To Beauty," Michael replied, clinking his bottle against Troy's. "A combat general, at the very least." As he took a swallow of the beer he looked around the barn's interior. "Did you keep your horses here?"

Troy nodded. "Before automobiles were invented they were the only way we had to get up and down the mountain. My father's favorite punishment was making me shovel manure." He looked down the rows of empty stalls. "I still miss horses. Damn Henry Ford. What do you miss from the old days? Singing in Latin?"

"May pole dances," Michael said, and smiled. "Remember how the prettiest girls in the village would weave flowers in their hair, and wear those skimpy little frocks? And when the sun shone behind them?"

Troy chuckled and raised his bottle again. "To pretty village girls, and their lack of under things." After they both drank he walked over to perch on the anvil where he'd once beaten iron into shoes for their mounts. "While we're alone, we need to discuss the problem we've been avoiding since we got here."

Michael eyed him. "Given that sleeping with both of us is her idea, what do you propose we do about it?"

"We could talk to her, together," Troy said and rubbed the back of his neck. "Point out that while we're both crazy about her, and lust after her, you and I are like brothers."

"I might compare it to incest, or remind her of my vow of celibacy," Michael said but didn't sound too confident. "Only I think she will hit me again." He frowned at Troy. "You have more experience with women. What do you think will persuade her to abandon this unseemly notion?"

"We could both refuse to have sex with her." He saw Michael's expression and grimaced. "Yeah, I know. I'd hold out for maybe thirty seconds before I caved."

The Templar regarded him steadily. "I could leave."

For a moment Troy was tempted to agree, so he could have Summer to himself. Yet even as he thought that, something inside him baulked over the idea of sending Michael away. Even before he'd nearly died protecting them from Alvis, the big man had been like a brother to him. A distant, estranged brother to be sure, but now that he'd left the Templars, that could change. He also had the feeling that if Michael left them, he wouldn't survive long on his own.

"Not happening, Paladin," he told him. "We've dealt with everything else. We can handle this. We just have to think of the right approach."

"You think too much, Pagan," Michael said, and drained his bottle. "There are enough bedrooms here for us to sleep apart. If we are not in her bed, nothing can happen. Just as nothing did last night."

"When I was sleeping on the couch," Troy said, "nothing could."

Michael was probably right. Avoiding a threesome might be as simple as keeping to their own rooms.

"All right," Troy said, "we'll try that. But what if something does happen?"

"Then we put a stop to it," the big man said. "No matter what she says, we are not her possessions, or her playthings. She cannot force us to do anything."

Troy nodded. "Except when she touches the two of us at the same time, and that green light shines in her eyes, and things start getting weird. Then she's definitely in charge."

"I'm glad you've finally realized that," Summer said and walked into the barn. She stopped to survey them. "I don't believe it. Hiding in here so you can drink beer and get out of the housework? What's next? Sneaking off to stripper bars?"

"We were just taking a break," Troy said.

Under his breath in Latin, Michael said, "Do not touch her" and elbowed him.

"What do you need, lady?" Troy asked.

Her eyes narrowed as she studied their faces. "Dinner's ready."

She turned on her heel and walked out.

• • • • •

Summer nibbled on a buttered biscuit as she sat back to watch the guys eat. Making the gigantic *tourtière* for dinner had been a good choice. Not only did the delicious meat and vegetable pie melt in the mouth, it was also very filling. She'd have to remember she now had two very large men to feed.

My men, she thought, feeling a surge of satisfaction blend with a pang of annoyance. She'd watched them sneak out to the barn and followed them, and had heard everything they'd discussed. *Why isn't it as simple for them to accept as it has been for me?*

Once they finished, the men insisted on clearing the table and washing the dishes.

"Go take a shower and relax," Troy told her. "You've earned it. We've got this."

"And we will not drink beer," Michael assured her with a straight face.

Since she was sweaty and dirty from the house cleaning and cooking Summer decided to give in gracefully and went back to the bath in the master suite, which had the only shower in the house. As she passed the king-size bed she paused and ran her hand over the duvet she'd spread over the clean sheets she'd put on it. She'd planned to sleep in it with Troy and Michael, but after what she'd heard them discuss in the barn now it seemed that she would be occupying it alone.

They're right. I can't make them do this if it's not what they want.

Summer went into the bathroom and turned on the shower before she stripped out of her dusty, grimy clothes. When she stepped into the old claw-footed tub and ducked her head under the spray she discovered the water was only lukewarm, but it still felt good on her skin. It grew warmer as she soaped herself, and then hot enough to fill the bathroom with steam. She rinsed herself clean and then stepped out onto the damp tile floor. She reached for the towel she'd tucked on the rack by the window.

Two baleful orange eyes peered in at her, making her scream. As she turned to run, her foot slipped on the damp floor, and she went down so fast she couldn't catch herself. After banging her head on the wall, she ended up sprawled in a heap.

"Beauty."

The door burst open and Michael came in, his mouth flattening as he saw her and bent down to pick her up in his strong arms. He looked over his shoulder at Troy.

"She fell."

"Damn it," Summer said and pressed a hand to her throbbing temple. "When I got out of the shower I saw someone outside the window looking in. I think he was watching me."

"Put her on the bed and stay with her," Troy said.

He slid past them and jerked open the window.

Michael carried her out into the bedroom and lowered her gently onto the duvet. He looked over her shivering, wet body before pulling the other half of the coverlet over her. He down beside her.

"Where are you hurt? Your head?"

"It's just a bump," she said. When Troy came out of the bathroom she sat up. "Did you see him?" He nodded. "Who was it?"

"It's more a what was it," he told her. "Big orange eyes, scary stare, right?" When she nodded Troy smiled a little. "It was an owl. A great horned owl, to be precise. I saw it sitting on a tree branch a few yards from the window."

Summer pressed her hand over her eyes and dropped back on the pillows.

"Great. Perfect. My first Peeping Tom, and it's a bird." She heard Michael cough to cover another sound and lifted her hand. "Oh, you're not laughing at me, are you?"

The Templar's broad shoulders shook for a moment before he told the ceiling, "No."

Troy touched the small bump on the side of her head.

"We'd better put some ice on this."

"I will get it." Michael rose and turned toward

the door.

"Wait." Summer reached out and caught his hand, and saw him go as still as stone. "Michael?" She glanced at Troy, who was now staring down at her, his expression blank, and his eyes filled with green light. "Oh, no, not again. Wait, I'm not doing this, Troy. I swear."

"No." Michael turned around to face her, and looked down at her with the same light filling his eyes. "We are."

Troy pushed the duvet aside to expose her damp, nude body before he regarded Michael. "It's time, Brother."

Summer's eyes widened as both men began stripping out of their clothes.

"Hold it. Stop. You're not in control of yourselves. It's the curse, or some kind of spell, or maybe it's me. But I heard you out in the barn. I know you two don't want to be with me like this, and I respect that." They were ignoring her entirely. "Guys, *please*."

Troy smiled down at her as he unfastened his trousers and let them drop.

"We are yours, lady. But you are not yet ours."

Michael walked around to the other side of the bed and climbed on beside her. He stretched out on her left as Troy lay down on her right. Both men faced her and looked at her, and both of them had huge erections. But they didn't try to touch her.

"What is your desire, Beauty?" Michael asked, his voice dropping to a low rumble. "We are yours to command."

"Okay, if I'm in charge, then I want both of you to do what you want," she told him firmly. "*Only* what you want. So it's okay. You can get dressed now, and leave me, and go sleep in another room by yourself."

Troy exchanged an amused look with Michael. "That is not what we wish to do."

They lay close enough that Summer could feel the warmth their skin radiated. Though her fingers ached to touch them, she knew she couldn't. But in a moment, it wasn't up to her. From the right, Troy cradled her breast with his hand and began laving his tongue over her hardened nipple.

She gasped as a shiver ran down her core.

From the left Michael bent over to give her a deep, wet, open-mouthed kiss, as his hand slipped between her trembling thighs. Summer groaned against his lips as she felt him press his fingers between her folds. He stroked them back and forth in her slick softness.

Troy lifted his head to watch Michael end the kiss. They tugged her upright, turning her, as Troy shifted back against the headboard and Michael knelt behind her.

"She is very wet now, Brother," Michael told him. "She needs to be pleasured."

Troy nodded and tossed him something small. "Thoroughly."

As a deep, aching need began to pound inside her, Summer tried one last time.

"What I need doesn't matter," she said, her voice breathy and pleading. "You're going to hate me for letting this happen. Please, I don't want that. I never wanted that."

"We know this, Beauty," Michael murmured against her ear as he briefly rested his hands on her shoulders. "We will remember it after we are done loving you."

"This is how it always begins, lady." Troy looked up at her, the green light still shining from his eyes. "You have bound us to you. Now we must bind you to us." He brought her hand to his stiff, swollen erection and curled her fingers around his thick shaft. "Your hunger is for both of us. We have what you want. We wish to give you what you need."

"However you need it," Michael told her.

When she glanced back at him she saw he was rolling a condom over his penis. Summer bit her lip, and then moaned as Michael gently eased her onto her hands and knees. Troy twined his fingers in her long, dark waves to cradle the back of her head.

This is going to happen. I can't stop it.

What was worse was, she didn't want it to stop.

Michael's hands gripped her hips as the heavy dome of his sheathed penis nudged against her sex. "Open your lips for him, Beauty. I want to see you put your mouth on him as I fill your sweet little pussy."

"Give it all to her, Brother," Troy told him as he guided Summer's mouth to his straining cockhead. "As deep and hard as she needs it." He watched her touch her lips to the smooth dome, and smiled. "Take it, lady. Open for me. Suck my hard cock while my brother fucks you from behind."

Summer's heart hammered in her chest as she parted her lips to take the tip of Troy's penis in her mouth. She felt Michael pushing as he lodged his heavy cockhead inside her. The sensations of being penetrated by both of her men at once made something dark and luscious streak through her. It curled in her breasts and pooled in her lower belly. She moaned around the girth gliding against her tongue, as Michael forged deeper inside her.

"So beautiful," Troy murmured. He gathered her hair and held it away from her face so he could watch her. "And so hungry for us."

Michael grunted as he worked another inch into her clenching opening. "We have made her wait too long. She will need us for the rest of the night."

"Is that your desire, sweet lady?" Troy crooned as he reached down to fondle her breast. "To be fucked by us until dawn? To have us ravish you over and over until none of us can move?"

Michael bent over and kissed her neck as he pushed into her to his root. "It will be our pleasure, Beauty."

Summer's eyelids fluttered as the men got down to business and began thrusting into her mouth and pussy with smooth, firm strokes. As she bobbed her head up and down, working her mouth over Troy's thickness, Michael pumped in and out of her in the same rhythm. Her slick tissues fluttered as the need to climax swelled inside her. It grew so huge that she wrenched her mouth away from Troy's penis and cried out, driving herself back against Michael to lodge him as deeply as she could inside her body.

"She needs release," Troy said, and clamped his hands over her breasts, massaging them roughly as he nodded to Michael. "Make her come, Brother."

Michael's big hand pressed between Summer's legs from the front, the pad of his thumb on her erect clit. He stroked it as he thrust even deeper.

Summer exploded with ecstasy, her whole body shaking uncontrollably as the pleasure poured through her. She clutched at Troy, and saw his hand tightening around his penis. She dropped down to take him with her lips, sucking him as his shaft swelled and then pumped jet after jet of his seed into her mouth. At the exact same moment Michael uttered a rumbling growl and shoved deep, his big frame shuddering as he came.

Mine, Summer thought, and surrendered to a second orgasm. It tore through her mind and body. Even as she writhed and quaked, the blinding climax whisked her off to a place where everything was warm, and lovely, and safe, where she lay cradled between her two loves like the most beautiful thing in the world.

That is what you are to them, a sweet voice murmured. *The most rare, and beautiful, and precious of all things they will ever know.*

They fell together onto the bed in a tangle of legs and arms, Michael against her back, and Troy pressed to her front. The two men stroked her with their hands and murmured nonsense to her as she slowly floated back down from that strange Elysium to the reality they shared.

"This is how it's supposed to be," she whispered, too tired now to do anything but cuddle with her lovers. "I just wish it could be forever."

A hard hand gently caressed her cheek, and one of them said, "For us, it is."

Summer slipped away, but she didn't dream, and she didn't remember anything. In the darkness she found only herself, enveloped in the warmth and smell of her men. For the first time in her life, she had finally found the place where she could lay her head. She could rest without fear, and know that the burdens she carried would never again be hers alone.

Birdsong stirred her from sleep, and when Summer opened her eyes she saw Troy's brilliant blue gaze, clear of the green light. Dark whiskers shadowed his jaw, and when she glanced down she saw he was naked and aroused.

"So that didn't go according to plan," she said, and waited for the disgust to show in his face. But when it didn't she wondered if she had ruined them instead of bringing them together. "I didn't do this on purpose, Troy. I tried to stop you."

"I know it wasn't you," he said softly. "I remember everything that happened."

His gaze shifted past her for a moment, then he kissed her brow and rose from the bed.

Summer wanted to call him back as she watched him gather his clothes and walk out, but nothing she could say would change what had happened. She turned to see Michael watching Troy leave as well, and caught her breath as he climbed off the bed.

"Michael, please don't be angry with me. I am so sorry."

The big man gave her an odd look before he bent over to kiss her in the same spot that Troy had.

"Go back to sleep, Beauty. There is nothing to forgive."

CHAPTER SEVEN

MICHAEL LEANED BACK against the barn to watch Troy, who was chopping wood with such ferocity the chips flew through the air like wooden shrapnel. The warlock paused to wipe away the sweat dripping from his brow.

"I thought you said you'd already stocked the woodpile," Michael said.

Troy surveyed the amount of short logs he'd split.

"Haven't you learned yet not to piss off a man using an axe?"

"Is that what I am doing?" Michael pushed away from the barn and walked over to pick up a length of oak and set it upright on the chopping stump. "She is blaming herself. I saw tears in her eyes before I left her."

Troy nodded and handed him the hatchet.

"Like she said last night, it's not what she wanted."

"I wanted it," Michael said and hefted the blade. He brought it down, splitting the oak with such force the two pieces soared away from the stump to land in the grass several feet away. "And so did you."

They took turns chopping away until an enormous pile of split wood surrounded them and there were no more logs left. Troy buried the blade of the hatchet in the stump and turned his head to glance back at the house.

"I know what you are thinking," Michael warned him. "I can hear it. I have since last night."

"Same here." The warlock dragged his hand through his disheveled dark hair. "But I still can't pick up on what's in her head."

"I do not think we are meant to." Michael shared his frustration for a moment before he added, "She would not keep us out. It is the power. It is somehow independent of her, like its own entity. We should be wary of it."

"You don't feel wary of anything," Troy told him. "Your head is like a kid in a candy shop." His mouth hitched. "Okay, so is mine."

"I thought the night I saved her from Gideon

was the happiest of my life," Michael told him. "Then I took her to my bed, and knew true bliss. In all this time I have never known anything that was half so fine and beautiful and joyful. I thought nothing would ever again make me that happy."

"Until last night," Troy said.

Michael nodded. "It is the same for you. No matter how many forests you chop down." He felt his cock harden as he recalled seeing Summer's mouth gliding along the warlock's shaft. "I could feel her tongue rubbing against you as she sucked you."

Troy nodded slowly. "When you plowed into her, I felt her tighten around you. She was so hot and wet I nearly came."

"We shared the sex as well as her," Michael said. "Do you think it will it be that way every time we take her?"

"I don't know," the warlock admitted. "Maybe we should test it again, see what happens. Right now."

Michael grinned. "After we bathe her together."

As soon as they entered the house, however, Troy frowned.

"She's not here." He turned around until he spotted a scrap of paper on the table, which he picked up and read. "She's gone for a walk. Hopefully not off the edge of a cliff."

"We can track her," Michael assured him. "Everything she touches grows green again."

Outside the house he was proven correct. A subtle path of frost melting into patches of tiny green grass shoots wound through the trees. They followed it until Michael picked up the sound of a rushing stream.

"She's up there," Troy told him and nodded in the direction of the northern tree line.

Michael had seen countless beautiful places during the many centuries he had walked the earth, but Troy's waterfall was one of the most spectacular. Partially frozen by the cold, the water pouring over the green and black rocks sparkled in the sunlight. It fell like a perpetual cascade of tiny diamonds to froth in the ice-edged pool below. There too sat Summer, her arms around her knees as she watched the water dance and ripple across the pond toward her, her long hair curtaining each side of her face. One of Troy's flannel shirts covered her body, but her legs were bare and Michael suspected she wore nothing under it.

Troy motioned for him to make a flanking approach, but before they reached her she said,

"Stop with the stealth. I heard you as soon as you came out of the trees."

Michael walked down and crouched beside her, while Troy did the same on her other side.

"We came to apologize," Michael said.

She picked up a stone and tossed it into the froth. "You mean, you ran out of wood to chop."

"We're sorry," Troy said, as he reached out and sent a surge of his power into the waterfall, freezing it solid and silencing it. "We know last night was due to circumstances beyond anyone's control."

She stood up and began unbuttoning the shirt.

"Would you make the water in the pool a little warmer, please?"

"Why are you still angry?" Troy asked as the ice around the edges of the pond melted away, and steam began to rise from the water's surface. "Michael and I are fine with last night. We'll just write it off to a random magic surge."

"Random. Right." She took off his shirt and tossed it in his face. "You're an ass, do you know that? And the same goes for you," she told Michael before she dove naked into the water.

Michael frowned as he watched her swim away from them. "That went well."

"I like your idea of bathing her better," Troy

said. He stood and began unbuckling his belt. "First one who reaches her gets to kiss her senseless."

Michael didn't bother to undress but dove in. He heard a shouted protest and a splash behind him as he swam out to Summer, who turned around and scowled at him.

"We made our peace with what happened," he told her as he touched bottom and held out his arms. "But because we're men we don't know how to put that in the words you want to hear."

"Then it's a good thing I love you as much as I do," Summer said, and swam to him. She curled her arms around his neck as she kissed him, her lips wet and faintly swollen and as sweet as honey.

Troy surfaced beside them. "You cheated."

Michael ended the kiss to reply with, "You did not say I had to be naked."

Summer released him and moved to the warlock, giving him a heartfelt kiss before she glanced at Michael.

"I want to make love with both of you again, and I think we can without the magic interfering. I want you to know how it can be when it's just the three of us. But if you still don't want it, then go back to the house and leave me alone."

"She's still pretty pissed off," Troy told Michael.

He shrugged. "She have no wood to chop." He gazed down into his Beauty's furious eyes. "We came here for the same reason. We want to make love to you."

"As opposed to calling it incest, or reminding me of your vow of celibacy?" she asked. "Why the change of heart now?"

"We love you," Michael said simply. He kissed her cheek, the tip of her nose and the space between her brows. "And now we know that we also belong to you. Together."

"Always," Troy told her as he kissed her other cheek, and the lobe of her ear, and her temple.

Summer slid her hand around Michael's neck, took a deep breath. She did the same to Troy with her other hand. She watched their eyes and then sighed.

"No green light this time, guys."

"Oh, we can still make magic happen, my lovely one," Michael assured her, slipping around her and pulling her back to his broad chest. He lifted her out of the water and cupped her breasts as Troy moved in to latch onto one beaded nipple.

Michael lazily caressed her other breast as he watched the warlock suckle her. She shivered as her bottom moved against the bulge of his thickened shaft. He reached down, opened his trousers and freed it. He pressed the throbbing length into the tight cleft of her buttocks, stroking his shaft over the tight pucker between them. He imagined how it would feel as Troy worked his big cock in her from the front.

The warlock lifted his head. "We don't have any condoms," he reminded Michael.

"Later, then." He picked up on Troy's thoughts and nodded toward the frozen waterfall. "Behind there."

As Troy melted the waterfall, which began noisily rushing down to splash them, Michael felt power stir within him as well. It flowed from Beauty and from Troy, but also from him. Though for a moment it occurred to him he ought to be alarmed, it felt as natural as being with the two of them.

He channeled the power through the pool and into the rocks behind the cascade. A warm golden light blended with the silvery blue of Troy's magic, turning the water a brilliant green before it faded away.

Summer ducked under the water and swam toward it, hoisting herself out onto the rocks. "What is this?"

Michael went after her, hauling himself out of the water at the same time Troy did. "I think it is a place where we can play," Michael said.

He'd somehow formed a cave in the rock. As they entered she turned around to take in the smooth, sparkling walls.

"Amethyst," she murmured. She touched the glass-smooth surface and smiled. "Michael, it's beautiful."

A thick carpet of green moss spread out beneath their feet, and covered a raised stretch of rock. Summer went to it, first sitting and then reclining on it as she watched them.

"I'm cold," she teased.

He and Troy quickly stripped out of their wet clothes, and went to lay on either side of her, pressing her between them, their wet bodies growing hot as the three sides of their desires came together into one urgent, aching wanting.

"We'll keep you warm," Troy murmured against the side of her throat.

Summer clasped her hands around their throbbing shafts as they fondled her and sucked her breasts and played with the little jewel-box of her sex. Michael felt again the wicked delight she gave Troy as well as him, and he couldn't resist penetrating her with his fingers and pumping them in and out.

"My turn to play with this pretty pussy, I think,"

Troy told him, shifting down to wedge his shoulders between her thighs. He began kissing her belly, his hands sliding under her hips to grip her bottom.

Michael rose to straddle her upper torso, and rubbed his thumb across her lips as he fisted his own swollen girth. "I want to see your mouth on me this time, Beauty."

She smiled up at him, and then began kissing her way up the length of his shaft, licking and nipping at him until he thought he would come just from those playful kisses. He groaned as she engulfed his cockhead with her hot, wet mouth, sucking steadily on him as she wrapped her fingers around the base of his shaft and squeezed.

"Yes," he breathed, watching her lips tugging on him.

He shifted to brace himself over her so he could gently thrust in and out of her mouth. The feel of her tongue curling around him made his thighs coil and his balls tighten, but so did tasting the sweetness of her in his own mouth. He could feel Troy's tongue stroking her little pearl, and the softness of her breasts under the warlock's hands as he reached up to tease her nipples. He felt her climax rising in her, and his own pleasure racing to keep pace with it. When she came, he jerked and poured his cream into her, groaning deep and shaking hard until the last pulse left him.

Michael rolled to one side as Troy knelt between her thighs, and brought her hand to his twitching penis. He used it with his to stroke his length once, twice and then held it as his seed jetted out onto her belly and breasts.

Summer snuggled between them as they lay down with her, and Michael thought he had never seen her look so content. When he wrapped his arm around her waist, Troy stretched his across her breasts, and the sight of their strong arms on her body made his heart clench.

This is why I came into being, Michael thought. *Not to be a warrior-priest. To be hers, and his.*

When he glanced over at Troy, the warlock nodded slowly.

• • • • •

Lachlan watched from the cover of the trees until Troy, his witch, and their Templar retreated behind the waterfall. Seeing both men chase after the little whore should have disgusted him, but instead he had gotten the biggest hard-on he'd had in years. It made him limp away, angry with himself for being aroused by a bunch of perverted breeders, until he had to stop and unzip his jeans and take it out. His cockhead was so engorged it was almost purple. The moment he touched it, he swore and shook, as his semen pumped out of him onto the ground.

Holding his cock and leaning back against a tree made Lachlan feel ridiculous, but when he heard footsteps crunching through the brush he had to scramble to tuck himself in and zip up before Wilson appeared.

"Hey," Lachlan said. "What are you doing out here?"

"Looking for that witch," Wilson muttered, his expression dark with resentment. "My father wants to talk to her. What are you doing?"

"Keeping an eye on them." He nodded in the direction of the waterfall. "They like to fuck outdoors, apparently, and they're doing her together now."

"I guess that's why they moved out here," Wilson said and turned and headed toward Troy's house. He glanced at Lachlan when he caught up to him. "I'll just wait at the old place until they come back."

"I'll keep you company," Lachlan said, trying to sound casual, and then had to skid to a stop when Wilson turned on him. "What? I don't have anything better to do anyway. I don't want to watch them at it."

"You need to give it up, Lach," Wilson said, and put a hand on his shoulder. "Aileen is my wife, and we're having a baby, and that's all I want. I know you've had a thing for me for years, but it has to stop. You need to find someone of your own who can make you happy."

"You mean I need to find another gay boy," Lachlan muttered sullenly. "What if I don't want to? What if I'm willing to wait?"

Now pity filled the other man's dark eyes. "It's never going to happen, man."

"You don't know." Desperate now, Lachlan stepped closer. "You've never tried it. You could, with me. You don't have to do anything." He reached down and cupped Wilson's crotch. "Just once, let me do it to you. Just so you know for sure."

"That's just it," Wilson said and gently removed his hand. "I do know for sure. I love Aileen. She's my whole life, and there will never be anyone else for me. If you can't accept that, then you need to leave the coven. I'm sorry."

Lachlan's eyes burned as he watched the only man he would ever love turn his back on him and walk away. His hand shook as he pulled his mobile from his pocket, and blindly thumbed it until the speed dial screen came up. Once he hit the number he lifted the phone to his ear. He blinked back the hot tears threatening to fall.

"Yeah, it's me again," he said as he checked his watch. "We need to talk."

CHAPTER EIGHT

ON THE WAY back to the house Troy spotted Wilson's pick-up truck sitting beside his Jeep, and eyed Michael.

"My brother's here."

"Yes, and I can tell how delighted you are," Michael said and wrapped his hand around Summer's. "Should we make ourselves scarce while you talk with him?"

"No," Summer said before Troy could reply. "We're together now, and they're going to have to accept it. Besides, he's the one intruding on us, and I don't trust him."

Troy produced a humorless smile. "My brother is a jerk, but he's not a traitor. He'd never endanger Aileen or the baby." He gave Summer a direct look. "Whatever he says or does, do not go green-eyed lady on him."

"All right, but if he punches you in the face again, I'm going to let Michael deal with him." She patted the Templar's chest. "Right, big guy?"

"I will crush him like a bug," he assured her gravely before he winked at Troy.

Wilson didn't wait for them to come into the house, but stepped outside and folded his arms as they walked up to the front porch.

"A little cold to go swimming, don't you think?"

"I'm a water elemental," Troy reminded him. "Which is the same as having a heated swimming pool wherever we go. What do you want, Wilson?"

"Father sent me to bring you back to the pavilion. Something's come up with the gathering." He nodded at Summer. "He also wants to speak with her." His eyes shifted to Michael. "You're not welcome."

"Neither are you, but here you are," Troy said. "Go back and tell Abel we'll be there tonight, after dinner."

"He wants you now—no, you know what? Fine. I'll tell him."

Wilson stalked to his truck and drove off.

Troy watched him go. "Trouble."

"Do you not have phones?" Michael asked.

"The Coven Master never uses them. He also

hates cameras, computers and most other types of technology."

He saw Summer was shivering and used his ability to pull the water from their clothes, sending it in a mist to settle down over the meadow.

She kissed his cheek. "You should have been a dry-cleaner."

Michael lifted his hand and touched the same spot on his face. "Keep doing that and you won't be wearing any clothes."

Summer chuckled. "I need food first."

While she went off to the kitchen to make them sandwiches and warm up a pot of soup Erica had sent with them, Troy built a fire in the old dining room. He showed Michael the effect Summer had had on his mother's old furniture, which was still covered with tiny twigs and new green leaves.

Michael crouched down to peer at the legs of one chair. "They have rooted themselves through the floor, did you notice that?"

Troy nodded. "I don't know whether I should leave them be or take them outside and plant them." He sat back on his haunches to watch the first flames of the fire flare up. "After this little chat with my father, all of us may have to leave,

Paladin. I'll have to resign from the Magus Corps, too. Any thoughts on where we should go?"

"Canada," Michael said without hesitation. He straightened and glanced at him. "We can try to track down Beauty's people."

"I think she may be from Quebec," Troy told him. "I went there once on assignment, and one of the witches from the local coven made that same kind of meat pie that Summer fixed for us last night. It's a specialty of theirs."

"The Templars are headquartered out of Montreal," Michael said slowly. "But they have a priory in Quebec, too."

"We're not going to Canada," Summer said as she carried in a tray filled with food. "We're staying here, with Troy's family. They're our best defense against the order, and I still need to find out who I am and why I was brought here." Before Troy could say anything she added, "I'll talk to your father, as a gesture of good will. Maybe I can even persuade him to see that we're not a threat to the coven."

"I hope you can," Troy said. "But I wouldn't count on it."

• • • • •

Before they left the old house, Summer changed into a pretty red dress Aileen had given her, and put up her hair in an attractive chignon. Red lipstick from a very chic woman in Central Park added the perfect touch of color to her face, and emphasized the rainbow colors of her eyes.

Michael appeared behind her in the mirror's reflection. "You look like a siren."

"Thank you, kind sir, and don't even think about it," she added as she saw his hands lift. "Later, when we come back, you can touch whatever you want."

"Does that go for me, too?" Troy asked as he looked in on them.

She nodded briskly. "Just remember to raid our room before we come back. We're going to need condoms. All of them. And maybe plan a trip into town soon because those aren't going to last us very long."

Michael dropped a kiss on her shoulder, and Troy chuckled.

When they arrived at the pavilion, Abel was waiting for them. After nodding to Troy and pointedly ignoring Michael he said to Summer, "If you'll join me in the library, I'd like a word with you."

"Come on, Paladin," Troy said as he brushed

past his father and headed to the rooms they'd used.

After giving her a warning glance, Michael followed him. Though she wanted nothing more than to follow the two of them, she accompanied Abel.

Summer saw Erica pacing in the kitchen as she passed it to go to the library with Abel, and noticed Lachlan doing almost the same thing at the other end of the corridor.

"Is something wrong, Coven Master?"

He ushered her inside and closed the door before he answered her.

"I've informed the other coven leaders of the Templar plan to attack the winter solstice gathering, and we've agreed on a new site for the celebration. I also told them about offering Michael Charbon sanctuary. They agreed that it was foolhardy of me to harbor a Templar traitor, but they will abide by whatever I decide to do with him."

Summer watched his face. "So what have you decided?"

"It's time for me to step down as Coven Master, and I intend to do so at the gathering," he said, surprising her. He walked over and poured whiskey from a decanter into two short glasses.

"Troy has obviously grown disenchanted with his service to the Magus Corps, and he has been thoroughly trained to take my place. It's time for him to assume leadership of this coven." He brought the glasses over to her and offered her one. "Which you will persuade him to do."

Summer didn't touch the glass. "And if I don't?"

"Your friend the Templar may be immortal," Abel said, and took a sip of his whiskey. "But he is not invulnerable. Accidents happen all the time."

Summer felt her temper spike. "Are you threatening to hurt Michael if I don't talk Troy into taking over as Coven Master?"

"I don't make threats, my dear." Abel gave her an unpleasant smile. "Only remember that your friend is a Templar among Wiccans. His kind have slaughtered our people for centuries. If the worst happens, no one will mourn his passing but you."

That was when Summer knew she had to walk out, or she might very well do something she'd regret. She turned on her heel and went to the door, jerking it open to find Lachlan standing just outside.

"Did you get all that?" she demanded. "Or do I need to repeat anything for you?"

Before Abel's apprentice could reply Wilson appeared.

"What's going on? Aileen's trying to rest."

"Your father just needed to threaten me," Summer told him before she headed for the room she'd shared with Troy, and found him and Michael packing up some clothes in a duffel. "We need to go, guys. Right now."

Lachlan and Wilson followed them out of the main house, but it was Lachlan who got in Summer's face.

"Troy is never going to be Coven Master. It's Wilson's place. If Troy tries to take over the coven I'll tell everyone about you perverts."

Wilson frowned at him. "That's enough."

Troy shouldered his younger brother aside and stepped up to Lachlan. "Piss off, you whiny little toad."

Michael tugged Summer back out of the way. "We should go," he said.

He repeated that in a louder voice for Troy's benefit, but the warlock was now arguing with his brother.

Summer saw Abel and Erica come out of the main house and felt the clash of different powers swelling in the air.

"Michael, get him," she said. "We need to go,

now."

Just as Michael stepped up beside Troy, Lachlan bunched his fist and launched it at Troy's face, only to have it smack into Michael's big palm.

"I think you should go and cool off, little man," the Templar told Lachlan.

But then Wilson pushed Michael away. At that, Troy launched a fist at Wilson that resulted in his brother sprawled on the ground and holding a bloody nose.

Lachlan bellowed in rage and pulled out a dagger as he hurled himself at Troy, but came up short as Michael stepped in front of the warlock.

"Oh, right, I forgot," the shorter man said as he backed away from the Templar. "You two are boyfriends."

"What are you talking about?" Abel demanded.

His apprentice nodded at Troy and Michael.

"They've been screwing the little whore together, Master. At the same time. I saw them doing it last night."

Troy closed his eyes briefly. "The owl."

Lachlan threw down his blade and strode off into the night while Abel stalked up to Troy.

"Is this true? Are you and the Templar sharing the witch between you? Without an initiation, or a ceremony, or any pledge between you?" When

Troy said nothing Abel stepped back, an ugly red color flooding his face. "It is a sacrilege."

"No, it's none of your business," Troy told him. "We're adults."

Michael caught Summer's eye. "Get in the car," he said under his breath.

"You're fools," Troy's father ranted. "I could expel all of you from the coven for this."

As Michael reached for Troy's arm, Summer turned and stepped toward the Jeep, but she didn't get far.

A soft, wet thud rocked her back on her heels, just as a sharp pain in her side made her gasp. She looked down to see the hilt of a dagger sticking out of her pretty red dress. A dark stain blossomed around it, spreading on the delicate fabric. For a moment, she could only stare. With a strange sadness, she realized the dress was ruined. Only when she started to sway, did it occur to her to scream for help. But she couldn't draw in enough air to breathe, let alone call for Troy or Michael. Instead something seized her, and jerked her into the shadows.

Summer saw trees blur past as she was dragged through the forest, but by who or what she didn't know. She scraped over rough roots, then through brambles and low branches. Pain shot through her as the blade was forced deeper. Warmth gushed down her hip and over her thigh. Though she struggled, she couldn't resist. Even in the darkness, she knew that no hands gripped her. There wasn't anyone to fight. As dizziness made her vision swim, she realized it had to be magic.

Suddenly, the forest gave way to rocky ground, and the edge of a cliff appeared. Terror gripped her as she recognized the icy gleam of the river below. With everything in her, she wanted to scream, to cry, to do something, anything at all—but it was no use. The magic released her with a final shove, and she sailed over the edge and down.

BETRAYED

SILVER WOOD COVEN BOOK FOUR

By Hazel Hunter

CHAPTER ONE

SURROUNDED BY ANGRY Wiccans outraged over his presence, Michael Charbon again considered leaving Silver Wood. Although he had repeatedly risked his life over the centuries to protect the innocent among them from the vicious wrath of his Templar brotherhood, to the pagans he would forever be an enemy witch-hunter.

"You take that Templar, scum lover of yours," Abel Atwater bellowed at his oldest son Troy, "and you get the hell off my mountain."

"He's not my lover," Troy shouted back, "and it's not your mountain."

The coven had been in an uproar ever since Troy had brought him to their hidden stronghold in the White Mountains of New Hampshire, so that Michael could recover from a near-lethal wound. He'd almost died shielding Troy, son of the coven's master, from a Templar assassin—not that it mattered to them. They certainly didn't care that he'd also wanted to protect Summer, the mysterious witch he'd discovered living homeless and without her memory in Central Park. Despising and fearing him was all he could ever expect from the pagans, especially now that they knew that he and Troy had become Summer's lovers.

Michael saw that hatred in Abel's eyes now, and knew there would never be peace between Troy and his father unless he left Silver Wood. He put a hand on the warlock's shoulder to draw him back, and then nearly doubled over as a sharp, fierce jolt stabbed into his side. He clutched at the newly-healed wound, expecting to feel a dagger buried to the hilt, but found nothing there.

At the same time Troy grunted, his hand pressed to the same spot on his abdomen, and staggered away from him. When the contact between them was broken the pain vanished.

"Paladin," Troy said. The man's brilliant blue eyes darkened with fury and pain as he looked over his shoulder. "It's Summer."

Michael looked at where their lover had been standing only a moment before, and saw only a splatter of something wet on the ground. He swore as he ran with Troy over to the patch of blood-stained dirt.

Abel strode up behind them. "I'm not done with you, boy."

"You are now." Michael stepped in his path before he could reach Troy. "Walk away."

The Coven Master lowered his head, and his breath came out of his nostrils as white as steam in the cold air, making him look like a bull ready to charge.

"You dare tell me what to do on my land, you bastard?"

"Walk away," Michael said again, dropping his voice low so no one else heard, "or I will show you what Templar scum like me can do."

Abel gave him an ugly smile. "This isn't finished."

He turned on his heel and stalked back into the main house.

Troy knelt down and touched the dark stain before he peered at the ground beyond it.

"Fresh marks," he said, pointing to where the soil was disturbed.

Michael followed them to the tree line, where he found another smear of blood and several long, golden brown hairs caught on bark at the base of a pine tree. He carefully pulled the hairs out of the bark and showed them to the warlock.

Frost rapidly spread out on the ground around Troy's feet as his power spiked.

"The bastard dragged her."

Knowing their gentle lover had been stabbed and treated like a carcass made Michael shift into the calm, cold focus he employed in battle. He studied the ground until he found more marks.

"He took her this way. Come."

They followed the trail into the woods, where it led them straight to the edge of a cliff overlooking the river. Troy stared over the edge while Michael crouched down and placed his hand on the soil where four faint furrows scored the surface.

"She was still alive when he threw her over." He gestured at the marks. "She tried to dig her fingers in here."

"We have to get down there. Too far to jump, and it'll take half an hour to climb down." Troy pointed down at a large flat rock in the center of the river. "Can you keep that level?"

Michael stared at it. It was one thing to channel the strange power he derived from the three of them, as when he'd created the amethyst cave. It was another thing by himself. But Beauty's life depended on it.

Michael nodded. "I can try."

Troy spread his hands, creating an arc of silvery-blue power. He sent it hurtling down at the river. It sank into the rushing waters and drew them up in a spout along with the stone. He raised the twisting column to the edge of the cliff.

"Now," he shouted over the sound of the roaring currents.

Michael leapt onto the stone, crouching to press his hands to the wet, cold surface. Whether it was sheer will or the connection he still felt to Troy, the giant stone stayed level. He nodded to the warlock, who jumped onto it with him.

"Easy," Michael warned him as the column of water began to descend back to the river. "If you knock me off, you will take a very cold bath."

"Water is my friend, remember, not yours," Troy said. He shifted the column to curl over and drop the stone on the bank, where he leapt off and looked downstream. "Gods. Even as cold as it is, she may have drowned by now."

"No," Michael muttered. There was a flutter of red in the water a hundred yards away. He pointed to it. "There. She is there."

He started running toward her, but before he could reach her body Troy used his power to pull her from the water. He deposited her limp form on the bank.

"*Beauty*," Michael whispered.

He dropped to his knees next to her. He caught his breath as he saw the gashes on her face and neck, and the strange angle of her left arm and leg. From a tear in her dress he could see the knife wound in her side. But the next thing he realized was far worse.

"She's not breathing."

Troy knelt on the other side, his mouth tight. He gently touched her throat.

"She has a pulse," he breathed, his face a mix of relief and confusion. "It's strong and normal."

"Why isn't she breathing?" Michael demanded. He lifted her chin to begin resuscitation, but as soon as he touched her he felt the strange power she possessed flooding into him. Then it drew energy from him back into Summer. "Pagan."

"I feel it," Troy said. "Don't resist." Troy's eyes narrowed as Summer's body began to glow with a misty green light. "Gods. It's happening again."

Michael flinched as her broken arm made a cracking sound and then slowly straightened. Her leg did the same as the lacerations marring her face and throat began to shrink and then disappeared. Only when her body was whole again did she gasp, and then choke out a mouthful of river water.

"Turn her on her side," Michael said, "and keep your hands on her."

Once she had coughed out all the water in her lungs, Summer went limp again. But the light enveloping her body continued to grow brighter, until it was almost blinding.

"What is this?" Michael asked as he watched the red fabric of her dress darken and shrink. It crisped and then fell away from her skin like so much ash. "Why is it doing this to her?"

"I don't know!" Troy said.

He squinted and turned his head away.

Michael managed to keep watching. Through the light he saw dark green marks appear on her naked body. They stretched into scrolling lines down the length of her torso. Once they had covered every inch of her skin from her collar bones to her hips the light faded, leaving only the marks on her flesh.

Troy checked her pulse, and they could both easily see the movement of her diaphragm. Despite the strange markings, they both exhaled in relief. But as they stared down at her, Michael recognized what they were seeing—writing. He exchanged a worried look with Troy.

"You know what that is?" Troy asked.

"Capetian, one of the oldest forms of French Wiccan writing," Michael said, scowling. "I have not seen it in centuries. I do not believe it has been used since the Templars drove the covens out of southern France."

"Can you translate it?"

Michael cocked his head to read one line that ran along her forearm.

"True, without falsehood," he read. "Certain when uncertain, by will I invoke–"

"Stop," Troy ordered, and spread his hand over the words. "That's a truth spell. If you read the rest you'll have me telling you what I really think of you."

Michael grunted as he examined more of the lines.

"There are more like that which mention water and earth and time. They all invoke some form of protection." His gaze shifted to a group of words set apart from all the others on her right shoulder, and then peered at them again. *"Troy Atwater."*

"I know my name," Troy told him.

"Yes, and it's written on her skin, here," he said, and pointed to it. "It says you are marked to be her sentinel mate, along with another name: *Michele Charbonneau.*"

419

As the warlock leaned closer, the writing of the second name blurred and formed a new name.

Troy glanced up at him. "Well? What does it say now?"

Michael dragged his hand over the back of his head. "It's my name. Michael Charbon."

"So someone incised our names on Summer in a form of Wiccan that hasn't been used since the tenth century." The warlock shook his head. "This night just keeps getting better and better." He shot Michael a look. "That other name, it had to be your birth name." He glanced back at the stone they'd used. "You have a Wiccan ability, and you've always been more like us than the Templars," he said excitedly. "Michael, I think they took you as an infant from a Wiccan family. They used to do that a lot back then."

"It does not matter now," Michael said, shaking his head as though that would help to clear it. "It is ancient history. We have to take care of her." Michael touched one of the words scrawled along her side. "These are tattoos, not cuts. I have touched every inch of her, and even if she had managed a concealment spell I would have felt the scars, and so would have you."

"She's starting to shiver," Troy said quietly. He took off his shirt and draped it over her as

Michael lifted her in his arms. "We'll take her back to the pavilion. Aileen and Erica should have a look at her–"

"No," Michael said flatly. "Whoever attacked her is among the coven. There was no one else on the mountain but your people."

"And that Templar spy, Baldwin, whoever he is," Troy countered. "I should go back and see who's missing, or if any of them saw someone near her."

"No. We cannot trust any of them." He cradled Beauty's soft but shivering body closer to his chest. "For now we will take her to your house, and tend to her ourselves. When she awakens, she can tell me who attacked her, and I will attend to him."

The warlock smiled grimly. "You're going to have to wait your turn, Paladin."

"You'll both have to wait," Summer whispered weakly.

Troy jerked his gaze down, but Michael realized the warlock was careful not to touch her. When Michael looked down, Beauty's dark opal eyes were open. They were tired and underlined with dark circles, but they were open. Relief flooded through him.

"Beauty?"

Slowly she looked up at him.

"You'll have to wait," she whispered, barely audible. "I didn't see anyone."

· · · · ·

Some hours later Summer sighed as Michael finished combing out the last of the snarls from her long hair.

"You should have quit the Templars and become a lady's maid."

The big man grunted as he parted her hair in three sections.

"It would be too hard to explain why I never age. Besides that, the only lady I am interested in caring for is you."

"Then you have your hands full."

As he braided her hair, Summer watched the flames dance in the bedroom fireplace, and wondered why she was so calm and content. She'd been like this since the men had brought her back to Troy's house. She didn't understand the attack or how she had survived it. Then there were the words that now covered her upper body. They didn't hurt or itch, but felt as if someone had wrapped her in a very thin, silky lace. Yet as shocking as her ordeal had been, it seemed utterly disconnected from her own experience, as if she'd read about it, or watched it happen to someone else.

"Why do you think my people tattooed me with these spells?" she asked Michael. "Could they have somehow known I'd lose my memory? And why hide the words until now?"

"I am not certain that anyone could have done this to you," he said, and tied the end of her braid neatly with a string before resting his hands on her shoulders. "The lines of the marks are as thin and delicate as true hand-writing."

She ran her fingertips over the writing on her forearm. "Someone had to do it."

"Perhaps." He covered her hand with his. "Or it may have been the green power within you."

They'd already told her what had happened after they'd fished her out of the water, and now she frowned.

"Michael, if anything does happen to me–"

"Shhh." He pulled her back against his chest, wrapping his strong arms around her as he kissed the top of her head. "Pagan and I won't allow this killer to come near you again."

Summer nestled against him, and sighed as the bedroom door opened. Troy came in with a tray filled with sandwiches and steaming mugs of tea.

"With you as my lady's maid, and Troy as my cook, I may never want to leave this room."

"I don't cook," the warlock told her as he parked the tray on the bed beside her and Michael. "I make sandwiches. Damned fine sandwiches, if I say so myself, but until you're feeling better, anything more involved will have to be filched from the coven or picked up in town." He picked up one mug and offered it to her. "Yours. I want you to drink all of it."

She took a sniff. "Well, it certainly smells pretty."

"It is," Troy said. "Chamomile, clove, saffron and rose petals, with a little honey to sweeten it."

Summer recalled what Erica had told her about certain tea blends the Wiccans used.

"Herbs for calming, something else, protecting and loving." She took a sip and sighed. "Very nice. What's the clove for?"

"Keeps the hostiles away," Troy said and handed Michael a mug of coffee. He sat on the edge of the bed and shared the sandwiches with them. "Eat," he said when Summer only nibbled at hers. "You want to grow up and be a big strong witch someday, don't you?"

"I might not be big compared to you two, but I'm strong enough." She handed the rest of her sandwich to Michael. "Or at least, I thought I was."

"You survived being stabbed and thrown off a cliff," the Templar reminded her. "While you are still mortal, no less."

"Can you remember anything more about what happened?" Troy asked.

"Only that I didn't see who it was. The attacker came up behind me."

Feeling restless now, Summer climbed off Michael and got up, bracing herself against his shoulder before she took a few tentative steps and then sat in the armchair in the corner.

"Still don't have my land legs yet. What I really don't understand is why. Why try to kill me now?"

"Since we came back from the city," Michael said, "you have either been with me, Troy or one of the women. Perhaps today was the first opportunity he had to strike while you were alone."

"But I wasn't." She turned around to face them. "You two were only twenty yards away from me, and everyone else from the main house was there, too."

"That little thug, Lachlan, ran off," Michael said. "Ewan and the pregnant witch were not there, either."

"Aileen can barely stand up on her own," Troy told him. "I saw Ewan inside the house earlier, and he wouldn't hurt a fly."

"Lachlan came at you with a blade," Michael countered. "When he could not prevail, perhaps he chose to vent his spleen on our Beauty."

"Hey," Summer said and frowned. She touched her side. "Wait a second."

"If it was Lachlan," Troy said, his expression darkening, "then he's mine."

Michael gave him a chilling smile. "You'll have to wait in line, Pagan."

"Guys." When they both stared at her, Summer stood up and pointed at the spot where she'd been stabbed. "The blade he used was still stuck in me when I went over the cliff. Did either of you see it when you fished me out of the river?"

Michael shook his head, while Troy said, "No, but if it's still in the water, I can find it."

Summer frowned as she touched her side again. She'd awoken covered in Troy's shirt.

"What happened to the dress I was wearing?"

The men exchanged an odd look before Michael said, "It was destroyed."

"What? How?" When neither of them answered her Summer got to her feet. "I liked that dress. Aileen gave it to me. So how—"

She staggered as a flood of memories poured through her.

• • • • •

"Beauty," Michael gasped, as he caught her before she fell.

Troy was immediately on her other side, both of them keeping her upright.

As she stared at them she saw another, fainter image of her limp, broken body in the sodden red dress. Two of her limbs were badly broken, and she wasn't breathing.

"I was dead," she whispered.

"No," Troy said firmly, as Michael gently cradled her. "You had a pulse, love. You just had some water in your lungs, which I got out, right away."

"And then you said to keep touching me." She stared at Michael through the blurry, flowing images. "You knew it would bring me back."

"I knew only that your power comes out when both of us touch you." He caressed her cheek, and when he took his hand away it was wet. "When the words began to appear on your skin, they burned off the dress."

"I'm not ready," Summer said lowly, her voice

quaking. She could hear herself speaking, but the words seemed to come from someone else. "*Maman* said so on the day they came for me. She begged me to forgive her." The memory fragment vanished, but this time something was different. "It doesn't hurt to remember anymore."

Both men guided her back to the bed, where Michael lifted her onto the mattress. A moment later they lay on either side of her, their hands stroking her and their voices soft as they murmured words of reassurance.

They wanted to make love to her, Summer could feel that, but they held back, afraid it would hurt her. Deep inside she could feel the bones that had broken knitting back together, and the stab wound now sealed, but still tender.

"I wish I could make love to you both again, but you're right. I think I need more rest."

Michael drew his finger down the length of her nose.

"I have waited hundreds of years for you." He lightly brushed her lips. "I can manage a few days more."

"I have a better idea," Troy said, eying Michael as he untied the belt of her robe. "Why don't you let us take care of you for a change?"

Being sandwiched between her lovers made

Summer feel more than safe, especially as their scents enveloped her. Troy smelled clean and cool, like the air after a light snowfall. Michael exuded a darker, earthier scent, like a grove of dark trees. Together they made her think of walking through the woods in the winter sun, with all the promise of spring waiting just beneath the snow.

Am I the promise of spring?

She felt an ache and glanced down to see that her nipples had grown so engorged they looked like two little, ripe strawberries.

"What are you two planning to take care of?"

"Watch," was all Michael said.

Her eyelids fluttered as both men shifted down and put their mouths to her breasts. Troy cradled her right mound in his long, beautiful fingers as he licked his tongue back and forth over her peak. Michael stroked her belly as he fastened his mouth over her left nipple to tug on it gently. The sensations of having both breasts attended to at once made Summer forget about everything but her men, and how sexy they made her feel.

"When you're feeling better," Troy murmured as he slowly fondled her. "We'd like to try something new."

"If you would like it, Beauty," Michael said and

gently rolled her over to face Troy. He moved up behind her to rub his big hand over her bottom. "We know we would."

They seemed to be entirely in sync now, and Summer felt their hunger for her like hot water flowing over her skin. Her own desires seemed to be blooming inside her like a secret garden of dark flowers.

"Why are we waiting?" she murmured, her head spinning.

"You need to rest," Troy said lowly as he rubbed her thigh. He slipped his hand between her legs to slowly stroke one finger against her delicate folds. "Just relax, and listen, and feel."

Though at first Summer thought Michael was rolling her back to him, he easily brought her on top of his big body. With her back resting on his broad chest, he cupped her breasts as he kissed the side of her neck. Troy bent over her to kiss her lips as he parted her and began working his thumb over the aching nub of her clit.

"When we take you next," Michael said, his soft voice thrumming against her back, "we want to be in you together."

Troy lifted his mouth as he pressed his finger into her clenching opening.

"I'll stuff this tight little pussy with my cock,"

he whispered against her lips. "I'll pump it deep and slow, the way you like it."

Summer shivered as she felt Michael caress her buttocks, and then trail a finger over the pucker of her rosebud.

"And while he does I will take you here," Michael told her. "You will like having my cock deep inside your lovely ass while Troy fills your pussy. You will feel both of our rods stroking inside you, and it will make you come harder than you have ever done, Beauty."

Summer gasped as their sensual threats added to the pleasure their hands were giving her. She imagined being between their big, muscular bodies as they both worked their shafts in and out of her.

"Now come for us," Troy said, and lowered his mouth to her breasts.

"Yes, Beauty," Michael added, pressing gently against her pucker. "Show us how it will be for you."

Summer's climax radiated inside her with the intensity of an inner sun. It burned through the fear and doubt and worry to consume her with the heat of their shared passion. She shuddered violently and uncontrollably, and felt both of her men stiffen as the pleasure spread from her to them. Their stiff, swollen shafts pulsed and jetted inside their trousers.

When it all drifted to a warm, loving glow, Troy glanced down and chuckled.

"I don't think I've come in my pants since I was a teenager."

Michael leaned close to whisper in Summer's ear, "I did it once while I was watching you in the park, but I admit, my hand may have helped a little."

Troy grinned at him. "This is why Wiccans don't have confession."

Michael nodded thoughtfully. "My mentors always claimed it is why all pagans are going to burn in Hell. Do you think there will be room for me, too?"

As Troy chuckled under his breath, Summer reveled in the small laugh that moved Michael's chest. She drifted in the moment, languorous and warm.

"I think I will take a shower now," Michael said after they had finished laughing. He gave her a quick kiss before climbing off the bed and heading into the bath.

"Do you want some more tea?" Troy asked as he stroked her hair. "I can go and brew a fresh pot."

"No, I'm good," Summer said, and sighed. "But there's something else I have to tell you about last night."

CHAPTER TWO

DAWN CREPT LIKE a ghost over the horizon as Troy sent a final surge of his power into the river. While searching the water he'd located innumerable coins, fish hooks, beer cans, and even an ancient tackle box still stuffed with lures, but no dagger.

"Son of a bitch."

The blade had either fallen on land or had been swept down river so far he couldn't sense it. Or the bastard had come back sometime during the night to retrieve it.

Troy worked on tamping down his temper as he climbed up the cliff side and walked toward the pavilion. He intended to have a civilized talk with his father—if that were possible—but first he wanted to see Ewan. He had once lived in France, and knew the covens there better than anyone.

Once he reached the yard he headed for the wood shop, where he found the older man measuring a length of golden oak.

"Troy," Ewan said, beaming as he gave him one of his hearty bear hugs. "Erica told me you'd left last night to look for Summer. Did you find her?"

"Yes," Troy said and filled him in with a brief recounting of what had happened, although he left out how Summer had transformed after they'd rescued her. "Michael is with her now, and we're not letting her out of our sight again."

"That seems wise, considering," Ewan said and sighed heavily. "Poor girl. She must have been so frightened. Well, I'm sure you and your friend will prevent anything more from harming her."

"Michael is also the reason I came to see you," Troy admitted. "We now believe that he was born Wiccan, possibly in France, and that his birth name may have been Michele Charbonneau."

Ewan looked surprised. "I thought he was a Templar."

Troy nodded. "He was raised by them since he was an infant. But it's possible the Templars killed his Wiccan family, or abducted him from them. Can you reach out to your contacts, and see if there are any Charbonneaus still among the covens?"

"Right away," the older man said and stroked his chin. "You know, if your friend turns out to be Wiccan as well as a Templar, it may create even more difficulties for the three of you, especially with your father. Perhaps we should keep this between us for now."

"Good idea," Troy said and glanced through the window at the main house. "One more thing, Ewan. Be careful around Lachlan. I don't trust him anymore."

"My boy, I am too old and useless to be of value to anyone but the dogs," the older man said. "But I think you should watch your back. Lately Lachlan has become very unpredictable."

Troy thanked the old warlock before he left the shop and entered the main house through a side door. He could hear Erica preparing food in the kitchen. But when he arrived there he only found Aileen working at the counter.

"Good morning," she said, eying him. "Are you looking for Wilson?"

"No," he said and closed the kitchen door. He inspected the bowl of strong-scented oatmeal she was mixing. "If you put anymore ginger in there it's going to bite you back."

"It's for Erica. Ginger is the only thing that settles her stomach when she's upset," she said.

"Would you get down the honey for me? You know she and your father spent half the night arguing about your new, ah, relationships."

He handed her the jar. "You disapprove?"

"Are you kidding? One woman with two handsome lovers? I'm jealous." She gave him a droll look. "I don't agree with your father's rather nasty, narrow-minded assessment, either, but then I know exactly how much you like women."

"That you do." His smile faded. "Where is Lachlan?"

"I don't know. I haven't seen him since the fight last night." Aileen reached out and touched his arm. "Don't get into another tussle with him or my husband, okay? It's not worth it."

"It's not about that," he said and told her about the attack on Summer. Aileen's eyes widened until he assured her that Summer was fine. "Lachlan disappeared a few minutes before she was stabbed and dragged through the woods. It's possible he was the one who tried to kill her."

"He's such a sniveling little coward I can hardly believe he'd work up the nerve." She scowled. "Spying on you and tattling to Abel is more his speed. Lachlan is a snake, always slithering around and poking his nose where it isn't wanted. But to stab and throw a woman over a cliff—that's truly sick and twisted."

Troy knew she didn't like his father's apprentice, but the bitter loathing in her voice made him frown.

"Aileen, did Lachlan do something to you?"

"No," she said and tossed the spoon she was using into the sink. "But if he ever does, I'll be doing some stabbing and cliff-tossing of my own." She immediately made a face and rested a thin hand on her swollen belly. "I'm sorry. I've never liked him, and I'm tired. Tired of all this conflict, bickering with my husband, worrying about a traitor among us—and if I don't soon have this baby, I'm pretty sure I'm going to detonate."

Troy kissed her brow. "It won't be much longer."

From the kitchen he went back to his father's study and knocked once before stepping inside.

Abel looked up from a scroll he was writing.

"So you've come back to apologize? Or are you looking for another fight–"

"Someone tried to kill Summer last night during the last one," he said flatly, and related the details of the attack before he added, "I want to talk to Lachlan. Now."

His father's dark brows arched. "My apprentice

438

did not attack her. Perhaps your pet Templar is jealous over the attention you give that little whore."

"Call her that again," Troy said softly. "Please." When his father said nothing he folded his arms. "Sex is sacred to us, in case you've forgotten, so why would you object to me sharing Summer with Michael? It isn't about Michael, is it? It's Summer."

"What kind of woman wants two men at the same time?" Abel countered. "She can't mate both of you. What if there is a child? Who is the father?"

The thought of seeing Summer's belly swell made Troy smile a little.

"I suppose any child of ours will have one mother and two fathers."

"There is no such thing," Abel said and got to his feet. "The covens will soon be arriving, and I have no more stomach for this."

"You're having the gathering here, at Silver Wood?" Troy almost gaped at him. "Why would you be so reckless?"

"Under the circumstances it is the safest place for it," his father said. "But what we do here is no more your concern. Just take your witch and your Templar, and go."

"And what if I want to stay, and take my rightful place, the place you've been training me for all my life? If I send Summer and Michael away, will you give me rule over the coven?" Troy watched his father's expression change from disgust to satisfaction. "That is why you told Summer last night that you'd hurt Michael, isn't it? So that she'd convince me to become Coven Master when you step down during the winter gathering?"

"I never said–" Abel broke off as the water from his glass rose and formed a circle around his head. It solidified into a halo of icy spikes. "What are you doing?"

"Actually I'm trying not to kill you," Troy said. He walked up to the desk and flicked his fingers. The razor-sharp shards of ice flew away from Abel's head to shatter against the walls and furniture around them. "It's becoming the toughest battle I've ever fought."

Eyes as blue and cold as his own stared back at him.

"You think it has been easy for me? Time and again you've gone out of your way to defy me, when all I have ever wanted was to see you become the leader you were meant to be."

Troy stared at him. "I may look like you, Father,

but I'm not you. I don't want power or position. I certainly don't give a damn about preserving your precious Atwater succession of coven master. I never have."

"Don't you dare speak of your birth right that way," Abel said and slammed his fist on top of his desk. "It is your destiny to rule."

"I'd rather dig ditches for the rest of eternity," Troy said and braced his hands on the desk and leaned over it. "My future is with Summer and Michael. We were brought together for a purpose, and I will never leave them."

"You'd give up the coven, and the chance to someday rule as Master of Covens, for endless perversions with a brain-damaged witch and a fucking Templar." Abel shook his head. "You are no longer my son. I disown you."

"Good," Troy said and straightened. "Then maybe you'll finally notice your other son. Wilson loves Silver Wood. He's taken a wife, and already begun the next generation of Atwaters. He's always supported you, no matter what you've done, even when he didn't agree with you—and all the while knowing he would get nothing from you for his loyalty."

Abel's expression grew shuttered. "Wilson cannot be Coven Master."

"Why the hell not?" Troy demanded. "He's a good man, devoted, fair-minded, strong—everything you always wanted me to be—and he loves this coven, and you. He's the one who will carry on your name. The son you've completely ignored. The brother who despises me only because I've forsaken everything he's dreamed of having. Wilson."

CHAPTER THREE

AFTER DISPOSING OF a trunk full of dismembered human body parts by gleefully chucking every bloody bit save one into a lovely reservoir, Gideon Edmunds continued his personal crusade into the White Mountains of New Hampshire. Cutting up the car's owner with his own chain saw had put Gideon in very good humor, and he was determined to hang on to his merry mood until he found the witch who could cure him.

"I am a very ill man, you know," he mentioned to the severed head of the car's owner, Nick. He had carefully tucked it face-up in the passenger seat. "My brain is being eaten by immortality sickness. Or perhaps it is a small army of bugs that have nested between my ears. It is difficult to say which, as much of the time I am mad."

Gideon glanced in the rearview mirror. His mouth twitch had grown so pronounced that he appeared to be either sneering or pouting. Yet he was still so handsome that the involuntary animation of his features could not truly detract from his good looks.

"Fear not, my friend, for my unhappy state is soon to end," he advised Nick's head. "I need only to find a pretty wench and rape her until she restores more of my mind, and tells me where I might find the green witch. Once the witch leads me to the Emerald Tablet, and uses it to heal me, then Gideon Edmunds shall be himself again."

I thought you were a fruitcake named Michael.

Gideon eyed his companion's gape-mouthed face.

"Extraordinary. How do you do that without moving your lips?"

I'm telepathic, you dumb ass. So, you find a girl and do her, and then suddenly she's so grateful she tells you what you want to know? Not a very good plan, pal.

Gideon frowned. "If you're going to be rude, I'll drive back to the water and reunite you with the rest of your parts."

Then you won't have anyone to talk to but the Almighty, and I gotta tell you, pal, at the moment, He's not real happy with you.

"What, for ending a gruesome fellow like you? You're a murderer for hire. You intended to kill me after I dug a grave for your last victim. You even shot me in the chest." Gideon sniffed as he rubbed the still-sore hole. "It was entirely self-defense."

It's not about me, Fruitcake. It's Michael. That traitor pissed on everything you believe in, and still you ain't done nothing about him, have you?

"Well, I do have to find him first," Gideon said. He took the foam coffee container Nick had left in the cup holder and shoved it in his open mouth. "Now shut up."

I'm in your head, moron. And you know what, Fruitcake? There aren't just bugs in here. There are leeches. Great, big, fat, slimy bastards, sucking away at you.

"Ha. You're lying. Unlike you I haven't been in the water, so no leeches could get in my head." Gideon peered at a sign that read "rest area" and felt a strong pull in his chest. He rubbed it and grinned. "I believe the Almighty is directing us to stop here. There must be many wenches waiting to provide me with the relief I need. It should prove an adequate resting place for you, Nick."

You can't leave me in a fucking toilet, Gideon.

Nick continued arguing with him from that

moment until Gideon parked outside the rest rooms. Aside from two young men standing between a battered pickup and a motorcycle, the lot was empty. Gideon tucked Nick's head inside his jacket and headed into the open entry marked "women." He found all the stalls empty, which greatly disappointed him.

"Well, it seems the Almighty is playing tricks on me. I shall have to look elsewhere for a wench," he told Nick's head as he carried him over to the men's side of the facility. "But I will put you in here so that you might rest now. It is proper, even if you haven't a cock or an ass anymore."

He decided to leave Nick in the very last stall, which was the cleanest, and took care to mount his head on the top of the flushing mechanism, which seemed the most dignified spot, and provided the best view.

"There. Perfect," Gideon said. He sat on the commode seat and arranged Nick's sticky hair around his cold, hard face. "I shall miss you, you know. You have been a good companion to me. I mean, aside from shooting me and those foolhardy threats you made before I chopped you to pieces."

Someone's coming, dumb ass. Shut up.

Gideon listened as the door opened and two

sets of footsteps crossed the tile floor.

"Why can't you come back to Portland with me?" one of the pair asked in a deep, cajoling voice. "We'll spend the weekend at my place."

"I have a million things to do for the winter gathering," the second man said.

Both men unzipped their trousers and began pissing in the urinals.

"Why don't you ever invite me to these parties? Is your true love going to be there with the wife he's breeding?" The man made a contemptuous sound. "God, you're pathetic, Lachlan."

"Fuck you, Jonah," the other man snarled.

Gideon was tempted to call out and tell them that he was fairly sure that the Almighty had already done so, by means that involved a whale, but he wanted to hear more about this winter gathering.

"You have, Lachlan, like every weekend since he knocked up the bitch," Jonah said. "When are you going to give it up, lover?"

"Don't call me that," Lachlan muttered.

Jonah heaved a sigh. "Look, man, you've got issues. I get it. First time my folks caught me with a guy, they threw me out. My old man still won't speak to me. But you can't hide what you are forever, and pretending you're not gay has already fucked you up. Big time."

One of the urinals flushed. "Then maybe you should find someone else to spend your weekends with, Jonah."

"All right, I will." The other urinal flushed.

"Wait, Jonah, I didn't mean it."

Once the men had left Gideon frowned. "Sodomites. We used to impale them with red-hot pokers, you know. Did that to one of the kings of England, in fact. One of the Edwards, I think."

Good times, huh, Fruitcake?

"That name, though. Lachlan. I swear I've heard it before now. Hmmm." He eyed Nick. "Did you feel that when he came in? He's like me."

You mean, he's out of his mind, too?

"No, he's immortal. Since there are no Templars assigned here that also means he's Wiccan. He must be part of the coven Nathaniel intends to attack." Gideon patted Nick's stony cheek. "It has to be why the Almighty had me stop here. So that I might follow him back to the nest, of course. Farewell, my friend. Oh, and thank you again for the car."

Look, pal, if you leave me here, you will be damned for all eternity.

Gideon chuckled. "Oh, my dear boy. I surely

was, long ago."

CHAPTER FOUR

WILSON CAME IN from doing his morning chores and tracked his wife to the garden. She was sitting and bundling sprigs from a basket of fresh-picked herbs.

"You should be back in bed," he said.

"You should stop telling me where I should be," Aileen said and smiled up at him. "Should I hold my breath?"

"Not unless you want to turn very blue," he said. He kissed the top of her head and sat down beside her. "After breakfast I thought I'd drive into town and pick up that wood Ewan ordered." He stroked his wife's narrow back. "Why don't you come with me?"

"I think we should stay home today." Her big gray eyes searched his face for a moment. "Someone attacked Summer last night. Troy thinks it was Lachlan. After the fight last night, he never came back."

"That doesn't mean Lachlan attacked Summer. He always runs off to sulk after he loses a fight. He's been doing that since we were boys." He saw the way Aileen was glaring at him. "What?"

"Nothing." She shoved the herb bundles back in the basket. "I'll go make some oatmeal for you."

"Wait." He caught her arm as she started to rise. "Lachlan was only trying to defend me."

She sat back down carefully. "You think I don't know how he feels about you? Wil, every time he looks at you I can see it—nd there's a very good chance he went after Summer."

"No way," Wilson said and tried to put his arm around her, but she shrugged it off. "Honey, Lachlan would never hurt anyone."

"Really," she said cooly and stared down at her hands. Then she faced him calmly. "Do you realize how many near-accidents I've had since I got pregnant? How many times I've almost tripped over the dogs, or caught my foot on a loose rug, or slipped on a patch of oil on the kitchen floor that I didn't see? I'm a lot of things, Husband, but I've never been clumsy or careless. In fact, if I wasn't constantly on my guard I might have lost the baby by now."

She looked as if she wanted to say more, and then pushed herself to her feet and went inside. Wilson followed her into the kitchen.

"You think Lachlan has been deliberately trying to hurt you? Why didn't you tell me about this before now?"

Aileen uttered a bitter laugh. "I *did* when it started. Remember? I told you about the dogs, twice. Both times you defended Lachlan, and said I was imagining things."

"I'm sorry," Wilson said, and pulled her stiff body into his arms. "I'll find Lachlan, and if he did this…he'll never come near you again." He kissed her cheeks and forehead until she stopped resisting him and hugged him tightly. "Where is Troy now?"

"In the study with your father," she said. "Wilson, please," she added as he headed in that direction. "Don't start anything with your brother."

"I wasn't planning on it," he assured her. "Troy knows this mountain as well as I do. Between the two of us we will find Lachlan."

When Wilson reached the study he began to open the door, but froze as he heard his brother's voice.

"He's a good man, devoted, fair-minded, strong —everything you always wanted me to be—and he loves this coven, and you," Troy said, his tone cold and furious. "He's the one who will carry on your name. The son you've completely ignored. The brother who despises me only because I've forsaken everything he's dreamed of having. Wilson."

After listening a few more minutes to Troy laying into their father about him, Wilson retreated from the main house, but glanced back at it. Troy was supposed to hate him, and envy him, not defend him. Why had he said those things about him to Abel? But as Wilson approached the scene of the fight, he forced himself to focus on his task.

He went directly to Lachlan's tracks from last night and began tracking him through the woods. Lachlan's every move left traces of his passage which appeared to Wilson's eyes like dappled light on the ground, leaves, and trees. His ability also allowed him to differentiate between human, immortal and animal energy tracks. While he couldn't identify any one person or species from the energy trails they left behind, he suspected Lachlan would be hiding out in his and Aileen's cabin.

He'd always known Lachlan loved him, but never dreamed he would try to hurt Aileen or the baby. Despite what he'd told his wife, he still wasn't convinced his childhood friend was capable of doing such evil. Lachlan was prickly and sneaky and secretive, and often annoyed the hell out of Wilson, but he wasn't a traitor. On some level Wilson had always known that Abel's apprentice had been trying to hide something from the rest of the coven, but he was convinced it was Lachlan's sexuality, not any betrayal.

The trail came to an abrupt end a few hundred yards from the cabin. Wilson found fresh tire tracks from Lachlan's truck on the ground. From the look of the ruts, and the direction they headed, the apprentice had driven out to the access road that went down the mountain.

Wilson stood and rubbed his hands together to warm them as he looked around. The tracks were too fresh to be from last night. He could still smell the exhaust from Lachlan's truck in the air.

"Why the hell would you come back here this morning?" Wilson muttered.

He decided to stop in the cabin to pick up some things for Aileen. Now that his brother and the Templar were staying with the witch in the old house, he felt better. Of course any time Troy put distance between him and their father Wilson felt happier. When Troy wasn't around, Abel actually noticed what he was doing.

I've hated my brother for years, and when he finally has the chance to take everything from me, he chooses a Templar and a strange witch over Aileen and the coven.

Once Wilson returned to the main house, he would have a talk with Troy. While they'd probably never be close, it was past time to put this feud between them to rest.

As he carried a bundle of clothes out of the cabin Wilson smiled up at the silvery-blue of the sky. He felt a contentment that seemed as odd as it was pleasant. He couldn't remember the last time he thought of Troy with anything but anger or jealousy. Now he was actually looking forward to talking with him.

That should be the shock of the century.

Wilson smelled something like a rotting carcass, and frowned as he stopped and sniffed the air. Whatever was putting off the stink had to be very close, but he couldn't see anything dead anywhere around him. The stench enveloped him just before a blade pressed across his throat.

"Now don't struggle, lad," a merry voice said, as a strong hand gripped his shoulder. "I might accidentally cut off your head, and we need to have a chat first. Unless you're telepathic as well as a filthy heathen."

Aileen's clothes fell from his hands as Wilson dropped to his knees and then lunged away from the foul-smelling man. He tumbled into a somersault and landed on his feet to take off at a flat run for the woods. He didn't glance back, not even when he heard the man gaining on him. But before he could reach the trees an enormous weight barreled into him from behind and knocked him face-first into the hard ground.

"Why did you do that?" the man demanded as he hauled Wilson to his feet. He shook him until his teeth rattled. He then dropped Wilson to the ground and paced around him in a circle. "Are you not fond of your head? Don't you wish it to remain attached to your little body?"

"Yes," Wilson told the dirt in his face carefully. "I do."

"Well, there you are." The man kicked him over onto his back and pressed a hand to his own chest before he bowed. "Gideon Edmunds, at your service. Or not, actually."

"I'm Wilson," he said, trying not to stare, but it was impossible.

"I am a Templar, you know, and we do not make threats," Gideon told him. "We make only promises. Now, can you guess what happened to the last man who tried to run away from me?"

Wilson's gaze moved from the Templar's red-streaked, twitching face to the blood-drenched clothes he was wearing. His stomach surged as he recognized a few shreds of skin and tissue still clinging to the front of the Templar's trousers.

"Yes, I can guess."

"I still have the chainsaw I used at my campsite, and I'm quite good with it." The man shook his finger at Wilson like a teacher scolding a pupil. "So behave yourself." He reached down with his free hand. "Up you go now. Let's take a walk."

When Wilson was back on his feet he tried to head toward the woods, but the Templar yanked him back.

"You're not going to be foolish, are you?" the Templar asked as he walked alongside him, and removed a gun from his jacket pocket. "Because I will blow holes in your spinal cord until it snaps like an old elastic band. Do you understand me?"

Wilson nodded as he thought frantically. "What do you want?"

"The green witch." The Templar gave him a serene smile. "You're going to tell me where she's hiding."

CHAPTER FIVE

SUMMER REFUSED TO stay in bed or indoors once Troy had left to search for the dagger. Ssince Michael had no intention of letting her out of his sight he agreed to take her for a walk.

"You will tell me if you feel chilled," he warned her as he buttoned up the front of her jacket, and pulled a knit cap over the thick waves of her hair.

Dark opal eyes glared up at him. "You're treating me like a little girl."

"Only until you have healed completely. Then Troy and I will treat you like a big girl." He watched the color flood her pale face and smiled slowly. "There, that is better."

"Don't make me think about sex," she grumbled as she pulled on her gloves. "Besides, I need to talk to you about something before we get distracted again."

Summer wouldn't say any more. Instead, they left the house and crossed the clearing to follow the stream into the woods. Only when they came upon a pile of rusty-orange and gray stone poking up from the ground did she stop to sit on one flattened edge. Michael could almost feel her thoughts tangling and snarling as she silently debated with herself.

"Whatever the burden is," he said, crouching in front of her, "it will be lighter if Troy and I help you carry it."

She nodded, and fussed with her gloves for a moment before she squinted up at the sun.

"Michael, my memories are coming back. They have been since that first night you and Troy and I were together. At first it was just bits and pieces but now it's more. It's so much more."

She sounded almost ashamed, he thought, or unsure.

"You do not know how much you should tell us yet," he said.

"Which is why I wanted to talk to you instead of Troy," Summer said. She pulled up her sleeve to expose some of the dark marks tattooed on her flesh. "My power didn't do this. My mother did. She tattooed me and bespelled the wounds so the marks would heal unseen and remain hidden until now. She also cursed me, several times, with different compulsion spells. The curses were layered and staggered in such a way so as to trigger at certain moments, and end at others."

Michael felt a hot flood of loathing stream through his veins.

"How could she do such terrible things to her own daughter?"

"They only seem terrible," she interjected. "The curse that compelled humans to be generous to me began when I woke up homeless in the park, and needed food and shelter. It ended when Troy brought me to Silver Wood, where I was safe." Her opal eyes looked deeply into his. "The desire curse triggered right after you left me, probably to draw you back, but maybe to attract another mate. The curses were never intended to harm me."

Michael considered for a moment, glancing at the tattoos. The tide of anger, though not gone, began to ebb.

"They protected you," he said.

Summer nodded.

"I can't be sure yet, but I think my mother knew what was going to happen to me." She paused and bit her lower lip. "Michael, someday I may need you to do something for me. I want you to know why. It's because you are the strong one.

You understand things that Troy never will. You have suffered and sacrificed and devoted your immortal life to protecting humanity."

The fierceness of her expression made him reach for her hands, and he frowned as he saw she had removed her gloves.

"Beauty, you unnerve me now. What is it you would have me do?"

"If I am taken by force, by Templar or Wiccan, you must come for me," she said softly. "And if you cannot free me, you will kill me." She pressed her bare hand over his heart, where it flared with green light. "So I command you, sentinel mate."

"What have you done?" Michael tried to back away, but something gripped his body and kept him from twitching a muscle. "Beauty, no."

"Worry and fear, all disappear," she said, her eyes glowing with the same verdant light. *"Memory of this talk, now a rest from a pleasant walk. Obey me in this, from the moment we kiss. So may it be."*

She leaned forward and pressed her lips to his.

As Summer kissed him, Michael felt something twist in his head, and then all the tension seemed to flow out of him. Her mouth tasted cool and sweet. He took his time kissing her back before he nipped her lower lip, and then grinned at her.

"Are you rested enough?" he asked. "Or shall

we spend the rest of the morning sunning ourselves here?"

Though she smiled at him, it was tinged with something that looked like sadness. He cocked his head at her, but the look vanished.

"I'll freeze before I tan, Paladin."

She pushed herself off the edge of the rock and took hold of his hand. Her touch felt like ice, and her fingers were trembling.

"Where are your gloves?" He searched her pockets before he found them, and put them on her. "Now leave them on. As pleasant as this walk is, I do not want you catching a chill."

"Let's go this way, through the evergreen grove," Summer said, tugging at his arm. "This way we can come up behind Wilson and Aileen's cabin."

He gave her a suspicious look. "And why are we visiting them when we are taking only a short walk?"

"We're not," she admitted. "But I can see the main house from there, and hopefully we'll spot Troy talking with his dad, not slugging it out."

Michael grunted and considered tossing her over his shoulder and carrying her back, but she wouldn't like it. Besides, this walk had been so pleasant thus far. But no sooner had he thought it, than he caught a faint but sickening, acrid odor of old blood and rot. He quickly scanned the area around them for any sign of animal remains.

"Beauty, do you smell that?"

She pulled him behind a fir, dislodging some of the snow powdering the branches. She lifted her finger to her lips. As she did, Michael heard the trudge of heavy footsteps and the panting breaths of two men as the stench grew stronger.

"How did you find us?" Michael heard Wilson ask.

"Lachlan showed me the way," a hearty voice replied. "Now, are you going to tell me where the witch is hiding? No? Well, perhaps after I introduce you to my chainsaw you will change your mind, and save an arm or a leg."

Michael's blood ran cold as he clamped his big hand over Summer's mouth and pressed her against his chest. Gideon Edmunds and Troy's brother emerged from the grove. The mad Templar looked as if he had been in a slaughterhouse, and held a gun pressed against Wilson's nape as he marched him toward the stream.

Summer's wide eyes met his. When he saw that she was composed he lowered his hand. He waited until the men were out of earshot.

"Run back to the pavilion," he whispered. "Tell them to bring every weapon they can carry."

"No," she said firmly. "I'm not leaving you. What will Gideon do to Wilson?"

"Exactly as he said he would."

Michael's hands went to the daggers sheathed at either side of his belt. All his instincts were shrieking for him to send Summer to the pavilion to get Troy. Yet without her help Troy's brother might be maimed or even killed. Given half a chance, though, Gideon would fall on her like a ravenous animal.

"Michael," she said lowly, and touched his shoulder. To his surprise, her eyes were glowing bright green. "I will not allow Gideon to harm me."

Power surged through her touch. As if her conviction were his own, he knew without a doubt that what she said was true. He clenched his jaw at the thought of not taking her to safety, but knew he couldn't let Troy's brother die. He nodded, took her hand, and followed the two men.

Summer proved as adept as any soldier at moving silently and taking advantage of the natural cover. He recalled she had spent several months hiding in Central Park as the police performed their nightly sweeps. But the smell of a campfire made Michael stop in his tracks, forcing Summer to do the same. Slowly, they crept forward, moving from tree to tree until they had a clear view of Gideon's back. Wilson hung suspended by rope from an oak branch. His face was white and his eyes huge as he looked down at the bloodied chainsaw the Templar was attempting to start.

"Wretched machines," Gideon muttered, and glanced at Troy's brother. "I don't suppose you'd give up the witch without being partially dismembered?"

"Please," Wilson said. "I don't know who you want. There are no green witches here."

Michael felt unexpected admiration for the warlock, who was facing the most gruesome of tortures, and yet refused to betray Summer. His wrists had been crudely but tightly bound together. The rope looped upward, stretching him to his tiptoes. Michael withdrew the daggers and handed one to Summer as he whispered his plan in her ear. She nodded and moved silently away.

The chainsaw bucked and blatted as Gideon nearly got it started, only for it to clatter to a stop a moment later.

"It seems it's your lucky day, heathen," the

Templar told Wilson as he threw down the tool in disgust. He drew his gun. "I will have to blow off your kneecaps instead of cutting off your legs. You may not even bleed to death. Now where is she?"

Michael emerged from the brush and strode to the edge of the campsite.

"A gun, Steward Edmunds? Where have you left your sword?"

"Who is that?" sad the mad Templar as he spun around. His mouth spasmed. "Michael Charbon, what a surprise."

He aimed the gun at Michael—or at least he tried. His arm and hand shook as violently as his lips. Though Michael tensed and crouched, the barrel of the gun jumped all over the place. When it went off, the shot hit a tree several yards away. Gideon seemed not to be bothered.

"Come closer. I want to shoot you, not the forest."

"Nathaniel sent me," Michael said and ducked back into the shadows. He moved laterally, circling. "Nathaniel has found the Emerald Tablet, and wishes to give you the cure for your sickness."

"How is it that you are a traitor and lie so poorly?" Gideon said, chuckling. He fired again, but with no better accuracy. "I'm mad, not stupid, witch hunter. If Nathaniel had the Tablet he would use it to take over the world, and kill all the heathens, and perhaps grow a bigger manhood." He reeled around, squinting up at Wilson, the sun in his eyes. "Did you know that he's hardly more than this?" he asked Wilson, and pinched the air.

"Gideon, I have seen the green witch," Michael said, stepping forward.

Gideon spun back around to face him. Summer came up behind Wilson and began cutting the rope. Michael reversed his dagger, clasping the blade between his fingers as he prepared to throw it.

"She is waiting for you," Michael said, jerking a thumb over his shoulder. "She is just through there."

"What do you say now?" Gideon said. His features contorted as his tic spread to the other side of his face. "If this is true, bring her to me." He began rubbing his crotch. "I must have the truth out of her. I must have…" He paused and sniffed the air. "You lie. She's here."

The ground all around the Templar's feet began to shake. He was knocked off balance and fell to his hands and knees. Wilson dropped to the ground, his hands still bound, but Summer helped him up as they staggered back. A cloaked figure stepped out into the sunlight. It raised gloved hands that were engulfed with what appeared to be black flames.

"What trickery is this?" Gideon shouted.

He rose up on his knees as something long and thick came flying out of the woods behind him, hurtling past Summer and Wilson.

Michael barely had time to register that the object was a tree, when it rammed into Gideon and impaled him.

Though the Templar's mouth gaped open, no sound came out. He choked on a liquid gurgle as the branches of the gnarled oak emerged from the front of his throat. His head jerked and his neck stretched as another branch surged through his forehead. Each arm and leg was impaled, then his torso. The tree burrowed its branches further into the man, spreading his flesh open in sickening pops and splats. When his body looked more wood than flesh, it finally flew apart, torn by the thickening branches. A broad swath of blood and gore flooded the ground where he'd knelt, and the tree fell with a crunching thump on top of it.

Summer put her arm around Wilson as she backed away from the campsite and looked around wildly.

"Who's there?" she asked. "Who did this?"

A shriek of savage laughter rang out through the woods, echoing over and over. By the time Michael reached Summer and Wilson, the cloaked figure had vanished, and the forest had fallen completely silent.

Wilson stared at the killing tree and grisly ground beneath it. "Summer, did you…"

"No," she said, her voice tight. "I could never do that to anyone."

"There was someone in a cloak, standing over there," Michael said, and pointed in that direction. "One moment he was there, and then he was gone."

Summer bit her lip. "Could Lachlan have done this?"

"No," Wilson breathed. He stared at her, his dark eyes still wide with shock. "But…but Ewan might have. It's his ability, you know. He can vanish from sight entirely."

• • • • •

Once they returned to the pavilion Summer thought it would be simple to confront Ewan, but he had been with either Troy or Abel all morning. Once they had gathered the other members of the coven in the large front room and informed them about the attack on Wilson and Gideon's hideous end, everyone began talking at once. Troy had immediately taken up position next to her, while Michael stood close as well.

"Troy and I will deal with disposing of the remains," Michael told Abel, raising his voice to be heard over the others. "But whoever attacked Gideon wielded great power, and used very dark magic."

"I don't care who killed him," Aileen said. She clutched her husband's hand tightly as she struggled to her feet. "But all of you heard what Wilson said. The Templar told him that Lachlan was the one who led him here. He's the traitor spying on us for the Templars."

"Aileen," Troy said, "that Templar was insane with immortality sickness. If you'd asked him five minutes later he probably would have said *you* led him up the mountain."

"Why are you protecting him?" Aileen screeched, and then gulped in a deep breath and spoke slowly and deliberately. "Lachlan tried to knife you last night, remember? He lies about where he goes whenever he leaves Silver Wood. Tell them, Ewan."

Ewan grimaced. "My dear, please. Ten minutes

ago everyone was convinced that *I* had killed the Templar. Let's not hurl more accusations until we gather some facts."

Summer saw how angry Aileen was growing, and slipped away from Michael and Troy to put her arm around the young witch.

"Maybe you and Wilson should go and rest for a bit. Let us deal with this."

"Lachlan hasn't been going to town every weekend," Aileen said flatly. "He's been driving hundreds of miles, hasn't he, Ewan?"

The rotund warlock shifted uneasily. "I did notice he was putting more mileage on his truck the last time I changed the oil. That's all."

"We should go and find Lachlan," Wilson said to Troy.

"I have a better idea," Erica said. She brought out a tray filled with steaming cups of tea. "Why don't you men go out and make sure there aren't any other Templars coming up the mountain? I mean, if you're not too busy arguing about mileage and oil changes."

Summer hid a smile as she went over to help Erica distribute the cups. "Nice one."

"I want Lachlan made to answer for what he's done," Aileen said, and stalked up to Abel. "He's been trying to hurt me and the baby for months.

He nearly stabbed Troy last night. Wilson could have died today. Gods, he probably killed the Templar to keep him from exposing him–"

"I'm not your traitor."

Summer winced and turned around to see Lachlan standing in the front entry. He ducked quickly as a ceramic cup came flying at his head and shattered on the door jamb.

"Let go of me," Aileen shrieked as her husband wrapped his arms around her. "I'm going to make him pay for what he's done to this coven."

"I'm not your traitor," Lachlan repeated. "I didn't bring that Templar to the mountain, and I didn't kill him." His mouth tightened as he looked at Wilson and then Aileen. "I would never hurt a pregnant woman, either. As to where I've been, I can prove that."

He took out his mobile phone and dialed a number, and then put the call on speaker.

"What the fuck do you want, Lachlan?" a male voice said.

"Jonah, my family thinks I've been doing something rotten every weekend," he said as he watched Aileen's face. "Would you mind telling them where you live, and what we do when I come to see you?"

"I live in Portland, and we fuck like bunnies,"

Jonah said and laughed. "So you're finally coming out to them?"

"Yeah. Everyone get that? Thanks, Jo." Lachlan switched off the phone. "I spent last night with him, too, and came back this morning. Maybe the Templar spotted me and followed me up. We had an argument and almost broke up last night, so I wasn't really paying attention."

"You're a liar," the pregnant witch said, almost in tears. "You could have paid that man to say those things."

Lachlan cautiously approached Aileen.

"You know, I don't like you any more than you like me. I never have. But I would never harm a woman or an unborn child. Especially not the woman Wilson loves more than life itself." When she wouldn't look at him, he nodded and glanced around the room. "The covens will be arriving soon for the winter gathering. So if you're not going to kick me out, I have work to do."

Summer frowned at Troy. "The covens are coming here?"

He nodded tightly. "My father elected to move the gathering to Silver Wood. He believes the mountain is the safest place for it."

"Unless Nathaniel has been tracking Gideon," Michael murmured.

At that moment Abel moved to the center of the room and held up his hands in a calming gesture.

"The magic used to kill the Templar is very specific. I will go through the dark grimoires until I find the spell, and then Erica will scry it back to the Wiccan who cast it."

"You needn't bother, my dear," the High Priestess said. She sat down in the armchair by the fire, and regarded them all. "I am the one who killed Gideon Edmunds."

CHAPTER SIX

EWAN WAS THE first to break the stunned silence that gripped everyone.

"Surely this is no time for jests, Sister."

"I'm not joking, Brother. I took his life." Erica's calm eyes shifted to Abel. "If you need proof, you will find the spell in the Night of Mind grimoire, and the preparation circle in my bed chamber."

Summer went to the High Priestess and crouched down by her chair.

"You knew he was here, and you didn't tell anyone?"

"I have scried his location every night since I escaped him." The older woman stared into the fireplace. "I always told myself it was so that I would never again fall under his power, but then I saw him coming here and knew what I had to do."

"They're going to want to know why," Summer said gently.

"It's time I told them." Erica's mouth tightened as she glanced over at the pregnant witch. "I should have, long ago."

Summer stood as Abel approached them.

"Before you say anything," she said, "you need to hear the entire story."

The Coven Master ignored her. "Was it him?" he asked Erica. "Was this the Templar who tortured you, and made you pregnant?"

Now it was Erica's turn to be dumbfounded. "You couldn't have known. Oh, please, Abel, no."

"Since we began sleeping together, love." He drew her out of the chair. "You have nightmares about him, and plead with him to stop hurting you. There have been some nights when you've screamed in your sleep."

Erica stared up at him in horror. "Why didn't you ever tell me?"

He touched her scarred cheek. "I was waiting for you to do that."

Summer saw Ewan's bewildered expression as the coven leaders embraced. She tactfully retreated across the room to stand with her men.

"I think there's one more revelation coming," she told Michael, and then glanced at Troy. "By the way, I don't hate your father anymore."

"Yeah," he said, and sighed. "Neither do I."

"You are the gentlest person I know," Aileen said when Erica turned to her. "Why would you do such a thing, even to a Templar? If you meant to save Wilson, you could have struck him down with a paralyzing spell, or even a curse to blind him. Is it because that Templar scarred you? Is that it?"

"Gideon Edmunds did more than beat me, and take a blade to my face," Erica said and touched the old scar that divided her features before she took hold of Abel's hand. "He raped me over and over in order to restore his clarity of mind. There came a night when I could feel something—a new courage and determination to survive. I didn't realize at the time that it came from the new life inside me."

Aileen paled. "Oh, no," she whispered.

"Until that moment I was prepared to die, but that night everything changed. On some level I must have known I couldn't let him harm my child." Erica hesitated before she added, "I couldn't let him kill you, Aileen."

"You're…you're my birth mother?" The pregnant witch sounded dazed now. "And that monster you killed…he was my–"

"He only made me pregnant, dearest. He was never your father." Erica took a tentative step toward her. "After I escaped Gideon Edmunds I was very ill in body and spirit. The way I was, I could not have looked after you, or given you the loving home you deserved. Nor could I tell my family what had happened to me." She gave Ewan an apologetic look. "So I arranged to have you in secret, and put you up for adoption."

Aileen pressed her hands to her mouth.

"My dearest, darling girl, when you came to us I wanted to tell you. But I needed to protect you more. I told myself that way I could be the mother of your heart as well as your body." Erica sank down in front of her daughter. "Can you ever forgive me?"

Aileen lowered her hands and then flung herself at Erica, sobbing as she clutched her tightly.

"I would say that is a yes," Michael murmured.

"Yeah." Summer leaned her cheek against his shoulder. "Me, too."

CHAPTER SEVEN

SUMMER CHECKED THE bubbling pot of pasta sauce on the stove before she went to place the big salad she'd made on the new dining room table.

The work involved with the final preparations for the winter gathering over the past few days had gradually dispelled the last of the shock and unease in the coven. Erica seemed to be at peace now that Aileen knew the truth of her origins. While some of the members of the coven remained disturbed about her use of dark magic, Summer suspected the High Priestess would never again resort to such measures. Learning the truth about her birth parents had transformed Aileen. She bloomed with happiness and contentment. Even Wilson appeared to have abandoned his usual sullen resentment of Troy.

He worked without a qualm alongside his older brother and father as they cleared several sites for the visiting covens to use as camps.

Things had never been better, and still Summer hadn't been able to shake off a sense that evil still lingered, and time was running out. Those feelings had prompted her to insist on joining Troy and Michael when they had gone to bury Gideon. Troy had set fire to the grisly remains, while he and Michael dug a deep grave to bury the ash. Once they had filled in the ground, Summer had sent a surge of her own power into the soil. It covered the grave with a carpet of tiny saplings that spread out over the entire camp site.

"By next spring these trees will be fully-grown," Summer had told Troy. "But I can feel the dark magic lingering. No one should ever camp here again."

He'd nodded. "I'll advise my father."

Now as Summer sliced one of Erica's fresh-baked baguettes to spread it with roasted garlic she looked out through the kitchen window at the light violet curtain that twilight had drawn across the horizon. Abel had grudgingly invited them to come back to the main house, but she was glad Troy had politely refused. Now that things had settled down with the coven they needed time alone together to attend to their business.

Summer saw the two of them as they came out of the old barn, each carrying an armful of split logs for the fireplaces. Troy was laughing and Michael grinning as they shared some joke. As their emotions flooded into her for a moment she thought her heart would burst with happiness.

You have to tell them.

Her smile faded as she felt the power roil inside her.

"Not yet," she whispered. "Not tonight."

Quickly Summer finished the bread so she could strain the pasta and top it with the savory red sauce she'd made. By the time she'd brought the last of the food out to the table Troy and Michael appeared. Eeach kissed her before surveying the table.

Michael gave her one of his slow smiles. "I knew you liked Italian."

"You must have been a chef in your previous life," Troy teased.

Watching them sit down on either side of her chair made her throat tighten, and for a moment she thought she might begin weeping.

Not tonight.

"More like a waitress who had a crush on the short-order cook."

Michael's light brows rose. "You remember that?"

"No," she said and forced herself to chuckle. "It just sounds more interesting than 'I can't remember.'"

The men ate hugely, as always, and talked about the gathering, which would begin in a week. Tomorrow they were both going to help with the makeshift arena. Abel would use it to perform the mass rituals and hold the magical contests planned for the celebration. Summer listened and nodded but said little. When the men volunteered to clear and wash up she retreated to take a long, hot bath and see if that would soak away her worries.

Reclining naked in the fragrant water only made her wish she had a tub big enough for three, and that thought sent shivery tremors of longing through her. She stroked her hands slowly over her body as she soaped herself, and then let out the water and used the shower to rinse off. When she finally dried off, she pulled on the T-shirt and leggings. As she walked out to the master bedroom, she yawned. Since the attack the men had been sleeping in other rooms. While she felt lonely by herself in the big bed, she understood they were giving her time to heal. That was why it made her jump to see both of them waiting for her, each man wearing only boxers.

"Oh," she gasped.

The sight of all that hard, muscular flesh made her heart flutter. Troy stood at one of the nightstands and set down a bottle of white wine he'd been pouring. He offered her a glass.

"We thought you might like some company tonight."

"And we are tired of sleeping in the other rooms," Michael said, as he placed a large box of condoms on the other night table.

Summer accepted the glass as her men approached. She took a sip, hoping it might calm her pounding heart. As they came closer though, she set the wine down.

"We can feel you," Troy said as he cradled her face between his palms. "Even from the other side of the house."

"You want us," Michael said as he came up behind her, and wrapped his arms around her waist. "We could feel your hands on your body while you were bathing."

"I was only washing," she assured him, her eyelids drooping as Troy began kissing his way down her neck. "Next time I'll have to do something else, something special."

"Let us do that," Michael murmured as he slid his hands under her T-shirt.

Us. We. Never me, or him, Summer thought as she closed her eyes.

They probably weren't even aware that they now only spoke of each other in the plural. She had done that to them, just as surely as she had used sex to bind them to her, and to each other.

Troy took his mouth from the front of her throat and brushed his lips over hers before he drew back, frowning down at her.

"Summer, why are you so sad?"

She tried to smile, but when Michael took his hands from her breasts and stepped away, she knew she couldn't fool either of them.

"I've taken too much," she blurted out, her throat tight and her eyes stinging. "I've stolen your lives from you. You'll never be free of me again."

Troy cupped her cheek and whisked away a tear with his thumb.

"And this is a bad thing how?" he asked.

"Some of my memory is coming back, and one thing I know now is that I can't give you sons. Women of my bloodline have only female children." She sat heavily down on the bed. "It's the reason we were chosen to be the guardians of the Tablet."

"So we shall have daughters." Michael sat down beside her and took her hand in his. "As my brother says, how is this a bad thing?"

"I will have one daughter," she corrected him. "I will train her to be the next guardian of the Emerald Tablet. Someday, when it's her time to replace me, she will take two lovers, two men who were also predestined to be her sentinel mates. She'll seduce them, and bind them to her, and ruin their lives." She saw how they were looking at her. "Don't you understand? None of us ever had a choice in this. Your names were tattooed into my skin before I ever met either of you."

"I see," Troy said. "So your mother chose us for you, is that right? How could she do that when, as far as we know, we've never met her?"

"I can't tell you," Summer said, hunching her shoulders as misery filled her heart. "That's part of what I still don't remember."

Michael studied her face. "In my mortal time, matches were arranged by parents for their children."

"Mine, too," Troy said. "I think that's how my parents got together, actually."

"Don't," Summer whispered. "Please, don't try to make light of this." She paused. "You can't even refer to yourselves in the singular anymore."

"You are wrong, Beauty. *I* despised my life so deeply that *I* considered ending it more times than I care to count," Michael said softly. "You brought me out of darkness, and gave me noble purpose. You gifted me with the first real, true love I have ever known."

Troy nodded. "Same here. I've never belonged to my father, my family or the coven. All these years I've been serving in the Corps, I've had nothing but my duty. The Magus Corps kept me busy and on the move, so I didn't have to think about how empty my life was. These last couple years I've just been sleep-walking through every day, and then you come along. Suddenly I'm alive, and in love. Finally I mean something more than Major. Finally I belong somewhere, with Michael, at your side."

"You did not ruin our lives, Beauty." Michael laced his fingers through hers. "You gave them to us."

If they were lying she would have known it, but they weren't. She could feel the truth in their touch, and saw it in their eyes. To keep from crying Summer kissed Michael, and then turned to Troy and hugged him close. Her men held her and stroked her and eased her down between them, holding her and comforting her until the joy and gratitude she felt flared into desire and need.

"Will you have me?" she asked them.

Troy answered her by covering her mouth with his, tasting her with his tongue and swallowing her moan, as his hand pushed up her T-shirt to cup her bare breast. Michael whispered something wordless against her shoulder as he reached down to tug her leggings down over her hips and drag them from her legs. Troy broke their kiss to pull her shirt over her head, and then she lay naked between them. Their skin rubbed and heated her as they peeled off their boxers to reveal the thick, straining shafts of their erections.

Wetness flooded between her thighs.

"I can't wait," she breathed.

"But you must, for a moment, " Michael said, as he rolled her toward him so he could nuzzle her breasts.

Troy rose and removed two condom packets from the box, tossing one to Michael, who caught it without looking. Troy retreated to the bathroom.

"Where is he going?" Summer asked, pressing herself against Michael's big body.

"We are going to take care of you, my Beauty."

That was all Michael told her as he rolled on top of her He pinned her with the delicious heaviness of his weight, while he kissed her deeply. His erection pressed hard against her, and she let her fingers dig into the hard slabs of muscle along his back. He lifted up as Troy came back to the bed. He smoothly shifted away as the warlock took his place, and immediately ravished her aching nipples with hard tugging pulls of his hungry mouth.

Summer felt Michael move up beside them, as Troy drew her onto her side. She shivered as the Templar caressed her buttocks before stroking a silky, warm, oil over her rosebud. At the same time Troy brought her hand down to his pulsing cock, and had her roll the thin sheath of the condom down the length of his shaft. While she did, he rubbed his fingertip back and forth against her clit.

The tease was maddening and for a few moments she didn't know if her trembling fingers could manage the condom. But finally she stroked it all the way down, and felt Troy shiver. Breathing fast, she gripped him with her fist and guided his broad cock head between her slick folds. But as Michael rubbed his bulbous head over the tight pucker between her buttocks, she gasped and went still.

"Don't be afraid," Troy said. "Trust us."

"We will fit perfectly," Michael murmured against her hair as he pressed in. "Relax, sweet Beauty, and let us inside you. Let us possess you."

Summer nodded and released the tension in her muscles, thinking only of being open for their pleasure. Troy penetrated her with a deep, sure thrust, and then held himself still inside her as Michael began to work his cock into the tight ring of her rosebud. For a moment there was an unfamiliar stretching and burning, and then the thick head popped inside her. She tightened around him reflexively, and felt all the rich nerves just inside the opening flare into life.

"Breathe," Michael said as he gave her another gentle thrust, and more of his shaft sank into her.

"Ah," Troy sighed and shuddered with pleasure as the pressure of Michael's slow strokes began working through Summer against the bulge of his own shaft. "Yes, Brother, like that. She can feel us both now."

"She makes me her maypole," Michael said, and groaned as he forged deeper. "All satin ribbons round me."

Summer couldn't move. Suspended between them and skewered by their thrusting shafts, she could only gasp with each glide and pump. Her nipples flooded with heat and aching sensation, plumping and tightening at the same time. A cry left her as Michael gripped her heaving mounds from behind and held them so that Troy could suck one peak and then the other.

When Michael had sunken into her to his root, Troy finally lifted his head to look into her eyes.

"We're going to fuck you now, Lady."

"How you need it, Beauty," Michael said, his breath whispering over her cheek. "Deep and hard."

Troy drew out of her almost all the way, and then thrust back into her pussy just as Michael began to glide out of her bottom. When he plowed back in, Troy pulled out. That set the rhythm of their fucking as they worked in and out of her with smooth, steady power.

Summer whimpered and writhed between them, her hips jerking first toward Troy and then back against Michael as she found their rhythm and followed it. She tightened and released them with muscles she'd never felt before. Her softness caressed their swelling shafts as she accepted their hard, deep strokes.

"Look at me," Troy breathed, his fingers tangled in her hair. "Let me see your eyes." He pressed deep, and the dome of his cock head nudged her cervix, sending a thrilling jolt through her pelvis that made her moan. "Together now, Brother."

Summer groaned as Michael matched Troy's movements. Both heavy shafts penetrated her simultaneously, stretching her and delving into her and filling her. Her breasts heaved against Troy as she shuddered and wailed.

"Oh, please," she begged, clutching at Troy when he stilled. "Don't stop, please, I need–"

Michael caught the lobe of her ear between his teeth.

"We have everything you need," he told her. "Every dream, every desire." He plunged hard into her. "We will bring you every delight you can imagine, my Beauty."

It seemed to go on forever, that intimate dance between them, and on them, the sweet friction inside her twining and expanding in a flush of feeling that rose and burned through her so wildly she almost blacked out. Michael brought her back by firmly pinching one nipple and then the other while Troy dragged the edge of his teeth over her bottom lip.

"You want to come on our cocks, don't you?" he said, his voice deep and a little ragged. "Go deeper, Brother. She needs to feel every inch of us taking her pussy and her ass before she gives herself to us."

Michael pressed in, filling her so completely she could feel the soft crinkle of his body hair tickling her tightly-stretched opening. For a moment Summer wanted desperately to feel their semen pump into her body. The thought of both of them coming inside her made a strange heat seep through her sex, as if it meant to burn away the protective sheaths. The sensation pushed her into a dark, frantic upsurge of hot pleasure that shattered inside her over and over. As the climax claimed her, she screamed their names until she couldn't get enough breath. Some primal rhythm possessed them all, their shafts pounding into her as she writhed, out of control. As Michael's hands squeezed her breasts, his shaft began to jerk. Troy's penis did the same in the tight clasp of her pussy.

"Summer," Troy groaned, spilling himself, as Michael did the same.

"Beauty," he whispered harshly beside her ear.

But it was several long moments before any of them could be still. The last bits of the shared orgasm spasmed erratically, hips twitching, as they all gasped for breath. When it finally ended, no one could move. For a long time, they simply lay there. But when her lovers began to carefully disengage their bodies from hers, Summer felt tears prick her eyes. They had been so gentle, and yet so passionate, and she had never felt sexier or more beautiful—but now she knew she would never be able to let them go. She caught the two of them frowning at each other over her head.

"Please," she said, "don't tell me I messed that up somehow. It was…"

She couldn't think of any word to describe it, and shook her head.

"There is something we would ask you," Michael said, and raised her hand to his mouth.

"When you are ready," Troy said, brushing the hair back from her eyes. "Michael and I would like to take you without using any barriers. No condoms, just us."

She stiffened. Had they been able to read her thoughts?

"When we do," the Templar said, "we will come inside you, and it will initiate you into your immortality. It is said there is no greater pleasure. But only when you are ready to join us in eternity, Beauty."

Summer wanted nothing more than to give up her mortality and make the final transition, but another part of her made her think that was the last thing she needed to do. She was afraid of the power inside her, the power that would manifest completely once she was initiated.

What if it takes over? What if I'm never me again?

"Beauty, if we have upset you, think no more on it," Michael said quietly.

She stared at him. "I'm not upset. I can't do this. I mean, I can't make the transition yet. Please don't ask me why, because I don't know. It's just one more thing I can't remember." She pressed the heel of her hand against her forehead. "And there's more, much more. I can feel it, hiding somehow in the back of my mind. Or waiting, maybe."

"If your mother hid the fact that she tattooed and cursed you, she was certainly capable of doing something similar to wipe your memory, or conceal it," Troy said, looking thoughtful. "There is possibly one way Michael or I might access it."

Summer frowned. "How can you get to memories I can't remember?"

"We try this again," he said, "but with an enchantment that will open your mind as well as your body." He traced the outline of her lips. "We use sex magic."

CHAPTER EIGHT

"TEMPLE MASTER."

ONE of the mortal staff entered the ready room and hurried toward Nathaniel Harper, who was studying a wall-sized map of New England.

The interruption sent a surge of fury through Nathaniel, but he ignored the human as he marked the next portion of Maine where he would send his men to search for the heathens. When the human didn't leave he gritted his teeth.

"I left orders not to be disturbed. Must I cut them into your forehead so you may remember them?"

"There was a call for you, my lord." The mortal held out Nathaniel's mobile with a trembling hand. "He said only that he is Baldwin, and you have five minutes to call him back."

Nathaniel snatched the phone and eyed the

mortal.

"Get out, and keep everyone else out."

He had to wait until the man fled before he pressed the call-back button. The line rang five times before a cold voice answered.

"You have ten seconds," Baldwin said.

"You called me," Nathaniel said in as kind a tone as he could manage. Inside he seethed with anger that he would have to be polite to a Wiccan, but if he lost Baldwin, he might never again find such a valuable source. "What is it?"

"Gideon Edmunds is dead," Baldwin said. "He was murdered by a witch last night. Would you like to know the sort of noble death she gave him?"

Nathaniel felt shame and relief, tied together with the tight rope of his hatred for all pagans.

"I'm sure you want to tell me."

"She filled him with a tree. Impaled every bit of him until there was nothing left," Baldwin said. He sounded gleeful now. "But you mustn't blame the witch. She was one of his many victims. She even bore his child."

"Gideon made a Wiccan female pregnant?" Nathaniel said. He thought quickly. "We must have that child. Was it a son?"

"No, a daughter. She's a grown woman now,

and carrying a brat of her own. Poor Gideon, dying before he could find out he was to become a grandfather." The Templar spy made a tsking sound. "Impalement was the very least he deserved for what he did to all those women. If he'd fallen into my hands, I would have impaled him on a spit and roasted him slowly over an open fire."

Nathaniel imagined doing the same to his spy, and was surprised by how much pleasure the fantasy gave him.

"I will send someone to collect the remains," Nathaniel said.

"Don't bother, he's already been burned and buried." Baldwin's tone turned sly. "You're still trying to find the new location of the winter gathering of covens, aren't you?"

"Yes," Nathaniel said and licked his lips. "If you will tell me, I can deposit ten times the usual fee in your Swiss account."

"I don't want money this time," the spy snapped. "I want the witch who killed Gideon to suffer."

Nathaniel had never known Baldwin to be interested in revenge. The traitorous Wiccan had only ever demanded money.

"Deliver her into our hands," Nathaniel said,

"and I will see to it personally. I can even video tape the interrogations, if you wish."

Perhaps he should supervise them as well. Alvis had always said that women were the daughters of Eve, doomed to repeat the sins of their ancient, thieving, lying whore of a mother.

"I will deal with her myself," Baldwin said. "I will arrange for you to capture the man she loves. His name is Abel, and he is the Coven Master of Silver Wood. Once you have taken him, you will torture him for the rest of his life. You will do it in such a way that he suffers all the pain you can inflict without killing him outright. I want him to live a very long and horrifying existence."

Nathaniel nodded eagerly, and then recalled that the spy couldn't see him.

"Yes, I will be happy to do so. Now where is the gathering to be held?"

"You Templars are always too quick to attack. I will call the Priory and give you the location once all the covens have arrived," the spy said. "Then you can be sure to wipe out all of them."

Nathaniel silently cursed before he said, "Very well. Thank you for informing us about Gideon's fate. He was much loved among the order."

"He was a much-loved monster, then," Baldwin said. "Goodbye, Temple Master."

"Wait, what about Gideon's daughter? Can you deliver her to us along with the Coven Master?"

The only thing that answered him was a click. It so infuriated Nathaniel that he threw the mobile to the floor, where the case shattered. Sullenly he bent over to gather up the device, and saw an image of his scowling face on the screen. He must have activated the camera when he dropped it. For a few moments, he studied his portrait. The corner of his mouth had lifted in a sneer that was completely at odds with his usually benevolent expression. He lifted his hand to touch that side of his lips.

"Temple Master," said Augustin Colbert, Nathaniel's clergy aide and acting steward. He propelled his wheelchair across the room. "What happened?"

"A minor accident," Nathaniel said and turned away from him. "Let the brotherhood know that Gideon Edmunds was murdered by a Wiccan last night. We will hold a memorial gathering for him in the morning at dawn. See to it that everyone not out on assignment attends. Now go."

Augustin wheeled closer. "My lord, you have had a bad shock. Perhaps I should summon–"

"Get out," Nathaniel shouted, the words screeching against his own ears.

He repeated them three more times before they echoed in the silence around him. When he turned he didn't see Augustin or his wheelchair. There was no one and nothing in the room with him.

Had Augustin even come in?

Nathaniel lifted his trembling hand to his face. He had been under a terrible strain these last months. Losing Alvis had been a terrible blow. The Norseman had been his most lethal, effective operative. Gideon's journey into madness had caused more harm and damage than anyone might have guessed. And Michael, whom he had treated like a son, whom he had taken from his filthy pagan family and raised to be a fine and noble Templar, had gone the way of Judas. Perhaps he should have expected Michael's betrayal, but to know that the boy whose soul he had saved had sacrificed everything to protect that little whore of a witch maddened Nathaniel.

"I will find her," he muttered, and wiped the sweat from his upper lip. "And when I do, I will make her pay for what she's done."

Will you rape her? That always worked well for me in the first stages. I think it's the wench's screams as it's done. They clear out the cobwebs.

Nathaniel peered at the apparition that gently

floated in front of him.

"It can't be you. You died last night."

This is how it ends, Temple Master, and how it begins. His dead steward grinned around the butt of the cigar. *We're going to have so much fun, you and I.*

Nathaniel pressed his hand over his lips to muffle his scream, and felt his mouth twitch.

CHAPTER NINE

TROY AND MICHAEL flanked Summer as they walked to the pavilion. After the passionate night they'd shared, they were all a little drowsy. But at least Troy could be glad that Summer had no idea that he and Michael were both silently swapping erotic memories as they made their way along the sunny path.

"Actually, I do," Summer said suddenly, tucking her arm through Troy's. "Not only can I read your thoughts, I can feel your emotions. I can also switch it off when I want to give you some privacy."

"I'm an open book," Troy said, and thought of putting his mouth between Summer's legs.

"As am I," Michael chimed in, his thoughts suddenly filled with his hands fondling her breasts.

"Very funny," Summer said, but stopped and frowned. "Whoa. Who are all those people?"

Troy followed the direction of her gaze to see a long caravan of cars and trucks coming up the mountain access road.

"I think the first coven has arrived. It's probably Crystal Lake. Their Coven Master hates to be late for anything, so he usually makes everyone turn up early." He lifted an arm and waved at the lead car before taking Summer's hand. "Father is probably going to need some extra hands to help sort out the vehicles at the camp grounds. Would you mind visiting for a bit with Erica and Aileen while Michael and I help out?"

"No problem." She rubbed the front of her jacket. "And Michael, if you don't stop thinking about sucking my nipples, I'm going to hurt you."

"You are right," the Templar said and grinned. He snatched her off her feet and rubbed his face against the front of her jacket. "I would much rather do it than think it. Unzip, please."

"I don't want to put a damper on things," an amused male voice said, "but you can't have sex on the lawn in front of the pavilion." It was Wilson. "At least, not until the rest of the covens get here and we make popcorn and get our video cameras."

Michael lowered Summer as Troy grinned at his younger brother.

"We'll try to restrain ourselves. Was that Crystal Lake I saw coming up the road?"

Wilson nodded. "The other covens should be right behind them. If you and Michael have some spare time, we could use help getting them squared away."

"I can take a hint," Summer said. "I'm going to visit your wife and her mom."

She looked up at Michael, touched the pull of her jacket zipper as if she meant to tug it down, and then sauntered off toward the main house.

Wilson joined Troy and Michael to watch her go.

"Is she always like that?" When they both made affirmative sounds he sighed heavily. "Gods, I wish my wife wasn't nine months pregnant right now."

A few hours later Troy finished stacking the last load of firewood for Crystal Lake's camp and hauled the empty cart back to Wilson's pick up. He saw Michael wheeling a barrow of stones toward the center of the encampment, where the women were setting up their cooking and ritual fires. The big Templar seemed oblivious to all the frank, admiring looks the witches were giving him, but he smiled whenever a child or pet crossed his path.

"We're finished here for now," Wilson said as he joined Troy by the back of the truck. He nodded toward Michael. "That guy just doesn't quit."

"Yeah, they never taught him that."

"We're not telling anyone that Michael was a Templar," Wilson said quietly. "We all agreed at dinner last night. If anyone finds out, it has to be from him."

"Or the spy," Troy said and dragged his hand through his hair. "I still think holding the gathering here is a bad idea. If the Templars find out and come for us—"

"We've got sentries posted at the beginning and end of the road on the mountain. If they come, we'll know. We're also armed and ready for them." Wilson scuffed the toe of his boot in the cold dirt between them. "Troy, I'm sorry."

"For what?"

"Pretty much our whole lives," his brother said. "I shouldn't have let Father and jealousy get between us. I know Aileen doesn't have any feelings for you. I called your woman and your friend ugly names, and despised them, and treated them like shit. Then they go and save me from being a chainsaw massacre." He cocked his head as he regarded Michael again, who had stopped to look at them. "I'm still not sure why he risked his life to save my ass."

Troy could feel Michael picking up on his thoughts, and nodded to the Templar.

"He understands how much brothers mean to each other."

"I didn't," Wilson said. "I'm an ass, and I know it, but I'd like to start over with you." He faced him and held out his hand. "Brothers?"

Troy ignored the hand and pulled Wilson into his arms, holding him close for a long moment. "Brothers."

CHAPTER TEN

SUMMER STOOD OUTSIDE the shadow book vault and shoved her hands into her jacket pockets. She watched Troy sort through the grimoire stored in the warded shelves inside, while Michael kept an eye on the door.

"Your father is going to walk in here," she said. "He'll find us raiding his magic book depository and toss us all off the mountain, you know."

"Erica promised to keep him busy for another hour at the coven welcoming ritual," Troy said as he emerged and shook some dust from his hair before he held up a small, silk-bound grimoire. "And I found it, so we can leave right now."

Michael scowled. "How can performing an evil spell do any good for Summer or us?"

"Sex magic can be unpredictable, and if done wrong even dangerous, but it's never been evil. It's one of the oldest sources of white magic known to Wiccans." Troy tucked the book inside his coat. "And if my father finds out the three of us are going to try it, he'll kill me before we can, so let's go."

On the way out of the main house they stopped to say goodbye to Wilson and Aileen. Summer immediately noticed the change in the way Troy and his brother regarded each other. She kissed Aileen's cheek.

"I think you actually have a brother-in-law now," Summer whispered.

"I'm claiming two from now on," the pregnant witch said and beamed at Michae. "Will you and the guys come to dinner tomorrow night? Erica is having a surprise baby shower for me, and yes, I'm not supposed to know, but I want you there."

"Count on it," Summer said, and gave her a hug.

On the way back to the old house Troy and Michael were quiet, and Summer could sense that they were thought-sharing, but decided not to listen in. The problem with always being able to know what her lovers were thinking was that she didn't want to know. When the time came for her to have a baby shower someday, she *did* want it to be a surprise.

One baby shower for a little girl, Summer thought.

While she still felt somewhat bitter over having her future so ruthlessly planned out for her, she was beginning to accept it. Surely her mother must have felt the same when she learned she was to be the next guardian.

We are born knowing it, Daughter.

Summer stood alone in the dark, snowy woods, and turned around to see Troy and Michael standing like statues behind her. Ahead of her a soft green light glowed, and her mother appeared, her two lovers standing behind her.

Why have you brought me here, Maman?

Her mother turned aside, indicating someone just beyond her lovers. Summer saw another woman with light brown hair and opal eyes.

My grandmother?

Summer stood on tiptoe as she saw yet another woman and two men beyond her grandmother, and a trio behind her, and another, and on and on until they disappeared beyond the horizon.

How long have we been doing this, Maman?

Since the first immortal tried to use the Emerald Tablet to rule over the world, her mother said. *It was decided then to use its power to create the blood line. We are not human or immortal, my darling. We are the children of the Tablet.*

"But if I'm not human, or immortal, what am I?" Summer asked, but the vision disappeared. She didn't realize she'd spoken out loud until she saw Troy and Michael staring at her. "Sorry. Just, ah, thinking out loud."

Troy shook his head slightly. "Come on, you two. I'm freezing."

"You are a water elemental," Michael complained. "Can you not melt winter or something like that?"

Neither of them seemed to know they'd been frozen in time while she'd had a mental chat with her mother. And why now, when they were simply walking through the woods to go home?

Once they reached the old house Summer went to the kitchen to brew some gingered orange tea, which always helped warm them up. She pushed the strange interlude with her mother from her mind. So she came from a long line of not-human, not-immortal women who liked threesomes and only had one kid. Everyone had to come from somewhere.

"You look worried."

She turned to see Michael watching her from the doorway.

"I'm not. I'm making tea." She took the kettle from the stove and filled the three cups she'd prepared before handing one to him. "Has Troy turned himself into a sexy little toad yet?"

"I heard that," Troy called from the dining room.

As Summer went to take his tea to him, Michael stopped her with a hand on her shoulder.

"You do not have to do this, if you would rather not. I will tell him to put the book back."

"You're worried. What is it? Is it the sex part?" she asked, and rolled her eyes when he gave her a very direct look. "Okay, aside from the sex part, what's bothering you about this?"

"I am not a warlock. I have never managed much in the way of magic." He ducked his head. "I trust Troy to cast the spell correctly, but if something does go amiss, you must help him before me. If you can help us. Or you can choose not to do this."

"Michael, every day I don't remember my past it threatens our future together." She covered his hand with hers. "I have to know the rest of it."

He nodded, and put his arm around her shoulder as he walked with her to the dining room. Troy had removed the tables and chairs, and had drawn a spell circle on the floor using thin lines of frost. The sex magic grimoire lay open on the table. When Summer glanced at it she saw an illustration of two men and a woman standing naked inside the same type of circle. When she blinked, the image changed to one of one man and a woman having sex standing up.

"Take off your clothes," Troy told her as he pulled his shirt over his head and unfastened his belt. "Don't touch me or Michael until you're inside the circle."

Summer felt another wave of doubt as she slowly undressed.

"I don't think I can have sex with both of you standing up."

"You'll only be having sex with Michael," Troy said. Now naked, he stepped over the circle's frost lines and stood in the center. "He's going to be your anchor while I use your pleasure to gain access to your mind."

"My old ball and chain," Summer teased the Templar as they stepped into the circle to join Troy. "So how do I—oooh." As Michael picked her up by the waist and held her effortlessly suspended, she glanced down. His thick erection, already sheathed in a condom, rose below her. She wrapped her legs around his waist, and gazed into his deep green eyes. "Hold onto me."

"Always, my Beauty."

He closed his eyes for a moment, and then

turned around, so that she could see Troy over his shoulder. The warlock began chanting as Michael positioned Summer over his erection, and let her softness sink down to envelope it by slow degrees. Being penetrated so gradually and completely made her dig in her fingers behind his strong neck. Once he'd buried his full length inside her she met Troy's hot blue eyes.

Michael moved his hands to her hips and lifted her a few inches before pushing her back on his cock. He worked her on top of him as if she weighed nothing. The delicious fullness of him inside her, the way she was completely at his mercy, made her rock against him. He grunted a little as he plunged upward, his rhythm increasing. Summer began to pant as Troy finished his incantation and moved closer, his hands sketching the air around her head with signs before his fingers sifted through her hair.

"All seeing to unseen, all of what has been, from the black to my sight, restore all this night, so may it be."

Summer fell into the beauty of Troy's eyes, and moaned as Michael pumped harder, his cock pistoning in and out. It kept her tethered to her body as she felt the warlock's power seeping into her like warm rain. The pleasure of having her body taken by the Templar while the Wiccan penetrated her mind made her writhe, pinned by spirit and flesh, until she felt Troy behind her eyes.

You would see what has been hidden from all, Elemental? The old crone deep inside Summer's mind laughed. *So shall you.*

Summer tried to push Troy out of her head, but the power welled up inside her, faster than it ever had before. It enveloped him in cold green light. Outside of her mind she heard Michael grunt as his body turned to stone. She hung in his arms, her body still skewered by his. The room around them began to fade away into darkness, and Summer desperately tried to reach out and hold something, anything to keep them in the real world. But all three of them were plunged into green darkness.

So may it be.

CHAPTER ELEVEN

"I DON'T WANT you shouting at Troy again," Erica told Abel as she followed him out of the main house. "If we make an effort, we can all be reasonable, rational adults."

"Sex magic. With three instead of two, and one who can do things like stop time." The Coven Master shook his head as he helped her into his car. "I'll be lucky to have a mountain left by morning. What was he thinking?"

"Don't ask me. I never thought sex was magical," she said, and regretted those words the moment they left her lips. "Except with you, of course."

Abel slammed the door and faced her. "You don't like making love with me. You fake every orgasm. You do it because you want to make me feel like a good lover, and keep me happy. I am the only man you've ever made love to. I knew these things, and I accepted them. The only difference now is I know *why*."

Erica stiffened. "Well, you certainly don't have to have sex with me anymore."

"Or maybe now that the fucking monstrous shit is dead, you'll stop thinking about him when we're making love." He leaned close and kissed her ear. "Also, I don't have sex with you. I make love with you. Now, can we go and stop my idiot son from destroying himself, his witch, his Templar, and our home?"

Erica had to press her lips together to keep from laughing as Abel raced along the road that led to the old house. As they passed the dirt road she had used to get to Gideon's camp site her smile faded. That day was still a blur of fear and loathing and fury in her mind. But from the moment she'd scried Gideon on the mountain she'd known what she would do. What she didn't understand was why she had been capable of such violence. Since Gideon had brutalized her she had always shrank from anything that reminded her of it.

"You were protecting your child," Abel said suddenly. "That's why you were able to do it. It wasn't about you. It was to keep Aileen safe from her father."

"I suppose it could be– " Erica sat upright and stared at him. "You're reading my mind. But you don't have that ability."

"With you, darling, I do," he said and glanced sideways at her. "I dipped into the sex magic book myself once or twice. Drew the circle under my bed, got you in it, and tried to sort out what had happened to you. It ended up being permanent."

Erica felt dizzy. "That means you know everything that man did to me. You knew about Aileen. You knew what a horrible person I am, and you still…oh, I will never understand you."

He stopped the car in front of the old house, shut off the engine, and reached over to pull her into his arms.

"I want you to be my mate. If you can't now, I'll wait for you. I'll wait forever for you. I love you, Erica Buchanan."

Abel kissed her again, and this time made it hot and sexy and entirely inappropriate in public. Yet as his mouth ravished hers, Erica felt a strange glow starting deep in her belly. When he finally lifted his head, for the first time in memory she wanted him to put his hands on her.

"Later," he said and kissed her brow. "Now stay in the car."

"If yesterday proved anything, dearest, it's that I don't stay in the car." Erica got out and peered at the house. "I don't see any lights."

He grunted and took her arm. "They may be in the middle of something, so don't make any noise or sudden moves when we're inside, all right?"

Erica felt a light sheen of sweat beading on her face as they quietly approached the house, but it wasn't from fear or dread. She still felt the needy ache in her lower parts, and now it seemed to be moving between her legs.

I'm past this nonsense, she scolded herself, and then saw the lecherous look Abel gave her. *Or perhaps not.*

He used his spare key to unlock the front door, and walked with her through the kitchen. Erica smelled the deep green scent of a lush garden. Abel pressed a finger to his lips before he eased open the door so they could look inside.

Troy, Summer and Michael stood naked in a spell circle, and from their positions and movements Erica could tell Michael was having sex with her while Troy moved in and peered into her eyes. She caught her breath as she felt waves of power suddenly radiate past the frost lines of the circle. She had to squint when a brilliant green light wrapped around all three of them. The sound of a high wind filled the room.

"Troy," Abel shouted above the din. "The spell is out of control. Neutralize it. Now, son, before it rips you to pieces."

Abel's son didn't seem to hear him, but his jaw tightened as he fought to lift his arm and use his hand to cover Summer's eyes. The moment he did all the air in the room went still. The green light drew back into itself, intensifying and growing hotter, until Erica was convinced it would explode.

Abel lifted his hands and hurled a burst of power at the circle as he uttered a containment spell. That, too, contracted in on the three. The light became so dazzling that Erica had to turn her head away until it vanished.

Abel made a hoarse sound of disbelief, and when she looked back she saw only empty space where the three had been standing.

"It took them," he said, and turned his horrified eyes on her. "They're gone."

As he staggered and Erica caught him in her arms, she heard something like an old woman's voice whispering. What it said made her blood run cold.

So may it be.

REVEALED

SILVER WOOD COVEN BOOK FIVE

By Hazel Hunter

CHAPTER ONE

LAST AUGUST

"I'M afraid I have some bad news," the driver told Eve after he'd finished talking on his mobile phone. He turned off the tinny, country music playing on the radio. "That was my contact in Quebec. He said someone set fire to your house."

Eve had felt the wrenching psychic pain last night, while Wiccan friends had been smuggling her across the border into North Dakota. But she had told herself that Marie could survive anything. She stared blindly through the windshield at the rapidly darkening sky. Lightning streaked through the dark clouds on the horizon.

"Is my mother still alive?"

"They don't know. They said she's missing." The driver, a reed-thin man with a name Eve couldn't remember, cleared his throat gruffly. "The two of you are pretty close, huh?"

The four of us, she wanted to correct him, and then her stomach clenched as she realized what Marie Lautner's passing would mean. Her mother's lovers, Jean-Paul and Christien, shared more than her affections.

If she was captured, mes pères will go after her. They will fight to the death to bring her back…but if she dies…

Eve choked back a sudden surge of acidic bile. "Please stop the car. I have to be sick."

"Oh, shit, hold on," the driver said and quickly pulled off the road.

Genevieve flung open the door and stumbled out, doubling over as she emptied her belly into the thick, brown weeds.

"You okay?" the driver called to her anxiously. "Uh, you need a napkin or something?"

She needed to go back to Quebec. She needed her *maman* and her *pères* alive. She needed to be a child again, little Genevieve Lautner, playing in the garden while Marie planted her herbs, Christien pruned the trees, and Jean-Paul raked the leaves. She wanted the cozy evenings of laughter and love. She didn't want to be left behind with the responsibility. She was too young.

She hadn't even completed her training. The only spells Marie had taught her were for healing.

All around her the weeds that had withered and been baked brown by the long, hot summer began to turn green and lush, as if to taunt her.

No. I cannot do this, Eve thought as she straightened, and her nausea receded into full-blown panic. *I cannot be this.*

Yet even as those frantic thoughts shrieked in the silence behind her eyes, she felt three bolts of pain through her heart. She staggered back to the car, holding onto the door as the psychic ties between her and her parents were abruptly severed. Heat and needling pain sank into her skin, stabbing into her from her hips to her throat. An icy dread crept down her spine as she realized it meant the last spells Marie had cast had been triggered by her death. They were spells cast in order to protect Eve, as well as the burden she had passed along.

It's mine now. Gods help me.

She managed to get back inside the car and clipped on her seatbelt to keep from falling over.

"How far away are we from the meeting place?" she whispered.

"It's only twenty miles or so from here," the driver said, giving her several quick glances.

"You're as white as snow, honey. Do you want to, you know, rest for a minute?"

"I feel better now," Eve lied, closing her eyes to focus on the spell she had to cast now to contain what was happening to her. Once her body ward was safely in place she added, "Please hurry. I need to see my people right away."

The driver nodded. Jim—his name was Jim, Eve finally remembered. He turned the radio back on. For a few miles he just hummed along to Hank Williams, and then he took out a pack of cigarettes.

"You mind if I have a smoke?"

"No." Although Eve hated the stink of tobacco, it wouldn't penetrate her spell shield. "You know you can't smoke around the coven."

"Yeah, I got the lecture," he said. He opened his window before he lit up, and then exhaled the first drag with a sigh of relief. "My girlfriend keeps nagging me to quit, but I've been puffing away since I was eleven. Hard to shake the habit."

Eve thought of what she had been doing at the same age: making bird houses with Christien, having snowball fights with Jean-Paul, and studying with Marie. She'd always wondered why her mother had insisted on her learning English when they only spoke in French to each other.

Did she foresee this? Is this the real reason she sent me so far away from home?

"So, you're a witch, too, right?" Jim asked. When she nodded, Jim gave an uneasy laugh. "Thought so. I couldn't believe it when I first found out about you guys, you know? I always thought witches were a bunch of Halloween bullshit, and then my girlfriend tells me she's one. Then she says a bunch of medieval priests want to torture and kill your kind. Next thing you know I'm helping move you people in and out of the country. Like I'm some magical coyote for illegals."

Eve heard a trace of disgust behind the false heartiness, and felt some of her own at his tone.

"I would have stayed in Quebec," she said, "if I could have."

And now Marie was dead, and so were Eve's two fathers, leaving her all alone with a burden she neither wanted nor entirely understood.

"Don't worry, honey," Jim said as he turned down a narrow road leading to an industrial complex. "I don't expect you'll have to stay for long. And hey, look. We're here."

Eve could see two large, dark cars parked in the lot between the warehouse buildings, but their headlights prevented her from seeing the faces of the figures standing around them. Her skin crawled with nerves and something else, and she felt a strong impulse to jump out of the vehicle. But that made no sense at all, unless the Templars had somehow tracked her to the states.

"You're sure this is where we are supposed to meet them?" she asked carefully.

"Absolutely positive."

He shoved his hand in his jacket as he parked a short distance from the other cars. When he turned to her, he took his hand out.

"Change of plans, though, honey. These guys will be real nice to you, as long as you stay calm, okay?"

Eve glanced down to see the gun he was pointing at her chest.

"What have you done?"

"I'm going to make me a pile of money, dump my witch girlfriend, and head to Miami Beach," Jim said with great satisfaction. "Now get out of the damn car."

She climbed out, squinting. The blinding, white-blue headlights dazzled her tired eyes. She glanced over at Jim's tense face, and saw beads of sweat glittering on his brow and upper lip.

He's afraid. But of them or me?

"Who are these men?"

"Nice guys, like I told you. Real religious." He came around the car and took her arm, hauling her forward. "Here she is. Bring me my money, and you can take her."

"Not yet." A large, heavyset man stepped out in front of the headlights. He leveled a shotgun at Jim. "She tells us where her mother hid the treasure, and then we'll pay you."

"Right," Jim said and looked at her. "Go ahead. Tell the man."

None of them were Templars, Eve realized dully. They'd sent their mortal minions to collect her.

"Whatever I say, you won't get paid," she said to the driver in a low voice. "They're going to kill you."

"Enough whispering," the big man said. He chambered a round in the shotgun. "Where is it?"

She spread out her hands. "Go ahead. Shoot me and the treasure will be lost forever."

"Hey, this wasn't the deal," Jim said. "I got a right to—"

The rest of what he said was obliterated by the blast of the shotgun, which blew the gun and most of the fingers off his hand.

Eve cringed away as the driver screamed and clutched his wrist. The heavyset man ejected the spent cartridge, chambered another, and aimed at her face.

"I'm not playing here, Frenchie," the man said calmly. "The next one will be a headshot. Where did she hide it?"

She blinked back hot tears as a strange calm spread through her.

"In a place where you'll never find it."

"Oh, god. Tell them," Jim said hoarsely. "Tell them now. You have to tell them where it is, you fucking bitch, or we're both–"

The man fired the shotgun, and Jim's face exploded. Blood and gore spattered Eve as the driver's body slammed into hers. It slid down to lay motionless at her feet. As the metallic stink of his blood filled her nostrils she stared down in horror. Though she wanted to scream, she was gripped by enchantment as the driver's death activated one of the spells branded on her skin.

Her maman's voice whispered in her mind.

To save you, all be condemned, as they would do, be done to them. So may it be.

"You have to stop right now," she said, but her voice came out in a thready whisper. "Please, if you don't, you'll die."

Her warning came too late. The headlights of both cars winked out, while the air in front of

Eve's eyes glowed green with building power. The light crackled through the air as it shot out, whirling around the shooter and his men as their faces emptied of all expression.

No, please, Gods.

Eve tried desperately to pull back the magic, but the power that gripped her rendered her helpless to do anything but watch.

One by one the men began taking out the weapons they carried, flicking off the safeties, and aiming them at each other. They still had their voices, and began yelling at each other to stop. As the first shot rang out they stared in horror at her, and began begging her to spare them even as they fired upon one another. Body after body fell to the ground, some dead before they landed, others screaming and writhing in agony before they finally went limp.

The last man left standing reversed the shotgun in his hands, and pressed the end of the barrel under his chin.

"Damn you, you fucking witch," he muttered as he reached for the trigger. "Damn you straight to—"

The shotgun fired, erasing his face in a blast of tissue, bone and blood.

With his death, her mother's spell ended. Eve

fell to her knees beside Jim's body. She put a trembling hand to her chest until she felt a warm wetness on her breast. She looked down at her blouse, which was soaked with the driver's blood. In disgust, she tried to pull it away from her skin. But green power whirled around her as the blood triggered the spell branded over her heart, the only spell Maman had never explained to her. Eve felt it burn into her chest and spread through her limbs as the green light grew blinding. Her eyes widened when she saw three more figures step out of the shadows.

One tall man with short-cropped golden hair and a brutally muscled form stood on the left. His eyes reflected the power suffusing the air. He surveyed their surroundings with the alert, cool detachment of an experienced warrior. On the right another, leaner man, as dark as the first was fair, studied her with eyes so blue it almost hurt to look back at them. He moved with the lethal grace of a skilled, silent predator.

Yet it was the woman who stood between them that held Eve's gaze riveted. Tall and elegantly slim, she had gilded brunette hair that cascaded over her shoulders in thick, soft waves. As she walked toward Eve, the moon came out from behind the clouds and silvered her lovely features, which Eve had seen every day since her eighteenth birthday.

"Stay back," she called out to them. "Please. Don't come any closer to me."

"She can see us," the golden-haired man said in a deep, stern voice. "We are present in this time. We must not interfere."

"There's hardly anyone left alive to interfere with," the dark man replied in a melodic tenor. When their female companion moved toward Eve, the man caught her arm. "Summer, wait."

"It's all right," Summer said and smiled at her. "We won't hurt you."

"No one can ever hurt me again," Eve told her.

Eve could feel her mind expanding as the power continued to alter her consciousness. She looked at the men on either side of her twin, and marveled over how one was as dark as Christien, the other as light as Jean-Paul. Some things never changed, it seemed.

"Why did you come here?" Eve asked.

"To understand this," Summer said, making an encompassing gesture. She came forward and knelt beside Eve. "And to understand you."

Eve almost laughed. "But you know everything about me."

"No," Summer said. "A few months ago I woke

up in Central Park with no name or memory of who I was. Since then little pieces of my life have come back, but I still don't know how or why any of this happened to me." She held out her hand. "Will you help me remember?"

"Don't touch her," the dark man warned. "She's warded with death spells."

"I am Genevieve Lautner," Eve said. Knowing she only had seconds before the transference spell triggered by Marie's death finished altering her mind, Eve grabbed her twin's wrist. *"Take from me my memories, all that I've known that you must see. So may it be."*

Green light filled Eve's eyes, and then the magic flung all four of them into the dimness between the stars.

• • • • •

Summer drifted in the darkness as her bruised mind struggled to make sense of what was happening. She tried to remember the sex magic that Troy had used in an attempt to recover her memory, but the spell eluded her. Everything was gone, and she was alone.

I don't want to be alone anymore.

Her own eyes stared up at her from the

darkness, the pupils hugely dilated. A tight voice perfectly imitated her own as it repeated something Summer had heard before. A spell, but not one that Troy had cast.

All that I've known.

The sound of a wail forced her to open her eyes, but the light blinded her. She was tiny and helpless, and cradled against a warm breast. She couldn't see clearly, but she could feel the gentle, thudding rhythm of the heart beneath her cheek.

You must see.

Her vision began to clear, and she looked up at the faces smiling at her: her mother, her golden father, her dark father. They whispered to her, and kissed her face, and fed her, and rocked her to sleep. Only then did Summer realize what was happening to her.

She gave me her memories, and now I'm reliving them, all the way back to her birth.

Day by day she experienced Genevieve Lautner's secluded life, first as an infant, then as a toddler, crawling and then tottering along the old oak floors of Marie Lautner's family mansion. Nearly every day she also accompanied her mother out to the beautiful back garden, which remained lush and green no matter how cold the weather turned.

"My little Eve," Marie said as they walked along the stone pathways through the flowers. "You're a touch of spring."

Eve also had two handsome fathers to adore and pamper her. Her lovely mother spent years teaching her everything about Wiccans, the Templars, and an outside world she had never seen. She listened to Eve weep with joy on her fourteenth birthday, when for the first time Marie had allowed her to leave their home and go into Quebec.

Eve had entered the modern world on that day flanked by her strong, protective fathers, who guided her through the streets while introducing her to the dirty, chaotic realm of ordinary mortals.

"So many people," Eve said as she watched a group of schoolgirls skipping along the sidewalk. "Why do we not live here, like them?"

Her fathers exchanged one of their odd looks before Jean-Paul said, "We could not have our garden here in the city, *cherie*."

While Eve's life had been quiet and idyllic, it had not been perfect. As she grew older she rebelled, arguing with her mother over her training, and the things Marie still kept from her. She knew that, like all the Lautner women, she would someday have to guard a secret. But all her mother would say was that, for now, it was her burden to carry, not Eve's.

"When it is time, you will know," Marie said. "Until then, enjoy your freedom, for it will not last forever."

As an older teen Eve had begun to feel imprisoned rather than free. Her mother refused to allow her to attend school, have friends or even go anywhere by herself, and they argued bitterly each time Eve tried to show some independence. After one particularly emotional fight, Eve had run away from home to spend a miserable day on Mount Saint-Alban. She stared for hours at the water, and wished she could sail across it to some faraway place where no one cared who or what she was. By sunset Jean-Paul and Christien had found her, and persuaded her to come back. When Eve returned, Marie had wept with joy, but she had also become even more controlling and secretive.

"Why don't you trust me?" Eve had demanded after another argument with her mother. "How can I be a guardian if I don't know what it is I'm supposed to protect?"

Marie had given her a sad look. "I wish you never had to, my darling."

Eventually Eve's three parents allowed her to

leave home to attend college and work part-time in the city. There she had her first love affair with a brash, handsome soccer player, who had awkwardly taken her virginity before dumping her for a gymnast. There would be two more young men after him who proved equally disappointing in bed, before Eve decided to stop dating. Her bad luck with love had made her confide in Jeal-Paul, to whom she had always gone with her secrets. After making sure she had used protection, he told her something strange.

"You do not have to look for your loves, *bébé*. They will find you."

Eve laughed. "So I will have two lovers, like Maman? I could not be that lucky, *mon père*."

He kissed the top of her head. "Lautner women are *always* so lucky."

After Eve came home for her last summer break, Marie had seemed remote and almost cold toward her, until one night at dinner when her fathers left them alone to talk. It was then that her mother had calmly told her about the secret she had been keeping from her for all those years.

Eve had been horrified to learn that she existed only to protect the oldest grimoire in the world, and to give birth to the next Guardian. At that moment she would have fled the house, and run as far away from her mother as she could. But when she tried to stand, her legs wouldn't work. The rest of her body grew heavy and numb.

"I never wished it to come to this, my darling," Marie had whispered as she lifted Eve into her strong arms and carried her back to the spell chamber. "But the Templars are closing in, and we have no time to relocate or finish your training. I must send you to a safe haven until the danger has passed."

Eve never completely lost consciousness that night. She felt every bolt of power Marie used to burn the protective spells into her skin. In the end she had been covered in blood and writhing in agony. Her mother scarred her one final time with a jar of emerald ink and a needle-tipped stylus, which she used on her scalp.

"Forgive me as I forgave my mother," Marie said when she finished. Her eyes glittered with a terrible green light as she stared down at Eve. "Should the worst happen, we will live on in you, Daughter."

She bent to kiss her brow, and that simple, affectionate touch sent a stream of power into Eve's mind, transferring the last of Marie's secrets to her memory. Only when the power faded did Eve finally understand why she had never seen the treasure that Lautner women had been protecting for millennia.

CHAPTER TWO

NOW

SUMMER AWOKE to hear the crunch of broken glass, and feel something warm and soft covering her stiff limbs. All around her the air smelled of a sunlit garden, but when she opened her eyes it was to darkness.

Strong arms lifted her from the hardwood floor and carried her to the bed she shared with her mates. They gently placed her on it before drawing the soft, old quilt over her shivering form. When she looked up she saw Troy Atwater's heavenly blue eyes gazing down at her from an older version of his handsome face.

"Welcome back," Abel Atwater, Troy's father, said as he turned to light a candle. "How do you feel?"

"Like I've been bounced against a brick wall." The croaking sound of her voice made Summer grimace. "What happened?"

"You blew all the fuses, and knocked out most of the windows in the front of the house, but that's all the damage we've found so far. You're not injured." He propped his hands on his hips. "No thanks to my son, of course, who also survived, along with your Templar."

"His name is Michael, and he's a Wiccan, not a Templar," Summer said. She felt her head pound in time with her racing heartbeat. "Where are they?"

"Here, Beauty." Michael Charbon staggered into the room, hauling Troy Atwater along with him. They both looked pale and exhausted. Once the Templar eased Troy down beside Summer he looked all over her. "Are you hurt?"

"I don't think so," she said and checked Troy, who gave her a groggy smile, and then looked up as Erica Buchanan came in carrying an oil lamp on a tray with mugs of tea. The high priestess looked haggard, and in the flickering light Summer could see the shiny traces of tears on her scarred face. "Come here, Michael."

The Templar hobbled around to the other side, where he lay down with a sigh of relief.

547

Both Erica and Abel looked as if they hadn't slept for a week.

"I'm sorry," Summer said. "Troy cast that spell earlier only to help me recover my memory."

"Earlier?" Abel said, his jaw tightening. "Summer, you've been gone for three days. Erica and I have been camped out here the entire time, trying every spell we could think of to bring you back. Now, would you mind telling me where you went, and how the hell–"

"That can all wait," Erica said, cutting him off. "Let the children rest now. I'll stay with them while you attend to the covens. Go on, Abel. By now they'll be wondering why we haven't held the opening ritual."

Abel gave Troy a sour look. "Well, I'm not telling them it's because my idiot son was fooling with sex magic."

"Appreciate that," Troy muttered as he pressed a hand to his head. "Could you also find out who tried to crack my skull open?"

"If I do, I'll give them a handsome reward. I'll be back in a few hours, love."

The coven master kissed Erica's cheek and left the room. Erica arranged the quilt over Troy and Michael before she handed out the mugs.

"Chamomile, with blue pimpernel, vervain and

feverfew," she told Summer. "It should help with the headaches from the backlash. There's soup and bread in the kitchen when you're ready for something to eat."

"You should go and get rest, too," Summer said. "You haven't slept in three days."

The older witch nodded toward the hall. "I'll leave the door open. Call if you need me."

Once Erica had left, Summer lay back and stared at the ceiling.

"Three days. How could we have been gone that long? Troy just cast the spell only three minutes ago, didn't he?"

"That wasn't my spell, lady," the warlock said, and curled his hand around hers. "That was all you."

Michael took her other hand. "Perhaps minutes for us were days for them?"

"Or we were spellbound for days and didn't realize the passage of time," Troy said, and grunted a little as he sat up and braced his shoulders against the head board. "Summer, that woman in the parking lot…"

"She looked exactly like you," the Templar finished for him.

"Eve was me," she said and looked over at Troy. "My name is Genevieve Lautner. You were right, Troy. I am from Quebec."

Now she somehow had to find the words to tell them the rest of it.

"Hold on," Troy said, frowning. "You can't be Genevieve Lautner."

Michael glared at him. "You knew about her before we met Summer?"

"The Magus Corps and every coven on both sides of the border was alerted last year when she disappeared." The warlock scowled back at him before he said to Summer, "I don't know what Genevieve looked like. The coven in Quebec never provided a photo of her. But back in September they alerted us that she was found dead, near the border in North Dakota."

"They knew by then that I had escaped the Templars' men. The lie was their attempt to protect me until I could find my way to a safe haven." She met Troy's doubtful gaze. "And they couldn't give the Magus Corps a picture because I've never been photographed, but I'm sure that they did tell you how to identify me."

"If I may?"

When she nodded, Troy gently lifted her hair above her right ear, and parted it until he saw the tiny green rectangle tattooed on her scalp.

"Summer—Eve—I have to tell you

something."

"I know the Templars murdered my family," she told him, swallowing against the tightness in her throat. "My mother sent me away because she feared they would kill me, too. Then the Emerald Tablet would be lost forever."

"You remember where it is?" Michael asked gently.

"Yes."

Summer brought her hand to her throbbing temple, and for the first time noticed that the spell brands on her skin were fading. In a few hours they would disappear, and only someone who touched her skin would be able to detect their presence. *Or someone who tries to harm me*, she thought, remembering the crumpled bodies in the parking lot.

"I have so much to tell you, but I don't want to."

"We do not have to talk about it now," Michael said.

His hand turned her face toward his, and she saw the unshakeable trust in his brilliant green eyes. He shifted close enough to brush his mouth over hers.

"You should rest."

"He's right," Troy said, and dropped a kiss on

her right shoulder. "Whatever it is, it can wait."

"I'm afraid it can't."

Summer glanced at the door, using a thought to close it soundlessly, and then lifted a hand and brushed it across the air as she murmured a spell that had not been used since Pompeii had been buried under fourteen feet of volcanic ash and pumice. The air glittered as an oval of mist condensed into an oval window.

The warlock went still. "Summer, I don't think another trip through time is a good idea."

"I'm bringing history to us this time." She took their hands in hers. "The only way for you to understand what's happening now is to show you how it began. Trust me, please."

When she felt both men relax, she focused on the portal. It expanded to envelope them, erasing the room and surrounding them instead with a primitive encampment of people dressed in crudely-woven tunics.

Michael reached out a restraining hand as a man walked toward them, and then through them.

"We are like ghosts here," he said.

"It's only a shared vision," Summer told him. "All Wiccans are descended from this first clan. These people were different from other humans in many ways, and not only in their minds and bodies. They gathered instead of hunting. They respected the natural world around them. They practiced a faith of peace and love."

The sun and moon began chasing each other across the sky as the encampment grew larger, and more people appeared with children and animals.

"As the first Wiccans discovered their natural abilities and powers, they began using them to improve their lives and their world," Summer told her lovers as they watched the settlement expand. "They eliminated sickness from the clan, and then they stopped aging."

Time moved forward faster around them, and the settlement became a village where the early Wiccans planted gardens, cultivated fields, and raised sheep. When night came, they gathered in circles in the moonlight and began using primitive magic to illuminate the darkness.

"So that they could share their abilities with others, the Wiccans created spells that when spoken would allow the transfer of magic from one member of the clan to another. This sharing increased the abilities of everyone in the clan." Summer smiled a little as two children ran in circles around them, and then looked at an approaching blur on the horizon. "Life was very good, until outsiders found them."

As a small group of humans leading pack animals entered the town. The strangers stared at the signs of the clan's prosperity. When one of the traders tried to grab a Wiccan woman, her mate knocked him away with a flick of his fingers.

"That's not good," Troy said.

"The Wiccans were just as shocked to discover that these humans had neither magic nor immortality," Summer said, and led her men to the home of an older man. He only shook his head as the leader of the caravan made violent, threatening gestures. "When the Wiccans refused to share the secret of the clan's powers with the traders, their leader returned to their homeland and gathered an army. A month later they attacked."

Michael made a low, appalled sound as they watched the traders and their crudely-armed men invading the town. They burned every home as they slaughtered every Wiccan who crossed their path.

"Of the clan just thirteen survived," Summer said. "They fled to live in hiding. Because so much magic had been lost with those who had died, they felt they would never be safe again. They began passing their spells down through the generations, making each child memorize them."

The three of them followed the small band into a forest where they lived first in caves and then in cabins hidden among the trees. The new settlement grew rapidly, as did the clan's numbers. More outsiders came, driving them out to find another retreat. The cycle repeated over and over, forcing the Wiccans to relocate endlessly. In time the clan slowly changed their appearance and their ways so they could infiltrate the mortal world. They hid in plain sight in vast civilizations and their enormous cities.

Summer opened the door to a chamber where an elder Wiccan sat working at a desk.

"As the clan had eradicated death, their magic grew as quickly as their numbers. Soon there were too many spells to be remembered. By this time the Wiccans had learned to read and write, so they began preserving their spells in one very precious, powerful book."

When the Wiccan reverently opened an enormous illuminated manuscript bound in green silk and jewel-studded silver, Troy took in a sharp breath.

"That's the Emerald Tablet."

Summer nodded. "It was the first true grimoire. Countless generations of Wiccans recorded all of their spells in it, and the spells of other magic-users. In time, the Tablet's power became so legendary that whispers of it reached mortal kings and conquerors. Wiccans were hunted mercilessly, captured and tortured to death. Countless wars were waged over the Tablet, until once more the clan was nearly destroyed. But this time the survivors did not flee or hide."

Time whirled around them, whisking them from the city to the desert, where a ragged, exhausted group of Wiccans gathered around the Tablet. In the distance, a vast army poured through the gates of a sprawling ancient city and began to advance on them. As the elder invoked a spell, the sand of the desert stirred, and then rippled and rolled with gentle waves that swelled and towered into a terrifying tsunami of sand. It raced toward the soldiers and their city. The golden waves crashed down, crushing and obliterating everyone and everything in their path. When the dust settled, the army and the city had vanished.

"I think it is Ubar," Michael murmured, nodding toward the dunes on the horizon. "We heard legends about it during the Crusades. The nomads in that region claimed it was destroyed in a single day by a sandstorm so fierce it scoured the city from the face of the earth."

"That was the first and last time the Tablet was used to kill. Once the Wiccans saw what it had done, they enchanted the grimoire so that it could never again be used for evil purposes." Summer sighed. "When the protective spell was cast, the Tablet vanished, and the Wiccans thought it had destroyed itself. They were wrong."

They were flung through time again, stopping in a village that had been sacked, where invaders drank and looted the homes. Summer entered one of the huts, and glanced down at the body of a young witch who lay dying among the corpses of the rest of her murdered family.

"Over the centuries the Tablet had grown so powerful that it had become a living entity, but it was trapped in its own inanimate form," Summer told her men. "The enchantment gave it the means with which it could determine its own destiny and protect itself."

Just before she breathed her last, the dying witch reached out to touch the grimoire, and then went limp. Spirals of green light crept out of the Tablet's gems and enveloped the dead girl's hand, sinking into her flesh.

"The Tablet decided to create a living Guardian who would always protect it," Summer said, and crouched down beside the girl to watch her dark eyes open.

The dead witch's face disappeared beneath a surge of the glittering green light, and when it reappeared the features had been changed. Her dark eyes lightened to a blue infused with flecks of every color in the rainbow as she sat up to take the Tablet in her hands.

"The Guardian had to be changed to contain the power and knowledge she would need to serve the Tablet," Summer said. "So the Tablet expanded her mind, and bestowed on her abilities that no other Wiccan possessed, such as the capacity to transfer memories to another mind. Because her body was still flesh, the Tablet could not make the Guardian completely inviolate. So it gave her the ability to bond two men to her as her own lovers and protectors—her sentinel mates. It also changed her organs, enabling her to give birth to one female child, who after one hundred years would be trained and ready to serve as the next Guardian."

Troy squeezed her hand. "Which is now you and us." He glanced down as the grimoire vanished in a brilliant burst of verdant energy. "After all that, it disappeared again? Did she hide it?"

"In a manner of speaking, yes," Summer said and flicked her fingers. Suddenly the ancient world vanished, and they were once more back in their bedroom. "But the grimoire didn't disappear. It destroyed itself."

"Then why would it make itself a Guardian?" Michael asked.

Troy stared at her. "It didn't need to exist as a book any longer, did it?"

Summer shook her head. "Before it disintegrated, the Tablet transferred every spell it contained to the Guardian's mind. After a century she transferred them to her daughter, who gave them to her daughter, and so on every century since the Tablet created the first Lautner."

Michael caressed her cheek as he gave her a sorrowful look. "And now you, my poor Beauty."

"Yes," Summer said and took a deep breath. "Like all the Guardians before me, I carry the burden, and protect the secrets. What no one but my bloodline and their sentinel mates can ever know is that the power and the spells, and all that was contained in the book, exist only in my memory."

Michael went still. "You mean… No, it cannot be."

"It is, and there is no escaping it." Summer met

his gaze. "I *am* the Emerald Tablet."

CHAPTER THREE

SUMMER SPENT THE night and most of the next day resting in bed while Troy and Michael repaired the damage inflicted on the house by their return from the past. Normally she would have insisted on helping, but she needed time to sort out the memories of her life as Genevieve Lautner. She was also now fully aware of the powers she possessed as the living embodiment of the Emerald Tablet. There were difficult decisions to be made.

Marie had not completed Eve's training, and waited until almost the last moment of her life to transfer her memories. Eve must have done something similar to Summer at the exchange, which might explain why she would later wake up in Central Park with no memory of who or what she was.

Could I have transferred my memories to myself, if that is even possible? Summer felt frustrated with how little she knew about the ability, but because Marie hadn't finished her Guardian training there were bound to be other problems. *And if I had no training, how am I supposed to train my own daughter someday? Must I do this to another child?*

One of the few things she did remember was the final bonding ritual she was supposed to have performed with her chosen sentinel mates. Until she completed the bond between them, neither Michael nor Troy would be able to know her thoughts. But given the current, chaotic state inside her head, did she want them to?

"You look unhappy," Michael said, as he appeared and sat down on the edge of the bed beside her. "I can brew more of Erica's headache tea, if it would help."

"It's just… There's so much I don't know about being the Guardian." She rubbed her temples with her fingertips. "I wasn't supposed to do this as a mortal. The Tablet is transferred only after the Guardian has attained immortality. Maybe that's why I can't control the power."

He pulled her onto his lap and tipped up her chin to study her face.

"When you are feeling stronger, Pagan and I

can do something about the mortality problem."

"That's not all," she said. She hadn't yet told either of them anything about their duties as her sentinel mates. Worse, she had bespelled Michael without his knowledge or permission. "You're right, though. As long as I am mortal I'm vulnerable in too many ways."

Michael skimmed his thumb across her trembling lips. "Beauty, what troubles you?"

"A lot," she said and closed her eyes. "Maybe it's too much for me. I have no memories of what to do. Michael, I could hurt someone."

"Figures I'd find you in here flirting with our woman," Troy said. He walked in with a hammer in one hand and plaster dust frosting his black hair. "Much as I would love to join in lap time, that last window isn't going to install itself."

Summer held out her hand to him, and when Troy took it she drew him closer.

"According to Erica the winter gathering is starting tomorrow morning, and with all the Wiccans around there won't be much time for us to be alone."

"So we won't go," Troy said, bringing her hand to his lips. "I'm fine with that."

"You are also fine with your father coming here to demand to know why?" Michael asked.

"Because that is what he will do if we stay away."

"What I mean is, I need to finalize our bond," Summer said. "I can only do that if I'm outside in the moonlight with the two of you." She grimaced. "Since we'll have to be naked, we might as well dispense with my mortality, too."

"Which means the two of us making love to you in the freezing cold, dark outdoors," Troy said and cocked his head. "We were hoping for something more romantic. You know, candlelight, wine, silk sheets, wonderful music to set the mood. Possibly large amounts of whipped cream."

"And the fireplace," Michael put in. "I have already chopped the wood for it."

"This isn't about romance," she said. "It's about protecting us." She kissed Michael and then Troy, but when they put their hands on her she shook her head. "There is one more thing that I need you both to promise me before we make the bond permanent tonight."

"Beauty, we would do anything for you," Michael said.

"Anything except what I think you're going to ask," Troy said, his expression turning grim. "Which is why you need our vows."

"You are my sentinels as well as my mates," she

said slowly. "With me you don't just protect a woman. You're watching over the Tablet, too." She eyed Michael. "You know the amount of knowledge the Templars have acquired about the Wiccans since they attained immortality."

"Too much," he agreed.

"They know about the Lautner bloodline, and have some idea of how powerful the Tablet is. If I am ever captured by the order, whether I am mortal or immortal, I can be drugged, raped, tortured, and maimed. I can be made to suffer endless, unimaginable horrors." Summer hesitated. "You were a witch hunter, Michael. You know what they're capable of, and that they would stop at nothing until their interrogators forced me to tell them everything. Isn't that true?"

His mouth flattened before he slowly nodded.

"It won't come to that," Troy said, his mellow voice sounding more like a growl.

"I hope it never does," she said, then ducked her head as shame crept through her. "Michael, I've already compelled you to make this promise to me. I'm sorry. I knew it had to be done, but I didn't think of the consequences." She moved her hand to his heart, and with a few words removed the spell.

"What did you make me promise to do?"

Michael demanded.

"Kill me."

She murmured a spell under her breath as she ran her finger along Michael's forearm, and then Troy's. Words in dark green glowed on their skin.

"This is the spell you must cast," she said as the words faded as quickly as they had appeared. "You have only to touch the place three times to make the spell reappear."

"But if you could make me or Troy do this thing," Michael said, sounding bewildered, "why are you asking us to promise?"

"She can't use the power of the Tablet for evil," Troy said before Summer could reply. "Our lives are now connected through this bond. If she forces us to kill her, we'll die, too."

"You're my sentinels, not my slaves. You will always have a choice." She rested her cheek against the warlock's shoulder and sighed. "It just isn't a very good one."

$$\bullet \; \bullet \; \bullet \; \bullet \; \bullet$$

That night Summer prepared carefully for the final bonding ritual. First she cleansed her body and then sat by one of the windows to watch the sky gradually darken. Though she tried to clear her thoughts, they had grown as tangled as long-neglected vines.

She wasn't alone in her disquiet. Through her bond with her men, she felt the turmoil of their emotions. After she'd revealed what she'd done, Michael was still out of sorts with her. Meanwhile Troy was trying to cope with the hard, cold reality of knowing his life was forever linked to her own. Since they had both been born predestined to be her mates, Summer couldn't alter their fate. Even if she went back in time, she couldn't change the paths that had brought them together, and then to her.

Being the Emerald Tablet sucks, she thought after a very silent dinner. Not even Erica's delicious soup and bread could dispel her lovers' dark moods. When the men refused to let her help with the clean-up, she retreated back to the bedroom to undress and don the heavy robe she would have to wear outside.

Of course I have to go skyclad in the middle of winter to do this, Summer thought as she quickly braided her hair and pinned it like a woven crown atop her head. *I just wish I knew why.* She stared at her reflection in the mirror and saw her own resentment glittering like ice in her eyes. *And I also should have had seventy-five more years of training—and freedom—before I had to do this. Why didn't you run, Maman? We might have gone anywhere.*

The image in the mirror shimmered and rippled as a faint green glow appeared around the edges. As Summer stared, her reflection changed to that of Marie Lautner's, who smiled sadly at her from the other side of the looking glass.

You are angry with me, and yet you know how much I wished to spare you this burden for as long as I might.

"I know it's why you waited so long to tell me about the Tablet," Summer said. She stepped closer and pressed a hand against the cool glass. "Maman, there are so many things I don't know. How can I be the Guardian when I am barely able to control the power?"

None of us could control the power entirely, Daughter. The Tablet still has a mind and will of its own, as it always will. Marie lifted her hand and pressed it opposite Summer's. *As for your training…all you must do is remember.*

She felt like punching the mirror now. "Remember what? My English lessons? The books you made me read? That's all the training you gave me."

When it is time you will know all that you need.

Marie's image vanished from the glass.

Summer stalked out of the bedroom, and then

came to an abrupt halt as she saw Michael and Troy waiting for her. Both men wore robes and held unlit torches, and Michael had a woven blanket tucked under one strong arm.

"You're ready for this?" she asked, looking from Troy's steady gaze to Michael's faint smile. "Okay, then let's go bond in the moonlight."

"This first," Troy said.

He came to her, tugged her into his arms, and bent down to give her a long, lingering kiss. The delicious taste of him filled her head, making her heart thump wildly. His desire poured into her and warmed her from within. As he lifted his head, strong hands turned her around and lifted her up. Michael took his turn, thoroughly ravishing her mouth as her feet dangled above the floor. He raked the edge of his teeth over her tingling lower lip, and then gently lowered her.

"Now we are ready, Beauty."

Summer cast one more longing look back at the bedroom, and she followed them out of the house into the icy night. Troy led them a short distance to a frost-covered meadow Summer had not yet seen.

"Every spring this clearing fills with wildflowers," the warlock told her as they stopped in the center. He glanced up at the tiny diamonds of the stars. "When we came to America I used to sit out here every night to watch for shooting stars, so I could make wish-magic."

"What would you wish for tonight?" Summer couldn't help asking.

"Nothing," he said and smiled at Michael and then her. "I have everything I ever wanted."

The Templar came up behind her and rested his big hands on her shoulders. "As do I, Beauty."

Pressed between them, Summer stopped shivering and let the last of the tension flow out of her.

"After tonight," she said, "we will be bonded in mind as well as body. There won't be any chance for us to keep secrets."

"No planning any surprise birthday parties. Got it." Troy's eyes took on a distinct tinge of green. "I am yours, my lady. Now and forever."

"As am I, my Beauty," Michael said.

Summer placed her hand over the warlock's heart. "My twilight magician," she said and turned to do the same to the Templar. "My sunrise warrior." She shrugged out of her robe, and when the men did the same she lifted her face and invoked the ancient name of her bloodline. "Lauten, first of the Emerald Guardians, look upon your daughter and sons. We bind ourselves in this triad, each to each, all to all."

She lifted Michael's hand and positioned three of his fingers facing to one side, and did the same with Troy's, pointing three of his fingers to the opposite side. She then placed three of her fingers between them to form the symbol of the triad: ƎME. Summer opened her mind and released the power within. It surged out of her and into her men, returning in a steady stream, to loop around and through their bodies.

"Name yourselves and make your vows before the Lord and the Lady," Summer said.

"I am Troy Atwater." Troy bowed his head. "I vow to serve the Guardian as sentinel and mate."

"I am Michael…Michele Charbonneau," the Templar said, and repeated the same vow.

Bright beams of moonlight drifted over their naked bodies as Summer drew the power back into herself. She staggered a little at the force with which it returned. She felt Michael's concern as he circled her waist with his arm, and heard Troy think in Welsh. Without thinking, he combined his power with Michael's to warm the icy ground beneath their numb feet.

In the moonlight the clearing lost its wintry glitter and took on a soft, lush appearance as thick grass and clusters of wildflowers began to spring from the rich soil. New blooms opened, making small splashes of color all around them, and a warm, sweet perfume suffused the air.

Summer's shoulders sagged with relief. "It's done."

As the Templar flung out the blanket he'd brought, the warlock lowered her onto her side. He spooned against her from behind as Michael stretched out and pressed her to his chest.

Summer felt the thick lengths of their erections rubbing against her thighs and buttocks, and reveled in the white-hot love for her burning in their hearts. Her own sex had grown so wet she could feel her fluids dampening the insides of her thighs.

"It's time for you to join us now," Troy said, pressing against the soft curves of her buttocks. He rubbed his shaft slowly in the narrow crease between them. "Nothing between us ever again, Summer. No fears, no barriers, no precautions. We're going to love you like this for the rest of our lives."

"We will fill you every time you have need of us, or we of you," Michael murmured as he nuzzled her throat. "And someday make your belly swell with our daughter."

Every word they said was true. She could feel it

through their bond. They had found her when she had been lost, protected her when she had been threatened, and loved her when she had felt more alone than any person in the world. The bond she had resented, doubted, and even feared, proved to be her heart's desire. After a lifetime of seclusion, and a solitary journey through terror after losing her family, she had found two new loves. They would see to it that she would never spend another moment of her life alone.

"Now," Summer gasped as she writhed between them. "Please, do it now."

Troy took hold of her hips as Michael lifted her thigh. Both men groaned at how wet she was for them. Michael fisted his thick shaft to work the swollen head of it against her clenching opening. He prodded it, nudged inside, and penetrated her. At the same moment, Troy dragged the head of his penis back and forth over her rosebud to make it slick with a silky bead of semen, and then pressed into the tight pucker.

As soon as the naked domes of their cocks moved inside her body, Summer began to tremble. She could feel the power coiling inside her as her lovers forged deeper. Change slowly unfurled in every part of her as she began to shed her mortality.

"You're made of pure satin inside," Troy said, grunting as he pumped another inch of his girth into her tight channel. "Brother, attend to her gorgeous tits. She needs them to be sucked."

The Templar bent his golden head to her full breasts, covering one pebbled peak and tugging it with his mouth as Troy roughly fondled the other.

"Troy, I can't take much more–"

She groaned as her lovers plowed deeper and harder, until both sides of her need were stretched and beautifully full of their hardness. At the same time she shivered at the feel of her own slick, velvety tissues and how she gripped her lovers with delicious firmness.

"Oh," she moaned. "Everything you feel…"

"We all feel," Michael finished, as he drew out an inch and then thrust back into her tightness. He licked the nipple of the breast Troy was squeezing.

They moved together with languorous wonder, the men gently sliding out of her and then pumping back in, their shafts as smooth as her silky flesh. The gentle friction soon stoked their needs, which they shared as intimately as the sensations. Summer whimpered as something burning expanded inside her, and she tried to impale herself on both of them.

"She is moving through the final stage," Troy told Michael. "You must give it to her hard now, Brother. Give her the pleasure to go with the pain."

A little shriek left Summer's lips as they plowed into her, working their cocks deeply into her ass and pussy. Michael sucked at her breasts, and Troy reached down beneath him to rub her clit. The moonlight turned golden and filled Summer's eyes as she felt an enormous, almost frightening climax billowing inside her.

"Come to us, Beauty," Michael said against her breast.

Troy nibbled on the curve of her ear. "Give yourself to us."

Lust and love and life streamed through Summer as she released her mortality. She flung herself into an eternity of pleasure that swallowed her in a sea of sensation and emotion. She felt every movement of her lovers' bodies, every thick pump of their cocks into her softness, and then both men stiffened and began to bathe her insides with jet after jet of their seed.

The moment they came inside her Summer transcended every want, every care, every worry of her former life, and immersed herself in pure bliss. No pleasure had ever given her such soul-deep satisfaction.

"I'm yours now," she said on the final, shuddering sigh. "Forever."

CHAPTER FOUR

"MY LORD, THE last of the scouting parties in the north have reported in," Augustin Colbert said as he wheeled himself into Nathaniel Harper's personal chamber. "They've found no sign of the coven gathering, and…my lord?"

"I found a full box of these in Gideon's room," Nathaniel said, puffing on the fat cigar once more before removing it from his mouth and inspecting it. "He had them smuggled in from Cuba, I daresay." He eyed his wheelchair-bound, clergy aide, whose jaw was still sagging. "You do know that I smoke on occasion, Augustin."

"Yes, my lord," he said. He took a mobile phone from his shirt pocket and tentatively placed it on a side table while keeping his eyes averted. "Baldwin indicated he would call tonight, so I thought I would bring your phone in here."

He turned his chair around and began wheeling toward the door.

Nathaniel sighed. He had no choice but to smoke now in order to conceal the annoying mouth twitch he'd developed—not that he intended to explain that to his clergy aide.

"Come back here, Augustin."

"I should leave you to your privacy, Temple Master," the younger man said without glancing back.

As Nathaniel snuffed out the end of the cigar, he imagined using Augustin's eye as his ashtray. *Would his eyeball sizzle, or explode?* It might be amusing to find out, although difficult to explain.

"You will get over here, at once, or you will become better acquainted with these cigars."

Slowly the clergy aide spun around and wheeled over to Nathaniel's chair, but stopped several feet away from the half-naked prostitute slumped at his feet.

"You needn't look at me like that," Nathaniel told him. He stood to pull up and fasten his trousers. "She tried to bite me, and I had to push her away. She lost her balance and struck her head on the corner of the table there."

"Yes, my lord."

Augustin eyed the body and muttered

something else.

Nathaniel stepped over the corpse. "What was that?"

"My lord, it is only…" Augustin pressed his knuckles to his mouth before he burst out with, "This is the third accident this week."

"You think I've committed the sin of murder," Nathaniel said in an encouraging tone. "Go ahead. Say it to my face."

"I think only that something is wrong, my lord," Augustin said and swallowed hard. "That you, and some of the other brothers…may be ill."

Nathaniel sighed.

"Of course you think that. You are a stupid human who understands nothing. Immortality sickness takes centuries to develop, Augustin, and is not contagious. I am not ill, nor in need of help. I have been impatient, yes, and somewhat heavy-handed with these filthy strumpets." He glanced at the corpse's head, which appeared misshapen due to the collapse of one side of the skull. Odd that she would hit the table quite so hard. "Nevertheless, I am not going mad, is that clear?"

"Yes, my lord," Augustin said, and then flinched as the mobile phone rang.

He quickly wheeled over to retrieve it and bring

it to Nathaniel, who snatched it away and squinted at the display.

"Get out," he told his clergy aide, and waited until the door slammed behind him before he answered the call. "Baldwin, how kind of you to call. How are your heathen lambs? All penned and ready for slaughtering?"

"They will be," the Wiccan spy said in a cold voice. "In two days. All of the covens will converge at one particular celebration. That will be the ideal time for you to strike."

"I am so glad I have you to give me strategic advice," Nathaniel said, not bothering to mask the irony in his voice. "Where is this celebration to be held?"

"Send your army to the Mahoosuc Ridge in Maine tomorrow," Baldwin said. "I will contact you with the exact location once your men are in place and ready to attack, and you have transferred triple the usual fee to my Swiss account."

"You told me you were doing this for nothing," Nathaniel reminded him. "Aside from the extensive torture of Abel Atwater, a service you should know we are happy to provide at no extra charge."

"Situations change, Temple Master. Pay me, or

you will never find them."

The line clicked as the spy hung up on him.

Nathaniel switched off the mobile and regarded the dead prostitute.

"You should have employed that tactic, you toothy slut. You might have lived to peddle your ass another day."

It's not her fault you've nothing but a limp peanut hanging from your crotch. The ghost of Gideon Edmunds appeared in Nathaniel's armchair, and smiled down at the corpse. *You know, that's one thing I never did.*

"Please," Nathaniel sighed. He took a fresh cigar from the box and snipped off the end. "You killed dozens of women."

Yes, and enjoyed it thoroughly. Gideon took the cigar from him and lit it, puffing away as he sat back in the chair. *But I never paid for sex, you miserable git.*

Nathaniel would have reminded his former steward that he'd also raped his victims, but a betraying metallic squeak came from outside his chamber door.

"Why, that little human skunk. He's out there eavesdropping on us."

Come in and join the party, Augustin, Gideon roared, and then peered at the door as if

582

expecting it to open. *Strange. No one ever hears me but you, Nate. Have you noticed that?*

"Unhappily, yes, and don't call me Nate," Nathaniel said. He hoisted the whore's body under his arm before he stepped out into the hall and dropped her in his bulge-eyed clergy aide's lap. "Augustin, how convenient to find you listening in on my private conversations." He deliberately wiped the blood from his hands on the front of the younger man's shirt and the metal spokes of one wheel. "Oh, no. I'm so thoughtless, aren't I? Now her DNA is all over you and your chair. What will the authorities think if I told them I saw you using a whore in the sanctuary?"

"Please, my lord," Augustin begged hoarsely. "I won't say anything, to anyone. I swear it."

Nathaniel nodded. "Once you've taken out this trash, assemble the men, all of them." He smiled brightly. "We're going to invade Maine tonight."

CHAPTER FIVE

MICHAEL STOWED THE last dish back in the cupboard. The morning after the final bonding and her initiation into immortality Summer had made a huge breakfast for the three of them. But rather than give them energy, all it seemed to do was sap it. As Troy hung the dish towel, he yawned. They were all still tired.

"Perhaps we should all go back to bed," Michael suggested, not sure that would necessarily mean sleep.

"I'd love to, Paladin, but we have to head over to the main house." Summer smothered a yawn. "Then Abel will probably want to yell at us some more."

Michael knew by now all the covens had arrived for the gathering, and imagined how crowded and busy the main house would be. This was their time to celebrate, but not his. For the most part the members of Silver Wood had accepted his presence since he and Summer had prevented Gideon from murdering Troy's younger brother. But word that he had spent most of his immortal life hunting witches was bound to spread.

"I should stay behind," he finally suggested. "It would be better if I am not paraded in front of the visiting Wiccans."

His lover's dark opal eyes shifted to the warlock.

"Were you planning to put him on a float?"

Troy shrugged. "I could tie him to the hood of the Jeep, if you want, but his heavy ass is probably going to dent it."

"You should not joke about this," Michael told them. "I was a Templar witch hunter, an enemy to your people. I do not wish to make anyone afraid to be here."

"You can be a little scary to people who don't know you. The thing is, you're the reason we're going over there." Summer held up a small object. "We need to see if Ewan can identify this symbol."

Michael frowned. "That is the little cuff you took from Nathaniel Harper's desk."

"Good memory," she said and gave him a sweet

smile. "Troy finally got a chance to look at it, and he says these things were common gifts given to Wiccan children back in your day. And since Nathaniel Harper isn't a Wiccan, and no one else in the North Abbey is, either–"

"We think it's yours," Troy said, and clapped him on the shoulder. "So let's go find out."

An odd surge of panic sizzled through Michael.

"What if you are wrong, and I am not Wiccan? Now that we are bonded, perhaps it is better not to know."

Summer slipped her arms around his waist.

"I don't care if you're a werewolf, or a vampire, or even a zombie, Paladin. You're ours."

"Okay, I hate the smell of rotting flesh, and things that eat it, so I *do* care if you're a zombie," Troy said, making them both laugh. "Come on. If anyone objects, we'll come home and go back to bed."

Summer stretched, parting the front of her robe and revealing the curve of her breast. Suddenly Michael hoped very much that someone would take offense. But at the main house, there was nothing of the sort.

Troy parked the Jeep on the drive up to the main house, which now stood swamped with various vehicles. Clusters of Wiccans from the visiting covens greeted each other and talked. Michael watched as dozens of children romped with Silver Wood coven's dogs, which were delirious with furry ecstasy to have so many new playmates. He spotted a pair of new mothers showing off their well-bundled infants to smiling admirers. Laughter continually rang out in the chilly air.

This might have been my life.

Over the long centuries, Michael had despaired of the grim duties demanded of him by the order. But now there was a strange new anger rising inside him.

If I am truly Wiccan, then Nathaniel took this from me as surely as he stole me from my home.

Troy nudged him with his elbow.

"Simmer down, Paladin. Remember, we're all wired to each other now, and you're about to stir-fry our brains."

He muttered an apology to his brother sentinel, but when he turned to Summer, he saw the love in her eyes a moment before he felt it wrap around him like the softest of cloaks. She held out her hand, and when he took it she twined her fingers through his.

"No one can take you from us," she murmured to him. "We're your home now, Michael."

587

Inside the main house Erica called a greeting to them from the kitchen, where she appeared to be preparing enough food to feed several covens.

"Troy, Ewan is looking for you. Lachlan also wishes to relate some details for the battle of the Holly and Oak Kings you two will be reenacting. Summer, you're positively glowing so I won't ask how your initiation went. Michael, Aileen is in the garden and she'd like to speak to you for a moment." As two children darted through the kitchen she called out, "Run outside, kids, but walk inside, please."

Troy snitched a biscuit from a basket and dodged Erica's spatula as he winked at Summer and Michael before heading off toward the back of the house. Michael took Summer's arm and accompanied her outside where the young, dark-haired witch was sitting in the spell-warmed garden.

"Morning," Aileen said, smiling and resting her hands on her protruding belly. "Summer, you look marvelous." She peered up at him with her solemn gray eyes. "I had a dream about you last night, Michael."

"Did you," he said. He always felt too large and clumsy around the pregnant witch. "I hope you did not tell your mate."

Troy's brother Wilson was Aileen's husband, and he tended to be very jealous of his lovely, young wife.

She shook her head. "It was a very special dream, and meant only for you." She gestured around them. "You were here in the garden, and surrounded by enormous, beautiful sunflowers. I counted fourteen of them. They twined around you, and then you turned into an oak."

Although Michael didn't believe dreams were anything more than fantasies, he kept his expression grave.

"So you believe it has some significant meaning?"

"The symbols do. The oak tree is sacred to all Wiccans, and represents strength, longevity, wisdom and prosperity," Aileen said, and then wrinkled her nose. "It's also what you'll be the king of for the battle tomorrow night. It was the sunflowers that made me really happy. They're spiritual guides that always point you in the right direction, so dreaming of you being surrounded by them is a very good omen."

"Why did you count the flowers, Aileen?" Summer asked.

"I'm not sure," the pregnant witch admitted. "But they made Michael very happy, and I think helped him finally become what he was meant to be."

"My destiny is to turn into an oak tree?" he couldn't help teasing.

"Come here, you two," Aileen said and held out her hands. Summer sat beside her and he knelt down before the bench. "I know being with us has been difficult for you both, and we certainly didn't make it any easier."

"I think you've had your hands full with Wilson and the baby," Summer pointed out.

"Yes, and I have the two of you to thank for that," she said. She gripped Michael's hand with surprising strength. "Despite our hatred of you, you still risked your life to protect the man I love. If you hadn't gone after them, Gideon would have crippled Wilson."

"You should not think about it," Michael told her, although he knew the mad Templar would have done that and much worse to Aileen's mate. "All that matters is that Gideon will never hurt anyone again."

She nodded, and turned to Summer. "We've treated you with suspicion since you came to Silver Wood, sister. But you saved my life, and the life of my unborn child, and then guided my mother back to me. Wilson and I always want to remember the blessings you have given us. So we have decided that if we have a son, we will name him Michael, and if we have a daughter, we will name her Summer."

Those names were not even theirs, Michael thought with a pang of bitterness, and then realized how foolish he was being. Summer and Michael were who they were to this girl, and that was to whom she wished to pay tribute.

"We are honored, Aileen," Michael said quietly.

Erica joined them and gave her daughter a loving look before she said, "I am sorry to interrupt, but you and the baby need nourishment." As she helped Aileen to her feet she smiled at Summer and Michael. "If you're hungry, there's more than enough for you two."

"Thanks, Erica, but we've already had breakfast," Summer said and watched the two witches disappear into the kitchen. "You know that girl adores you almost as much as I do."

"She does not really know me, or what I have done." He stood and stared at the profusion of basil sprouting from a large container. "But you do now."

Summer tugged him down to sit beside her. "After last night I know everything about you, Michael, and from now on I always will. I know that you've never harmed an innocent, or tortured the helpless. Every witch you hunted was one who was in some way harming mortals. You tried to be true to the only family you've ever had, but you shrank from their cruelty and blind hatred. Even when you battled Troy in the Saracen's arena, you were merciful. You and I both know how strong and quick you really are. You knew what you could do to end his life. You could have easily killed him a dozen times, but you didn't."

He thought of the daily battles he'd fought with the warlock.

"In the beginning I despised him, but he was like me, a prisoner made to fight. I would not give our captors the satisfaction."

"I'm very glad you didn't," she said and snuggled against him. "Whatever Ewan discovers about that symbol on the cuff, Michael, you are Wiccan in your heart. I promise you, we will never let the Templars take you from us again."

CHAPTER SIX

TROY FOLLOWED EWAN Buchanan's rotund form into his chamber, which was crowded with old books, wood carvings and baskets of scrolls.

"I appreciate your help with this, Ewan."

"It's the least I could do for our new hero," the older warlock said. He went over to a shelf and selected a thick volume bound in cracked, curling leather. "Has Michael suffered any guilt over his comrade's very unpleasant fate?"

"No, and considering how much death and destruction an insane Templar could have inflicted on the coven, and how he was prepared to torture my brother, I doubt anyone feels any remorse. Although the way he died…"

Troy hesitated to say any more, since Ewan's sister had been the one to kill Gideon by using dark magic to impale him with a pine tree.

"You and all the others were so shocked by her confession," Ewan said as he carried the book over to his desk. "My father used to tell me that a Buchanan never forgets the injustices done them, and will wait a lifetime or two to take vengeance. Now let me see this trinket you have."

Troy handed over the cuff. "We think it belonged to Michael when he was an infant."

"It's the right size and age. I'd say Celtic, from the engraving style." The old warlock set it down beside the book and began looking through the pages of hand drawn symbols. "Last night your father asked my sister to become his mate. She accepted, so they will be performing the ritual tomorrow night, after the battle of the kings."

Ewan sounded slightly peeved at the prospect, Troy thought.

"Surely you don't object."

"Since I have been trying to find Erica a mate for more than twenty years now, how could I?" His pudgy face grew serious as he stopped thumbing through the pages and compared the symbol on the cuff to one in the old book. "Here, this looks to be it."

Troy eyed the two symbols, and then read the inscription under the drawing.

"It belongs to the Parisii."

"Ah, I was correct," Ewan said. "They were one of the pre-Christian era Celtic covens who settled in northern France after the third great exodus." He peered at the cuff. "Among other things, they founded the city of Paris. They were also great survivors who never left the region, if I remember correctly. If your Templar truly belongs to them, he may yet have family there."

"Would you contact the Parisii and inquire if they have any members named Charbonneau among them?" When the old man nodded Troy touched his shoulder. "Thank you, Ewan. We couldn't have done this without you."

The warlock gave him a benevolent smile. "I am always happy to help."

"Now that your sister will be looked after," Troy said, "perhaps you can find a mate."

Ewan's smile disappeared. "Would that the Lord and Lady so bless me, but it would be a fruitless match. An illness in my mortal childhood rendered me sterile. Since we have no other living relatives, I fear the task to carry on the Buchanan bloodline falls on Erica's shoulders."

"You have Aileen now," Troy pointed out. "Her child will be the first of the next generation of Buchanans and Atwaters."

"Yes, of course," Ewan said, nodding his

agreement. "The next generation is almost here." The old warlock laced his hands and rested them on the upper curve of his big belly. "I look forward to watching you and Michael in the arena. I'm sure you will do the Kings proud."

Lachlan appeared in the doorway. "Troy, can you come out to the barn? Your father and I are assembling the gear for tomorrow night, and he wishes you to choose the weapons."

Troy followed his father's apprentice out of the house and across to the big barn where Abel Atwater was sorting through a collection of open trunks filled with weapons.

"You look as if you're going to wage war rather than stage a battle, Father."

"I thought I'd give you a proper selection," Abel said. The Coven Master straightened and gazed at the swords, knives and clubs around him. "Hard to believe we once were obliged to arm ourselves with these day and night. We'll have to blunt the blades to prevent you from hacking each other to pieces."

Troy picked up a pair of long swords with two-handed grips.

"You needn't bother. If there's one thing Michael and I can do, it's put on a convincing show with deadly weapons. Where have you decided to hold the bout?"

"I thought we'd use the west clearing out by the old pavilion." His father saw his expression. "If you don't want us on your property, son, just say so."

"That's not it." He glanced at Lachlan. "Would you give us a moment, please?" He waited for the younger man to leave. "We finalized our bond and initiated Summer at that clearing last night. It wasn't my idea. I would have stayed in our warm, comfortable bed, but she insisted."

Abel grimaced. "Romping naked in these temperatures? You'll get frostbite where you really don't want it."

"That's the thing. The bonding and the transition pushed Summer's ability into overdrive." He tried to think of how to describe it, but gave up. "Want to take a ride with me?"

His father agreed, and a few minutes later Troy stopped the Jeep on the edge of the clearing. He climbed out and watched Abel as he walked around the car and surveyed the hundreds of thousands of wildflowers nodding above the thick carpet of new meadow grass. Every tree within sight was budding not only with leaves but acorns, nuts and berries. Around the base of each trunk small saplings had sprung up by the hundreds.

"She did all this?" his father murmured as Troy came to stand beside him. "How far does it reach through the forest?"

Troy thrust his hands in his pockets. "All the way down to the valley on this side, and it's still spreading."

Abel stared at him. "You mean…"

He nodded. "I'd say by tomorrow night the whole mountain will be green again."

His father said nothing for several minutes as he walked across the meadow, and then he stopped and shook his head.

"And I thought I had my hands full." The amusement faded from his expression. "You won't be able to stay here at Silver Wood after the gathering, will you?"

"I'm not sure," Troy said. "Probably not." He reached down to pluck a dandelion from the ground, and watched it swell and then silently burst, its wispy seeds floating away on the breeze. "What I do know is that we have to keep her safe, Father. Whatever it takes."

Abel nodded. "I've given a lot of thought to what you said to me the last time we discussed the future of this coven." He gave him a wry look. "You won't change your mind about taking over as Coven Master, will you? With your power and wisdom you could very well lead all the covens in the world one day."

"My path lies in a very different direction," Troy said. "I'm sorry."

"So am I, but I had to ask one more time." The older warlock studied the horizon. "Now that Erica has finally agreed to mate with me, I'm ready to step down and simplify my life. So when we hold the closing ritual, I'm going to name Wilson as my successor."

Troy grinned. "Excellent choice."

CHAPTER SEVEN

THE NEXT TWO days passed in a whirlwind of fun and pleasure for Summer, as she joined in the nonstop activities of the winter solstice. Witches from all the visiting covens converged on the main house with evergreens, food, and gifts for the members of Silver Wood, who in turn visited each encampment with baskets of food and gifts. Individual rituals honoring the season took place hourly, and Summer often found herself watching with wistful envy as the children of the coven were taught the traditions and practices of Yule among the Wiccans.

"My mother always had a lovely meal, and my fathers would hide gifts for me in the garden, but we never had anything as grand as this," she told Troy after they came home from a long day of celebrating. "What about you, Michael? How do the Templars celebrate the season?"

"In prayer at the chapel, or on Crusade," he said and grimaced before he placed another log in the fireplace. "Mostly on Crusade. The season always brought out the Temple Master's determination to wrest the Holy Land from the Saracens."

"Yes, I have so many fond memories of how the Templars party," Troy said as he sat down with them to watch the flames dance. "Stingy and mean, the whole lot of them. I think De Sonnac celebrated Christmas on the journey by ordering an extra beating for me—which I remember you gave me, Paladin."

Michael shrugged. "So you admit that Templars can be generous."

That they could joke about such a terrible time in their lives made Summer's heart melt a little, and she stood up and held out her hands.

"I have a present to give both of you tonight."

"Really?" Troy's dark brows arched. "Do we get a hint?"

Summer extended her arms and allowed her outer clothes to unfasten and remove themselves from her body. That revealed the very skimpy, black lace lingerie she wore beneath them that had been a Yule gift from Aileen.

"You'll have to unwrap the rest of it yourselves, but we have to decide something before you do."

She let the question that had been hovering in the back of her mind flow into their bond.

Michael frowned. "I thought we did not have to use condoms now that you are immortal."

"There are other reasons to use them," Troy reminded him.

"My bloodline must continue." Summer made a helpless gesture. "I was created to want that as much as the two of you, so I am definitely ready. We can put it off for a little while if either of you aren't. But it means no unprotected sex, or there will be consequences…nine months from now."

The men looked at each other as if they were having a silent conversation.

"I understand if you want to wait," she added, feeling anxious now. "I know it's a lot to ask."

"Not really." Troy regarded her. "I was ready for this last night."

"I was ready in Central Park," Michael said, getting to his feet. A second later he tossed her gently over his shoulder. "Bed," he said to Troy. "Now."

Once her mates had unwrapped their gift they took their time admiring it, and touching it, and then kissing every inch of it. Summer squirmed between them as they teased and caressed her with their strong hands, pressing her between their hard bodies until she thought she would climax just from the intensity of the foreplay.

"Guys," she muttered, dodging Troy's hungry mouth. "Time to stop admiring your present and start using it."

As Michael pulled her on top of him Troy crouched behind her. He ran his tongue from the small of her back to the nape of her neck, sending a burst of shivering delight into her breasts.

"Did you feel that?" the warlock asked Michael as he brought his hands around to cradle her swollen mounds.

"Yes," the Templar said, and drew Summer's mouth down to his. "Do it again."

During all the others times they'd made love the men had felt each other's sensations, but never hers. Something shifted inside her as a peculiar ache began pounding between her thighs.

"It's time," she said and spread her legs as the power grew inside her. The two heavy shafts pressed against her soft, wet folds. "Come into me."

Michael groaned as his cockhead rubbed against Troy's, both nudging against her entrance.

They danced back and forth along her slick folds. But as the ache between her thighs mounted, she pressed down on them both. The connection was electric, and a moan rose from deep in her throat.

"I must take you together," she breathed, almost not believing her words.

"No," Troy whispered hoarsely from behind.

"We will hurt you, Beauty," Michael said, gazing up at her.

"No," she moaned, rubbing her breasts against his chest and her buttocks against Troy's belly. "I was made for this, made to take you both. It's how you make me pregnant."

She felt the tension in their bodies as they hesitated. She ground herself on them, making both men hiss.

"Gods above," Troy moaned, but she could feel his hand positioning his thick shaft at her entrance.

Michael shifted his hips in response, doing the same.

"Oh," the warlock groaned as their hard shafts began to sink inside her. "This is too good."

She gasped for a moment as, incredibly, they surged deeper.

"Yes," she breathed, feeling the sweet stretch. "Please, like that. Fill me up with your seed,

Pagan, Paladin. Give me our daughter."

They stroked harder into her, each thrust in perfect unison. Though they were a tight fit, Summer had never felt so complete. She writhed between them, pressing down as she accepted them into her body. She clasped them sweetly with her softness, until she felt the power merge all three of them in a white-hot meld of delight.

Deep, hungry sounds spilled from Michael's throat as he pumped hard into her, urging Troy to do the same. The warlock drove into her just as relentlessly, his hot breath on her neck as he growled his pleasure.

Summer felt her womb warm as if bathed from within with sunlight, and cried out as she felt them stiffen and surge into her one last time. Then all three of them groaned as the seed from both men flowed into her and joined with the heat of her passion. As they shuddered through the last of the ecstasy, a tiny flicker of life burned into their hearts. The next Guardian had been conceived.

CHAPTER EIGHT

AT SUNSET THE following night, the covens began arriving at the clearing. Abel and Erica had arranged blankets and seating for everyone around a large arena marked off by red and white silks tied around posts of oak. Around each post a garland of holly had been carefully wound, and topped with a hammered disk of gold.

"The circles represent the sun, and the promise of spring," Erica told Summer as they came to join the others. "Although thanks to your ability, we didn't need to bring any flowers. Did your mother teach you about the two kings?"

"A little," Summer said, recalling one of Marie's stories. "I know that the Holly King represents winter, and the Oak King summer, and they battle twice each year so that the wheel of time might turn."

"That is the traditional story among all Wiccans," Erica said, as she spread a quilt over a patch of thick grass. "The battles are held on the equinoxes of Yule and Litha. Some legends say the kings battle for their right to reign over the land, but my grandmother always said they were two halves of the Lord, who forever fought for the hand of the Lady."

"That's a lovely alternative," Summer said, although she was glad neither of her men had ever really fought over her. Some movement from the trees caught her eye. "Oh, here they come."

Summer smiled as two grand processions came out of the forest on opposite sides of the clearing. One was led by Troy, who was dressed in a red velvet robe trimmed in pure white fur, while at the head of the other was Michael, who wore a golden silk robe trimmed with emerald satin. Both wore wreaths on their heads to represent crowns, with Troy's made of holly leaves and Michael's fashioned from oak twigs bearing acorns. Wiccan coven masters and high priestesses from every coven carried evergreen boughs as they followed the two men. Seeing her sentinel mates looking so handsome made Summer sigh with pleasure.

"You know, if Troy were a lot heavier," Erica said, "he'd look just like Santa Claus."

Aileen appeared with a large, soft cushion in her hands.

"Some Wiccan scholars claim the Christians based their Saint Nicholas on our Holly King," she said. "May I sit with you? Wilson is helping Abel with the boys."

Summer and Erica supported the pregnant witch as she gingerly lowered herself onto the cushion.

"Ewan was supposed to bring a folding chair for you," the High Priestess said. She frowned as she scanned both sides of the clearing. "I don't see him. Are you sure you should be out in this weather, dearest? You're so close to your time now."

"I'm not missing this chance to see our boys duel," Aileen said, and grinned at Summer. "Who are you rooting for?"

"Both of them, of course," she said. As she sat down beside Aileen, she eyed the two swords that Abel placed in the center of the circle. "This does end in a draw, right?"

"The Oak King has to win," Aileen advised her. "If he doesn't, we have twelve more months of winter."

"So I'm rooting for Michael," Summer said brightly, making the other two women laugh.

The procession of Wiccan dignitaries broke off as Troy and Michael stepped into the makeshift arena. They handed off their robes to Lachlan and Wilson before pulling the swords from where they had been thrust into the ground.

Summer admired her mates' bare chests for a moment. "I love seeing them partially undressed. It's almost as good as naked."

"If you start talking about sex, which I can't have for another eight weeks," Aileen warned, "I'm going to hurt you."

Abel entered the circle as well, and after applause from the assembled covens raised his arms toward the night sky.

"Welcome, brothers and sisters, to the celebration of the Yule equinox. Tonight the sons of Silver Wood, Troy and Michael, will take on the roles of the Holly and Oak Kings, so that we may honor the two sides of the Lord, long may he rule." He bowed in all four directions before retreating from the circle. Once outside, he lifted his hand, and swept it downward as he shouted, "Let the battle begin."

Troy and Michael exchanged a formal bow, and then immediately lifted their swords and began circling each other. For a moment Summer's smile faltered as she imagined them being forced by the

Saracens to do the same, and then she heard their thoughts.

I'm going to kick your oversize ass, Paladin, Troy thought as he moved in with a quick thrust.

Michael dodged the jab easily and made a fluid rolling movement as he countered. *Are you tall enough to reach it, Pagan?*

"There's my brother." Erica stood up. "I'll be right back with a chair for you, Aileen."

As the older witch hurried off, Summer looked across the clearing at Ewan, who was standing and watching his sister's progress. The old warlock's round face looked different in the moonlight, she thought idly, and then frowned as she felt a prickling sensation crawling across her skin. She rolled back the cuff of her right sleeve, and her eyes widened as she saw her spell brands darkening.

"What's wrong?" Aileen asked.

Summer felt pain stab into her arm and bit her lip as she watched Troy stagger back from Michael as he grabbed the same spot on his arm.

"Something's gone wrong," Summer said.

Her gaze shifted to Erica, who had just reached Ewan. He touched her face and then clouted her over the head, knocking her to the ground.

"Aileen," Summer said, "stay here."

As Summer got to her feet she nearly doubled over as she felt something slice across her belly. Michael was clutching his bloody abdomen. Abel entered the circle.

"Stay back, Father," Troy shouted. "The weapons have been enchanted. We can't control them."

Summer flung off the psychic pain and ran for the circle, her heart filling with fury. She drew on the power within her to protect her mates. It rose up inside her, but as it began radiating off her limbs she groped desperately for control. Silently she cursed her mother for not training her properly. How could she be expected to function as Guardian if she had no idea of how to protect herself and her mates?

All you must do is remember, her mother had told her from the mirror, and her voice echoed that final word over and over in Summer's mind: *Remember.*

Suddenly time stopped. Everyone froze except for her. She reached deep inside herself, this time not for the memories that Eve had transferred to her, but for the memories her mother had given her of her own life. She raced back through every year of Marie Lautner's life until she had absorbed everything Marie had learned as Guardian from

Summer's grandmother.

Newly-armed with almost one hundred years of Marie's training, Summer released her subconscious grip on time, and ran for the circle. She leaped over the silks as she sent two bolts of power at the enchanted swords. It ripped them from her mates' hands and drove them so far into the earth that all that remained were two quivering, blood-stained hilts. As she reached them, Summer sent out her thoughts.

Michael, are you—

It is not serious. My brother managed to reign in the attack.

Summer looked out into the shadows.

"Abel, the Templars are coming up the mountain. Get your people out of here."

"No," Ewan said and appeared out of thin air behind Troy's father. He whipped a dagger across the back of the Coven Master's knees, sending him toppling. "He's not leaving. He has an appointment in the Templar's torture chamber, where he's going to suffer for the rest of his miserable life."

"Ewan?" Abel gasped and stared up at him. "What are you doing, man?"

His head snapped to one side as a heavy boot connected with his jaw.

"Taking vengeance for the bloodline you nearly wiped out, you murdering bastard."

Ewan kicked him again.

Summer scanned the horrified faces of the Wiccans watching them, and sent out a compulsion spell that sent them running for their encampments. She then glanced at Michael, who nodded to her before he disappeared into the shadows. Troy moved toward his father.

Ewan planted his boot on Abel's chest as he drew a sword from beneath his cloak.

"Stop where you are, Troy, or I'll slice his head off before you can reach him."

Troy halted several feet away. "Ewan, don't do this," he said. "My father is not a murderer."

"He killed every member of my family five hundred years ago," Ewan said. He smiled down at Abel as he rested the tip of his sword under his chin. "You remember that, don't you, Atwater? When the Templars came for you, you sent my brothers out to fight them. You hid behind your wife's dead body and watched them being slaughtered, you fucking coward. You didn't lift a finger to defend them."

"I was in shock," Abel said, and then grunted with pain as the sword tip drew blood. "Ewan, I had just lost the love of my life. I couldn't move. I couldn't think. All I remember was wishing that the enemy would come and kill me next."

"Yet here you are, still alive." The old warlock drove his boot into Abel's ribs.

"Brother, please, stop." Erica stumbled toward the circle, her scarred face streaked with blood. "You can't do this."

"And you, you whore," Ewan growled. He bared his teeth at her. "Pretending to hate men while all this time you've been screwing our family's killer. That Templar should have hacked out your traitorous heart after he was done cutting up your face."

"Ewan, stop," Troy said quietly. "The Buchanan bloodline has not been wiped out. Aileen lives, and her child—"

The old warlock interrupted him with a laugh.

"Do you truly believe I would name the get of a rapist Templar as my kin, boy?"

"Why not?" Wilson appeared on the other side of the circle. "You've been working for them all this time, haven't you, Baldwin?"

Ewan's belly bounced with his hearty laugh.

"Very good, Wil. Yes, I'm your traitor, and I've made a good living at it. But before I go I have one last mission. I'm going to cut your brat out of your slut wife's belly and feed it to your dogs." He smiled down at Abel. "Along with your father's balls."

Summer heard the choking sound Aileen made, and then felt the rapidly-approaching Templar multitude before she sent a thought to Troy.

"Take my life," Abel said quietly. "If I am the cause of your pain then my life is yours. Just let the others go."

"Nothing will end my pain," Ewan told Abel as he lifted the sword, "but I would like an ear."

"Down," Troy shouted.

As Summer and everyone else dropped to the ground hundreds of owls burst out of the trees. A heartbeat later the huge birds swooped down on Ewan, clawing at his face and hands as he screamed and writhed. He dropped the sword and thrashed his arms trying to drive them away. The dogs came running into the clearing and launched themselves at the old warlock, knocking him onto his back.

Wilson lifted his hand and the dogs retreated to surround him, their muzzles wet with blood and their chests heaving with deep, ugly growls. Troy went to his father, who nodded, and then went with Summer to Ewan. Her stomach clenched as she looked down at him, and how his mouth worked as he tried to speak. Only a gurgling sound came out of him before he went still and limp. He stared with blind eyes at the stars, as the blood slowly stopped pumping from the terrible wound in his throat.

"Wilson," Aileen gasped. She held her arms around her belly as she managed to stand, but nearly collapsed again as Erica reached her. "Mother, please, help me, I think…ah."

She bent over, gasping with pain. Erica touched her belly with a shaking hand as Wilson strode quickly to his wife.

"She's gone into labor," she told him. "We have to get her back to the main house."

"You cannot," Michael said, emerging from the shadows, his expression grim "It has been surrounded by the Templar army."

• • • • •

"We're securing all the women and children at the old pavilion," Abel said as he handed out the last of the weapons they'd amassed in Troy's barn. "Tell your watchers that if the Templars overrun us, they are to fall back and lead them through the forests and down to the valley."

Summer stood with Troy and Michael as they watched the Coven Master passing out maps.

"If we fail," Summer said, "they'll never reach safety, will they?"

Michael shook his head. "Nathaniel has brought his best trackers. They will not permit anyone to escape."

A young warlock came up to Troy, mismatched daggers in his thin hands and terror in his gentle eyes.

"Do you know why they haven't attacked yet, Major?" His voice cracked on his last words.

"They're waiting for dawn," Troy told him, and then took his arm and led him away to talk with some other youths.

"They're so young," Summer said and wrapped her arms around her waist. "Barely more than boys."

"They are still mortal," Michael murmured, and rested his hand on the back of her neck. "Troy will send them to guard the old pavilion, where you should be, Beauty."

"I know, I'm going," she told him, masking the lie with the psychic barrier she had learned to build through her mother's memories of training. "I just need to see the battlefield before I go." She smiled faintly at his glare. "With Troy's help we can make some water traps that will slow them down."

619

"He and I can see to that," Michael said. He pressed his hand over her flat belly. "You are going to keep our daughter safe."

"That is your only job, by the way," Troy said as he rejoined them.

"I could always zap both of you with my green mojo and go do it myself," she said. She took their hands in hers. "Please. I'll feel better if I can do this with you."

Troy exchanged a look with Michael.

"We have less than two hours before sunrise," Troy said. "We'll have to make it quick."

Summer followed them out to where Wilson had parked his pick-up truck, and climbed in to sit between her mates as Troy started the engine. The air smelled of wildflowers instead of death. Ewan's body had been taken away, leaving only a dark stain on the grass. For a moment she stared out the window at where the old warlock had died, and wished she could have foreseen what he had been planning.

"Everything about Ewan was a lie he created to protect his dream of revenge," Troy said, accurately reading her thoughts. "Not even Erica knew what was really in his heart."

"He was vile," Michael said, sounding as if he wanted to spit. "All smiles and kindness outside, but rotten and dead inside." He sat up and peered through the windshield. "Troy, stop the truck, and turn off the engine and the lights."

As soon as the warlock pulled over to the side of the road and shut down everything Michael climbed out. He made a stopping motion when Summer began to follow. He slipped into the shadows, re-emerging a short time later to lean in the door he'd left open.

"Nathaniel has moved his forces forward," he said and pointed across the road. "Their tents are just beyond those trees, there."

"Then we can't do this," Troy said. "Get in and I'll turn around."

Summer touched the dashboard briefly, and when he turned the key only a clicking sound came from the truck.

"The battery must have died," he said, but his blue eyes narrowed on her face. "Or it had help with its demise. Don't fool with us, Summer."

Michael tugged her out of the truck and clamped an arm around her waist.

"We can go back on foot," he said and frowned down at the ground for a moment before he gave her a wild look. "Beauty, no."

"I'm sorry, Paladin," she said and slipped out from under the weight of his still arm. She glanced over at Troy, who had also turned into a statue of himself. "I have to do this without you."

Summer walked across the road and made her way through the trees until a sentry stepped out to block her path.

"I am Genevieve Lautner," she told him calmly. "The green witch your Temple Master has come here to find. Take me to him."

The sentry's muddy brown eyes took on a brief green glow before he shouldered his automatic rifle and led her to the Templar camp. As she walked through the gauntlet of heavily armed, staring men, Summer saw eyes widen, fists clench and other signs that the Templars could not be permitted anywhere near the Wiccans.

The sentry ducked inside a large white tent marked with a red cross, and re-emerged a minute later with a coil of rope in his hands.

"You are our prisoner now. I am to bind you."

If she ordered him not to do it he wouldn't, but Summer had to keep up the farce a little longer. She offered him her wrists, and waited patiently as he fumbled with knotting the rope. Standing in the middle of so many angry, seething souls made her skin crawl, but it also cleared her mind. When he was finished she addressed the tent.

"You may come out now, Temple Master. I will

not attack you. I have come here to give you what you want, in exchange for the safety of all the Wiccans gathered here."

CHAPTER NINE

"YOU HAVE MADE a very wise decision, my dear," Nathaniel said as he emerged from the tent. His mouth worked for a moment as his gaze crawled over her. "Well, now, look at you. I hadn't expected you to be so young and lovely. Genevieve Lautner, isn't it? Did you come here to truly surrender, or do you intend to do some mischief?"

"I'm called Summer now, and I will not hurt anyone." She glanced at the men crowding around them. "There are too many of you for my people to fight, and I don't want anyone harmed on either side because of me."

"Such compassion," Nathaniel said, beaming at her. "Not that I believe a word that comes out of your heathen mouth, you understand. There is something very familiar about you, however. Have we met before tonight?"

It was as she suspected. "Yes, I think we have. I will give you what you want, Temple Master. In return all I wish is to ask a question. One that you will answer honestly."

Nathaniel chuckled. "I should have my men cut out your tongue for such impertinence. But I remind myself that you were good enough to surrender to us. Go ahead, witch. Ask your question."

She glanced back to where she had left Michael and Troy before she scanned the grim faces around them.

"Do your men know that you're suffering from immortality sickness, Temple Master?"

No sooner had the words left her mouth than Nathaniel gave her a vicious backhanded slap that knocked her to the ground. He reached for his belt as he stood over her.

"Carry her into my tent. I fear I will have to personally interrogate her."

"You mean rape me?" she said. As two of his men dragged her up on her feet Summer used her bound hands to wipe the blood from her mouth. "When Gideon attacked me in Central Park that's what he intended to do."

Nathaniel yawned. "Yes, yes. All my men know

that Gideon had immortality sickness."

"What you don't know is that his actions activated a curse that was branded into my skin. A curse that reflects all evil back to its source, and spreads it to anyone in league with him. Since his illness was the source, the curse caused it to rapidly advance. It's why he went insane so quickly, and by now it's infected the rest of the brotherhood." She regarded Nathaniel. "Including the man he served as steward."

"You're a whore and a liar," Nathaniel said. He yanked his belt from his pants and doubled it over in his fist. "I'm going to enjoy beating the skin off you."

"Master, I think she's right," said a man's voice. One of the Templars pushed forward until he stood before Nathaniel. "I have been growing sicker every day since Gideon abandoned the order. So have many of the others."

The Temple Master lashed out with his belt, which the warrior caught in his hand. Another two came up behind Nathaniel and seized his arms.

"I will have you all tortured," Nathaniel shouted. "Right alongside this evil slut–"

A heavy gauntlet struck the back of his head, and he went limp and sagged between the men.

"We hoped the Emerald Tablet would provide a cure," the first man said. The Templar's tired eyes met Summer's. "I have not harmed you. Neither have any of my brothers. Take this curse from us, and we will release you."

For a moment she almost felt sorry for him, until she remembered the reason why she had been branded with so many deadly spells.

"It's not my curse. It was cast by my mother, Marie Lautner. Since it was her magic, only she could remove it from you. Maybe she even would have, but your order murdered her in Quebec." Summer saw expressions of horror and frantic murmurs spread through the assembled Templars. "Nothing can stop it now but the end of your life. But how you die is still your choice, for now."

The Templar studied her face. "The only honorable death for a warrior-priest is in battle."

"My people cannot give you that," Summer said, and held out her wrists, using her power to burn off the rope binding them. "But I can."

As the burnt remnants of cord fell to the ground, muted mutters rose from the gathered soldiers. But there was no anger in the faces that Summer slowly turned to see. Instead, there was a strange hope. Finally she faced the first Templar.

"I can give you the end you seek," she said

quietly.

"Yes," he whispered. "Please."

The air crackled with tiny sparks of emerald energy as she walked back through the woods to the field. The Templars followed her, their faces blank and their eyes glowing bright green. When she glanced over at her sentinel mates she could feel the weight of their gazes on her, and the frantic twisting of their thoughts as they struggled against the power binding them.

Don't be afraid, my loves, Summer thought to them. *It's almost over now.*

Two Templars dragged Nathaniel out of the forest between them. As he stirred, they brought him to her. She had them release him, and watched as he dropped to the ground.

"I have not bespelled you," Summer told him when his dazed eyes met hers. She swept her hand across the field. "I want you to be aware, and know what I have done."

His gaze shifted to the bright glow of the time portal she had opened, and his jaw sagged as he saw the men in white tunics marching across the sands.

"That is Fariskur," Nathaniel murmured. "De Sonnac's final battle."

She nodded. "Everyone who fought in this

battle died, except Michael and Troy—and you. You were watching that day, from the place where you hid from the battle. Do you know why they survived?"

"You," he said and gave her an ugly look. "You were there. You saved them that day."

Summer nodded, and walked up to the portal. She waited as all the Templars marched through it, even the two who had to drag Nathaniel Harper in with them. Then she followed them in, and the portal vanished.

CHAPTER TEN

"FIVE," MICHAEL HEARD Troy mutter before he brought the axe down on the log, splitting it in two. "Only five."

Summer had vanished into the portal to the past, taking with her Nathaniel Harper and every other Templar on the mountain. He and Troy had watched it, unable to move until the portal closed. Then the pain had washed over them, and they had fallen to their knees and wept. That had been five days ago.

Wilson walked up to stand beside Michael, his newborn daughter cradled in his arms. He surveyed the enormous pile of split logs Troy had tossed to one side of the stump.

"Is he trying to chop up every tree on the mountain?"

"He needs to do this," Michael said, smiling

down at little Eve, who looked up at him with her mother's solemn gray eyes. "How is Aileen?"

"Sleeping better, now that we've moved back to the main house." Wilson's mouth hitched. "Erica insisted on cleansing and blessing every inch of it before we did, but I think the coven is finally feeling safe again. Are you coming to the closing ritual tomorrow night?"

Michael watched Troy split a log with such force it exploded into toothpick-size splinters. "I would say not."

"When he's in a better mood, tell him his niece wants to see him."

The warlock rolled his eyes before he walked back to his pickup, buckled his daughter into her car seat, and drove off.

Michael went back inside the house long enough to retrieve two beers before he went into the barn, where he twisted the top off one and tossed the other to Troy.

"Stop reading my damn mind, will you?" Troy said. But he drank from the bottle until he'd drained half of it before he heaved a sigh and dropped down on a hay bale. "Five, Paladin. She could survive five minutes on a Crusade battlefield, right?"

Michael went over to sit beside him. "She is

perhaps the most powerful being in existence, so yes, she could."

Troy nodded. "She's just taking her time, that's all. Making sure that we're all right back then." He rubbed his forehead. "So it's my turn to watch the battlefield tonight, right?"

"No," Michael said and drank some beer. "But you can watch it with me."

A shadow passed in front of the barn door.

"I don't believe you two. Drinking beer again? It's not even noon."

Michael got to the door a split second before Troy and flung it open to see Summer standing outside. Her clothing was filthy, her hair dusty with sand, and her pretty lips now looked dry and cracked.

"*Beauty.*"

She flung herself at them, curling her arms around their necks as she kissed Troy and then him with her chapped lips.

"I love you. I missed you. It took a while to sort things out back then. Oh, and I have morning sickness, really bad. I think on the way back I threw up on the Dark Ages."

They hauled her into the house, where they stripped her and bathed her and fed her, and took turns kissing and holding her in their big bed as she told them about the Templars' final battle.

"I had to stay to make sure they all died," she admitted. "Nathaniel tried to tell De Sonnac that he was from the future, at which point he was relieved of his head. Then I had to make sure you two didn't die, and got captured by the right Saracens. It took forever. The sand fleas drove me crazy."

"You couldn't have done all that in five minutes," Troy said, and then he saw how she was looking at him. "Okay, *you* could have, but the last time we traveled back it took three days to return after three minutes."

"That would be because I was lugging two guys through time with me. By myself I can move pretty fast. Also, I don't have to return at the same time I left." She stretched her arms over her head and yawned. "I'm really tired, though. Would you mind if I sleep for a week or two?" Before either of them could reply she sat up and stared at Michael. "Aileen had the baby and you didn't tell me?"

He nodded. "It was a very long labor for her, but she and the baby are fine. It is a little girl, but she said that she wouldn't call her Summer until you returned."

"So they call her Eve," Troy said, his eyelids

drooping. "I like Summer better…"

Michael and Summer watched him drift off.

"He has not slept since you vanished with the Templars," Michael said quietly. "He has chopped enough wood to keep us warm until the baby graduates college, I think."

"I'm sorry for what I did to you two. But if I had explained, you would have tried to stop me, or talked me out of it." She bit her lip. "I was so scared, Paladin. The only thing that kept me from losing it entirely was thinking of you two, waiting for me back here."

He pulled her close, and pressed her cheek against his heart.

"You will never do that again. Troy would not survive it. Neither would I. While he has been chopping wood, I have been punching trees. I have made another clearing, do you know that? Even bigger than the wildflower meadow."

He eased back to see her slumbering face, and carefully reached over to switch off the lamp. Only then did he let the tears of joy run down his face.

• • • • •

Summer attended the closing ritual of the winter

solstice gathering flanked by her lovers, and surrounded by nearly every member of Silver Wood coven. She also held in her arms the tiny, precious bundle of Wilson and Aileen's daughter, whom everyone had agreed should keep the name Eve. In the center of the wildflower meadow, Aileen stood proudly beside Wilson as Abel handed him a beautiful old compass, and named him his successor as Coven Master of Silver Wood. Then they introduced their daughter to the assembled Wiccans.

Summer stepped forward to carefully transfer the baby to Aileen's arms, and smiled as the proud grandfather announced her name and bestowed a lovely old blessing on the baby and her parents.

"Your brother looks very handsome when he's happy and sleep-deprived," Summer mentioned to Troy. "I expect you to be the same when our little girl makes her debut."

Troy nodded. "I resigned from the Magus Corps today, so I'll have plenty of time to practice." He leaned over to look at Michael, who was frowning at his mobile phone. "More texts from the Parisii?"

The big man nodded absently. "They have finished locating the rest of my family. There is a problem." He glanced up at them. "I have fourteen brothers and sisters. They all wish to come here and meet me and you and Troy. They ask if we can Skype."

"Skyping is good," Summer said. "Lachlan can show us how to do it when he gets back from Portland. So what's the problem?"

He blinked. "Nothing. I am very happy to know that I have…that I am still… Beauty, how am I ever going to remember that many names?"

Troy grinned. "We'll make a list."

A short time later they walked back to Troy's house with Abel and Erica, whom Summer had asked to join them for a drink. Once inside Summer brought out a bottle of wine, which they used to toast the newest addition to the coven.

"She's as beautiful as her mother and her nana," Abel said, lifting his glass to Erica. "And as stubborn as her father and granddad." He eyed Summer. "And none of us would be here if not for you, my dear. Thank you for my family, and our future. We want you to know that no matter where you go, you will always have a home with this coven."

Summer exchanged a look with her mates.

"We won't be leaving the mountain, Father. We've decided to stay here, on Troy's estate."

Erica frowned. "I thought it was traditional for

the Guardian and her mates to live in seclusion."

"It has been, until now," Troy said. "We do have certain responsibilities to watch over all the Wiccans, and assure that no one abuses the gift of power. Michael is also going to monitor the Templars, and in time we hope to begin settling our differences with them. We both have to protect Summer from those who would try to seize her power. But we don't want to spend our lives in solitude, nor do we want to raise our child away from her kin."

"Michael and I have had enough of being alone," Summer added. "It's time for us to be part of a real family, and we'd love to join yours."

"Oh, dearest." Erica kissed her cheeks. "You already are."

"Indeed," Abel said gruffly. Something glittered in his blue eyes. "That you would ask is the best Yule gift I've ever been given, Daughter."

"I'm glad you feel that way."

She raised her glass, followed by the rest. Summer's eyes glowed briefly as she smiled at each of them, focusing finally on Erica and Abel.

"*Worry and fear, all disappear*," she said, her eyes glowing brighter. "*Memory of my ancient link, now a warm glow from a lovely drink. Obey me in this, from the moment we sip.*" She paused, raising her glass and voice higher. "*So may it be.*"

As Abel and Erica took their drinks, all knowledge of the Emerald Tablet and her guardianship was removed. Once they saw Abel and Erica off, Summer closed the door and leaned back against it, smiling at her mates.

"That's everyone."

Troy shook his head. "They had no idea. It's incredible, how easily you can remove memories."

"I really just edited out a few details," she admitted. "Their perceptions of us remain basically the same. So to everyone who knows us we're simply a witch and two warlocks who mated for love. Only the three of us will ever know the truth."

Michael gave her one of his slow smiles. "Mating for love *is* the truth, Beauty."

Summer smiled back at him, and then at a beaming Troy. She couldn't agree more.

• • • • •

THE END

• • • • •

Book 6 Excerpt:

LOST
Silver Wood Coven Book Six

To protect her lovers Summer funneled the power through the strongest connection they shared: their mating bond. It poured out of her and into them as love and desire, and their touch changed as they absorbed it. A moment later the green fire faded, leaving Summer wedged between the men, with Michael gripping her waist from behind and Troy cradling her face from the front.

Her dark warlock checked her eyes before he looked over her head. "She's back behind the wheel."

Michael slowly took his hands from her. "I think I will take a cold shower."

"Yeah, and maybe I'll go for a swim in the nearest frozen river." Troy stepped back, revealing the heavy bulge of his erection.

"Stay." Summer lifted her hands to her blouse and began unbuttoning it. "I need you both. Right now."

For a moment Troy looked as if he wanted to rip off her clothes and push her over the desk.

"You're still… We can wait, love."

"I can't," she confessed as she peeled off her blouse and bra.

"We know your body is ready for us." Michael came up behind her and nuzzled her hair. "But what of your heart, Beauty?"

"There are other parts of me that need attention." She reached for his hands, and brought them up to her bare breasts. The moment his rough palms touched her nipples they began to pucker and throb. "Maybe you could do something to make them feel better."

"Yes." Troy's eyes narrowed as he looked at Michael. "We can handle that."

He bent his head to cover her mouth with his.

Summer opened for his cool, deep kiss, and groaned as she felt Michael stripping her jeans and panties down her legs. In a heartbeat her need for her lovers shot from frantic to furious. She tore open Troy's shirt to run her fingernails over the tight, small coins of his nipples. At the same time she rolled her hips so that her backside nudged the ripped muscles washboarding Michael's lower abdomen.

"She will not wait any longer for us, brother," the big man said, and gently lowered Summer to the top of the desk.

She heard him unzip as she unfastened Troy's jeans to free his shaft, which was so swollen and stiff she had to use both hands to bring the straining, satiny head to her lips.

Troy hissed something as she took him in her mouth. He gathered her hair up in his fist as he watched her lave his cockhead.

"Gods, you're so beautiful when you suck me."

Summer moaned as she felt Michael nudge her slick folds, and lifted her hips to give him better access to her wet softness.

"She feels like a sun-kissed peach, all sweet and warm and wet," her golden lover said, and grunted as he used short, hard strokes to penetrate her. "Can you lift her from the desk?"

Troy nodded, and slipped his hands under Summer's upper arms to support her as Michael did the same with her hips. Their strength suspended her between them, and Michael made a low, excited sound as he shifted her forward and then back.

Summer trembled as she surrendered to the rampant demands of her lover's thrusting shafts. She took Troy into her mouth when Michael moved her toward him, and squeezed the big man's thick girth as Troy eased her back against him. The air around them grew as heated as their skins, and Summer surrendered herself to the thrill of being loved and filled and taken by her magnificent mates.

"Change," Michael murmured, drawing out of her and coming around the desk as Troy lifted her into his arms.

• • • • •

Buy REVEALED: Book Five of the Silver Wood Coven Series Now

MORE BOOKS BY HAZEL HUNTER

THE HOLLOW CITY COVEN SERIES

A daring quest. A deadly enemy. A protector who won't quit. Although Wiccan Gillian Granger's life's work is finding a legendary city, her research in musty libraries hasn't prepared her for the field, let alone a gorgeous escort. Shayne Savatier knows he's on a milk run, especially after he meets his beautiful charge. But when enemies attack her, everything changes. Passion intertwines with protection, and duty bonds hard with desire.

Possessed (Hollow City Coven Book One)

Shadowed (Hollow City Coven Book Two)

Trapped (Hollow City Coven Book Three)

Sign up for my newsletter to be notified of new releases!

THE SILVER WOOD COVEN SERIES

Though she's taken the name given her by a kind stranger, Summer can no more explain waking up homeless and covered in blood, than she can the extreme attraction drawing people to her. Amnesiac, confused, and frightened, she's not even aware that she's a witch. But help arrives in two very different forms: the cool and restrained Templar Michael Charbon and his centuries-long friend Wiccan Major Troy Atwater.

Rescued (Silver Wood Coven Book One)

Stolen (Silver Wood Coven Book Two)

United (Silver Wood Coven Book Three)

Betrayed (Silver Wood Coven Book Four)

Revealed (Silver Wood Coven Book Five)

THE CASTLE COVEN SERIES

Novice witch Hailey Devereaux had resolved to live life as an outsider. Possessed of a unique Wiccan ability, her own people shun her. But that all ends when two very different men enter her life: the brooding Major Kieran McCallen and Coven Master Piers Dayton. But their training and tests are only the beginning. As she struggles to fulfill her destiny and find her place in the world, Hailey also discovers love.

Found (Castle Coven Book One)

Abandoned (Castle Coven Book Two)

Healed (Castle Coven Book Three)

Claimed (Castle Coven Book Four)

Imprisoned (Castle Coven Book Five)

Sacrificed (Castle Coven Book Six)

Castle Coven Box Set (Books 1 - 6)

THE MAGUS CORPS SERIES

Meet the warlocks of the Magus Corps, sworn to protect Wiccans at all costs. As they find and track fledgling witches, it's a race against an ancient enemy that would rather see all Wiccans dead. But where danger and intimacy come together, passion is never far behind.

Dominic (Her Warlock Protector Book 1)

Sebastian (Her Warlock Protector Book 2)

Logan (Her Warlock Protector Book 3)

Colin (Her Warlock Protector Book 4)

Vincent (Her Warlock Protector Book 5)

Jackson (Her Warlock Protector Book 6)

Trent (Her Warlock Protector Book 7)

Her Warlock Protector Box Set (Books 1 - 7)

THE SECOND SIGHT SERIES

Join psychic Isabelle de Grey and FBI profiler Mac MacMillan as they hunt a serial killer in the streets of Los Angeles. Even as their search closes in on the kidnapper, they discover not only clues, but a fiery passion that quickly consumes them.

Touched (Second Sight Book 1)

Torn (Second Sight Book 2)

Taken (Second Sight Book 3)

Chosen (Second Sight Book 4)

Charmed (Second Sight Book 5)

Changed (Second Sight Book 6)

Second Sight Box Set (Books 1 - 6)

THE EROTIC EXPEDITION SERIES

Travel the world in these breathless tales of erotic romance. Each features a different couple in fast-paced tales of fiery passion.

Arctic Exposure

A young couple is stranded in an Alaskan storm.

Desert Thirst

In the Sahara, a master tracker has the scent of his fiery client.

Jungle Fever

A forensic accountant blossoms under the care of a plantation owner in Thailand.

Mountain Wilds

A beautiful doctor on the rebound crashes with her pilot in British Columbia.

Island Magic

Two treasure-hunting scuba divers are kidnapped in the Caribbean.

THE ROMANCE IN THE RUINS NOVELS

Explore the ancient world and the new in these standalone novels of erotic romance. Each features a hero and heroine who come together against all odds, in exotic and remote settings where danger and love are found in equal measure.

Words of Love

Set in the heartland of the ancient Maya.

Labyrinth of Love

Set on the ancient Greek island of Crete.

Stars of Love

Set in the rugged Pueblo Southwest.

Sign up for my newsletter to be notified of new releases!

NOTE FROM THE AUTHOR

Dear Wonderful Reader,

Thank you so much for spending time with me. I can't tell you how much I appreciate it! My newsletter will let you know about new releases and *only* new releases. Don't miss the next sizzling, hot romance! Visit HazelHunter.com/books to find more great stories available *today*.

XOXO,
Hazel